To Denise,

with love and

from.

DEVOTION TO MURDER

Steve,

10 August 2018

DEVOTION
TO
MURDER

STEVE EASTWOOD

Matador
9 Priory Business Park,
Wistow Road, Kibworth Beauchamp,
Leicestershire. LE8 0RX
Tel: 0116 279 2299
Email: books@troubador.co.uk
Web: www.troubador.co.uk/matador
Twitter: @matadorbooks

ISBN 978 1789013 450

British Library Cataloguing in Publication Data.
A catalogue record for this book is available from the British Library.

Printed and bound in Great Britain by 4edge Limited
Typeset in 11pt Adobe Garamond Pro by Troubador Publishing Ltd,
Leicester, UK

Matador is an imprint of Troubador Publishing Ltd

Acknowledgements

I would like to offer my grateful thanks to those who gave so generously of their time, expertise and advice during my research and the writing of *Devotion to Murder*. In particular, I'd like to express my gratitude to my old friend Tony Oswick, a talented writer in his own right, and David Evans, who is an award-winning crime writer. Their unstinting support and guidance gave me the confidence to keep working towards a, hopefully enjoyable, product. I would also like to thank my friends, Adina and Ray Titchmarsh, Steve Savage, Martin Chipchase, Jeremy John (Lord Roding), Sue Jacobson (Lady Fanny), and my son, James Eastwood, all of whom were players in my *Murder Mystery group* and provided the inspiration for the tale.

Finally, I would like to thank my friends; Brian Prater, 1940s enthusiast who lives the lifestyle and appears with his Wolsley on the cover; and Robert Wong, a highly talented professional photographer who took the images and has kindly given his permission for them to be used.

Steve Eastwood
Clacton-on-Sea
2018

Prologue

It was July in the year of our Lord 1949. After six years of conflict, most of Europe had settled down to something akin to peace and normality. There were still international tensions, of course, but these were of no real interest to the inhabitants of Beaumont, a small village on the Essex coast. For many of these people, life had already altered fundamentally. Having to come to terms with the loss of loved ones, scraping a living and food rationing, they were doing their best to shake off the effects of the war. There was some optimism, for those who could find it within themselves, but there was hardly a spirit of forgive and forget. It was against this background that Sister Margaret, a Carmelite nun, arrived in the village. She had been sent on a mission by the Vatican to help the lord of the manor in his conversion to Catholicism. Jeremy John Beaumont, the 7th Lord of Roding had been a devout Christian, but his faith was shattered when his first wife, Bettina, was killed during an air raid, and again when Edward, his only son and heir, later died in a road accident. Desperate to find solace, Jeremy had remarried in haste, to Francine, a woman who was twenty-six years his junior. She soon tired of the marriage, and, when Jeremy became ill, they began to live virtually separate lives. It was to be Sister Margaret's mission to guide Jeremy back to the path.

As for the indigenous population of Beaumont, they were not big on Catholicism or religion of any stripe. So, when they saw her about the village, they found her something of an oddity. In their eyes, she was, at best, an anachronism, but some of the people resented her presence deeply. Their reasoning was simple. If God is love and Jesus really exists, then, surely, they would not have suffered for the past ten years and would still have the loved ones who had been so cruelly taken from them. How, then, did this "Bride of Christ" have the nerve to show her face in their village? As if this were not enough, she was living it up at Beaumont Hall with his lordship, if you please!

1

DAY ONE

Tuesday 12th July 1949

'Do try to relax, Jeremy,' said the nun. 'Sometimes the Lord God makes us ill to test our faith.'

'Well, if that is true, I wish he wouldn't test me quite so rigorously, Sister.'

The nun crossed herself, as a precaution.

Lord Jeremy Roding was propped up in his four-poster bed, surrounded by books and newspapers. Sitting alongside him was Sister Margaret. A tall, attractive and elegant woman, whom his lordship estimated to be in her late twenties. He observed her as he lay on top of the eiderdown, and he imagined that, confined beneath the shapeless habit, there had to be a healthy libido the young nun was fighting to control. However, he was no longer in any condition to put his theory to the test. Had she come into his life twenty years ago, well, things would have been very different indeed. He would have done his best to tempt her and satisfy his curiosity. But, for now, as he was a deeply troubled man, she was trying to comfort him by quoting from the scriptures. It wasn't really working, so he tried to divert her from her efforts.

'Anyway, my dear, how are things with you?'

'Good, Jeremy, but, I have found that the people in the village don't like me very much. Probably because I am a foreigner.'

'You must forgive them, Sister. They have been through a lot in recent years. They are very suspicious of strangers in general, let alone foreigners,' his lordship chuckled to himself. 'I firmly believe that one has to have been born and bred in the village to ever be accepted at all. They are a funny lot, really.'

His lordship bent forward, and his laughter turned into a fit of phlegm-laden coughing. The nun got to her feet, turned and reached across to pick up a jug from the dressing table. She poured a glass of water and handed it to him. He accepted it and drank it down greedily.He continued, 'No you mustn't let them worry you.'

At the age of sixty, Jeremy was suffering from a respiratory illness that had left him relying on full-time nursing care. Although not totally bedridden, he was quite immobile, and reliant on sticks and a wheelchair to get himself around. Once a powerful and charismatic individual, his shock of red hair and beard were still as thick and lustrous as ever, but he was greying, and, with his lack of mobility, he had put on another three stones in weight.

'So, Jeremy, where is the Lady Fanny today?'

'Fanny has gone up to our London house for a few days.'

'She goes there a lot, does she not?'

'Yes. She spends much of her time up there pursuing her business interests. The art gallery, exhibitions and whatnot. She is very ambitious, you see, and she does have her own network of friends in London. She finds life here, at

Beaumont, rather tedious, I'm afraid. One would definitely say that she is her own woman.'

'I often wonder why you call her Fanny and not by her real name, Francine. I think it is a very pretty name?'

'Well, she doesn't like it for some reason. And, it seems, all her friends call her Fanny. It sums her up totally, I think,' said Jeremy with a hint of bitterness.

The nun did not understand the reference and was unable to comment. She just nodded and gave a smile.

'Anyway, Jeremy, I think you need to get some rest. I am going to go into the garden for a while to do some more of my painting.'

'Right you are, my dear. Try to create a masterpiece for me, will you?'

She got to her feet and helped him get under the covers, then left the room, closing the door quietly behind her.

In despair, his lordship picked up a newspaper and tried to read in the hope that this would have a soporific effect. He was bored and had tried hard to get off to sleep. In fact, he had tried too hard and it was working against him. Jeremy was now staring at the ceiling, pondering over the remaining years of his life and what they could possibly hold for him. He was in quite a philosophical frame of mind and he told himself that, compared to other people, he had no real reason to complain. There were always plenty of staff about the place, so he was not exactly alone at Beaumont Hall. He had a reliable butler, cook, and gardener, and there were one or two youngsters working on the estate. No, there were many people considerably worse off than him.

But it was a sad fact that Jeremy had begun to prepare for the end of his life and he was in receipt of spiritual counselling, which was being provided by the fair Sister Margaret. She had already been staying at Beaumont Hall for a couple of months and he had found her to be a source of great comfort.

It was also quite fortuitous that, when Jeremy had fallen ill, he had managed to engage the services of a full-time nurse in the person of Adina, the wife of his butler, Raymond Jenkins. She was already living at the Hall and had been at something of a loose end. She had been trained as a nurse, and, after the war, she had served in Vienna with the Red Cross, which had led to her meeting her husband Raymond, who was serving there with the British Mission.

Jeremy had warmed to Adina and found that she was ideal for the job. She was very attentive, thoughtful and she cared for all his physical needs. She had a lively sense of humour and was charming company. She was also damned attractive.

'You are late again, young man,' shouted Beryl Aldis, 'by fifteen minutes, and that's the third time this week. I shall be having words with Mr Jenkins about you, unless you buck your ideas up.'

'I'm sorry about that, Mrs Aldis. My mate Alfie and I got into a shoal of roach, and they just kept coming and coming. I suppose I just lost track of time.'

'You're lucky to have this job you know. There's them who fought in the war and came back to nothing. Just you keep your eye on the time in future.'

Beryl Aldis was a matronly figure and, as the cook, she ruled the kitchen area with a rod of iron. She had been employed at Beaumont Hall for most of her adult life and knew the workings of the place, inside out. Compared to the years before the war, they now operated with a relatively small number of staff. Beryl knew that discipline had to be strictly maintained, if the household was to function at all efficiently.

James Davidson was kitchen porter at "the big house", as the villagers called it. He and Beryl had a good relationship, but he knew exactly where he stood. He was the nephew of Ruby Gedge, an old friend and colleague of Beryl, who had recently retired after many years in service at the Hall. She, therefore, felt that it was incumbent on her to keep an eye on young James, and to make sure that he stayed on the straight and narrow.

The trouble was that James was something of a dreamer and all he could think about was his fishing. He was a handsome young chap of eighteen years of age, medium height, and with blonde hair that always looked as though a comb had not passed through it for days. He was quiet and sensitive, and, despite his poor timekeeping, Beryl had found James to be a good worker.

James' daily kitchen duties revolved around the serving of meals to the household, beginning the process by lighting the ovens when he arrived for work at 6.00am. He would be given a series of tasks by Beryl, which ran alongside serving breakfast and lunch, and the subsequent clearing down. After luncheon duties had been carried out, James would usually be permitted to leave the Hall for the afternoon.

So far, this Tuesday had been rather quiet, and he had finished his work quite early. It was a lovely, clear sunny day and James had spent his afternoon on the riverbank. Yet he had been expected to return to perform dinner duties at 4.00pm and had arrived back late. Again.

Beryl set him to work immediately.

'James, go and see Mr Jenkins, will you? And ask him to find out whether his lordship wants to take his dinner in the dining room, or whether he is going to remain in his bedroom and take it up there.'

'Yes, Mrs Aldis.'

'And I suppose we'd better find out what our Mary Magdalene wants for her dinner.'

'Yes, Mrs Aldis.'

He found Raymond Jenkins in the study, where he was replenishing the decanters. The butler advised him that Sister Margaret was in the garden, busy with her painting.

James made his way outside where he found the nun sitting in his lordship's Bath chair, which was parked in front of the summerhouse. She was staring into the middle distance. Her easel had been erected and mounted on it was a half-completed landscape scene. Her palette and brushes were by her side. She was an attractive young woman for a nun, and James regarded her with a mixture of awe and admiration. He was reluctant to disturb her as he assumed that she must be thinking through some aspect of her artwork. She looked quite serene, and, although her feet were bare, she was fully clothed, wearing the habit, wimple and the large metal crucifix that he always found intimidating.

'Excuse me, Sister, but I have been told by Mrs Aldis to find out what you'd like for dinner and whether you want to have your meal in the dining room.'

'Where will his lordship be?'

'I have an idea that his lordship might be dining alone in his bedroom, but I won't know until Mr Jenkins has spoken to him.'

James considered the artwork. 'That's very good, Sister.'

Sister Margaret ignored his comment.

'Nothing for me, can't you see I'm busy?' said the nun, in what James took to be a rather dismissive and brusque manner. She did not even turn her head to look in his direction.

James felt humiliated and was upset by her attitude. He said nothing further and decided to leave her to her painting. *Why would she want to speak to me like that?* he thought, as he walked away from her. He reminded himself that she didn't really know him and so her response couldn't have been personal, so James decided he wasn't going to let it upset him. 'Miserable, ignorant cow!' he said to himself, as he walked back to the kitchen. James would have liked to have told her where to get off, but he knew he'd lose his job over it. He just walked back inside the kitchen.

Although the sister had been a guest at the Hall for several weeks, James had had little to do with her in that time. He was aware that other members of staff had formed the opinion that she was stern to the point of rudeness. They didn't like her at all, and they all took the view that she was best avoided. He wondered how she had found herself taking holy orders to become a nun in the first place. It certainly didn't suit her personality.

James was still smarting from his encounter with the nun, but he made a conscious effort to replace thoughts of Sister Margaret with his plan to prebait a stretch of the river where, during the afternoon, he had seen a few nice chub.

Back in the comfort of a dream, he just started to peel the potatoes, deep in thought.

'Well?' said Mrs Aldis.

'Well what, Mrs Aldis?'

'Well, what does she want for her dinner?'

'She doesn't want anything, Mrs Aldis.'

'Really!' she said, as she slapped a ball of dough down on the kitchen table and started kneading it, vigorously applying extra pressure.

'She's a strange one and no mistake. She hardly touched her lunch. We had to throw it away in the end. I really can't stand to see perfectly good food going to waste, it's criminal.'

'Perhaps she's fasting or maybe sickening for something.'

'I don't think so.'

'Maybe she's got worms.'

'Don't be rude, now, young man,' said Mrs Aldis, giggling to herself.

James just carried on with his few remaining spuds. He was away again with the chub, anticipating that he would get an early night, and once away from the Hall he would be straight back down to the river to meet his friends.

'I still can't get off to sleep for any length of time, Adina.'

'Perhaps you are worrying too much. Try to empty your mind and relax.'

'I've tried. I seem to be able to go off for an hour or so, then my mind switches on and I start thinking.'

'Would you like me to make a hot drink for you, my lord? Perhaps a mug of cocoa might help to calm you.'

'No, thank you, Adina. It's good of you, but that will just make me want to go to the lavatory.'

'If that is all for now, my lord, may I go back to our apartment for a while to do some housework?'

'Yes, of course, my dear.'

'I must do some washing and ironing. It's starting to pile up. We will have no clothes to wear if I don't. You will be all right here on your own?'

'I will be fine, but, before you go, it would help me if you were to give me your special treatment. It would help me relax, you know.'

'I am happy to try, my lord. If you think that it will help.'

'Yes, I really think it might.'

Adina sat on the side of the bed and pulled back the covers. She then went about her business with skill and dexterity. It did not take long before she relieved his tension. Jeremy soon went off to asleep.

Adina left his lordship's bedroom and she walked to her apartment at the other end of the building. She came back to his lordship's room, for ten minutes or so, at around 4.00pm, and, although Adina was reluctant to wake him, she needed to give him his medicine. He soon dropped off again.

About 4.30pm Jeremy was woken from his slumber by the sound of shouting, which appeared to be coming from outside in the garden. He couldn't tell whether the voice, or voices, were male or female, but on recalling that Stephen Savage, the gardener, was carrying out some work in the immediate area, he reassured himself that the noise was due to Savage's efforts, and, not feeling inclined to go to the window to investigate the matter, he stayed in his bed. The noise didn't appear to go on for very long and he had soon dismissed it from his mind. Jeremy continued with his newspaper, and, after a short while, he managed to drift off to sleep again.

Just after 6.00pm, James left the kitchen to take some slops out to the bin area. As he got to a point near to the bins, he cast his gaze over to the summerhouse, which was some fifty yards away across the lawn, to his right. What he saw threw him totally. Sister Margaret was lying prostrate on the grass.

'Sister! Are you all right?'

She gave no response as she was rolling on the ground in front of the summerhouse. James realised that something was amiss, so he ran across to investigate, and gasped in horror when he approached her and saw that the nun's wimple was lying on the floor beside her and she was bleeding heavily from a head wound. She was staring at James, almost beseeching him to end her misery. Her lips were moving as if to speak, but James could hear no words. Very soon, he realised that she was still.

He was stunned rigid and wanted to do something to help, but he didn't dare touch her. She was a woman after all. The lad suddenly felt very exposed and vulnerable. He left the sister where she lay and ran back to the kitchen to fetch Mrs Aldis, but she was nowhere to be found. He began to panic. *What if people think it was me?* James ran through the house and started shouting 'Help! Help!' at the top of his voice. Finally, he found Jenkins, who was in the dining room. 'Mr Jenkins. Come quick. I think the nun's dead! Will you come outside with me and have a look, please?'

'What do you mean, she's dead? If this is your idea of a joke, young man, then it's in very poor taste!'

Beryl then stepped into the room, having been attracted by the sound of James' shouting. The two men rushed outside and without having any notion as to what the fuss was about, she followed on behind them. They found Sister Margaret lying on her side in something akin to the recovery position. Raymond Jenkins bent over her and gently tapped her face, almost as if he was trying to wake her from her slumber. 'Sister, Sister. Come on, up you get.'

The nun made no response to his pleading, and, in view of the extent of her wounds, Jenkins realised that she was unlikely to do so.

'Her cross has gone. It was definitely around her neck when I saw her earlier on,' observed James.

'She might be lying on top of it,' said Jenkins.

Beryl took control of the situation. 'Never mind the bloody crucifix! Ray, go and call for the doctor and then call the police!'

Jenkins rushed away to the house to use the phone in the study. While James stood watching, Beryl tried to resuscitate the sister using the limited training that she had received a long time before as an auxiliary nurse. She knelt across the nun, and, for what seemed like five minutes, she pumped her chest and checked for a pulse. But, Beryl's heroic efforts were to no avail: Sister Margaret was gone and there was nothing she could do to bring her back.

After about fifteen minutes, an ambulance arrived on the scene. The crew were soon joined by the local GP,

Doctor Graham Stevenson, who examined the unfortunate lady, but he reached the same sad conclusion.

Sister Margaret was dead. She had gone to meet the boss.

Jesus Christ, I'm shaking. But I've never felt so alive. Stupid, evil bitch. How dare she say that the war was God's way of keeping the population down? Didn't she understand that we all lost family? She probably never had any family of her own, and she certainly won't be having any now. I know I probably went too far, but at least it will stop her from spreading her poison. No regrets. The bitch deserved it.

Lord Roding was woken by Jenkins, who was tugging at the sleeve of his pyjamas.

'My lord. Wake up, please. I'm sorry to disturb you, but there has been a serious incident in the grounds.'

'What kind of incident, Jenkins? I've only just managed to get to sleep, damn your eyes!'

'Sister Margaret has been murdered!'

At this news, Jeremy sat bolt upright in his bed. 'She's been what?'

'Murdered.'

Jenkins went to the window and he drew back the curtains to allow some light into the bedroom. He continued to speak as he did so. 'The nun, Sister Margaret. Young James found her about a half hour ago; she was lying on the floor outside the summerhouse. She had wounds to her head and to her neck, and there's blood everywhere. It looks like someone has beaten her to death with a garden spade.'

'Who? Who has beaten her to death? Did Savage see what happened to her? He was out there this afternoon, I'm sure he was. I heard him out there earlier on.' The shock overrode the tears he might have had.

'I have not seen Savage since early this morning, my lord.'

'Has someone called an ambulance or a doctor?'

'Yes, my lord. The ambulance is here, and Doctor Stevenson is with Sister Margaret as we speak. I also called the police, but they haven't arrived yet.'

'What about young James. Is he all right?'

'Yes, my lord. Just a little shaken up, but he'll be fine.'

'I need a cigarette, Jenkins. Light one for me, will you?'

'Is that wise, my lord? The doctor was very firm on the point that you shouldn't smoke,' pleaded Jenkins.

'Don't argue man. Just get me one, will you?'

The butler did his master's bidding; retrieving a packet of cigarettes from the inside pocket of his tailcoat, he lit a Park Drive and handed it to Jeremy, who took a long and satisfying drag.

'That's better.'

Jenkins helped Jeremy into his tweeds and he selected a shirt from the wardrobe. After finding some footwear, he sat him in his wheelchair.

'Right, Raymond, let's go and see what is happening outside, shall we?'

They left the bedroom.

Once downstairs, Jenkins wheeled his lordship to the study, parking him next to the french doors providing access to the garden. He would, from this point, be able to monitor events without becoming embroiled in what was happening around the body.

Jeremy could see that the cook was standing talking to the doctor. She had an earnest expression on her face. Jenkins had told his lordship of her desperate efforts to save the sister. The poor woman looked devastated, and he could see that her apron was covered in blood. He admired her and felt sorry for her in equal measure. His lordship instructed the butler to call the doctor over to him, in order that he might enquire as to Sister Margaret's present condition and seek his opinion as to what might have caused her death. As the master of the house, he wanted to hear the facts from Stevenson for himself.

After hearing the doctor's account, Jeremy was overcome with grief, and, seeing his master's distress, Jenkins took him back to his bedroom so that he could rest and regain his composure.

About ten minutes later, Police Constable (PC) Alfred Lewis, the village constable, sped onto the scene by bicycle. He looked for all the world like Fatty Arbuckle in a cinematic trailer for *The Keystone Cops*. As he entered the garden, he dismounted from his machine with such haste that he very nearly plunged into a nearby flowerbed. He was beetroot red in the face and fighting for breath.

'Sorry I'm late, but I was at the other end of my beat when my wife got word to me about this incident.'

At once, Doctor Stevenson outlined the situation to the officer and the sequence of events as far as he understood them. He showed PC Lewis to the body, gave him an explanation of his findings and, having earlier been badgered by James, he told the constable about the missing crucifix. The doctor stood over the body and explained his conclusions as to the cause of death.

'Sadly, Officer, the lady is deceased. She most likely succumbed to the wounds sustained to her head and neck, although we will not know for sure until a post mortem has been carried out. In my opinion, it is a clear case of unlawful killing, so I would advise you to leave the body where it lies and protect the scene of the crime from any interference. I think we must inform the coroner about this one.'

The doctor pointed to a garden spade that was lying on the floor of the porchway to the summerhouse. 'There's your weapon, I would suggest.'

'Doctor, would you mind remaining with the body just while I telephone the CID [Criminal Investigation Department] and the rest of the cavalry.'

The doctor agreed, and PC Lewis went off to the house to find a telephone. As he got to the kitchen door, he was met by Jenkins and the constable told him he should assemble all members of staff in the kitchen, where he wished them to remain. This was apart from Mrs Aldis. PC Lewis explained that, due to the amount of blood on her apron, she should remain in the dining room to prevent blood transferring from her garments to those of other staff. Lewis escorted her to the dining room, where she removed her apron and sat down. He then went to use the telephone.

On his return to the garden, he found the doctor seated at a table completing some notes of his own. As Lewis approached him, the doctor remarked, 'I just need to go to my surgery to collect something. I will be back in about ten minutes, if anybody wants me.'

About 7.20pm, PC Lewis was still standing guard over the body when he was joined by Detective Inspector (DI) Albert Cooper and Detective Sergeant (DS) Brian Pratt of the Essex Constabulary. They had been met at the front door by Jenkins, who had directed them towards the murder scene. Doctor Stevenson had just returned from his surgery. Introductions were unnecessary as he was known to both detectives.

'Intriguing one this, young Cooper,' said the doctor.

'What are we dealing with here then, Doc?'

'Looks very much like a murder to me. Someone gave her a few hefty whacks with that, I would imagine.' The doctor indicated the spade, which was still in position on the floor. He continued, 'Anyway, that's for you and the pathologist to confirm, Alby. Obviously, I'm not at liberty to issue a death certificate at this stage, and I'll have to report it to the coroner.'

He indicated the victim's wounds, which consisted of deep lacerations to her head and neck, and the wimple that remained on the floor next to the body.

'I am given to understand the lady's religious name is Sister Margaret, and that, by all accounts, she was not all sweetness and light. In due course, the coroner will need her birth name. Still, I expect the diocese will be able to provide you with that.'

Albert Cooper had served with the constabulary both before and since the war. He enjoyed the sobriquet of "Alby", which had been given to him by school friends. He was a large man of thirty-six years of age. He stood six feet three inches in his stockinged feet and was of a strong, lithe build. He had a full head of black hair, which was neatly cut in a "short back and sides" and smoothed with Brylcreem. Alby was quite a handsome individual with a strong chin, although he did have a boxer's nose, which was a souvenir from his army days.

Cooper's "bagman", Brian Pratt was thirty-five years of age. He was slightly shorter at five feet eleven inches tall, and of a thin build. In terms of physical stature, he was a shadow of his boss. Unfortunately for Pratt, he had inherited the balding gene. What was left of his hair was blond, as were his eyebrows and moustache.

Whatever their shortcomings were in the looks department, Cooper and Pratt were regarded by their colleagues as thorough and capable detectives.

Alby Cooper knew his ground and the people on it. At the outbreak of hostilities, he had been a serving officer in the Colchester Borough Constabulary as well as an army reservist. He was one of the first to be conscripted into the army, serving with the 12th Lancers as a part of the British Expeditionary Force.

At Dunkirk, he was captured, and he spent the next four years as a guest of the Germans. Those years had taught him a lot about human nature. When he was finally released, he was a shadow of his former self and he was left with scars, not all of which were physical. At the outbreak of war, he had had a girlfriend, Jennifer, to whom he had been engaged to be married. Unfortunately, she had tired of waiting for him and she had become involved with an American airman, whom she married in quick time. She now lived with her husband in Arkansas. Cooper's trust in women was severely damaged by this experience and he had become embittered.

Cooper rejoined the police force after the war had ended. He channelled his bitterness into sheer hard graft and a dogged approach to investigations, allowing himself little time for a private life. As a result, he had rapidly risen to the rank of detective inspector. He was now faced with a murder and he was determined to get a result.

Cooper and Pratt were standing in the rear garden of Beaumont Hall, surveying the scene; the sun was fast disappearing below the horizon, Doctor Stevenson had departed, and they had been joined by Brendan Withers, a forensic scientist.

A dead nun lay before them.

'It definitely looks as though the weapon was the spade. We shall have to take care to bag it and keep it clear of the body. Then, later, at the lab, the blood on the spade will be compared with that of the victim. The pathologist will also do a physical comparison of the spade against the wounds during the post mortem,' said Withers. 'Do we know the origin of the spade, sir?'

'Yes, Brendan. Apparently, it was left in the ground over there earlier this afternoon by the gardener, a Mr Savage.' Cooper pointed to what looked like a large half-dug flowerbed adjacent to the summerhouse.

'What does his lordship say about all of this?' said Withers.

'He's deeply shocked. In fact, he's taken to his bed. Seems to be one tragedy after another with his family, and now this. His lordship appears to have been quite fond of the woman; she was something of a companion for him. We'll have to arrange to take a witness statement from him when he's settled down a bit.'

Cooper pointed towards the deceased and gave Withers an instruction, 'Brendan, I want you to supervise the removal of the body from the scene to the mortuary, and arrange for someone to travel with it, so that they can prove continuity.'

'Yes, sir,' said Withers. 'I will keep you informed of the time and date of the post mortem. I imagine that you'll want to be there, won't you?'

'Yes, I will. Thanks Brendan.'

'Brian, we'll also need Brendan and his team to carry out a careful search of her bedroom in the house, but, for now, will you just make sure that it's locked, and that an officer is stationed outside the door.'

Cooper called across to Sergeant Scott, a uniformed patrol sergeant, who was lurking on the periphery of the scene.

'Sarge, I need you to cordon off an area, say, a fifty-yard circumference of the scene, and post the most confident member of your section to act as gatekeeper. They'll need to have the wherewithal to be able to stop people entering the cordon who have no business being there. That might even include the chief constable, or any other senior officer who happens to be curious or just want to put their snout in.'

'I think we can manage that, governor. I've got a few smart alecs on my section who could cover it.'

'Well, whoever you designate, they'll need to keep

a log and they must be able to stand their ground. In the meantime, the forensic team will be busy within the cordon, but I want the security of the cordon maintained even after the body has been taken away.'

'Leave it with me, governor.'

'We should also organise a search of the grounds, so we must call some extra bods in to help with that. May I leave it with you to organise?'

'Will do, governor. It'll be getting dark shortly though.'

'Do what you can, Rob. If you need to carry on in the morning, then so be it.'

'But what are we searching for?'

'Any other weapons, blood, a possible exit route indicated in the long grass or footprints; that kind of thing.'

'Brian!' shouted Cooper, calling Pratt across to him again.

'Brian, I need you to get somebody to speak to the school caretaker to ask him if we can set up our incident room in the school. The kids are on holiday for a few weeks, so it should be OK. Any argument, come back to me and I'll have a word with the headmistress. I'm off to speak to the boss to update him and ask for some more staff. For now, I'll leave you, Rob Scott and his section to supervise the scene.'

Cooper climbed into his Wolseley and drove the six miles to the town hall where the office of the superintendent of the Colchester Division was located. It was mid-evening. He realised that he was being somewhat optimistic given that he was already aware the superintendent was due to attend an evening council reception. He thought there might just be a chance that he could get a message passed to him.

A short while later, a note having been duly delivered,

Superintendent Tom Stockwell emerged from the council chamber. He had assumed the need for him to leave the event was for a good reason and he appeared in quite good spirits. Was that a whiff of Scotch Cooper could smell on his breath?

'Good evening, Albert. What brings you here?'

'A murder, sir. At Beaumont Hall.'

'Not Lord Roding, I hope,' said an alarmed Stockwell, ushering Cooper into a side room.

'No, a house guest. In fact, it was a nun, sir. Beaten to death with a garden spade. I thought I'd better inform you. I wouldn't want you to be asked questions about it later and be taken by surprise.'

'Quite right, Albert. Thank you. Good God! What is the world coming to? Has anyone been arrested for it?'

'No. Not yet, sir, I'm afraid. We haven't any suspect either. I hate to say it, but I think this one might go on for some time.'

Cooper then explained the circumstances in more detail. When they had finished their discussion, Cooper agreed that he would further discuss the case with the superintendent the following morning.

Cooper returned to Beaumont Hall and caught up with Brian Pratt.

'Most members of staff have made a witness statement now, governor, but we haven't taken one from his lordship yet. I think he'll want you to be present when he does make one. It's something to do with rank, I think. He mentioned it when I went to speak to him in his room, although, to be fair, I think he's still in shock. He was in bed all day and unable to provide anything useful other than the fact that the deceased was a house guest who was giving him spiritual guidance.'

'Really? 'said Cooper sceptically.

'Yes. Apparently, she was helping him convert to Catholicism. Anyway, I took the liberty of assuring him of your presence when we finally put pen to paper.'

'Thank you, Brian. Were you able to carry out any house-to-house enquiries?'

'No, unfortunately we weren't, governor. There are no other premises directly overlooking the Hall, so it wasn't possible. One or two of the staff live in tied cottages on the estate itself, but they and their families have been interviewed. The next nearest houses are over a mile away.'

Cooper looked across the lawn to the scene that had been illuminated and covered by a large tent. He could see that, within it, the Scenes of Crime officers were still carrying out their examination of the victim's body, which remained in situ.

'OK Brian. We'll let the servants go home now. After Scenes of Crime have finished we'll need to keep the scene and her bedroom guarded overnight. I will see his lordship for a more detailed chat tomorrow. The briefing of the team will be first thing tomorrow morning, in the CID training room, after I've been to see Mr Stockwell to update him. Can I leave you to spread the word?'

'Will do, governor.'

Cooper then cadged a lift back to town with one of the uniform police cars, leaving the Wolseley with Pratt. After booking off at the police station, he checked his watch and realised there was no chance of his grabbing a late pint as it was past closing time and even the governor of his local, the Hole in the Wall, was averse to doing "afters" on a Tuesday. Cooper decided to go straight home to try to get a good night's sleep. *No bad thing,* he thought to himself. He would need clarity when he started in earnest the following morning.

2

DAY TWO

Wednesday 13ᵗʰ July 1949

'I'm glad you told me about this last night, Albert. The more I think about it, the angrier I get. It's outrageous! outrageous!' said Superintendent Stockwell at the top of his voice.

'A nun murdered on our patch. What is the world coming to?'

'Grim times indeed, sir,' said Cooper.

They were standing in the superintendent's office, which was still located in the town hall. The Colchester Borough Constabulary, of which they had been proud members, had just been subsumed into the Essex Constabulary and the power base had shifted to Chelmsford.

The superintendent had been the head of the old force, and, in the process of amalgamation, he had suffered a reduction in status, but, whatever politics lay behind the change, the ethos of the old borough force was still intact. It remained steadfastly independent and any acceptance of change by the staff would not happen quickly.

'We must find the person responsible and clear this up, or we won't hear the last of it.'

'Well yes, quite, sir.'

'And another thing, it seems that the *East Anglian Recorder* have got a hold of the fact that a nun has been murdered on our patch. Some woman called Munson. How did that happen, do you think?' said Stockwell pointing an accusatory finger.

'I don't know, sir. It didn't come from our side, I can assure you.'

'Well, I damned well hope not.'

Cooper was quietly seething, and he wasn't so sure. *If one of my lot have made themselves busy, I'll kick their arse all around the car park.*

'I had the Munson woman on the phone first thing this morning. To be fair to you, Albert, were it not for the fact that you kept me informed, I would have been completely nonplussed and made to look as if I have no grip on what goes on in my own force's area. I told her we had no comment to make at this stage,' said Stockwell, who continued, 'This investigation, do you think you could handle it yourself?'

'Me, sir?'

'Yes, you, man. You have the necessary investigative experience, and, who knows, a successful outcome might give you a chance to project yourself for higher rank.'

'Well, I'm pleased you have faith in my ability, sir, but won't Essex Headquarters have something to say about it?'

'Just you leave them to me Albert. It's a matter of principle. We don't want the Metropolitan Police or anyone else's murder squad treading all over the borough, do we? We are still quite capable of managing our own affairs.'

'Well, of course, sir.'

'Tell me, how many staff do you think you would need?'

Cooper thought out loud. 'Oh, an incident office manager, DS Mills would be ideal for that; a couple of office staff on the inside; and I'll need DS Pratt and six detective constables on the outside enquiry team. That should be enough for now, sir.'

'Well, I can give you most of them. We do have other crimes in the borough to deal with. As for the constables, you can have four instead of six, and two of them will be female officers on secondment from the Women's Police Department: WPC Jane Stewart and WPC Linda Collins. Both are good officers. Miss Collins is particularly bright. She served in the WRNS [Women's Royal Naval Service] during the war. Regard it as a kind of experiment. I want to see how women would get on with serving in the CID.'

'Very good, sir. I must just also tell you I have already taken the liberty of informing the coroner about the case?'

'Who is the coroner these days?'

'Doctor Cunliffe, sir. He was quite content with the situation when I spoke to him.'

'Very well, then. Keep me posted on any progress, will you, please.'

'Yes. Thank you, sir.'

Cooper had been dismissed.

Well, that was remarkably painless, he thought, as he left the superintendent's office. He'd anticipated getting much more of a grilling than he'd received.

He felt surprised and quite chuffed that the boss had expressed such faith in him. *On the other hand,* he thought, *could it be that I'm being set up as a possible scapegoat should it all go to rat shit?* He decided to take a positive attitude to the appointment and tried to dismiss any thoughts of failure.

'Well, that's a feather in your cap, Alby, my lovely,' said the boss's secretary.

Her sudden outburst made him jump. He hadn't seen her lurking behind the superintendent's office door.

'Bloody hell Mavis!' he said through gritted teeth.

'You been listening at the door again, nose ointment? He'll catch you at it one day, you know.'

'Just being attentive,' she said. 'You know how much I care about you boys. Besides, if he invested in one of those intercom things I keep asking for, I wouldn't have to creep around half as much as I do.'

Cooper chuckled to himself as he left the management suite.

Nosy mare! he thought.

Mavis was a very attractive woman, it had to be said. About thirty-five years old with blonde hair and a good body, long shapely legs and an ample bosom. She had lost her husband during the war and she was still on her own. Mavis had a good handle on the office gossip and she liked to think she held a position of power. People in the force were loath to upset her; she knew it and played on the fact.

A few of the men fancied their chances with her, including Cooper himself, although he had never been tempted to ask her out. He was very wary of women. As a single man, he was quite entitled to throw his hat into the ring, but he shuddered at the thought of what could happen to his career should any personal relationship with her turn sour. For now, he just played along in a state of mild amusement and flirtation.

On leaving the town hall, Cooper crossed the High Street to "Sadie's", his aunt's greengrocery shop. Sadie was serving behind the counter as usual.

'Morning auntie!'

'Keep your voice down! It does nothing for me image you know, letting customers hear I'm old enough to be your aunt.'

Sadie was a widow and a mere twelve years older than him.

'What time was it this morning, then?'

'Been up since 5.00am to take the delivery from the market. Jim normally does it, but he's in hospital with appendicitis.'

'Bloody hell, Sadie! I don't know how you do it.'

'At my age. You mean?'

'No. Now I didn't say that, did I?'

'No, I know. Just teasing. I've got good workers who can usually take care of things, so I can get a couple of hours on the settee in the afternoon. That's not going to happen today though. Never mind.' She yawned into her clenched fist. 'Anyway, have you spoken to Brenda yet?'

'Blimey. Here she is again with her Brenda!' said Cooper, with mock indignation. 'No, I haven't managed to identify her yet. I'm beginning to wonder if she really exists or whether she's some figment of your imagination. Have you actually met the girl yourself?'

'Not as such, but, from what I hear from speaking to her mum, she would be ideal for you, Alby. She even works at the police station.'

'Yes, I know. You told me, but I haven't been able to place her yet.'

Sadie was always trying to steer him in the direction of, what she always referred to as "nice girls". For some time, she had been talking about her friend's daughter, Brenda. Unfortunately, Sadie wasn't good on detail and the only Brenda he knew at the police station was a woman who worked in the canteen and was in her late fifties. All right for her age, but she was heavy on the lipstick and, given the state of her teeth, if she had a white one, she'd have a snooker set. He certainly wasn't going to get involved with her.

'Anyway, auntie, apart from the early start, everything all right?'

She threw an apple to him, 'Yes, thank you, ducks!'

He had little time to stop for a chat, so he left her and dived straight into Fred's Café next door, where he indulged in his morning ritual of an egg sandwich. Fred, who was standing behind the counter with the ever-present fag hanging out of his mouth, acknowledged him with a nod and a smile. 'We've had a murder then, Alby? The papers are over there if you want to find out more about it.'

Fred was well known for his dry sense of humour. Cooper laughed. 'Thanks Fred. It's where I get most of my information from.'

He ordered his sandwich and a mug of tea and sat down at one of the tables. He picked up an abandoned copy of the local paper, which was lying on a nearby counter. Splashed across the front page in large letters was the headline "Nun murdered at Beaumont Hall". He read the article, which, disturbingly, contained quite a bit of detail purportedly penned by one Gladys Munson. It provided no clue as to the reporter's journalistic source. As he read the article, he began to understand the superintendent's anger. *Where the bloody hell had she got all this information from?* It was disturbingly accurate. After eating his breakfast, Cooper got up from the table, and, as was his habit, he took his cup and plate back to the counter.

'All right if I take the paper with me, Fred?'

'Help yourself, Alby. Just make sure you get the bastard!'

Cooper walked around the corner to the police station, entered via the front door and climbed the stairs up to the main CID office, where some officers were busy at their desks and one was using the telephone. Those who saw him enter the room stood up.

'As you were. Finish off what you're doing, folks. We'll kick-off the briefing in a couple of minutes.'

The team consisted of two experienced detective sergeants, in the persons of Ian Mills and Brian Pratt, and four constables, two of whom were the trainee detectives, Jane Stewart and Linda Collins. After they had finished their tasks they gave Cooper their undivided attention.

'Thank you, ladies and gents. Before we start, I'd like to welcome Miss Stewart and Miss Collins who will be acting as temporary detective constables on secondment. Welcome aboard, ladies. Please come and see me for a chat after the meeting.'

After these greetings, he ran through the circumstances as far as they were known. He then issued a warning: 'All evidence and information must be passed through DC Terry Cook in the incident office. He'll keep me up to speed.' All eyes focussed on Terry Cook, who was sitting at a desk at the rear of the room. He acknowledged them with a perfunctory salute.

Cooper continued, 'You may be aware that we've already had some coverage in the *East Anglian Recorder*, which was worryingly accurate. However, it doesn't name the source of the information. So, it comes to this: nobody in this room is to speak to the press, whether they are local or otherwise, without my say so. We need to be very careful about what detail goes into the public domain. If I find out anyone from within the force has talked to the press without authorisation, there will be major consequences, and by that, I mean dismissal!'

'Bloody hell. They were quick off the mark, governor,' said Pratt.

'Yes, they were, Brian, but I was going to say that the information in the paper, detailed as it was, had to have come from someone who had attended the scene. I strongly suspect it may have been a member of Lord Roding's staff,' Cooper continued, 'OK. So, moving on, these are our priorities, ladies and gents. Before we run through witness statements taken from the staff at the Hall yesterday, I'll detail the urgent enquiries we need to get covered. Firstly, we want to know more detail about our victim and why she was staying at the Hall. I'm hoping the information from Lord Roding and a search of her room might provide us with this, and it could well be key to solving the case. We need to establish the motive for this murder. I'm hoping if we can do that, it will provide us with a clue as to the identity of the killer.'

Cooper turned to Pratt. 'Brian, I want us to cover the victim's room this morning. So, will you notify Brendan Withers at Scenes of Crime and tell him we'll meet them at the Hall at 11.00am, please? We will require them to carry out a full forensic search of the bedroom.'

'Yes, governor.'

'The post mortem needs to be covered, so I'll do that,' said Cooper. 'when we get a time from the pathologist. Right, search of the grounds. We were unable to carry out a search of the grounds before it got dark last evening. Sergeant Scott and his team were out this morning at first light. They found nothing in the garden or grounds, and there was no sign of the exit route taken by our murderer in the long grass.'

Cooper then turned and addressed his remarks to DS Mills.

'Ian, I want the incident office to remain, for now, up at the village school. We'll run it there for a week to see if we can pick up on any of the local gossip. After that, we'll have to reassess the need for it to be there, as twenty-four-hour security would be quite a commitment for the uniform branch.'

'Yes, sir.'

'One last thing before Sergeant Pratt summarises the witness statements: Mr Stockwell, the superintendent, has just told me he wants us to handle this enquiry entirely ourselves. That is, without importing a murder-investigation team from outside to take over from us. It's quite a vote of confidence, in my opinion.'

The room erupted with ironic cheers.

'I thought you'd be pleased with that. So, we'll try not to let him and ourselves down then, eh? Now, listen in, boys and girls. There is a lot to do. Over to you, Brian.'

'Thank you, governor,' said Pratt. 'Sister Margaret, was a house guest at Beaumont Hall, which is the home of Lord and Lady Roding. Her body was discovered on the ground outside the summerhouse, in the garden, by a kitchen porter named James Davidson. He estimates this to have been around 6.00pm. She was still alive when he found her, but she died after only a few minutes. We believe that she had been struck around the head and neck with a garden spade; this was found nearby. For now, we have young Davidson as the last person to have seen the victim alive. He also said he'd been sent out to speak to her earlier, by Mrs Aldis, the cook, to ask her what she wanted for her dinner. That would have been about 4.25pm. Apparently, at the time, she was doing some painting in the doorway of the summerhouse and she was OK. After he had found her on the floor later, he ran back to the house to get help and the cook, Mrs Aldis, tried to resuscitate her, but it was too late.'

'What's the lad like, Sarge?' asked Linda Collins.

'He was in shock, obviously, but he comes across as a bit naïve, simple even. When I was taking the statement from him, I asked him whether he'd tried to render first aid. He dismissed this because he'd not been trained in first aid and, anyway, in his words, "I didn't like to because I've never touched a nun before."'

'Neither have I, Sarge, but it wouldn't make him a bad person if he did!' offered DC Tom Rogers, the office clown, to peals of laughter.

'Yes, thank you for your contribution DC Rogers,' said Pratt dismissively, 'This isn't *Workers' Playtime.*'

Pratt continued, 'The young man's account is corroborated by Mrs Aldis in her statement. She was in the kitchen virtually all day.'

He surveyed the team over his spectacles. 'By the way, a typed copy of these statements will be in the incident room. I want you all to read them in full. And, I know I'm repeating what the governor said, but I stress this because it is of the utmost importance. Everything must pass through the incident office, so they have the most up-to-date picture.'

He continued, 'Next, we have the statement of the butler, Raymond Jenkins. He states he was cleaning the interior of the Rolls Royce and was carrying out some maintenance on the vehicle for most of the day. He went to the garage around 7.30am and stayed there, apart from going back to serve breakfast in bed to his lordship at 9.30am. A couple of times during the day he went to his own apartment in the house for meals. Around 4.30pm he drove into Colchester to make a few purchases at the wine merchants, before returning to the Hall about 5.10pm. He had dinner in his apartment with his wife Adina. About 5.35pm he went to the dining room of the Hall, where he set about replenishing the decanters. About 6.00pm, young Davidson ran into the room to report finding the victim.'

Cooper turned to Ian Mills, saying, 'Ian, we need to make an enquiry with the person who served Mr Jenkins at the wine merchant's. If they remember him, it would be good to get a statement to corroborate the time of his visit. Also, we need to know whether he was alone or had somebody with him.'

Pratt nodded and continued, 'We have yet to get witness statements from the cleaners and Adina Jenkins, his lordship's nurse.'

'Name sounds foreign,' said Rogers, stating the obvious.

'Well done, Sherlock,' mocked Ian Mills. Rogers' face reddened.

'Right, Brian, what about Stephen Savage who owns the spade?' asked Cooper. 'He states he was working on spare ground next to the summerhouse, doing some digging. He left the spade dug into the ground about 3.30pm and went to his workshop. At 4.15pm two women called Baker visited him by arrangement and they went into the greenhouse to get flowers for a wedding. They stayed with him until 5.30pm. He then went home.'

'And he didn't go back to the summerhouse at all that day?'

'No, governor.'

'OK. In due course, we'll need to speak to the Baker sisters and get a corroborative statement from them.'

'Will do, governor. Linda, I want you with me this morning at the Hall,' said Pratt, 'We'll see if we can get those outstanding statements.'

'Tom and I will call in at the wine merchant's,' said Mills, nodding to Terry Cook. 'So, mark that enquiry down to us please, Terry.

'OK,' said Cooper, 'unless there's anything else, folks, that's it for now. Let's get on.'

The meeting having concluded, Cooper made his way to his office and, having first grabbed a cup of tea, he sat down at his desk facing a large pile of paperwork. It was a fact of life that, whether the DI was running a murder or not, the flow of routine paperwork was relentless.

A knock came on the door and Cooper looked up to see Jane Stewart.

'Come in, Jane, close the door and take a seat.'

Jane was a couple of years older than Cooper. She had been in the force for twelve years and Cooper knew her well. She was five feet ten inches tall and, although she was what some might call "big boned", she was a handsome woman with auburn hair styled in a bob. Cooper knew she possessed a lively sense of humour and was a popular member of the force. Though he also knew her to be something of a worrier.

'Welcome aboard, Jane. This is a bit of a departure for you, being attached to the CID. Think you'll enjoy it?'

'I'm sure I will, governor.'

'Well, for what it's worth, we've worked together before and I know you are more than capable. I'm going to attach you to Ian Mills. Anything you are not sure about, just ask him or Brian Pratt. OK?'

'Will do. Thank you, governor.'

Cooper could see Jane had a very troubled look on her face.

'Would you do something for me, Jane?'

'Yes, governor.'

'Just remember that there's nothing in law that says you can't do your job well and have fun while you're doing it.'

She smiled, 'Thanks governor.'

Jane left the office. The next officer to arrive was Linda Collins, who stood in the doorway. Cooper looked up from his desk before she had the chance to knock on the door.

'You wanted to see me, sir?'

'Yes, Miss Collins, come in and take a seat.'

Cooper hadn't really been able to take a good look at her during the meeting as she had been seated behind a desk, but here she was standing before him: She was twenty-nine years of age, around five feet eight inches in height – shorter than Jane, but still quite tall for a woman – and of slim build. She had black hair, tied back in a french roll. Brown eyes and an exquisitely pretty face. She was smartly dressed in a two-piece, dark-grey suit, underneath which was a white, open neck, blouse. In short, Linda Collins was stunning.

'I understand you were in the Wrens. Is that correct?'

'Yes, sir. Three and a half years, in all.'

'What did you do?'

'I was in Portsmouth for training, at first, then Gosport, as a radio operator. After that I was posted to Malta, where I worked mainly in the radio room on shore.'

'Then after you were demobbed, you joined the police. How much service have you got in?'

'About four years now, sir. I was stationed at Chelmsford and then I was posted to Colchester just after the amalgamation.'

'Dealt with much crime?'

'Shoplifters and domestic assaults. That's about all really.'

'And now you want to be a detective?'

'Yes, sir. I would relish the challenge of being on the CID and I'm sure you'll find that I am a hard worker.'

'What gave you the idea?'

'Well, I've always fancied myself as a detective from the day I joined. But it was Mr Stockwell who suggested my secondment to me, sir.'

'Really? Well, let's do our best not to disappoint him, shall we? I'll attach you to DS Pratt who'll be your first line supervisor. Anything you don't understand, make a point of asking him or DS Mills, OK?'

'Thank you, sir.'

'Once again. Welcome aboard.'

Cooper had two new and welcome additions to his team. He suddenly felt invigorated.

'Jeremy, what the bloody hell is going on down there?'

Her ladyship was on the telephone, having been tipped off by a friend about the murder of Sister Margaret.

She was in full rant and his lordship knew it was best just to say nothing, and let the rant blow itself out before daring to open his mouth.

'Why didn't you call me and let me know what had happened?' asked Fanny. 'Don't I have a right to know?'

'Well, I knew you were busy up in town and I didn't want to disturb you, my darling,' said Jeremy, pathetically.

'You know I was dead set against the idea of that woman staying at the Hall from the very first.'

'I needed her expertise, darling.'

'I told you though, didn't I? I knew she'd be trouble,' scolded Fanny. 'Her and her superior attitude, turning her nose up at me. She was a complete bitch.'

'Oh, do please keep a modicum of respect, my darling. The poor woman's just been brutally murdered.'

'She probably opened her bloody mouth once too often.'

Jeremy was shocked at this diatribe and momentarily lost for words.

'Why didn't you just go to church like normal people?'

'Well, I needed more than that, my precious.'

'And who paid for all her food and drink? Answer me that?'

'She didn't eat a lot, dear; anyway, *noblesse oblige*, what?'

'You're a fool, Jeremy! A fool!' shouted Fanny. 'You just let people take advantage of your good nature.'

'Well, anyway, when are you coming home, dear?'

'I'm not. I have things to do up here in town.'

'But the police may wish to see you,' said Jeremy.

'I can't imagine why they would want to see me, but if they do, they can come here, can't they?' She slammed down the receiver.

Jeremy sat alone in the study in his wheelchair. He wondered why he had ever married the bloody woman.

'Good afternoon, gentlemen,' said Jenkins, as he opened the front door of the Hall to Cooper and Pratt. 'His lordship is expecting you. If you'll come with me, I'll take you to him.'

The officers followed the butler through the ground floor of the house to the study, which was at the rear of the building. The room was light and airy, and there were large french windows, which afforded a view onto the terrace and gardens. Cooper caught sight of the summerhouse, which was only about thirty yards away across the lawn. As they waited, he stood and inspected the framed photographs that were on the mantelpiece of a high stone fireplace. There were several pictures of a young man in uniform, whom Cooper took to be the late Honourable "Teddy" Roding, but there was not one of the current Lady Roding. He thought it rather strange.

They were soon joined by Lord Roding, and, following introductions and the offer of tea, they all sat down.

'Tragic circumstances, my lord.'

'Yes, indeed, Inspector. Sister Margaret was a good woman and an immense help to me. She'd been with us for a couple of months and we had become very used to her being around the place,' said Jeremy.

'What was her purpose for being here, my lord?' asked Cooper.

'Well, with my illness, I now have a lower expectation of life extending beyond more than a few years. Naturally, I have prayed, and I have managed to find solace in Jesus Christ. I find the true "Lord" gives me comfort.'

Oh no. Not another God-botherer, thought Cooper, but instantly scolded himself for his cynical lack of compassion.

His lordship produced a handkerchief and blew his nose loudly. 'I am making it my mission to convert to Catholicism, and, to that end, following a consultation with my school friend, Monsignor Tarquin Crecy, I was able to secure the help of Sister Margaret, who came highly recommended and rightly so.'

'If we should need to speak to him, where could we find Monsignor Crecy, my lord?'

'I have his address in London, Inspector. That is, I have his place of employment. He works from an office in Westminster Cathedral. I'm sure they could put you in touch with him,' said his lordship.

'Only, we'll want to know more about Sister Margaret's background. Put simply, we need to know who we're actually dealing with,' explained Cooper.

'I see. I'm sure Tarquin could answer your questions for you. He's a very kind and resourceful man.'

'How did you get on with her, my lord?'

'Very well. She was at my side almost constantly and she was a great comfort to me. It was a little difficult with her at first because I did have some trouble understanding her accent and so did the staff. But we became more used to it over time, and I helped her with her English pronunciation.

She was due to return to Rome next month, but, alas, that will no longer happen, poor girl.'

'Obviously, we need to know where everybody was at the time of the murder. Would you please tell us your movements during the day, yesterday, my lord?'

'Surely, you don't regard me as a suspect, Inspector?' said his lordship, defensively.

'No, my lord. Not as a suspect. But, then again, we have no suspect at this stage of the enquiry, and we need to establish where everybody was and whether anyone saw anything suspicious; that kind of thing.'

The explanation seemed to pacify his lordship, and he gave his account, albeit reluctantly.

'My day started at around 9.30am, when I received my breakfast tray, which was brought to me by Jenkins. While I was eating, I received a visit from Adina, my nurse, who came to administer some medicine and she remained with me for a short while. Later in the morning, Sister Margaret came and sat with me for an hour or so. I was tired after a restless night and so I decided I would remain in bed.' He continued, 'That put Sister Margaret at something of a loose end, so she said, as it was such a fine day, she would go into the garden to continue with her painting. She was a very talented artist, you know. It's so sad. I had it in mind to offer to speak to my wife to see if she could get some of her work exhibited.'

'And where was Lady Roding, my lord?'

'She was at our London address in Bedford Square. She has her work at the art gallery in Kensington during the week.'

'Did you speak to the sister after she went out into the garden?'

'No. I'm sorry to say, that is the last time I shall ever see or speak to her. In this life, anyway.' He began to weep. 'I'm sorry, Inspector. Who could have done such a thing? She was only a slip of a girl.'

When he had composed himself, his lordship's account was taken down by Pratt in the form of a witness statement. Cooper then informed him that they would like to make a detailed forensic search of Sister Margaret's bedroom. Although his consent was not a requirement, his lordship agreed that, under the circumstances, a thorough search of her room was entirely necessary. On the instructions of his lordship, Jenkins led the officers to an upper floor where they came upon a young constable, who, having been tasked to stand guard, had clearly made himself comfortable and was sitting outside the bedroom reading a copy of Moriarty's *Police Law*.

As if embarrassed that he had somehow been caught out, the constable leapt to his feet. 'Good morning, sir. Just studying for the sergeant's exam.'

'That's all right. I'm pleased to see it son. Everything quiet up here?'

'Yes, sir. Nobody has been near or by apart from Emily and her sister: the two girls who do the cleaning.'

'You didn't let them enter the victim's bedroom, did you?' said Cooper, only half joking.

'No, sir.'

'Good man. How long have you been here?'

'I've been here since taking over from the night-duty man at 6.30am,' said the young constable, buttoning his tunic.

'Good,' said Cooper, 'We are going to carry out a search of the bedroom when Scenes of Crime arrive. Will you enter us on the log and give me the key, please?'

'Yes, sir.' The constable handed over the key, took a pencil from behind his ear and wrote the details down on the log book, as instructed.

'And while we're carrying out the search you can nip round to see Mrs Aldis in the kitchen for ten minutes and get a well-earned mug of tea.'

'Thanks very much, sir.'

Cooper turned to Pratt. 'Brian, will you just go down and look for Brendan? We won't enter the room until you return.'

He waited and chatted with the constable for five minutes or so until Pratt ascended the stairs with Brendan Withers and one of his colleagues. They were laden with metal cases, cameras and other paraphernalia.

After unlocking the door, Withers and his colleague entered the room. Remaining outside and not wishing to get in their way, Cooper poked his head through the doorway to observe their activity. As expected, the sister's bedroom was quite spartan in content and layout. It was a single-sized bedroom with a high dormer window, and with just enough room for a single bed, small wardrobe and dressing table. It was basically a cell with enough available floor space to fit in a small rug.

Following a short briefing by Cooper about the parameters of the search, Withers and his colleague began examining the various surfaces of the furniture and fittings, in a search for fingerprints and blood.

'Right, Brendan, I'll leave it with you,' said Cooper, 'Brian and I have got a post mortem to go to.'

Pratt's face fell. This was news to him. He hated attending post mortems and Cooper knew it. It wasn't a fear of dead bodies per se, after all, he had seen plenty of them in his time. No, Pratt's tolerance altered the day he went to his first post mortem held for a child. This came within a year of Pratt and his wife Marjorie losing a child in infancy. He found that he was unable to remain dispassionate and the experience had totally floored him.

Since then, Cooper had consciously followed a policy of trying to get Pratt to as many post mortems as he could to break his aversion to them. However, Cooper had decided that, henceforth, he would cover any child cases himself.

They walked, in silence, back along the gravel drive towards the Wolseley, and Cooper could sense Pratt was mentally preparing himself, so he grabbed the keys from his sergeant and got behind the wheel. They set off through the country lanes to get back into the town, and, during the drive, Cooper thought he might try to diffuse the tension.

'Did you notice that pair of pink, frilly knickers lying on the floor of the bedroom Brian? Methinks there's more to our nun than meets the eye.'

'Yes, governor,' said Pratt.

'What a woman. What is it they say? You can kiss a nun once, you can kiss a nun twice, but you mustn't get into the habit.'

Brian was just staring out of the window. Even black humour wasn't going to shake him from his reverie.

Cooper and Pratt entered the mortuary twenty minutes late, and they were hit by the sickly-sweet aroma of death, which gripped their throats. The mortician issued each of them with a gown and mask and led them to the examination room. Already present was Arnold Fairweather, forensic pathologist and all round pompous arse. He was not in the best of moods.

'Ah, Inspector, I'm so glad you could grace us with your presence. We have waited long enough, so I have already made a start.'

'Good afternoon, sir,' said Cooper not rising to the sarcasm. 'This is my sergeant, Brian Pratt. We were unavoidably detained.'

Fairweather spared Pratt a nod.

They turned their attention to the cadaver laid on the table before them. Clearly female, as evidenced by her genitalia, she was without discernible facial features as her scalp had been pulled forward over her head. The rib cage had been cut open and the vital organs had been removed.

'I am just about to remove the top of the skull.'

They were subjected to the tormenting whine and grind of the electric saw as the pathologist cut into the bone. It set Cooper's teeth on edge, and he could smell and almost taste the decay emanating from Sister Margaret's body.

Cooper made a point of checking on Pratt and observed that, although he was wearing a slightly pained expression, his colleague had a stoic countenance and had clearly decided that the best approach was to try to take a professional interest in the proceedings.

Cooper had often wondered how the mortuary staff could become so inured to the horrors of their workplace. He recalled an occasion when, as a junior detective, he had witnessed a pathologist eating a ham sandwich, at the body, while conducting a post mortem. The very thought of it caused the nausea to flow back and tighten his throat.

Meanwhile, adding to the unpleasantness, Cooper caught the full putrid smell as her organs were being dissected and examined by another assistant at a separate table.

'An interesting one this. A Carmelite nun, was she?'

'Yes, sir.'

'Well, she's not typical. Not typical at all.'

'Why so, sir?'

'You might be surprised when I tell you that I have already established that she was no longer *virgo intacta*.'

'Jesus Christ!' said Cooper, 'I didn't expect that.'

'I know she was a "Bride of Christ", Inspector, but I don't think it could have been him. Probably more recent than that,' said the pathologist, laughing at his own blasphemy.

'Does that mean she's had sexual intercourse at some time in her life?' asked Pratt, who was catching up fast.

'Yes, Sergeant, that's exactly what I mean. Obviously, they didn't teach Latin at your school,' sneered the pathologist. 'I can also tell you she has given birth to at least one child, possibly even two.'

Cooper was quite taken aback by this revelation. He wanted to be sure that Fairweather was not in error, but he didn't dare question the professional expertise of a pathologist. Particularly not this one.

'There's one other thing you might be interested in, Inspector. There is some old scar tissue inside her left arm. I must say I'm a bit dubious about it.' Fairweather grabbed the sister's left wrist and pulled the arm up into a vertical position. He then indicated the scar tissue, covering an area roughly measuring one inch in width and three inches long, in an irregular oblong shape.

'What do you make of it, sir?' asked Cooper.

'It's difficult to say with any certainty. Although we do see a lot of bodies bearing a variety of scars caused by wartime bombing. I suppose nuns were just as susceptible as any other members of the population. This is several years old though and can't have been caused at the time of death.'

Fairweather dropped the arm unceremoniously, as though he was dealing with a lamb carcass in an abattoir.

The great man carried on with a lengthy and thorough examination of the sister's body, making various observations that were rigorously recorded by a junior colleague for the report.

'Time of death I would put between 4.00pm and 6.00pm yesterday. Cause of death was due to a stroke / cerebral haemorrhage following trauma to the left temporal lobe of the skull. This is entirely consistent with blows from the edge of a heavy instrument. I have been shown the garden spade (BP/1) found at the scene and I can say that this item, given my findings, could well have been used to inflict the fatal blows. I will let you and the coroner have my full report as soon as I can.'

'Thank you very much, sir,' said Cooper, who had to admit to himself that, although he was a nasty piece of work, Fairweather knew his stuff.

Cooper and Pratt left the mortuary for the car park and climbed back into the car to return to the office.

'Blimey, governor. Would you Adam and Eve it? She was a right little minx, wasn't she?' said Pratt.

'Not necessarily, Brian. Yes, this development does raise a lot of questions, but nuns don't always enter the Church straight from school or even as young women. She probably took holy orders having had a different kind of life beforehand. Perhaps there's even a husband somewhere.'

'And what happened to the child?' mused Pratt. 'I would imagine they're probably back in Italy with the father, or some relative or other.'

'Or maybe they were even killed during the war. Who knows?'

'Hopefully the Church can help us with that.'

'By the way, do you fancy stopping off at Fred's for a bacon sandwich?' said Cooper, laughing.

'Not bloody likely, governor!' said Pratt.

3

DAY THREE

Thursday 14th July 1949

Cooper had put on weight recently, mainly due to alcohol consumption, and living on a diet of fish and chips. He had decided a keep-fit regime was needed, and, that morning, he had jogged the half mile to work and even this short distance had proved to be a bit of a struggle. He resolved to start small and build the distance up gradually. One thing he did find irritating was that, following his shower, it took him twice as long as the duration of the run to stop sweating and cool down before he could get dressed for the day.

He was finally engaged in the business of changing his shirt and doing up a tie, when Pratt put his head around the office door.

'I've just been passed an urgent message from the control room for you, governor. It's from Lord Roding who requests that you telephone him urgently on a matter of some importance.'

Cooper reached for the telephone and spoke to Raymond Jenkins, who told him that his lordship would be available to see him at 11.00am.

❖

At the appointed time, Cooper and Pratt arrived at the Hall. They were shown to the dining room, where they found his lordship sitting in his wheelchair. He was holding a large glass of Cognac. He greeted the officers with the offer of "a snifter", which they both politely declined. He had what looked like tear stains on his puffy cheeks.

'I'm afraid I have some grave news for you, Inspector. My old friend, Monsignor Tarquin Crecy passed away a couple of weeks ago; I have only just learned of the fact. To pave the way for your enquiry, so to speak, I telephoned his office at Westminster Cathedral and I was told the sad news by one of his colleagues.'

'That's unfortunate.'

'Yes. I agree, Sergeant.'

'Do you know how he died, my lord?'

'Some type of seizure, apparently.'

'Do you know where it happened?'

'No, other than the fact that he was in London at the time,' Lord Roding continued, 'Although the thing that surprised me almost as much was that the person I spoke to was adamant they had no knowledge of Sister Margaret or any arrangement that might entail a nun being posted to stay with me. I just cannot fathom it.' He shook his head.

'With the greatest of respect, my lord, are you sure you weren't speaking to the wrong person about it?'

'No, no, I'm quite sure. I spoke to his former colleague, Father Michael Thomas, who is a priest himself, and he assured me he had no knowledge of a nun called Sister

Margaret, or indeed any other nun, being sent to help me with my conversion.'

'Well, we were intending to follow this up and make our own enquiries with the Church in the next day or so,' said Cooper, 'but this presents us with something of a quandary.'

'Yes, I suppose it does, Inspector.'

'My lord, do you know what Monsignor Crecy's job actually entailed at Westminster Cathedral?'

'I don't know, specifically. I took it that he was just a high-ranking priest. He did tell me he'd been in Africa earlier in his career, doing missionary-type work and he'd been in the Vatican throughout the war.'

'How did you come to meet Monsignor Crecy again after so many years?'

'It was quite strange really, Inspector. I ran into him quite by chance in Covent Garden when I was up at the RAC club in town a couple of years ago. "Tarkers" and I go back a long way. We were at Marlborough School together, you know. He's from a noble Irish family. The Crecy's have estates in the west of Ireland.'

'So, it was just by way of a chance meeting in the street then, my lord?'

'Yes, it was. Why he should have gone into the Church and even become a senior clergyman puzzled me, since he was a bit of a rogue when we were at school. Up to all sorts of mischief. That would have been the last occupation I'd have thought he'd take up. Anyway, we started to meet for drinks whenever I was up in town. Tarkers always liked a drink. He could certainly tuck it away, for a clergyman.'

'What about Sister Margaret? Did she tell you anything about herself? Her family? How she came to the Church?'

'No, Inspector, she didn't say a lot, really. She played her cards very close to her chest. I used to think she was rather a shy person. She didn't like to talk about herself at all and she was rather evasive on the subject. It was almost as if she felt her life was of no importance in the general scheme of things. She seemed to regard herself as a non-person.'

'Did she tell you where she was during the war?'

'She did tell me she'd been in the Vatican during the war and that was where she had first met Tarquin.'

'What about where she was from originally?'

'She told me she was brought up in Switzerland. The Italian part, around Lake Lugano, I believe.'

'My lord, can you think of anyone who might have had an axe to grind with Sister Margaret?' asked Pratt.

'No, not all.'

'What about your wife, Lady Fanny? How did she get on with her?'

'Oh, Fanny, yes.' Jeremy went quiet for a few seconds as though in contemplation. Then he rallied. 'Well, Fanny has her moments, it's true, but she wouldn't hurt a fly, really. She's absolutely no time for religion, that's for sure. She thinks it's all mumbo jumbo. But as she spends most of her time up in London anyway, she wasn't too troubled by Sister Margaret's presence at the Hall. Out of sight, out of mind, I suppose.'

Jeremy went silent again and stared out of the french windows.

'Anyway,' he asked, with a sudden tone of impatience in his voice. 'May I ask how long your officers will be at the Hall, Inspector?'

'We still need to take statements from one or two members of staff, my lord, and some fingerprints for elimination purposes. Why do you ask?'

'I simply ask, Inspector, because I want things to get back to normal as soon as possible. We are all finding the situation rather difficult.'

'I appreciate that, my lord, but would you really have us do half a job?'

'Don't be impertinent, Inspector,' said Lord Roding, with menace.

'I am not being impertinent, my lord. As I am sure you know, I am bound by law to do my duty. Whether you find that convenient or not is neither here nor there. Thank you for your information. I'll let you know when we have completed our enquiries with the staff. Good day.'

Cooper turned on his heel and marched out of the room with Pratt trailing in his wake. They went back to the car.

'What the bloody hell was all that about, governor?'

'He seemed to suddenly turn nasty, didn't he?'

'He appears to be a worried man, all right.'

'Did you take note of the name of the priest his lordship said he'd spoken to?'

'Yes, governor. Father Michael Thomas.'

'I think we need to have him seen. Not only that but we must give them formal notification of the death of Sister Margaret, in the form of a letter signed by Mr Stockwell. Will you compose something for me please, Brian, as soon as we get back to the nick? I just have to run a short errand in the town.'

'Righto, governor.'

❖

On arrival back at the police station, Cooper left Pratt at the rear door and walked off into the town centre. He was intent on getting to the bottom of the woman "Brenda", as the intrigue was beginning to dog his thoughts.

He made straight for the greengrocers to see Sadie.

'Hello, ducks. Unusual to see you here this time of day.'

'Yes, Sadie, I know. I wanted to speak to you about this girl Brenda.'

'Haven't you found her yet then?'

'No, I haven't. You know, it might help if you were to give me a clue. A surname would be good.' Cooper didn't mean to sound sarcastic, but on reflection he realised he probably had.

'Well, let's see. I was at school with her mum, what was her maiden name? It'll come to me in a minute. She married Arthur Collins. So, Collins. Will that do?'

'It's a start. But I can't think of a Brenda Collins. Maybe she's a recruit.'

'Anyway,' said Sadie, 'it shouldn't be too hard to find her; her uncle Tom works for the police as well.'

'Where?'

'Colchester, of course.'

'Mum's maiden name?'

'Yes. Yes, it was Stockwell,' she said triumphantly.

The shock hit him, as he made the connection, with the likelihood that Brenda was in fact Linda.

'Sadie! For heaven's sake. What have you got me into?'

'Do you know him then?'

'Do I know him? He's only my divisional commander, that's all!'

'See, I told you she was from a good family, didn't I?'

She just didn't understand the significance of her revelation.

Cooper had. The hair was standing up on the back of Cooper's neck, and, after visiting Sadie, he left feeling as nauseous as he had been at the post mortem. Sadie had obviously confused the name Brenda with Linda. He would have to be very careful indeed.

Cooper walked back to the police station in something of a daze. He climbed the stairs to his office, shut the door and sat at his desk. Remembering that he had a quarter bottle of Scotch in his draw, he fished it out and poured himself a sensible measure. It was only just after 1.00pm, but he felt the need. After he had barely managed one swig, a knock came on the door. He hid the glass under the desk.

'Come in.'

The door opened. It was Brian Pratt. 'I've done the letter, governor. Thought you'd like to give it the once over.'

'Come in, Brian, and shut the door.'

Brian handed over the draft letter, which was written in his own hand.

'Sorry, governor. I know my handwriting's not the best, but I thought I'd write it out first and agree the content before attempting to type it. Do you want me to read it to you?'

'Good idea, Brian.'

Brian could tell that Cooper was not in a good frame of mind but kept it to himself. 'I quote, "Addressed to His Eminence Archbishop Mahoney, Westminster Cathedral, Victoria Street, London SW1.

"Dear Archbishop Mahoney, I am writing to convey the sad news that officers of this force are investigating the murder of Sister Margaret of the Sacred Heart of Jesus. The murder was committed on the estate of Lord Jeremy Roding at Beaumont Hall, Beaumont, Essex, on Tuesday 12th July 1949. The investigating officer is Detective Inspector Cooper, who is based at Colchester Police Station. We understand that Sister Margaret was seconded to Lord Roding, for a period of three months, to prepare him for his conversion to the Roman Catholic faith. Furthermore, the secondment was arranged by the late Monsignor Tarquin Crecy, a friend of Lord Roding. The body of Sister Margaret is presently resting in the mortuary of the Essex County Hospital, Colchester, Essex. To enable our officers to investigate the murder, and bring the murderer(s) to justice, we need information and assistance from the Catholic Church. Furthermore, the coroner will require details of a Church representative with whom we can liaise over this sad matter. We look forward to hearing from you. Yours sincerely, Thomas Stockwell, Superintendent."

'Good. I think that hits the mark all right, Brian, don't you?' said Cooper.

'Yes, governor.'

'Right. Get one of the girls to type it for you. In fact, better still, give Mavis a ring at Mr Stockwell's office. He's got to sign it, so she may as well type it. When that's done, I want you to deliver it this afternoon. We need a response from them ASAP.'

Brian withdrew and went on his way, wondering what was troubling his old friend.

4

DAY FOUR
Friday 15th July 1949

Cooper was intent on getting into the office as early as he could to read the witness statements in preparation for the morning briefing. So, he called in at Fred's Café for an egg sandwich, to be consumed at his desk.

As he made his way along the High Street, he was thinking about the previous day's exchange with Lord Roding. *I'm sure he's going to make a complaint to the chief constable's office, but it's too bloody late now. Perhaps I could have been a bit more diplomatic, but his sense of superiority and entitlement gets right up your nose.*

Then he remembered the revelation made by Aunt Sadie that had led him to realise that Linda Collins was the niece of Tom Stockwell. *I'll have to keep that piece of information to myself, for now. In fairness, she can't help who she's related to. Still a bloody tricky situation, all the same.*

Cooper entered the foyer of the police station and exchanged greetings with the front-office constable as he was let in through the wicket door. He made his way up to the CID office and hung up his jacket. It was too early for the trolley, so, after retrieving a mug and the makings from his locker, he made himself tea from the hot-water tap in the gent's toilet. *I really must stop drinking this crap,* he thought to himself. He wondered about the hygiene aspect of drinking straight from the hot-water tank.

He got to his desk and started on the witness statements sitting in his in tray.

Later that morning Cooper convened a meeting of the murder team.

Brian Pratt spoke first and related the details of his visit to Westminster Cathedral. Once again, Father Thomas was not available and so he had left the letter with his secretary, who confirmed the fact by signing his pocket notebook. He also provided a summary of the witness statements taken since the last meeting.

This was followed by Brendan Withers giving an account of the search of Sister Margaret's bedroom. 'Initially, we carried out a search for fingerprints and traces of blood on the various surfaces. There was a complete absence of blood as far as we could see. We lifted some fingerprints from the inside of the bedroom door, the window, the sill and the dressing table. We still need to complete taking elimination fingerprints from a few of the staff. There's only a couple left to do.'

'Fine. Thank you, Brendan. Sounds as though you are making progress.'

'Oh, and there was another thing that occurred to me, governor. Do you want us to ask his lordship for his fingerprints, leave it, or do you want to broach the subject with him yourself?' enquired Withers.

'Of course, we need them. You can ask him Brendan. Why should he be treated any differently? But be careful. He's a bit prickly at present. We will need to do the same with Lady Fanny as well, when we finally get along to see her. Dignity is a fine thing, but their prints are essential.'

'Right you are, governor. Getting back to the room, we carried out a physical search. There wasn't a lot there, really. A spare habit and wimple were hanging in the wardrobe with another pair of "sensible" shoes. There were no civilian clothes present, apart from some underwear in the drawer: a brassiere, slips and things. Quite surprised me, really; they were sexy, pink, frilly jobs. Not what one might expect a nun to wear underneath her habit. But then who am I to speculate about that?'

DC Rogers, the office wag, had a mischievous glint in his eye, stifled a titter and nearly made an inappropriate remark about rude habits, but he thought better of it. In anticipation, Cooper and Pratt both gave Rogers a menacing stare as there were female officers present; they would have leapt on him as soon as he opened his mouth. But there was no need for them to do so. The lad, for once, pulled himself up just short of embarrassing himself.

Withers ploughed on, 'Pair of dirty knickers on the floor under the bed. We have taken those, and we are testing them for any traces of semen. What else? The religious books one might expect, a Bible and a book I think they call a catechism. Also, there was a diary and a letter you'll be interested in, sir. The letter purports to be from Lady Fanny and is quite threatening in its tone. I have it here. Would you like me to read it out?'

'Please do, Brendan,' said Cooper.

Withers read aloud, 'I quote. "Sister Margaret, I am writing to you to give you a warning. Someone told me that you have been talking to his lordship about the state of our marriage. This is something that I won't put up with. It's got nothing to do with you. You are a guest in our house and you are here to give my husband advice about the Church, so he can become a Catholic. Nothing more! If you carry on talking about our marriage, I will deal with you!" signed Lady Francine Roding and dated 4th July 1949.'

'Thank you, Brendan,' said Cooper. 'It does sound quite an angry letter. It's certainly the nearest sign we have of a motive and it gives us a line of enquiry. We need to see her as soon as we can and ask her whether she can prove her whereabouts for the time of the murder.' He continued, 'Ian, will you have a good look through the victim's diary, please? Obviously, if there is anything of interest, let me know.'

'Yes, sir, will do,' replied Mills.

Withers chipped in again, 'One other thing. It did strike me as odd that there was a total absence of any personal documentation, such as a passport, identity card or any ration book. There was no validation for her being in this country at all.'

'Really?' said Cooper. 'She must have travelled to the UK using some form of documentation. As for a ration book, if Lord Roding was going to feed her while she was here, but didn't want to explain her presence, then she may not have needed to apply for one of her own.'

'Maybe Lord Roding has locked her documents away in his safe,' speculated Pratt.

Cooper acknowledged the possibility. 'Brian, perhaps you would check that and have a word with his lordship?'

'Will do, governor. I'll go there with Brendan. That way we can back each other up if he has one of his tantrums.'

'What about the murder site, Brendan? Was anything else found there?'

'No, nothing that wasn't mentioned during the post mortem. There was no blood found or bodily fluids other than those of the victim. The murder weapon certainly appears to be the spade. The victim's blood was on the leading edge, and, as you know, sir, the pathologist was quite satisfied when he carried out a physical comparison between the spade and the wounds.'

'What about the crucifix?' said Pratt, 'Did you find it when you moved the body?'

'No. That's still missing. We did find a couple of chain links that appear to have been broken off during the attack. They were underneath the body. It looks as though it was snatched from her neck.'

'Anything else?'

'That's it for now, sir.'

'Sorry, governor, there were a couple of other things I was going to mention,' said Pratt, 'I telephoned the office of Father Thomas at Westminster Cathedral this morning to follow up on the letter, but he wasn't available to speak to me. So, I left a message with his secretary for him to give us a call. The other thing was that there is quite an interesting statement from his lordship's nurse, Adina Jenkins. Shall I read it out, governor?'

'Please do, Brian.'

Pratt read the statement aloud, '"I live within the main house on the family estate of Lord and Lady Roding at Beaumont Hall, Beaumont, near Colchester, Essex. I live with my husband, Raymond, who is his lordship's butler. Our apartment is located on the south side of the Hall. The summerhouse is on the other side of the building. I have lived on the estate since 1945, but I have been employed on the estate as Lord Roding's nurse since 1947. I am aware Sister Margaret has been staying at the Hall for a few weeks as a house guest. I have spoken to her on a few occasions as she spends a lot of time with his lordship. I have found her quite pleasant although a bit shy. I did not speak to Sister Margaret on the day she was found dead. I have been asked by the police where I was during that day. His lordship spent most of the day resting in his rooms. I was with him for two short periods, although I returned to our apartment afterwards to do some washing and prepare Raymond's meals. One thing that does occur to me is that, about 4.30pm, I went to the bedroom and gave his lordship his medicine. As I was doing so I looked out of the window that faces onto the lawn and the summerhouse. I saw Savage, the gardener, who was seated on the bench with Sister Margaret. They were chatting in quite a friendly way. I have been asked about whether I could be mistaken. I am sure it was Savage. The weather was fine and clear, and I had a clear view of him, which was not obstructed in any way. I have spoken to Savage on several occasions as I enjoy his company. He is a bit of a joker and he has been teaching me how to swear in English."'

'Mr Savage didn't mention he had been speaking to Sister Margaret in the statement you took from him, did he, Brian?'

'No, governor. He didn't,' confirmed Pratt.

Mills handed a typed copy of Savage's statement to Cooper.

'We'll have to interview him about that. It was his spade that was used to kill her and, according to this statement, he was one of the last to see her alive. There is still the question of blood-stained clothing, so we need to get into his house and the buildings he uses on the estate to search for them.'

'Do you want me to nick him then, governor?'

'I think we'll have to, Brian. I don't want any fanfare or anything appearing in the press, so we need to do this discreetly. That includes keeping it low key within the station. Brian, you took his original statement, so I want you to carry out the arrest of Mr Savage with Miss Collins. Ian, DC Rogers and Scenes of Crime will carry out the searches. I'll be there as well. I'll speak to Lord Roding to let him know what is happening and the grounds for the arrest. Bearing in mind our star witness, Adina, is still on the estate, we'll need to alert his lordship to the possible staff problems that might arise, if or when Savage is bailed. I also want to get his consent to search the buildings.'

'Do you want us to bring Savage to Colchester or take him to Harwich, governor?'

'We'll bring him here, Brian. I'll go and speak to the station sergeant and explain the need for it to be kept as quiet as possible. I'll only say this once ladies and gents: I want us to keep this to ourselves. We might have the right man, but we might not. So, we say nothing to people outside of the team and we assume nothing. I'm off to inform Mr Stockwell. I want us all back here, ready to leave, at 11.30am.' The team dispersed to get their things together.

Early that afternoon, the front door of Keeper's Cottage was opened by a bewildered-looking Stephen Savage, who was fighting to prevent two barking black Labradors from bursting out into the front garden. Brian Pratt was on the doorstep with Linda Collins. The other officers were in a second car parked further up the road, but in sight of the officers at the front door.

'Sergeant Pratt, just a minute. Let me deal with these two!' He slammed the front door shut, and, through the translucent glass of the front door, Pratt watched him struggle with the two dogs, finally managing to shut them in the kitchen. He then returned to open the front door.

'Sorry about that, Sergeant. They are a lively pair of buggers, but they don't bite. More of a nuisance really. How can I help you?'

'Stephen, is it all right if we come in?'

'Yes, please do come in. Would you like a cup of tea?'

'Not now, thanks. There is something I need to explain to you,' said Pratt.

'Come through.' Savage led them into the front room.

'Stephen, when I took your witness statement from you a few days ago, you told me you were digging near the summerhouse until about 3.30pm. Then you left that area and went to the workshop. Is that right?'

'Yes, that's right.'

'And you left the spade dug into the ground?'

'Yes, I did.'

'Did you go back to the area where you left the spade at all, later in the day?'

'No, I didn't.'

'We have a witness statement from somebody who says

they saw you sitting talking to Sister Margaret later, at around 4.30pm, outside the summerhouse.'

'Well, that's not right.'

'What we must do now, Stephen, is formally arrest you and search your premises. Then you'll be taken to the police station to be interviewed by me and my colleague Linda. It'll be very discreet, so don't worry. So, Stephen Savage, I am arresting you on suspicion of the murder of Sister Margaret,' Pratt cautioned him.

Savage was stunned; he stumbled back against a wall and started to hyperventilate. Pratt took his arm, eased him onto a chair in the hallway and urged him to take a series of deep breaths to regulate his breathing. *"Don't worry?" Brian knew he'd said something stupid as soon as the words had left his lips. To have to arrest Savage was an unpleasant duty and he felt sorry for him. How was Savage supposed to not worry?*

After a few minutes, Savage seemed to recover his senses and Pratt escorted him to the living room.

'What about the dogs?'

'Don't worry, Stephen. We'll have them looked after.'

'Please don't put me in handcuffs, Sergeant Pratt.'

'That won't be necessary. We're going to the police station where I intend to interview you straight away. Stephen, please be assured, we're not in the business of locking people up and throwing the key away.'

Savage didn't look at all convinced.

'Thing is, Stephen, to do the job properly, we're going to have to search the house. I'm sure you understand.'

Savage was still dumbstruck and just nodded.

Pratt turned to Collins and said, 'Linda, will you nip outside and call the others in, so they can get on with the search?'

Collins left the house.

'What about the dog's food?'

'Don't worry about the dogs, we'll arrange to have them fed if necessary.'

Brian Pratt was a man who was outwardly bluff. A man's man. Inwardly, he was intelligent and sensitive, and he was very good at reading people. To him, the arrest of Savage didn't seem right. It was a procedural necessity, of course. But, in his heart of hearts, Pratt didn't really believe that they had arrested their murderer. Collins returned a couple of minutes later.

Leaving Ian Mills and his team to carry on with the rest of the search, Collins and Pratt drove Savage to the police station, where, on arrival, the facts surrounding the arrest were related to the station sergeant by Linda.

'Do you want to place Mr Savage in a cell?' asked the Sergeant, 'Or do you want to go straight to interview?'

'Straight to interview, please, Sarge.'

'You've done what?' said Lord Roding, indignantly.

'We have arrested your gardener, Stephen Savage, for the murder of Sister Margaret,' said Cooper.

'But why? He can't have done it. He's been with us for years.'

'What prompted his arrest, my lord, is a witness statement given to us by Adina Jenkins in which she states that, while she was giving you your medication during the afternoon of the murder, she looked through the window and saw Savage outside speaking to Sister Margaret. They were apparently both seated on the bench in front of the summerhouse. This was about 4.30pm.'

'She didn't mention it to me at the time.'

'Well, I would imagine, at that time, it was of no real consequence, my lord.'

'No, I imagine it wasn't.'

'And, of course, those circumstances, taken together with the fact that it was his spade that was the murder weapon, means we really should consider him a suspect.'

'Yes, I see,' his lordship sighed. 'Oh dear. Bloody tragedy if it does turn out to have been Savage. He's a good man and a damned fine gardener. No, I can't believe he's capable of such a thing.'

'It's not a foregone conclusion, my lord. In all cases, we are required to prove guilt by adducing evidence and although we had grounds to arrest him we are a long way from having enough proof to charge him with anything. We will keep an open mind.'

'So, what happens now?'

'He'll be interviewed at the police station.'

'Does he need a solicitor?'

'As we're investigating an offence of murder, I would say he does, my lord.'

'Please tell him, Inspector, that I'll cover his legal costs. I'll speak to Geoffrey Green, who is our family solicitor, and arrange for him to receive representation, if it becomes necessary.'

'Which company of solicitors would that be, my lord?'

'Green and Green, of course. Will he get bail, do you think?'

'Too early to say, my lord.'

'I understand. I imagine these things take time.'

'They do. Also, there are a couple of other matters I need to discuss with you.'

'And what would they be, Inspector?'

'First, my lord, we need your consent to search Savage's places of work. The workshop, greenhouse and anywhere else he might have regular access to. We'd be looking for blood-stained clothing.'

'Yes, you have that, of course. Obviously, I don't want you to enter staff living quarters or even my own rooms, come to that. Nor do I want you rooting around in my study. If it becomes at all necessary, then speak to me about it.'

'I will, my lord. Thank you. The other matter I wish to speak to you about is the question of discretion and the ongoing harmony within the Hall, as far as witnesses are concerned. It might seem to you to be an alien term, but most of your staff come into that category. We're inclined to keep Mr Savage's arrest low key for now, but, should he be charged with the murder, then, of course, the situation will change. We would apply to the magistrates to have him remanded in custody, and the fact of his arrest would be in the public domain, with coverage in the national press being a distinct possibility.'

'Why should that present a problem?' said his lordship, haughtily.

'Apart from the adverse publicity, it shouldn't present a problem. The problem might come if Savage is not charged and he is released on bail.'

'I don't quite follow you.'

'At some point, he'll become aware of Adina Jenkins' witness statement and what she said about him. That being the case we'll need you to ensure that there's no strife between Savage and Mrs Jenkins.'

'I see what you mean. Well, please let me know if he does get bail. I'm sure we could keep him busy and away from the main house.'

'I will, of course. Thank you, my lord.' Cooper took his leave and Jenkins ushered him to the front door. After seeing the detective off of the premises, Jenkins returned to his lordship in the study.

'Well, Jenkins. What do you make of that?'

'My lord. I really can't see that Savage would be capable of something like that. I don't think I've ever heard the man as much as raise his voice.'

'Yes. Completely out of character, I would say. We must get him some legal representation. Will you get Green and Green Solicitors for me?'

Jenkins did his master's bidding and returned with the telephone, which he placed on the desk next to his lordship's wheelchair. He handed him the receiver. 'My lord, I have Mr Geoffrey Green on the telephone for you now.'

'Thank you, Jenkins.' Jenkins withdrew and closed the door behind him.

'Hello Geoffrey.'

'Good afternoon, my lord. How are you today?'

'Surviving, thank you. I have been meaning to contact you about some amendments that I wish to make regarding my will. However, I also have a criminal matter that I wish to discuss with you involving one of my staff who has just been arrested for murder.'

His lordship gave the solicitor a summary of the circumstances surrounding Sister Margaret's murder and the arrest of Savage.

'My lord, it's been a few years since I dealt with criminal cases. However, if you are content, I will instruct our junior partner, Reginald Cohen, to act for Mr Savage. He is a good man. He can start by attending the police station, and I would be happy to deal with the amendments to your will.'

'Fine. When do you think you could come and see me?'

'I could come to the Hall at 5pm, if that would be convenient, my lord?'

'Yes, that would be good. Would you have time to dine with me afterwards?'

'I would indeed, my lord. Thank you.'

'Splendid. I will see you then.'

After leaving the Hall, Cooper made his way on foot to Keeper's Cottage where he met Ian Mills, who was standing in the front garden eking out the last few draws from a cigarette. On seeing his boss walking up the path towards him, he stubbed it out on a gatepost.

'How are you getting on with the search then, Ian?'

'We're about half way through, governor. Nothing of interest downstairs. The others are upstairs at present. There's not much in the way of clothing, but what little there is we're going to take for forensic examination. We still need to search a couple of small outbuildings at the back of the place. The dogs seem to have finally settled down though, which is a blessing. They're a bit of a nuisance.'

'Good. I've spoken to his lordship and he's given his consent for us to search the other buildings, the greenhouse and workshop. So, I'll leave you to it then, Ian. Let me know if you need anything.'

On his return to the police station, Cooper caught up with Brian Pratt. He informed him of the fact that Lord Roding was arranging legal representation for Savage, which was to be provided by his own solicitors.

'Yes, governor. Their Mr Cohen has been on the blower already. I gave him a run down on what Mr Savage is saying. Basically, Savage has provided an alibi. Apparently, on the afternoon of the murder, he was in the company of a Mrs Ivy Baker until 5.30pm.'

'Then we need to visit the lady to check his alibi straight away, Brian. Take young Miss Collins with you.'

Later that afternoon, having made their enquiry, Pratt and Collins returned to the inspector's office. By this time, the search team had also completed their business and so Cooper debriefed them all.

'How did you get on, Brian?'

'We got statements from Mrs Ivy Baker and her sister Agnes, and they seem entirely genuine and respectable. They both, quite independently of each other, corroborated Stephen Savage's statement in every respect. So, he has a firm alibi up to 5.30pm on the day of the murder.'

'That leaves him with a window of half an hour up to 6.00pm, but it certainly puts to bed any notion of Savage being in the sister's company outside the summerhouse at 4.30pm,' observed Cooper, 'Ian, what's the position on your side?'

'We've completed a search of all of the relevant premises on the estate, governor. We found nothing of any startling interest. We have taken all his clothes for forensic examination, just in case. But there are none with any visible signs of blood on them.'

'OK. Brian, have you taken the clothes he was arrested in?'

'Yes, governor. There was no sign of blood on them either. I must say, whenever I've seen him, he's been wearing the same clothes and he told me, in interview, they were the ones he was dressed in on the day of the murder.'

'Yes. He's not exactly Mr Sartorial Elegance, is he? Anyway, we'll need to send them all to the lab for examination, but he's got to have some clothes to be going on with. What's he wearing now?'

'He's wearing an old boiler suit at the minute.'

Cooper turned his attention to Collins. 'Linda, will you get ten quid out of petty cash, go into town, and get him some new clothes and shoes? If you hurry, you should just be able to catch the shops before they shut for the day. Please keep it modest, mind!'

'Will do, governor.' Realising there was no time to lose, Linda Collins left the meeting to go to the cells to get Savage's clothing and shoe sizes, and then she would dash up to the High Street. The station sergeant would obtain the cash for her while she was speaking to the prisoner.

'Right,' continued Cooper. 'We need to get a witness statement from Mr Savage based on what he's saying about his alibi. Then I'm going to arrange for him to be released without charge. What we have now is only circumstantial evidence. He isn't completely in the clear, mind you. He would still have had a small window of opportunity, but we'll have to wait a while for the forensic results from the examination of his clothing. If we get anything more tangible later, we can always rearrest him.'

Later that evening, Stephen Savage was released on bail pending further enquiries, to return to Colchester Police Station at a date in the future. During the interview, he had been shown the witness statement of Adina Jenkins, so Cooper made a point of telephoning Lord Roding to explain the position before he was released from custody.

Linda Collins appeared to have spent the ten pounds wisely and, on his release, Savage was the smartest he had been in a long while. He was driven home by Pratt and Collins, and on his arrival, he was welcomed by the two Labradors, like a returning hero.

It was mid-evening, and Cooper wasn't intending to stay in the office for much longer and run the risk of getting involved in anything else. He knew he'd had enough for one day, and if he was needed, they could always dig him out from home.

'There's not really a lot more we can do tonight, Brian. I think we could both do with an early night. So, don't hang around too late, will you? Stand the team down until the morning. We'll have a briefing and catch up around 10.00am.'

Cooper strode off through the town centre and eventually stopped off at his local, the Hole in the Wall.

His body ached for refreshment, having not eaten since breakfast, but, as he couldn't find a chip shop that was still open, he'd have to make do with a pint of Double Diamond and a pickled egg. He settled at a table in a corner of the bar and reflected on the day's events. The next thing he was aware of, was somebody gently shaking him.

'Alby, Alby, time to go home, mate.' It was the barman. Alby had nodded off.

He left the pub, took the few short steps along the path to his digs, and quietly entered the house. Errol, the dog, had got used to the sound and smell of him by now, and he didn't turn a hair, but Cooper, despite his best efforts to remain silent, had registered on his landlady's radar.

A shout came out of the darkness, 'Who's that?'

'Pearl. It's me, Alby. Sorry to disturb you.'

Pearl, his landlady, lived at the rear of the house. She was loud, brassy and ample bosomed, but strangely attractive, and she was constantly in search of a man. Cooper's better judgement told him that he should keep their relationship business-like and that it would be best he didn't get involved with her socially, now or at any time.

The hall light came on, and there she stood, dressed in her finery and holding her stilettos, one in each hand. She had obviously only just come home from a night out. She didn't look too bad, or was Cooper weakening?

'Ah, it's you, Alby! Had a busy day, darling? Why don't you come and have a nightcap with me?'

'Oh. I don't think so, Pearl. I've got to be up early in the morning.'

'Oh please, Alby.'

'All right. Just the one.' He didn't want to upset her.

Pearl led him to her accommodation at the back of the house and shut the door behind them. When Cooper had first taken up residence, she had let it be known that she was available to "turn down his sheets", should he ever feel the need. He thought the old "sauce box" was just pulling his leg, so he had ignored her remarks. He was about to find out that she wasn't. There was nothing cultured about this Pearl.

5

DAY FIVE

Saturday 16ᵗʰ July 1949

Cooper was restless. The house and its residents were silent, which suited him well as he was hoping to avoid bumping into the "she devil", who had so comprehensively taken advantage of him the previous evening.

He quietly got dressed and tiptoed along the hall to the kitchen where he nearly fell over Errol, his landlady's springer spaniel. Although, according to his certificate of pedigree, the dog's name was "Flynn of the East", Cooper had bestowed on him the nickname "Errol", which seemed more appropriate, since he tried to have sex with everything that moved. Errol had got to his feet, in excited expectation, the moment Cooper had stepped into the kitchen. After a quick rinse and shave in the sink, he took the beast over to Castle Park for some much-needed exercise.

And exercise they did. After twenty minutes of chasing the dog around the park, they emerged from the Castle Park gates with Cooper panting and sweating. *No need to jog to work today*, he told himself. He turned right and walked along the High Street, with Errol finally back on the lead.

He'd struggled to round up the little bugger, who as soon as he was released, had scampered off into the undergrowth to chase rabbits without as much as a backward glance. On reaching his digs, Cooper returned Errol to the kitchen, had another quick wash and went on his way.

He dutifully made a point of checking on Sadie at the shop, but, once again, she started using the B word, "Brenda". He had certainly resolved that conundrum to his own satisfaction, but it still had worrying prospects for him, and, for now at least, he wasn't prepared to discuss it further. He caught the apple that was thrown to him and moved on swiftly along the High Street to the police station. He got to the office, made himself a cup of tea from the tap, and settled into work mode.

Cooper later spoke to the troops and set out his plan for the day.

'Brian, I want you and Miss Collins with me. We need to go and see her ladyship up in London. But, first, I'm going to have to see the boss to bring him up to speed regarding Mr Savage.'

'Are we going by rattler or using the car, governor?'

'Car, I think, Brian.'

Cooper made a telephone call to the superintendent's office and spoke to Mavis whose turn it was to work on a Saturday morning.

'Is, his nibs in, Mavis?' asked Cooper following a brief and quite unnecessary introduction. She knew his voice well enough by now.

'No. He's out with the borough surveyor at present, Alby. They're having a site meeting about the new station. He'll be back about 10.30am, I expect. Let me just check what he's doing after that.' Mavis inspected the diary. 'He's playing golf at midday, with members of the police committee,' reported Mavis.

'He's what?' asked Cooper, incredulously.

'Playing golf with members of the police committee.'

'Blimey. Nice work if you can get it.'

'If you come in around 10.45am, you should catch him. Shall I tell him what you want to see him about?'

'We need a search warrant for an address in London,' said Cooper.

Cooper later walked up to the superintendent's office. After she had announced his arrival, Mavis ushered him into the *inner sanctum*. He found the superintendent lacing up his brown brogues. He was wearing a casual, collared shirt with short sleeves, and plus fours. He reminded Cooper of Stan Laurel.

'Good morning, Albert. Is this about the murder? Only I haven't got long to chat. I have an important meeting at midday.'

'Yes, it is, sir,' said Cooper, smiling to himself. *Lying old git.*

He quickly brought the superintendent up to date regarding the arrest of Savage, but he seemed somewhat preoccupied, ambivalent even.

'Fine, fine. Before you go on, what is the current situation regarding the theft of Councillor Davis' chickens?' *What the bloody hell is he worrying about that for?* thought Cooper, *We have got a murder on our hands.* 'Young Rogers is dealing with that, sir. I must confess, I'm not aware of any progress at present.'

'Well, it happened well over a week ago and I haven't seen the crime report yet. Who is his sergeant?'

'That, would be DS Mills sir.'

'Well, get a grip of him, will you? It smacks of a "lack of supervision", all round.'

'Yes, sir. If I may just return to the murder for a moment, we have another line of enquiry. When we got Scenes of Crime to carry out a forensic search of the victim's room, they came across this letter, which, as you will see, purports to have been signed by Lady Roding on the 4th July. It is threatening in its tone, and it shows there was quite a rift between her and Sister Margaret.' Cooper handed the original letter to the superintendent for his perusal.

After a few seconds of reading the letter and a couple of minutes of procrastination, Stockwell took off his spectacles and looked him in the eye. 'I see the point you are making Albert, it is quite threatening, but what action are you proposing to take?'

'Sir, we've been trying to establish a motive for the murder and this gives us a strong indication that Lady Fanny Roding may have had one. I would like your permission to apply to a magistrate for a warrant to search the Roding's house in Bloomsbury for evidence. Specifically, blood-stained clothing and any other letters that might be there.'

'Do you really think that a search warrant is absolutely necessary?' asked Stockwell, visibly wincing.

'Yes, sir. I do.'

Stockwell got up from his desk and walked across the room to close the office door. He then returned to his seat.

'Precisely what grounds do you think you have to justify a search warrant?'

'The threats contained in the letter give us reasonable suspicion that Lady Roding had a motive for a murder that actually took place in the grounds of her family estate. The signs of blood dispersal at the scene indicate the murderer would have some spattering of blood on his or her garments. The murder only happened a few days ago, and I believe we still have a chance of recovering the clothing. So, in my opinion, there isn't a moment to lose.'

'Well, I think you need more than just this letter to give you enough grounds. I really cannot authorise it on this basis.'

Cooper tried to argue the case further, but to no avail.

'Albert, you said yourself the murder only happened a couple of days ago, it's early days yet.'

'Sir, if we leave the search much longer, the clothing, if it is indeed there, will have been laundered or disposed of. I realise the connection is somewhat tenuous, but we're investigating a brutal murder and by any objective assessment the letter amounts to a threat. So, I think this gives us the reasonable suspicion we require, and enough to justify a warrant,' he said with all the vehemence he dare employ.

Stockwell shook his head and remained intransigent. He was simply not having it. 'No, Inspector. Are you seriously asking me to let you apply for a warrant to search the home of a peer of the realm based on such flimsy evidence as this? The force would be sued into bankruptcy! Just go and see her, man. Who knows? If you ask her, she might even let you look around!'

Cooper withdrew and returned to the police station. He was crestfallen, deflated and bloody angry. He told himself he would make a detailed note of the conversation in his policy book so if he was called to account for failing to carry out the search, he would be covered. By his estimation, he had more than enough evidence to take the action that he'd proposed. The law didn't require certainty, just reasonable suspicion.

Cooper mulled over the manner of his rejection, but reminded himself that, like many senior police officers, Stockwell had no experience of dealing with serious crime since he'd spent all his police service in uniform. This was just a fact of life and quite understandable. Unfortunately, Stockwell also, apparently, had no backbone, which, in Alby Cooper's opinion, was not. He was now beginning to understand the nature of the *poisoned chalice* that Stockwell had presented him with.

After arriving back, Cooper walked into the main CID office and found Pratt sitting at his desk using the telephone. On seeing his boss, he replaced the receiver on its cradle, and gave him his full attention.

'No joy with Mr Stockwell then, governor?' said Pratt, who had worked with Cooper since they were constables and could almost read his mind.

'What makes you think that?'

'Well, you don't look very happy.'

'Yes, well, Stockwell doesn't seem to think we have enough to justify a search warrant.' He swore under his breath.

'So, does that mean we're not going to London to see the lovely Lady Fanny then?' said Pratt, disappointed.

'No, Brian, we're still going. We'll take Miss Collins with us as well. I think we'll need a female officer with us, and she'll benefit from the experience. Lady Fanny is a bit of a challenge, apparently.'

Within the hour, the three of them climbed into the Wolseley and headed off towards London. While in the car on the way up to town, Cooper briefed Pratt and Collins about the approach that he intended to take with her ladyship.

'Even though we didn't manage to get our search warrant, I still think it would pay us not to give Lady Roding any advanced warning of our visit,' explained Cooper. 'So, we'll have to play it by ear and take a chance on her being at home. If she isn't, we'll sit it out for a while and just hope that she returns. I'm pretty sure if we were to go to the front door, speak to a member of staff and tell them the reason for our visit they would only find some way of tipping her off.'

Cooper was soon to find out that Linda Collins was not only a strikingly attractive young woman, but that she also possessed a sharp mind. Certainly, he and Pratt were both impressed by her attitude, and were pleased to have her as a member of the team. There was just one thing troubling him about her.

They got to Bedford Square and after a short tour around the adjacent streets, they finally found a parking space nearby.

The Roding's London residence was a large, white Georgian house of four floors (including a basement) with a portico at its front. It had black railings bordering onto the pavement, which had only recently been restored after having been commandeered by the Government during the war.

Pratt pulled the triangular bell handle that hung down the wall next to the front entrance. He pulled it several times more as he was unable to hear any bell within. After what seemed like five minutes, the front door was opened by a young maid who was dressed in traditional uniform.

The inspector introduced himself and his colleagues as police officers and asked to see Lady Roding. The maid admitted them to the hall, where they were required to wait while she disappeared off into the house to notify her mistress. About five minutes later, she returned and led them to the drawing room.

After ten further minutes of waiting, Cooper was beginning to become rather impatient. He didn't like being kept waiting by anyone. This was but one manifestation of the effects of four years spent incarcerated in a German prisoner of war camp.

When Lady Francine Roding finally entered the room, politeness and respect prompted the two junior officers to get to their feet and join their inspector, who was already standing having been pacing the carpet.

Her ladyship was a woman in her mid-thirties, tall and slim with blonde hair cut to shoulder length in a pageboy style. She was wearing a flared skater tea dress in navy blue, with black stockings and high heels. She was elegant, fragrant and beautiful. Both Cooper and Pratt were smitten. They might have been enamoured of the lovely Fanny, but the image was shattered as soon as Lady Roding opened her mouth. What came out was the sound of an affected *upper-class* accent covering pure *cockney,* which, as much as she tried to moderate it, kept escaping at the edges of her speech. It sounded ludicrous.

Lord Roding had clearly married her for her looks. And who on earth could have blamed him?

'Good afternoon, my lady. I am Detective Inspector Cooper; my colleagues and I are from Essex.' He showed her ladyship his credentials.

'We are investigating the murder of Sister Margaret at Beaumont Hall.'

'What's that got to do with me? I've been in London all week,' said her ladyship loudly, and immediately taking a defensive position.

'I appreciate that, my lady—' said Cooper managing only to get out half of what he wanted to say before she interrupted him.

'Listen, squire, don't bother with all that "your ladyship" nonsense otherwise we'll be here all bleedin' day. I'd be a lot happier if you'd just call me Fanny.'

'Well, we need to ask you a few questions, Fanny, and establish your whereabouts on the day in question. We are speaking to everyone connected to the estate, just to work out where they were and whether they might have seen anything suspicious.'

'Which day was this?'

'The murder happened on Tuesday of this week. Were you here, then?'

'I was in Kensington running an art exhibition with my friend and business partner Marcus Devaux. We were there from 9.00am to about 8.00pm. Waste of bloody time, if you ask me. We didn't sell a thing, although some people said they were interested; time wasters! Anyway, he can vouch for me.'

'Anybody else?' asked Pratt.

'Obviously, Marcus knows the guests who were there, and I know most of the people, by their first names at least, but, I hope you're not going to start bothering them and embarrass me?'

'Well, we would be very discreet, of course. It is not our business to try to embarrass anybody, my lady.'

'Inspector, I don't want to be awkward, but I come from quite a humble background, as you probably realise, and it has taken a long time for me to be accepted by anyone in polite society.'

'What about the press?' said Collins with a flash of inspiration. 'Would they have sent somebody along to cover the exhibition? Might they even have taken a few photographs?'

'Yes, of course,' said Fanny. 'Quentin Smallpiece, the society reporter, was there from *Tatler* and he had a photographer with him.'

'Good,' said Collins. 'How long were they at the exhibition for?'

'They got there around 4.00pm and they both stayed until the end of the evening. Mainly because we were serving free cocktails, the greedy buggers. They took lots of photos and I'm sure you'll find me in most of them because I spent all of my time working the room, speaking to people and trying to drum up business.'

'Have you any contact details for Mr Smallpiece and his photographer?'

'Marcus will have their details. I'll have a word with him for you.'

She left the room to use the telephone.

Pratt took the opportunity to speak to his boss. 'Governor, are we going to ask her about searching the house?'

'No, Brian. I think I know what the answer would be if we were to ask her permission. Let's just concentrate on her alibi for now and try to keep her on side. Oh, and not a word to her about the threatening letter. We'll keep that for later.'

Cooper decided he would question her about Sister Margaret, but in oblique terms.

After a few minutes, Fanny returned. 'He's not answering his phone, Inspector. I'll try him again later.'

'Thank you for trying, anyway, Fanny.'

'Did you know much about the nun, Sister Margaret, at all?'

'No, not really. She was at the Hall for a couple of months, but as I don't go there much these days, I didn't see a lot of her. She was my husband's guest really. Not mine,' she said, dismissively.

'Did you get on all right with her?'

'No. She was a bit of a bitch, to be honest. I didn't take to her at all. Just because she was a nun, she thought she was the bee's knees and a cut above everybody else. Know what I mean?' Fanny flicked the end of her nose with her index finger.

'Did she have any friends at the Hall?'

'I don't know. I doubt it. She spent most of her time either with my husband, on her knees praying or both.' Fanny sniggered in what Cooper took to be a callous disregard for the victim. This Lady Fanny was a hard cow and no mistake.

'Why do you spend so much of your time here in London and not at the Hall?'

'Work mostly,' she said. 'That, and because I've got family and my friends here. People I've known since my days at the Windmill Theatre. It seems my husband doesn't want to do anything these days except, pray, read the Bible and lie in bed, so I just stay here and get on with my own life. I go to Beaumont most weekends, though.'

'Can you tell us anything about the sister at all?' asked Collins.

'One thing struck me as odd about her. For a nun, she didn't go to church much.'

'Perhaps, she preferred to worship in her own way,' said Cooper. 'You know what they always used to say at school. God is all around, and you don't have to necessarily go to church to praise him.'

Blimey! thought Cooper. *Where did that come from? I must have been paying attention after all.*

'Well, they didn't say anything like that at the school I went to, but anyway. She came from Italy; Rome, I think. She spoke reasonable English, I suppose. Certainly better than mine at any rate,' Fanny laughed. 'She was a very good artist. I will say that for her, and if she got rid of that religious garb she would scrub up quite well, I would imagine. She had a very pretty face and with some make-up, well… a bit of a waste, really.'

'Fanny, I would be grateful if we could just put into writing what you have told us in the form of a witness statement,' said Cooper.

'I haven't really got time to start writing statements.'

'You wouldn't have to write it yourself, Fanny. Sergeant Pratt here will take it down. It wouldn't take long.'

Her ladyship agreed.

'There is also the small matter of our taking a set of fingerprints from you. These would be purely for elimination purposes and you could request to see them destroyed in due course.'

Fanny allowed herself to be fingerprinted, and that surprised them all. She called for the maid and arranged for tea to be served to her guests.

About three-quarters of an hour later Lady Fanny was being guided by Pratt as to where she should append her signature on the pages of the statement.

'OK,' said Cooper, 'we'll leave it there, I think. If you can, just let Sergeant Pratt have your friend Marcus' contact details before we go. Please don't talk to anybody else about our visit, particularly the gentlemen of the press. No doubt they'll try to contact you at some stage.'

'Well, they can piss off. I'm not talking to them.'

Strangely, Cooper was quite reassured.

Their business being at an end, Cooper thanked her ladyship and the maid showed them to the front door. They left Bedford Square and set out on the return drive back to Essex.

'What do you think?' asked Cooper.

'Very attractive, governor,' said Pratt.

'Not really what I meant, Sergeant.'

'The sergeant's right, sir. She is attractive. But she's also quite a tough customer,' said Collins. 'And she's very forthright, but if she had murdered the sister, I don't think that she would be able to hide the fact very easily.'

'Hard, she is,' said Cooper. 'Anyway, let's see how her alibi pans out.'

On the return journey to Colchester, not much, by way of conversation, passed between them. They were each subsumed in their own thoughts. In Cooper's case, he was reflecting on the campaign that was being waged by Sadie, who was clearly intent on finding him a suitable mate. The name "Brenda" came back into his mind. He had been wondering about his young colleague, *Is now an appropriate time to put to her the fact that she is the boss's niece?*

'Miss Collins.'

'Yes, sir.'

'I need you to give me a few minutes of your time when we get back, please.'

'Certainly, sir.'

Linda Collins was intrigued. She knew better than to question a senior officer and she was left to mull over the possibilities for the remainder of the journey. Instinct told her there was more behind the inspector's request than mere work. She didn't mind though. He was rather dishy, after all.

'You wanted to see me, sir?'

'Yes, Linda. Come in and take a seat.'

Linda Collins had come to Cooper's office armed with two cups of tea, which he took to be a conciliatory gesture.

'I thought I'd bring you a cup of tea, sir. I didn't know whether you take sugar or not, so, I've sugared one of them. Hope that's OK?'

'That was thoughtful of you. No sugar for me, thanks.'

Linda chose one of the cups and placed it on the desk in front of him. She then sat down with her cup in her lap, smoothing out her skirt with one hand as she did so.

'I know that you've only been with us for a couple of days, but how are you settling down?'

'Fine, thank you, sir. The team have been supportive, particularly Sergeant Pratt.'

'Good. Linda, there was something that I particularly wanted to speak to you about, that has been causing me some concern.'

'Really, sir. What's that?' A pained expression came across her face.

'I understand from my aunt Sadie, who runs a greengrocer's in the town, that she was at school with your mother. It seems that Sadie has been speaking to your mother recently, in the shop, and they came to the realisation that we both work together. Unfortunately, it's a small world.' Cooper withheld any reference to Sadie and her matchmaking.

The penny dropped instantly with Linda, who could sense where the conversation was leading. She decided to volunteer some detail on her family background ahead of the inevitable question that was obviously coming her way. 'Yes, she's a local girl. Her maiden name was Stockwell.'

'And, as I understand it, she has a brother named Tom.'

'Yes, sir, that's right. Superintendent Tom Stockwell. He's my uncle.'

'Hence, his interest in your career and your attachment to the CID.'

'Yes. I know how it might look, sir,' she said defensively, 'but he would insist on helping me. I mentioned to my mum that I've always wanted to be a detective, and she went behind my back and spoke to him about it.'

'Were you going to tell us about your connection?'

'To be perfectly honest, governor, I hadn't made my mind up what to do about it. I've been worrying about it since I started, and it's left me in something of a quandary. Whatever I do, no matter how hard I work, if people know the connection, I could always be accused of benefitting from favouritism.'

'I can see the difficult position you are in, Linda. The question is, what, if anything, do we do about it?'

'I want to stay on the team, sir, but I don't know whether to just tell people and have done with it. I don't want to make things worse.'

'Do you really want to be a detective?'

'Yes, I do.'

'It's important, then, that you work hard and try to keep your contact with Mr Stockwell to a minimum. You know what it's like. If your colleagues see you in his company, coppers being coppers, they'll want to know why he's taking an interest in you.'

'Yes, I know, sir.'

'Keep it to yourself for now and we'll see how we get on. If you encounter any problems, come and speak to me. I'm sure you've just found yourself in an invidious position and didn't intend to take an unfair advantage on the back of your family connections. I will mark Sergeant Pratt's card so that he can watch out for you.'

'Thank you, sir. I appreciate that.'

'You've made a good start on your attachment, Linda, and I'm pleased with your progress. I would hate for this to spoil things for you. If you get any problems, speak to Sergeant Pratt and then the three of us can talk about it. OK?

'I will. Thank you, sir.'

Cooper now had a decision to make. Should he raise the issue with Stockwell or keep it to himself? Whichever way it went, he felt quite protective towards her.

6

DAY SIX

Sunday 17th July 1949

The two men were strolling through the Giardini Vatican, the gardens of the Vatican City, with its baroque fountains and sculptures of Roman figures, who appeared to be monitoring their progress. It was a warm, balmy evening and there were very few people in the vicinity. Cardinal Pat O'Mara, head of the Vatican Special Assignments Unit, had a visitor. O'Mara was a very busy man and he had not welcomed the intrusion.

'What is so important that you wanted to see me so urgently?'

'I have received some unfortunate news from our man in London and I thought I should inform you, your eminence.'

'Tell me, my son. What is the problem?'

'Monsignor Tarquin Crecy died of a heart attack in London a few days ago, and, as if that is not enough, his latest project, Sister Margaret, has been murdered.'

'That is very sad. Do we know who was responsible for her murder? Please tell me it wasn't Tarquin Crecy?'

'No, your eminence. It certainly wasn't. The British police have no idea who was responsible. Apparently, they wrote a letter to Archbishop Mahoney, although it did not reach his office.'

'Has anything appeared in the newspapers?'

'Very little. The police have made no official statements on the matter.'

'Good, good. Let us hope that it stays that way. Do you think this will bring a problem to our door?'

'No. I think it is most likely to have been one of the villagers who murdered the sister. A domestic matter, so it will be solved locally.'

'She was put in place by Monsignor Crecy, was she not?'

'Yes, your eminence, she was.'

'Then the party line must be that the Church has no knowledge of her. Make sure our man in London knows this.'

'I understand, your eminence.'

'Tarquin Crecy's death will be a major blow and he will not be easily replaced. But at least the real reason for her being in place will die with them both. Thank you for telling me, my son.'

7

DAY SEVEN

Monday 18ᵗʰ July 1949

'I'm sorry, governor, but you're not going to be very happy with this when I tell you,' said Mills.

'Go on then, Ian. What have we done now?' said Cooper with a tone of resignation.

Mills spread out a newspaper on the desk before him and read aloud, "*East Anglian Recorder* – Murder team visit Lady Fanny Roding.

"The enquiry in relation to the murder of the Catholic nun who was found in the gardens of the Roding estate at Beaumont Hall appears to have taken an interesting turn, according to our correspondent, with the police searching the London address of Lord Roding where his wife, Lady Fanny Roding, spends much of her time. We are given to understand that no arrest was carried out. An attempt was made by the *Recorder* to contact Lord Roding; however, he was unavailable for comment.

"Readers might recall that, during the war, Lord Jeremy Roding married the former actress and society beauty, Fanny Dyson at St Bride's Church in Fleet Street after a whirlwind romance. Lord Roding's first wife, the late Lady Bettina Roding, died under somewhat strange circumstances, and, following an air raid, her body was found in the auditorium of the Windmill Theatre. In April of this year, Lord Roding's only son and heir, the Honourable Edward "Teddy" Roding, was tragically killed in a motoring accident.'"

'Bloody hell! That's all we need. Does Mr Stockwell know about this, Ian?'

'We haven't heard anything from him yet, governor, but I'm sure it's only a matter of time before we do.'

'How the hell did the *Recorder* get hold of this?'

It was a rhetorical question anyway, but Mills and Pratt were certainly not going to offer an answer. They knew that suspicion would inevitably fall on the team. Not only that, it did not reflect well on the force; Lord Roding would most likely complain to the chief constable and pressure would surely come from above to call in the Metropolitan Police to continue with the investigation.

Cooper grabbed the paper and read the article for himself. He then threw it down in exasperation.

'It's not bloody right, anyway. We didn't search Fanny's house and we didn't make any suggestion to her that we were going to.'

'It won't have come from her then, governor, will it,' said Pratt.

Cooper got to his feet and straightened his tie. 'Right! Nothing else for it. Let's seize the bull by the horns and go and see Stockwell before he comes to us.'

Cooper marched along the High Street towards the town hall and found that it was raining heavily. He ignored the rain. He was on a mission. By the time he had arrived, and to make his day complete, he was drenched from head to foot. He took the stairs to the superintendent's office and he approached Mavis, who was sitting behind her desk absorbed in something she was typing on her typewriter. She looked up at him as he entered the office, and she appeared to be quite pleased with the distraction.

'Is Mr Stockwell in, Mavis?'

'No, he isn't, my lovely. He's gone to Headquarters for a meeting. Is there anything I can help you with?'

'No thanks. It's an operational matter, really. Bit of a decision required. How about Chief Inspector Hopkins, is he about?'

'No, he's not. He's taken a day's leave. They're both back in the office tomorrow morning, though,' she looked at Cooper. 'Oh dear, Albert, I'm not much help to you, am I? May I get you a towel or something?'

Cooper ignored the offer, 'Not to worry, Mavis. It'll keep.' Cooper remained business-like and tried not to let his face express his frustration. He knew that Stockwell would catch up with him sooner or later.

He returned to his office and to the briefing, where he related details of the visit to Bedford Square. He explained that, in the absence of a warrant, they had, in fact, been unable to conduct a search of the premises despite what the *East Anglian Recorder* had declared.

The team didn't appear at all surprised by what he had to tell them, thereby giving Cooper the impression that they had all read the article for themselves.

'Rest assured, I have no doubt in my mind that the

information being churned out in the *Recorder* is not coming from this team. I want you all to know that.'

Despite his reassurance, the team were resigned to the fact that they were bound to come under suspicion from some quarters.

'Anyway, boys and girls, it's not all bad,' Cooper continued, 'It seems there are photographs in existence that were taken by journalists showing Lady Fanny at an art exhibition in Kensington. The event was held while the murder was being committed at Beaumont Hall. If we can verify those, we can eliminate her as a direct suspect. So, enquiries are needed with her colleague Marcus Devaux. Apparently, he has the contact details for the photographer and the journalist who were present on the day. Brian, I would like you and Linda to go back up to London to see Mr Devaux. Give me a call with the details of the journalists when you get them.'

'Do you want us to pay the *Tatler* a visit while we are up there, boss?'

'No, Brian. We need to hold off and consider our position before we go to see them. I just want to speak to Mr Stockwell about the kind of approach we are going to take, bearing in mind that, whatever they call themselves, we'll still, basically, be dealing with the press. I only hope to God that they don't feel free to share what we tell them with Reuters or start to become a nuisance. If that happens we'll have to try to get a court order. Give me a call later and let me know how you get on.'

Cooper then continued with other more mundane matters.

'Boss, there is one other unfortunate development,' said Mills, 'It's the usual anonymous letter, probably from a crank. It was received this morning at the station by post. It bears a Colchester postmark and is addressed to you by name. Do you want me to read it out loud?'

'Oh no! What have I been up to now?' said Cooper in mock horror.

The team laughed.

'No, it's nothing against you, boss.'

'Go ahead then.'

Mills began, 'I quote, "About the murder at the Hall. You should know that the boy James was caught a couple of weeks ago, by the nun; he was snooping around the house in an area where he shouldn't have been. He said he had seen an intruder. He is not to be trusted."'

'Is that it, Ian?'

'That's it.'

'Well, we won't lose a lot of sleep over that then, will we? But we'll bear it in mind. Ian, will you raise a job for a member of the team to have a word with the lad about it, please?'

The meeting over, the team dispersed to carry out their various tasks. Pratt and Collins went to the rear yard of the station, and, having fired up the Wolseley, they set off in the direction of London.

Jenkins waited until after breakfast before going into the study to make the telephone call.

As usual, he had taken a tray up to his master with his copy of the *Times*, but the *East Anglian Recorder* that had also been delivered he had left in the kitchen. His lordship hadn't missed it and Jenkins was grateful for the small respite that this afforded him. There had been an unfortunate and disturbing article in the *Recorder*. Beryl Aldis was the first to have spotted it and she had drawn it to his attention. The butler knew that, if his master had read it, it would have angered him and would probably have gnawed away at his pride for the rest of the day. Luckily, for now, Jenkins had managed to suppress the information. However, there was one other duty that he needed to perform.

Having satisfied himself that he was quite alone, he picked up the receiver and called her ladyship at the Bedford Square address.

'Morning, my lady. Everything all right with you?'

'Yes. Why shouldn't it be Raymond?'

'Well, there's an article in the *East Anglian Recorder* about the police going to London and searching your house to do with the murder. I wanted to make sure that you were aware of it.'

'*What?* No! The bastards! The police did no such thing.'

'Not true, then?'

'No, it's not. Yes, they came to the house to see me. They asked me about the nun and they wanted to know my whereabouts for the time of the murder. But, as for a search of the house, that's complete tosh!'

'Where do they get this rubbish from, then?'

'No idea. Does his lordship know about it?'

'No. I've managed to keep it from him for the moment. He's in bed having his breakfast. I only took the *Times* up to him, but I expect that sooner or later he'll want to know why he hasn't got the *Recorder*.'

'Good. I suppose I had better speak to him about it first, before he finds out from someone else. He'll be quite calm about it, I expect, if it comes from me. I'll explain what really happened and I'll play it down a bit.'

'I'd better go and get him ready then.'

'Yes. If you can get him into his wheelchair in about an hour's time, I'll phone him. Thank you, Raymond, darling, I had better get my backside in gear and get ready myself.'

Jenkins replaced the receiver. *Good girl,* he thought. *She took that rather well.*

Since taking up his position as a "gentleman's gentleman" at Beaumont Hall, he and Lady Fanny had forged something of a bond. He wasn't too sure about her at first, but Jenkins had made himself available to her as a source of comfort and support. Now, he was slowly cultivating their relationship and exploiting the situation by stealth. As for Fanny, she made good use of him in return, creating reasons for his presence at the house in Bedford Square to do her bidding. The relationship between Fanny and Jenkins was now becoming more than that of employee and servant.

As for Adina, she seemed to be quite content with her husband's frequent trips to London. There was a benefit for her in that they occasionally provided the opportunity for her to get a lift in the Rolls Royce to Shoreditch, where she would meet a friend. A "Romanian exile" who worked in the City of London.

Adina and her friend would meet for lunch, and she would pass over a sum of money to be sent to her mother in Romania. The remittances were never large, but they were sufficient, given the parlous state of the Romanian economy, to ensure that Adina's mother could sustain herself and live in relative comfort.

Jenkins knew about the arrangement and the fact that she was meeting her friend to pass over the money, but he did not realise that there was more on the agenda than his mother-in-law's subsistence. The "friend" was part of an organisation that had a global reach.

Cooper was seated in his office, mulling over various documents and making entries in his policy book. He had just reread the anonymous letter, mentioned at the last briefing, and he was now considering it, along with the narrative of a telephone log of an anonymous call that had been reported to him by the control-room sergeant. He read the dialogue to himself:

"Received at 13:25 hours on Friday 15th July 1949.

"Caller: Anonymous Female.

"Receiver: PC 2030 Smithers, Essex Constabulary HQ, control room.

"Caller: 'About the murder at Beaumont Hall – I've just read the local paper and you lot are barking up the wrong tree!'

"PC Smithers: 'Can I have your name please?'

"Caller: 'No. Just listen to what I have to say. The butler, Raymond Jenkins, is a smarmy so and so who thinks he is God's gift to women. He was fascinated by Sister Margaret and he paid her rather too much attention, in my opinion. He probably thought that he could tempt her into betraying her vows. Pervert! Also, it might pay you to ask why Jenkins often stays overnight at the Bedford Square house with her ladyship.'

"The caller hung up. The call was made from a telephone kiosk. Apparently, it was from a woman who spoke with a London accent."

Cooper suspected that, since she had referred to various "goings on" at Beaumont Hall she was likely to be a member of staff. But what was her motivation? She had pointed the finger of suspicion at young James Davidson and at Raymond Jenkins, and she had also made an oblique reference to the report in the local paper. Things were starting to become rather messy. He would have to make it a priority to identify and interview the woman caller and find out who it was that was leaking information to the press. Could they, in fact, be one and the same person?

He was amazed that he had still not heard anything from Superintendent Stockwell or Lord Roding regarding the anticipated complaint. Cooper decided to just bury himself in his work and attempt to put them both out of his mind, lest paranoia should set in. He was still in the office when he received a telephone call from Kensington Police Station. It was Pratt.

'We've been to the art gallery to see Mr Devaux, governor, and we took a short statement from him. Strange cove, bit light on his feet. Know what I mean? Certainly, no chance of him being a love interest for Lady Fanny. Makes you wonder what makes some people tick.' Pratt continued to describe Devaux in disparaging terms and he was starting to go into a rant.

Cooper became impatient, 'OK, I get the message, Brian. Spit it out mate. Did he have the details of the photographer or not?'

'Yes, governor. Both employed by *Tatler*. Quentin Smallpiece is the journalist and the photographer's a bloke called Harry Grimes. I have their office number. Are you sure you don't want us to call and see them while Linda and I are up here, governor?'

'No, I'm sure. Just pass their details over for now, thanks, Brian, and I'll call them in due course. I'm going to have to square it with Mr Stockwell first and he might even decide to speak to the chief. If you and Linda want something to do, you can go to Westminster Cathedral and see if Father Thomas is available.'

'Will do, governor.'

'Then, when you're done, you make your way back. I'll see you in the office first thing tomorrow morning. By that time, hopefully, I shall have managed to speak to the superintendent, and maybe he'll have given me a decision.'

Cooper called Mavis. 'Is he back yet, Mavis?'

'He's been and gone I'm afraid, my lovely, but he'll be back in the office tomorrow morning for a few hours, then later in the day he's got to go to a meeting about this year's Oyster Feast. He tells me that, this year, they're trying to get Tommy Trinder.'

'That should liven things up a bit. I heard that the Oyster Feast can be a bit boring with some of the stuffed shirts that get invited.'

Mavis laughed. 'Anyway, darling, what are you up to this evening? Doing anything nice?'

Cooper found her interest unnerving and he hesitated before giving her a reply. 'No, I shall be at work for the entire evening,' he lied.

In truth, he had planned an early departure from the office, and he had promised himself fish and chips followed by a couple of pints in the Hole in the Wall. He certainly wasn't going to get involved with her, if that was what she was hinting at.

'Have you been invited to the Oyster Feast?'

'No, Mavis. I've never been to it and I don't think I ever will either. It's not really for the likes of me.'

The Colchester Oyster Feast was an annual event held at the town hall to celebrate an important part of the local fishing industry. Hosted by the mayor, it was attended by the "great and the good" with a smattering of invited guests from the world of entertainment. As for Tom Stockwell, he was expected to be there and would most likely be one of the last to leave. It was an integral part of his position as the local chief of police and seemingly a perk of the job, although, in Cooper's opinion, his boss did tend to "tear the arse" out of the many opportunities that came his way.

Cooper left the office and wandered off along the High Street in the general direction of his digs. He stopped in Head Street for some fish and chips, which he took around the corner to sit beneath "Jumbo", the huge water tower that dominated the Colchester skyline. He opened the newspaper wrappings and tucked in, wolfing down what he realised was his only meal since his two rounds of toast that morning. He scolded himself for the fact that he wasn't looking after himself properly. Then, having lined his stomach, he walked the short distance to the pub.

On entering the saloon bar of the Hole in the Wall, Cooper was greeted by some of the regulars, most of whom he had known for a few years, but only on first name terms.

Cooper had always tried to make it his practice not to ask unnecessary questions or pry into people's lives when he was in the pub. He was only there to relax, and he had developed a style of conversation management that was friendly but superficial. The other regulars knew what his job was, and they would, on occasion, seek his advice on matters that might be troubling them, but they usually just let him be. But then there was always the local toe rag known as "Nobber" Gibbs.

'You caught that nun murderer yet, Cooper?'

'Not yet,' answered Cooper.

'Lord Roding was giving her one, I expect,' said Gibbs.

This was proclaimed at the top of his voice for the benefit of everyone in the room. Some laughed, but most were appalled at his ignorant outburst. Cooper felt compelled to defend his lordship's honour and that of Sister Margaret.

'Let me stop you right there, pal!' said Cooper, 'We have got no inkling at all of Lord Roding or the good sister indulging in that kind of behaviour. Do I make myself clear?'

'OK, keep your hair on, mate. I was only joking.'

'Well don't!' said Cooper who tensed up and fixed Nobber with a stare that burned deep into his eyes, his fists clenched automatically and, on realising this, he put his hands in his pockets to prevent himself from lashing out.

'Well, anyway, the press think it's a possibility.'

'Come again,' said Cooper, not quite believing his ears.

'The press think it's a possibility.'

'How do you know that then?'

'They were in here at lunchtime asking questions,' said Tim, the landlord, interceding before things turned ugly.

'This woman from the press, Munson I think her name was, came in with another one, a bloke, and they were having a drink at the bar. They spoke to a few of the lads and bought them drinks. She asked me if you drink in here. I couldn't lie, could I? So, I said that you do, sometimes.'

'Yeah. And I said that I wish that you fuckin didn't!' said Gibbs, determined to have his say.

'What else was she saying?' asked Cooper, doing his best to ignore Gibbs.

'Does anyone in here know you or drink with you? Does anyone know about the nun at Beaumont Hall?' said Tim, 'General stuff apart from that. Fishing, she was.'

Cooper was incensed at this intrusion into his private life, which was completely out of bounds as far as anyone else was concerned.

What was her game? What could he look forward to in the next edition of the local paper?

Having suddenly lost the taste for alcohol, he left the pub and went home. He knew that he would have to do something about this woman.

8

DAY EIGHT

Tuesday 19th July 1949

Once again, Cooper had had a terrible night's sleep, but it was nothing to do with Nobber Gibbs. Well, not directly, anyway. Awake at 5.30am, he had lain in bed just thinking about the case with his mind totally focussed on the problem of putting a stop to the series of leaks that were being made to the local press. They troubled him greatly. He knew from experience that these situations were not rare within the police force, and that they could have a very corrosive effect on the morale of the staff, causing unnecessary suspicion and bad feeling. Leaks could sometimes be just due to careless talk, but, in the more extreme cases, down to long-term corruption with somebody copping backhanders. Cooper realised that he needed to get to grips with the problem urgently. Rather than lie in bed and watch the clock, he washed and dressed, skipped breakfast and set off for work early.

The first port of call was Sadie's. He knew that he had to have words with her and he was just in the right mood to get it out of the way.

'Morning, ducks!'

'Don't you, "morning, ducks", me.'

'Oh dear, Alby. Whatever's the matter? Get out of bed the wrong side, did we? Tell Auntie Sadie all about it.' She stroked his hair as though he was the child she'd known all those years ago.

'You and your matchmaking. Brenda, as you call her, has only turned out to be my boss's niece. Her name is Linda Collins and she is one of my team. I had to have a word with her about it.'

'What's she like? Is she as pretty as her mum says she is?'

'Yes, she's gorgeous, but that's not the point. It makes things very awkward.'

'Sorry, Alby. I really don't understand what all the fuss is about.'

He spent the next few minutes explaining the difficult position that her meddling had placed him in, begged her to use more discretion and to cease her campaign of matchmaking. After he had delivered his rebuke, Cooper turned on his heel and left the shop in despair. He wasn't at all sure that Sadie had taken his plea seriously.

Cooper strode off along the High Street. He was in a foul mood. An argument waiting for somewhere to happen. As he reached the news vendor, he picked up a copy of the *Recorder*, and his humour lifted slightly, as he realised there was nothing about the murder either within the paper or shown on the billboard.

Then, as he wandered off in the general direction of the police station it struck him. It was only the germ of an idea, but he was sure it had potential for development, and the more he thought it through, the more feasible it seemed. At last, he had discovered a means of attack. He would have to run it past Stockwell, of course, and gain his approval. As an approach to the situation, the proposed action would be quite lawful, if somewhat irregular, but desperate situations called for desperate measures.

As Cooper entered the foyer of the police station he noticed the familiar sight of the front-office constable dealing with a member of the public at the counter. The officer, without thinking, acknowledged Cooper and turning to the lady said, 'Here he is now, as a matter of fact, madam.'

The woman, approached Cooper and held out her right hand. She was tall and slim, with mouse-coloured hair that was worn in a bun. Wearing a tweed suit with brown woollen tights and brown sensible shoes, she had "head girl" written all over her.

'Inspector, I'm Gladys Munson from the *Recorder*. May I speak to you about the murder of Sister Margaret?'

Cooper was taken aback, he felt his pulse quicken, and his foul mood was restored, having been ambushed by the journalist whose approach had been facilitated by the constable, who should have known better. He took a deep breath and summoned all the self-discipline that he could muster.

'Ah, Miss Munson. I have been following the progress of your investigation. Perhaps you'll let us get on with ours. I understand that you were enquiring about me in my local pub, the Hole in the Wall.'

'Just trying to get the story, Inspector. You shouldn't take it personally.'

'Well, I do. I don't appreciate you asking about my private life. That is out of bounds. As for the murder, if there is anything to release to the press we will let you all know in due course. Good day.'

He turned on his heel and nodded to a chastened constable, who immediately left his position behind the counter to open the wicket door.

'When you get relieved from the front counter, I want a word with you, young man.'

Cooper ascended the stairs to his office. He was fizzing, although he had now had the pleasure of meeting the dreaded Gladys Munson.

He made himself a cup of tea and settled down to read the contents of his in tray. It took him some time to calm down and concentrate on what was in front of him.

About 9.30am, Cooper walked up to the town hall to see Superintendent Stockwell. As he entered the outer office, he could see that Mavis was not at her desk and that Stockwell was on his feet, busily watering his plants. He was humming to himself, a picture of contentment, quite oblivious to Cooper until he heard him knock on the open door. A tall, spare man with receding grey hair, Tom Stockwell was entering his final years of service. Cooper noticed that, unusually for him, Stockwell was wearing civilian clothes, a three-piece suit, which made him appear rather stylish and even sophisticated. It was certainly much sharper than the old "demob" suit that he himself had been reduced to wearing since being back in the CID.

'Ah, Inspector, come in. I wanted to see you. How is the murder investigation going?'

This general question put the ball well and truly in Cooper's court. He considered his position. *Can I, for now, possibly get away with not mentioning the press leaks unless he asks me about them? Perhaps I can just play them down? That wouldn't do any good though. He wouldn't accept that. They are a severe problem, after all.*

As Cooper needed to discuss with Stockwell the potential risk involved in speaking to *Tatler*, he knew that, at some point, he would also have to talk to him about the leaks to the press and his encounter with Munson. But he hadn't yet thought his tactics through and was not quite prepared for the inevitable grilling that his suggestion was likely to receive.

Instead, Cooper began by outlining the reason for Sister Margaret's presence at the Hall, the death of Monsignor Crecy and the lack of any acknowledgement of her existence by the Church. He overlaid this with the findings of the post mortem. In short, he hit the boss with a barrage of old information to satisfy the moment.

'She was quite a mysterious woman, wasn't she?' observed Stockwell.

'Yes, sir. She certainly was. But I am convinced that if we can find out more about her background and reason for being here, it will hold the key to the reason for her murder. We still haven't received a response to your letter to the archbishop, I take it?'

'No. They haven't responded yet.'

Then Cooper really chanced his arm. 'I wonder whether it would be possible to take a direct approach and make enquiries at the Vatican ourselves through an interpreter.'

'I don't think the budget would run to that, Albert. It's also highly irregular.'

'Radical sir, yes, but it could save us an awful lot of time. We're getting little or no response from the Church in London. In fact, when he spoke to them, they told Lord Roding that they had no knowledge of a Sister Margaret being sent to help his conversion.'

'I'm not convinced that it's necessary and I'm sure that the chief constable will take the view that we should be able to achieve our objective by speaking to the Catholic Church authorities in London. You'll have to keep chasing them, that's all.'

Realising that he was wasting his time pursuing this point any further, he changed tack. 'Sir, as you will recall, we went to Bedford Square to see Lady Francine Roding.'

'And did you carry out a search?'

'No sir. She provided us with an alibi for the afternoon of the murder. Apparently, she was hosting an art exhibition in Kensington with a colleague. Also present were two men from the society magazine, *Tatler,* who took a series of photographs which should establish her presence and support her alibi.'

'So, you didn't require a search warrant after all then?'

'No, sir.'

'There you are. I told you that it wasn't necessary.'

'You did, sir.' Cooper bristled. The words *"pompous prat"* came to mind.

'What are you going to do about *Tatler?*'

'Frankly, sir, I don't think we could pursue the matter of her alibi any further without making an approach to them, although I recognise that we would have to tread carefully. Journalists being what they are.'

Stockwell sat in silence, nodding his head in agreement.

There was an awkward silence as the superintendent mulled over the pros and cons.

Cooper rescued him from it. 'It would serve to confirm or break her alibi, sir.'

Then, thinking aloud, the superintendent responded in a way that totally surprised Cooper. 'Yes, I agree,' he said decisively. 'It's clear that we'll have to speak to the people at *Tatler* if the investigation is to progress, Albert. There is nothing else for it. It will carry a risk, of course, so I want to be with you when the visit to *Tatler* is carried out, and, time being of the essence, I think that we should contact them at 9.00am tomorrow and try to get up there to pay them a visit later in the day.'

'I'll get on to them first thing, sir.'

Finally, Stockwell broached the subject of the leaks. 'What does concern me are these unauthorised disclosures of information. I'm beginning to think that they are coming from somebody within the force. I expect you to get to the bottom of them. Do I make myself clear?' said Stockwell, stridently.

'Crystal, sir.'

Cooper left Stockwell to his plants and returned to the police station.

Cooper could hear loud voices and hilarity as he placed his foot on the bottom tread of the stairs and started up to the CID office. He could tell that most of the noise was coming from DC Tom Rogers, and, as he entered the door of the office, he could see why. Rogers, who had not realised that his boss had arrived, was standing, with his back to the door, with both empty pockets protruding from the sides of his trousers. He was in the process of explaining his elephant impression. Linda and Jane were doubled up with laughter. The noise level dipped and when he finally spotted Cooper in the doorway, Rogers squeaked the words 'Sorry, governor,' and scuttled to his desk. This made the girls laugh even more.

'Right settle down, you lot. We've got a bit to get through. Brian, will you kick-off and tell the other members of the team about the visit to Lady Fanny.'

Brian Pratt gave a brief outline of their visit to Bedford Square and the *Tatler* alibi, which led on to Cooper adding his news about the meeting that had just taken place with the boss. The team let out a collective groan in recognition of what they perceived to be Stockwell's overcautious attitude. But Cooper felt compelled to put them straight, particularly as Linda Collins was in the room.

'Let's keep it respectful, boys and girls. He does wear the King's uniform after all. Whatever you might think, he is the boss and must take responsibility for what goes on in his division. I can tell you though, he does have our best interests at heart.'

None of the troops dared to comment further.

'Anyway, let's get on. Ian. Was there anything in that diary found in her room?'

'Yes, governor. The diary is an Italian one and there was an entry made under Domenica 10 Maggio 1949 – that is, on Sunday 10th May 1949 to you and me – which said, "speak to Father O'Leary at St Saviour's".'

'Very impressive,' said Cooper, smiling, 'Can you sing it to us, Ian, in the form of an aria?'

'I will if you want me to, governor.'

The team laughed.

'You know there is a church of that name in the village and the priest is called Father O'Leary,' said Jane.

'Are you happy to have an enquiry made there, governor? To see whether they know our sister?' said Mills.

'Yes, definitely a job for somebody. Go ahead, please, Ian,' said Cooper. 'Thank you, Jane, I didn't realise you were that religious.'

'She's not really, governor,' said Tom Rogers. 'She was the one who told me about the elephant impression in the first place.'

Cooper laughed and then they all laughed.

'Anyway, An impressive bit of Italian there, Ian.'

Mills was showing off, but Cooper didn't mind at all. He knew that he had a personal tutor in the form of his rather beautiful and voluptuous Italian wife Rosa, whom he had "liberated" during the war and had managed to bring back home to Blighty.

'Brian, have you had any reply from Father Thomas at Westminster Cathedral?'

'No. He wasn't in the office when we called in to see him, governor, although, to be fair, that was just on the off chance. I'll keep trying, though.'

'So, we still have no recognition of the existence of Sister Margaret on the part of the Catholic Church. I think it's crucial that we speak to them and clarify the position. OK, if there is nothing else, have a good day, boys and girls.'

The team dispersed and went about their business.

9

DAY NINE

Wednesday 20ᵗʰ July 1949

It was shortly after 9.00am when Cooper telephoned the office of *Tatler* in London, introduced himself and asked for Quentin Smallpiece. A few seconds later a very fruity, *upper-class* voice came on the other end of the line. 'Good morning, Inspector. Quentin Smallpiece speaking. How may I help you?'

'Good morning, sir. We were given your name by a Mr Marcus Devaux. I understand that you and a colleague covered an art exhibition in Kensington for him and his business partner Lady Fanny Roding on Tuesday last. Is that correct?'

'Yes, indeed we did.'

'I was given to understand, by her ladyship, that you took a series of photos of the event?'

'Yes, or least my colleague Harry Grimes did. He's the photographer. I'm just the hack.'

'I see; only, we are investigating a murder that was committed on the same afternoon as the art exhibition and we need to establish the whereabouts of certain individuals who knew the deceased. Lady Fanny being one of them. We are hoping that your photographs will help us in that regard.'

'Yes, I see what you mean. I'm sure that we could make them available to you. When would you like to come and see them?'

'How about this afternoon, say, 3.00pm?'

'I would say, yes, Inspector, but I haven't yet had chance to view the shots and select those that we would like to go to print. However, what about the contact prints. Do you think that they would be sufficient for your needs?'

Conscious that Cooper was not likely to be familiar with them, Smallpiece explained that contact prints were compilation pages of individual shots, from which pictures can be selected for future use. 'Well, I think that, provided the imagines are large enough for facial recognition, they would certainly be enough for our purposes.'

'Yes, Inspector, they are perfectly large enough for that.'

Before ringing off, Cooper obtained details of *Tatler*'s location. 'Thank you, Mr Smallpiece. I'll see you at 3.00pm.'

Cooper then telephoned the management suite and squared the arrangement with Superintendent Stockwell.

He had a few hours to kill before leaving for London, so Cooper got on with some paperwork. After a short while he heard the telltale squeak of Doris, the tea lady, coming along the corridor in his direction. She was a delightful woman, with a cheery disposition, who gamely fought a daily battle with a tea trolley that had three cooperative wheels and one that defiantly refused to conform to the general direction of travel.

'Morning Alby, would you like a cup of tea, dear?' said Doris, standing proud with the trolley blocking his doorway.

'Good morning, Doris. Yes, tea with no sugar, thanks.'

She looked like an Amazon warrior, complete with matching scarf- hat and pinafore.

Upon payment of a threepenny bit, she did the honours and brought the mug to his desk. As was often the case, Doris sat down opposite him for a couple of minutes and lit up a Woodbine. She offered him one, which he politely declined.

Doris was around fifty years of age and, although slightly overweight, she was attractive in a mature way. She was always good for a chat, but he never knew her to indulge in malicious gossip, which was a pleasant change from the back biting that some of the staff tended to indulge in.

After she bemoaned her varicose veins and following her usual complaint about the tea trolley being the potential death of her, they exchanged pleasantries. 'Anyway, you're looking pleased with yourself this morning. You in love or something?'

'Only with you, Doris, light of my life.'

She laughed heartily. 'How you getting on with your murder then, ducks? Caught anyone yet?'

'No, but things are going quite well. It's early days yet, Doris. It's an interesting one though, that's for sure. You don't have Catholic nuns murdered very often these days, so we must be breaking new ground.'

'You know, my old man Vic and I were only talking the other day about how the Catholic Church must be the richest club in the world. All that gold in their churches and cathedrals. It does make you wonder where it all came from in the first place. He says that it was mostly stolen by those Spanish matadors in South America, and that they made it on the backs of the poor. I bet there were a few wrong-uns among them as well, lining their own pockets. There usually is where money's concerned. And you can't trust anybody these days. Makes you think, doesn't it?'

'It certainly does,' said Cooper, almost overwhelmed by her outburst. She had been referring to conquistadors, but he wasn't going to correct her.

'Anyway, Alby, I can't be sitting here gossiping with the likes of you all day,' she said, with a chuckle. With that, Doris stubbed out the cigarette on the sole of her plimsole and stashed the dog-end in the pocket of her pinny for later. Then, almost in one movement, she stood up and kicked the frame of the trolley, as if inflicting some form of punishment on a capricious beast. It immediately jumped into life and she continued on her way along the corridor towards the big office.

Soon after midday, Cooper started to prepare for his departure to London. As Brian Pratt was to be left behind to hold the fort, Cooper would be the driver for this journey, so he took the Wolseley up to the town hall to collect the superintendent.

Cooper needed to be alone with him to discuss his idea for tackling the press leaks. To ensure success, it would be imperative for very few people to have prior knowledge of the action he was intending to propose. Although Cooper trusted Pratt implicitly, he did not need him to be cognisant of the plan.

During the journey up to London, Cooper was pleasantly surprised to find that the further his boss got from his patch, the more pleasant and chipper he seemed to become. It was as if a heavy weight was gradually being lifted from his shoulders. Stockwell did most of the talking as Cooper feigned total concentration on his driving. This was a deliberate ploy on Cooper's part, which afforded him thinking time and enabled him to word his pitch with care. In the past, he had learned to his cost that Stockwell had a propensity for leaping on unguarded or injudicious comments. Now, with several hours of exclusive access to the boss, he might have the chance to get through to him, whereas, previously, Stockwell had always seemed too preoccupied to hold a detailed conversation on any given subject.

Cooper was quite looking forward to visiting *Tatler* and witnessing at close quarters how Stockwell would approach the situation. Dealing with the press was always a tricky business. It could make or break a senior officer's career: "Damned if you do and damned if you don't." There was a healthy distrust on both sides. Senior officers, with little or no training, just had to use their own judgement, common sense and do their level best. In some cases, this led to unholy alliances and in others it led to antagonism. It was an extremely difficult balance to strike so, for selfish reasons, Cooper was very happy that Stockwell would be taking the lead on this aspect of the investigation.

Upon arrival in the *Tatler* building and after introducing themselves at reception, they were both shown to the waiting area where they were given tea.

As they sat waiting, they were treated to the sight of several *bright young things*, who came and went with files under their arms. Cooper felt that the whole place had an atmosphere of style and positivity. This was an invigorating and pleasant experience, after so many years of austerity and strife. It certainly gave a strong indication of the kind of lifestyle being enjoyed by much of the upper echelon of British society and their familiars. *Cooper reflected that it was a shame that the same level of opportunity had not yet been extended to the wider population.*

After a few minutes, Quentin Smallpiece appeared before them.

'Good afternoon, gentlemen,' said Smallpiece with his cut-glass accent and a slight lisp.

Cooper carried out the introductions, and, in their turn, they shook hands with Smallpiece. He had the grip of a Girl Guide.

'If you would care to follow me, gentlemen, I will take you through to the studio.'

Cooper observed the man as they followed him along the corridor. He was about six feet in height, and was of a very slim build, clean shaven with blond hair. He was coiffured to within an inch of his life. To have said that he was effeminate would have been a gross understatement. *Still, one can't always judge by appearances,* thought Cooper. The man was clearly of service age, and this made him wonder what contribution Smallpiece might have made to the war effort.

After walking through a maze of corridors, they finally arrived in the studio. Cooper saw that the walls were festooned with photographs of the rich, famous and notorious. Already in the room was the photographer, who, upon their arrival, looked up from his work and, with a smile, stood up to greet them. Thrusting out a sturdy hand, he introduced himself as Harry Grimes.

He was altogether different from Smallpiece: tall and well-built with spectacles. He spoke with a heavy cockney accent. *Bethnal Green,* sprang to Cooper's mind.

'Afternoon gents, how can we help you?'

'Mr Grimes, as I explained to your colleague on the phone, we are investigating the murder of a Catholic nun, which was committed last Tuesday; the same day as an art exhibition that was covered in Kensington by both of you, I believe.'

'That was for Mr Devaux, wasn't it, Skip?'

'Yes, that's the one,' said Smallpiece.

'Only, we did two last week. The other one was in Knightsbridge. They seem to be all the rage at present.'

'The murder was in the grounds of Beaumont Hall, the home of Lord and Lady Roding,' said Stockwell.

'Really? Well, we know Lord Jeremy and the Lady Fanny of old, don't we Skip?'

'I must stress that she is not a suspect as such, but, like several key individuals, we are seeking to establish the whereabouts of Lady Fanny Roding at the time of the murder. She told us about the exhibition and the fact that she was present throughout the event. We're hoping that this can be confirmed by recourse to your photographs.'

'Yes, Superintendent, I am sure that we can assist you. The thing is, as you know, we are a business and in the spirit of police-journalist cooperation, I wonder whether we could come to some arrangement. Maybe, *Tatler* being able, in due course, to produce, say, an exclusive article,' said Smallpiece.

'Well, I'm not sure that we can do that,' said Stockwell.

He was almost interrupted by Smallpiece, who appeared quite anxious to get his point across. 'We could agree content and you could have full editorial rights before publication. You see, the thing is, Lady Roding is a person of interest as far as we are concerned. She married into money. She is not of the *nobility* and she is a rather colourful character. One might say that she is something of a gift for a society journal such as ours. We really have heard quite a bit of gossip about her,' said Smallpiece tantalisingly, 'and, of course, we could give you access to our extensive archive.'

Yet again, Stockwell was to surprise Cooper with his response as it was quite apparent that he was not going to dismiss the proposal without some consideration.

'Clearly, we appreciate your cooperation, Mr Smallpiece; I would have to seek authority from our chief constable. But if you would leave your proposal with me, I will see if anything can be agreed.'

'Happy with that, Skip?' said Grimes.

'Yes, indeed,' said Smallpiece.

'Then the contact prints are over here on the table, gentlemen. You'll see that Lady Fanny's image is splashed across most of them,' said Grimes.

He guided Stockwell and Cooper across the room to a long table where they examined the images.

'Blimey!' exclaimed Cooper, 'She told us that she'd "worked the room" and she wasn't joking, was she? She's on nearly all of them,' said Cooper.

'Yes, she does get about, does our Lady Fanny,' commented Smallpiece with a wry smile.

Cooper then turned to Grimes and almost as an aside he said, 'Of course, Mr Grimes, we'll need a short witness statement from you producing the sheets in evidence, and that might mean you having to attend court.'

'That's fine by me,' said Grimes, 'I spend half of my life at the Old Bailey as it is.'

'What time did you take the final photographs?'

'That would have been about 6.30pm, wouldn't it, Skip?'

Smallpiece nodded in agreement, then said, 'We both stayed on until about 8.30pm.'

'They were serving free cocktails and it seemed a bit of a shame to let them go to waste,' said Grimes laughing, 'It was a good night, from what I can remember of it.'

'Peasant!' said Smallpiece, with mock indignation. 'Please do forgive my working-class colleague, Inspector.'

'In fact, these events give me a good opportunity to engage the guests in conversation and collect some gossip for the journal,' said Smallpiece. 'We meet a lot of *high society* figures in our line of business, and we do tend to run across the same people time and again. This adds to the gossip factor, of course, which is fundamental to *Tatler,* and one has to try to keep up with it all.'

'Was Lady Fanny still there when you left?'

'Yes. In fact, she was the one who locked the door behind us. We were the last to leave the gallery apart from her ladyship and Marcus.'

After taking witness statements, Stockwell and Cooper were escorted to the front of the building by Grimes.

'Just one thing, Harry. As a matter of interest, why do you refer to Mr Smallpiece as "Skip"?' asked Cooper.

'We served together in the RAF during the war, Inspector. We were in Lancasters. He was my skipper and I was the bomb aimer. You wouldn't think so to look at him, but underneath all that foppery, he's a tough customer and a bloody good bloke.'

One can't always judge by appearances, indeed, thought Cooper, as they bid Grimes farewell and descended the steps into the street.

As they walked back to the Wolseley, Cooper turned to his boss.

'Are we really going to give them their exclusive, sir?'

'Shouldn't be a problem, Albert, provided we can edit the content and influence the time of its release so as not to comprise any court proceedings. Besides, I'd like to see what they have in their archive about Lady Fanny.'

'Yes. That lady has a colourful history, I should think.'

'Anyway, Albert, judging by the photos, and the witness statements you've just taken from Messrs Grimes and Smallpiece it does look as though our Lady Fanny could not have been the killer.'

'No, sir. Not in person, perhaps. But she has money and influence, and, according to the letter, she's the only person we've found with any kind of motive. She could still have murdered Sister Margaret by proxy.'

By the time Cooper had got back to the CID office, Brian Pratt had stood the murder team down for the day.

Cooper and Stockwell had left Central London shortly before 5.00pm; consequently, they had copped the full inertia of the rush hour even before reaching the Strand. They got a bit further on, but then it had taken them the best part of an hour to travel the few miles from Aldgate to

Stratford. It was now almost 8.00pm and they had only just arrived back in Colchester.

On returning to the police station, Stockwell and Cooper went their separate ways. Cooper had partaken of quite enough intrigue for one day, and he told himself that it was time for a well-earned pint of Double Diamond.

He thought he'd give the Hole in the Wall a swerve lest he bump into the pain in the arse that was Nobber Gibbs. He certainly couldn't be doing with any more banter from that quarter. It might develop into *fisticuffs*, and where would that get him? The sack, probably.

No, he would go to the George Hotel, a much more salubrious establishment altogether.

The George wasn't busy. In fact, the saloon bar only had a few customers and they were seated in a couple of small groups. As was his habit, Cooper quickly sized them up and subconsciously evaluated them during his visual sweep of the room. He was content that they posed no threat as they appeared to be a mix of local traders and hotel guests.

Cooper bought his usual pint of beer and he noted, without surprise, that it was a penny more expensive than that sold by his local, *one and six* [one shilling and sixpence] *that's bloody scandalous. Still, only to be expected,* he told himself.

He sat with his back to the wall at one end of the bar, which, again, was something he did automatically. This gave him a chance to see everything before him, thus allowing for no unwelcome surprises.

Good, he thought. *A nice pint. That's all that's needed to initiate the relaxation process. But one and bleeding six? It ought to be bloody good for that price.* Cooper sat and supped his beer quietly, while ruminating over the day's business.

He then became aware of a group of men walking into the bar area from the dining room. They appeared particularly well refreshed, and he soon realised, from their banter, that they were journalists working for national newspapers.

Fortunately, the barman had given no sign of recognising him, so he reasoned that he'd be fine if he just drank, relaxed and kept his own counsel. *This could prove to be an interesting and informative exercise.*

As the evening progressed a couple of members of the group gravitated along the bar in his general direction. This was, apparently, more by way of drunken momentum than any intent on their part. Although he could monitor their every word, he studiously avoided making eye contact. He soon picked up on the fact that they were attempting to engage the barman in conversation about the murder.

After a while, they finally understood that the barman was playing dumb and that he didn't want to be drawn on anything in relation to the murder, so they gradually lost interest in him.

The room slowly emptied of other patrons until Cooper became the only punter in the bar other than the journalists. He had removed his jacket, collar and tie, and they were lying in a pile on the bench next to him.

One of their number had obviously decided that he would move along the counter and approach Cooper, who was reading that day's copy of the *Daily Sketch* and was still intent on minding his own business.

This man was a corpulent, ruddy-faced individual with an arrogant manner, and, as soon became clear, an overblown sense of his own importance. Cooper did his best to ignore him, but then he was tempted to have a bit of sport. The man introduced himself, but did not have the good grace to even attempt to ascertain Cooper's identity.

'I'm Robin Grosvenor of the *Daily Sketch*. You'll probably have heard of me. We're covering the murder. Are you a local man?'

Here we go, thought Cooper. 'Yes, I am, boy. Born and bred.' For the purposes of this exercise, Cooper adopted a broad North Essex / South Suffolk accent.

'Have you heard about the murder?'

'Which murder is that then, boy?'

'Which murder is that then?' said Grosvenor mockingly, 'The murder of the nun, of course!'

'Yes, I've heard about that one.'

'What have you heard?'

'Yes, I have indeed, boy.'

'I'm sorry. What did you say?'

'Yes.'

'I'm sorry. I don't understand. What are you trying to say?'

'I said yes!'

'What did you mean when you said yes?'

'I answered yes. Just confirming what you were a saying.'

'So, you meant yes then.'

'Yes, I did.'

'Somebody killed her. Do you have any theory as to who might have killed her?'

'Yes. Matter of fact, I do.'

Grosvenor moved in closer, hoping to be taken into Cooper's confidence, 'Who was it then?'

'Yes, I do, boy.'

'Can you tell me who murdered the nun?' said Grosvenor, losing patience and starting to raise his voice.

'No, but I know someone who can.'

'Who is that then?'

'Her husband.'

'Whose husband?'

'The nun's husband.'

'But surely, she wasn't married, was she?'

'Of course, she was!'

'Who to?'

'The Lord.'

'Lord Roding?'

'No. Don't be a blooda fool! He's already married to that Fanny woman! What are you loik?'

'Who then?'

'The Lord Jesus.'

'You're a bloody idiot!'

'I know. Thank you. Good night, boy. Nice talking to you.'

With that, Cooper downed the dregs of his pint, walked out of the bar and made his way home.

10

DAY TEN

Thursday 21st July 1949

'I'm sorry to have kept you waiting, Sergeant, but I wasn't expecting any visitors. How may I help you?' Father O'Leary was rather flustered. A large man of well over six feet in height, he was somewhat overweight. He was wearing a black suit, the jacket of which he would have struggled to button up, even if he'd wanted to. Below a thick head of black, curly hair, he had a ruddy complexion, and beads of sweat had broken out across his forehead. A Dubliner, he had been the parish priest at St Saviour's for over twenty years. He was obviously an ardent drinker.

'I've been given to understand that you have had contact with a Carmelite nun called Sister Margaret. Is that correct?' asked Ian Mills.

'Yes. My housekeeper informed me, only yesterday, that she has been murdered. It's so very sad. I've only just come back from a retreat in Norfolk, where I was totally cut off from the world for a week or so, and I've only been back a day. I had no idea about this tragic situation until she told me.'

'How did you know Sister Margaret, Father?'

'I was contacted by Cardinal Pat O'Mara of the Vatican Special Assignments Unit and told to expect her arrival.'

'The Vatican Special Assignments Unit? What do they do, Father?'

'I must say, I have no idea really. Special projects for the Vatican, I would imagine. But I have known Pat O'Mara for many years. We were young priests together in Dublin.'

'So, why did she come to Beaumont in the first place, Father?'

'To help Lord Roding with his conversion to Catholicism. I did think that it was somewhat unusual, but I supposed that, as a lord, he must count as a *special project*. Tell me, Sergeant, how was she killed?'

'She was attacked in the grounds of Beaumont Hall by a person or persons unknown and beaten to death with a garden spade.'

'Good Lord. The poor girl. How terrible. I do hope that she didn't suffer. Do you know who was responsible for the attack?'

'No, Father. We don't have any idea at present, but I can assure you that we're working on it, and that we're using the maximum resources at our disposal. Can you tell me where she came from or anything about her?'

'She was sent to us from the Vatican.'

'Did you know of her before she came to this country?'

'No, Sergeant. I had never met her or heard of her. You will appreciate the Catholic Church is a vast organisation.'

'Can you tell me how she got here?'

'Yes. In the event, she arrived at the parochial house by taxi and I took her by car to introduce her to Lord Roding.'

'But how did she get to the UK?'

'I seem to recall her saying something about arriving at Harwich by ferry.'

'What did she tell you about herself?'

Father O'Leary was silent for a few seconds and was obviously considering the question. 'She was born in Switzerland. She told me that. She originated from the Italian part. She had only been a nun for about four years. Oh, and her given name was Irma Caro. That was told to me by Pat O'Mara, and, come to think of it, on the phone he said that she was Italian.'

'Did she sound Italian?'

'I'm terrible with accents. I thought she sounded Italian.'

'What role were you expected to fulfil in respect of your dealings with her?'

'My role was to provide spiritual and logistical support for the duration of her stay. She was due to be here for about three months.'

'Did she make any mention to you about having any problems when she was at the Hall?'

'No, none. She never reported any problems to me, anyway.'

'What did you make of her?'

'She was quite shy. An earnest young woman, anxious to do well, I think.'

'Why didn't she stay with you at the parochial house?'

'Apparently, Lord Roding wanted her to be available on tap, so to speak, and, anyway, we simply would not have had the room to accommodate her. She would have had to share a room with me and the Catholic Church does rather frown on that sort of behaviour,' said Father O'Leary tongue in cheek.

'Did you ever visit her at the Hall?'

'I had no reason to. She did pay me one visit here at St Saviour's, but she only came to tea and she didn't mention any problems then.'

'Did Cardinal O'Mara come to see you?'

'No, he only spoke to me on the telephone. Apparently, he was in London at the time. I said before, I have known Pat O'Mara since we were ordained as young priests. He's done well for himself and now occupies an influential position in the Vatican. It is said that he has the ear of His Holiness the Pope.'

'Can you recall the date of Sister Margaret's arrival?'

'Yes, Sergeant, I remember exactly when she arrived. It was my housekeeper Mrs Maloney's birthday: the 19th May.'

There being no further questions or information, Ian Mills took a witness statement from the priest.

11

DAY ELEVEN
Friday 22nd July 1949

Cooper made sure that he got to the office bright and early, as today was the day that he would launch his operation to flush out the person responsible for making unauthorised disclosures to the press. He had agreed a plan of action with Stockwell after much discussion, and, although they had more than one suspect in mind, for that day's operation, there was one primary target. Hopefully, this suspect would not be able to resist the temptation of divulging the details of the gift that was about to be placed in front of them.

Buoyed up by the prospect of success, he went about his duties with a smile and took the opportunity to call young Miss Collins into his office to check on her morale.

'Close the door and take a seat, Linda.'

He noticed that she was wearing a white, open-necked blouse, which showed a hint of cleavage, above a dark-green pencil skirt. She was gorgeous.

'How are things?'

'Fine, governor. Though, I still can't help thinking that I

ought to say something to the others about my relationship to my uncle Tom.'

'I'll leave it to you to decide whether that's necessary. But Sergeant Pratt and I are both happy with your work. I would give it a bit more thought before saying anything.'

'I'm wondering whether I should speak to him about it.'

'I wouldn't do that yet, Linda. We don't want him thinking that there is a problem when there isn't one. And I wouldn't want him to replace you with somebody else.'

Linda smiled and tilted her head slightly to one side, coquettishly. 'Thank you, governor. That's nice.'

'Anyway, we'll leave it there for now.'

Linda thanked him again and she left the room. He did indeed need to leave it there. He was finding it very hard to remain dispassionate and professional. Cooper knew, deep down, that, somehow or other, the team would have to be told about her relationship to the boss and it would be best if that fact was divulged by Linda herself. However, the timing was troubling him, as was the possibility that the team would suspect that she had been fed in by Stockwell to spy on her colleagues in relation to the leaks.

Cooper later left the police station to walk to the bus station café where he had arranged to meet his old colleague and mucker DI Arthur Brown. Arthur was a contemporary of Cooper, both at school and within the force. They were recruited by the Colchester Borough Constabulary at the same time and they had cut their teeth together as junior detective constables (DCs). Arthur was about six feet in height and, in boxing terms, one would describe him as a "light heavyweight". He had black hair that was in crew-cut style. He was a wily customer who possessed a ready wit, and Cooper trusted Arthur as much as he ever dared trust anybody. He had worked at Colchester Police Station in the past, and he was well known by staff and locals alike. The café seemed the best place to meet to avoid the inevitable questions that would be asked of Arthur, by his former colleagues, about his reason for being there.

After a lengthy chat and some careful planning, they walked to the office of Superintendent Stockwell.

On their arrival, they entered the outer office where they were met by Mavis, who was sitting behind her desk, painting her nails. Cooper detected that, today, she had quite a different fragrance about her and she was dressed as if she was going out on a lunch engagement. Clearly the boss had left her with little work to be getting on with and she appeared to be taking advantage of the fact.

Cooper greeted her and made a point of introducing Arthur. She quickly acknowledged him, but she did so with a rather dismissive tone. Cooper then reminded himself that she and Arthur had worked together in the past. It occurred to him that Arthur might have been yet another one of her failed romantic targets, and that her bitterness and disappointment were now being manifested.

'Mavis, I know that the boss is away at Headquarters this morning. I need to discuss some sensitive cases with my colleague DI Brown. Mr Stockwell has agreed to our using the office in his absence so that we can get some privacy. Did he tell you?'

'Yes. He told me about it first thing this morning, then he went straight out for a meeting with the chief constable,' said Mavis.

'Any idea when he's likely to be back?'

'I have no idea. He doesn't tell me everything, you know,' she said, moodily.

Cooper realised that all was not well with her. She was speaking in clipped tones, trying to affect an air of superiority, and she was behaving in an unnecessarily defensive manner. As Cooper's landlady, Pearl, would have said, "She's putting her parts on!"

Her demeanour was not soothed by Cooper's next request.

'Fine, we'll crack on then. Any tea going?'

Mavis put on her best "I'm not your sodding tea lady" face, but nevertheless she put the kettle on and supplied the two detectives with the necessary beverages. They closed the door, separating Stockwell's room from that occupied by Mavis, and they carried on their sensitive case meeting in "secret".

'Well, I must say, Arthur. I'm bloody grateful to you for your help, mate. We were struggling badly. How did you get to find out that it was this man Bernard Connelly?'

'I must admit that it wasn't due to classic detective work. I'd love to be able to claim that it was. But it was down to the fact that, having committed the murder, he couldn't live with himself and his conscience got too much for him. He went to see a friend of his who is a Salvation Army captain and he made a full confession.'

'Well, he couldn't very well go and see a Catholic priest about it, could he?' Cooper laughed, irreverently.

'No, I suppose not,' Arthur continued, 'That put the Salvation Army bloke in a difficult position, see. After a while he talked Connelly into going with him to the police station so that he could confess and get it off his chest. It fell to me to deal with him and I gave him a quick cursory interview, before he had a chance to think about it and change his mind. Oh, he's your man all right and he told me how it all came about. I didn't want to go too deeply into it, with my limited knowledge of the case and confuse the issue, so he's sitting in the cells in Braintree for you to take over, mate.'

'So, Arthur, what has this bloke Bernard Connelly said to you about the way that the murder was committed?'

Brown explained, 'Apparently, he is something to do with maintenance in the graveyard at St Saviour's Church in Beaumont. A gravedigger or some such thing. That's where he met her, and, apparently, he came to the Hall to pay her a visit.'

'A bloody gravedigger! What the bloody hell was she doing getting involved with a gravedigger?'

'Well, apparently, he's a bit of an amateur artist himself and she had told him about a summerhouse, in the grounds of Beaumont Hall, that she uses as a studio. Does that mean anything to you?'

'Yes, it does. She was murdered in the summerhouse.'

'Well, it seems she invited him to visit her so that she could show him her paintings, and he wanted to take her up on the invitation. So, they arranged for him to visit her at the Hall that afternoon.'

'For her to show him her etchings, I wouldn't wonder,' said Cooper laughing aloud.

'Something like that. Anyway, he said that she told him to come straight around to the back and she would meet him there. So, he did. He fancied her, and he thought that she was giving him the old come on, so he tried it on with her. She started to scream, he panicked and shut her up in the only way that he knew how.'

'And how was that?'

'With the first weapon that he could find.'

'Yes, and what was that?'

'I didn't tell him anything about the murder myself. It had to come from him.'

'For Christ's sake spit it out, Arthur,' said Cooper raising his voice, almost to a shout.

'He said that he was so mad at her that he punched her around the head with his fists.'

'Is he a time-waster, or do you think he actually did it?'

'Oh, I think he's your man all right.'

'Is Bernard Connelly known to the police in Braintree? Does he have any previous convictions at all?'

'No. No convictions,' said Brown, 'but he does come from a large family, and one or two of his brothers have been done for drunkenness and fighting. His father was a wrong-un. He was from County Cork originally, and came across with the army.'

'Thanks Arthur. I am very much obliged, mate. You've saved us a lot of leg work, I reckon. I just need to get hold of my sergeant; we'll be over there with you this afternoon, and we'll carry on with him.'

They then had a brief discussion about procedure, Connelly's home address and the possibility of recovering the blood-stained clothing.

After a session that had lasted some thirty minutes, the meeting was finished.

Arthur left the building and Cooper, who was close on his heels, returned to the police station, where he sought out Pratt, and allocated him a task to take him out of the division for the rest of the day. Cooper then busied himself in his office. He received periodic updates on the phone from Arthur, who, with his team, was carrying out surveillance on their suspect. This whole business of the leaks had recently dominated Cooper's thoughts to the extent that it had diverted him from concentrating on the murder enquiry. He looked forward with eager anticipation to finally nailing the person responsible and closing off the problem.

12

DAY TWELVE
Saturday 23rd July 1949

Cooper and Pratt were sitting at one end of the canteen having breakfast. Pratt was busy demolishing a plate of egg on toast and Cooper, who was merely nursing a mug of tea, was looking on enviously. He was fighting the urge to order a sausage sandwich, having already breakfasted at Fred's, but, on reminding himself that he had not been eating regularly of late, he placed his order.

They had been discussing the progress of the murder enquiry, or at least, the lack of it. They were now well into the second week and it seemed, to Pratt at least, that they were no further forward. No real suspect. No motive, no hypothesis. To add to their frustration, they were now coming under pressure from other departments for the return of their staff. They were joined at the table by Ian Mills.

'Morning Ian. Everything done at the school?'

'Morning governor. Yes. I spoke to them yesterday afternoon and it's all sorted. It does make sense to shut up shop there now. We weren't getting any more callers at the incident room, and local enquiries have all but dried up. We can carry on back here at the nick.'

'OK, Ian. Will you remind me in due course that we send along a bunch of flowers and a force plaque to the headmistress? Perhaps Linda and Jane would do the honours.'

'Will do, governor.'

Cooper appreciated Mills' reassurance that his earlier decision to close the incident room had been the right one, but his heart still sank with regret.

'The other problem was,' continued Mills, 'that I was having my earhole bent by uniform, because they're so short of staff and were having to provide security for the school at night.'

'We're due a large slice of luck, I think, governor,' said Pratt. 'But at least the *Recorder* has left us alone for a few days.'

'Yes. That's probably because if we make no progress, there's nothing to be leaked. And, anyway, they don't go to press at weekends,' said Mills.

'God, Ian, you can be a miserable sod at times,' said Pratt.

'Now, now. Play nicely, children. Let's not get too downhearted. There are still things that we can be doing. At least we now know the victim's real name. That gives us something to go on. Anyway, apart from that, as things have gone a bit quiet, I think it gives us an opportunity for us all to take tomorrow off. I'm sure we could do with a break, and then on Monday we can all come back to work refreshed and crack on.'

'Yes. I like that idea, governor,' said Pratt, 'It's not as if, after twelve days, we'll lose anything by it.'

'No. And it's not as if Sister Margaret and Lord Roding will be going anywhere now, is it?' said Mills.

'Take a day off, Ian, for Christ's sake,' said Pratt.

'Thanks Brian, I think I will,' said Mills.

They laughed, downed their tea and walked to the training room where the rest of the staff were assembled. As Cooper cast his eyes around the room, he saw Linda Collins, who, for once, was wearing a uniform, but even in an outfit of blue serge, she still managed to look chic and beautiful. They exchanged smiles.

'Morning all. You're in uniform, I see, Miss Collins. We're not losing you, I hope?' *Oh dear, that did sound cheesy.*

'No, governor. I've got to go to a colleague's long-service award ceremony at the town hall this morning. It's a long-standing commitment.'

'Good. Right, let's get on then,' said Cooper, hoping that he hadn't embarrassed himself. 'For those of you who might not be aware, we now have a name for our victim, as provided by Father O'Leary, the local parish priest at St Saviour's. It was Irma Caro, apparently. And if it wasn't for you, Jane, suggesting that we go and see him, we wouldn't have got that. So, thanks and well done.'

An acknowledging murmur of "well done" went around the room. Jane curtsied and smiled.

'Sergeant Mills took the statement. Ian, if you would just read it out loud, please.'

Mills duly complied. 'We still have a gap to fill in respect of the journey taken by Sister Margaret to the point where she arrived at the parochial house, so I had Linda go back and make further enquiries. Mrs. Maloney, the housekeeper, is ninety percent sure that the sister arrived by taxi, but she can't remember which firm the cab came from,' said Mills.

'Surely the driver will remember her. We just have to find him,' said Jane Stewart. 'I mean, it's not every day that a cab driver picks up a nun, is it?'

'No. You're right. Ian, will you raise an action, please, to have all cab companies in the town visited?'

'I must say that I'm intrigued by this Cardinal Pat O'Mara bloke of the Special Assignments Unit of the Vatican. He sounds like something from the Spanish Inquisition, doesn't he? What does the term "Special Assignments" mean anyway?' asked Pratt.

'And does it involve torture?' said Rogers.

'Absolutely, and secret activities of an unspeakable nature,' added Mills.

'Well, for heaven's sake, what's so special about converting to Catholicism?' said DC Rogers. 'I mean, who gives a shit about that, anyway? It's all one big fairy story.'

'Language, Rogers!' said Cooper. 'Have a bit of respect. Ladies present.' He nodded towards Jane Stewart and Linda Collins, who were standing at the back of the room, grinning sheepishly.

Mills continued, 'It's good we now have a proper name for our victim, though. How are we spelling that?'

Pratt searched around for a stick of chalk and wrote the name on the blackboard.

'That's her name. Irma Caro, or at least that's what Father O'Leary was told,' said Pratt, 'Hopefully, we can rely on it.'

'We haven't much choice but to run with it,' said Cooper. 'I suppose it does give us a bit more to go to Immigration with. They ought to have details of her entry to the UK.

After all, nun or no nun, she is a foreign national. Although, I've no idea what details a nun would have to show on her passport. Another job for somebody, Ian.'

'Don't nuns get paid, governor?' said Ian Mills, thinking out loud.' Surely Monsignor Crecy's people in London must have provided her with the rail fare to get to Colchester, at least.'

'Well, Ian, you'd like to think so, but I wouldn't bet on it. Maybe Lord Roding can fill us in with the details about her rail fare. As for her funding, well, I think we'll have to speak to the Vatican about that one.'

'Not sure they'll be in the phone book,' said Rogers, flippantly.

'Another silly comment from you, Rogers, and you can be the first to go back on shift work,' said Cooper.

'Sorry, governor.' Rogers resolved to keep his mouth shut.

'OK, if that's all for now folks, you will be pleased to know that earlier the sergeants and I had a meeting during which we decided that the team will all take tomorrow off as a rest day. You've all worked hard. Let's try to get as much done as we can today, and we'll start fresh on Monday morning.'

The troops murmured their approval and the briefing was ended. Cooper and Pratt left the room and the remainder of the team stayed at their desks.

'Tom, come with me. I want a word.' Mills led Rogers into the sergeant's office and told him to shut the door.

'Tom, why don't you try to engage your brain before opening your mouth?' said Mills. 'You're going to drop yourself in the shit if you carry on making stupid comments all the time.'

'Sorry, Sarge.'

'Your work's good. It's just your silly attitude. You don't have to act like the office clown. I know the governor has his eye on you. Just wind your neck in.'

'Sorry, Sarge.'

'Anyway, the boss had his ear bent by Mr Stockwell about that case of chicken rustling, from Councillor Davis' allotment. That's your job, isn't it?'

'Yes, Sarge.'

'Right. Well, I want to see that crime report on my desk within the next hour as he wants it by close of play.'

'Yes, Sarge. If he wants to see it, how many copies do I need?'

'One top copy, one for CID admin and one for you. Now get on with it and think about what I've just said.'

Rogers left the sergeant's office and, before returning to his desk, he walked to the admin cupboard. He collected a typewriter and placed it on the desk in front of him. Reaching into the filing cabinet, he selected the necessary blank forms and carbon paper, which he shuffled and carefully wound onto the carriage. 'Right. Name: DC 35 Rogers.' The details were keyed onto the page with the slow and deliberate use of one finger. Rogers also displayed an irritating tendency to mouth the words as he typed them.

Linda Collins, who was sitting at the adjacent desk smiled to herself. She was skilled in the arts of shorthand and typing, but she wasn't about to interfere. Over the next half hour Tom Rogers slaved away on the machine, gradually completing the various fields, including a lengthy explanation of the enquiries carried out with the local traders. On completion, he gave the report an extra careful read. He was satisfied and not a little pleased with his efforts. He removed the pages from the typewriter and examined them.

'Oh, bollocks!'

Linda looked up, 'What's the matter Tom?'

'I put the sodding carbon paper in the wrong way around. What a waste of time. I'll have to do it all again.'

She laughed heartily, 'Give it here, Tom. I'll do for you. We don't want you getting done for "wasting police time", do we?'

13

DAY THIRTEEN

Sunday 24th July 1949

Rest Day.

14

DAY FOURTEEN

Monday 25th July 1949

Cooper could hear banging on his bedroom door. *Bloody hell! What time is it?* He looked at the alarm clock, *8:40am, shit! I knew I shouldn't have had that drink last night.* It was obvious to him that he'd forgotten to set the alarm clock.

'You in there, Alby?' shouted Pearl, accompanied by the barking of an excited Errol.

'Yes. Thanks, Pearl. I'll be out in a minute.'

He thanked God, that Pearl was taking an unhealthy interest in him, otherwise he might have slept on until lunch time. Cooper quickly grabbed his dressing gown, shrugged it on and unlocked the bedroom door in one swift movement. He washed and shaved in record time, dressed, and left the front door by 8.55am, to the disappointment of Errol, who was denied his morning rabbit hunt.

He had felt better, but he was a "trained soldier" and knew that a little Scotch from his desk draw would set him right. Besides, he had high hopes for the day and was eager to get to work. As far as the press leaks were concerned, he would learn, one way or the other, whether they had been offering their bait to the right suspect. The answer was likely to be on the front page of that day's edition of the *Recorder*.

As Cooper strode along the High Street, he avoided Sadie's and Fred's Café, in case they had read the paper already and would want to ask questions of him. He didn't want to get into that conversation. Furthermore, he simply didn't have the time.

As he reached the Castle Park gates, the answer to the question was made clear. Written across the news vendor's billboard were the words, "Nun Murderer Arrested".

Charlie, the paperman, spoke before Cooper could open his mouth, 'Morning, Alby. Been busy I see.'

Cooper was non-committal, 'Yes, Charlie. We're getting there, mate.'

Charlie handed Cooper a copy of the paper. 'Have this one on me.'

Cooper thanked him and carried on along the pavement, reading as he went. At first glance, he could see that the necessary ingredients were there. He was thrilled to bits. "Bernard Connelly of Braintree" was named and the author was Gladys Munson.

As he arrived at the front entrance of the police station Cooper saw that Ted Glover, the station sergeant was behind the counter. He was vigorously waving a copy of the *Recorder*.

'Morning governor. Seen today's edition of the *Recorder*?'

'Yes, thanks, Ted. I've got a copy already.'

'Front office is getting inundated with calls from the papers asking to speak to the senior investigating officer. We need to know what to tell them.'

Cooper took an executive decision. 'I think for now, Ted, we'll just have to tell them that a press statement will be given in due course.'

'Thanks, Alby. Leave it with me.'

Cooper made his way up to the CID, called Brian and Ian into his office and shut the door.

They and the other members of the team had been completely unaware of the fact that there were moves afoot regarding the so-called "press leaks".

Cooper gave his sergeants a brief outline of the situation, and told them that everything would later be explained in more detail to both themselves and the team. Cooper was about to make his way to the town hall to see Stockwell.

There now being something of a distraction, Pratt postponed the daily briefing.

After a couple of hours had passed with no news, curiosity got the better of Brian Pratt and he went off to locate his boss, tracking him down to the Superintendent's office. As he entered the management suite he was greeted by the sight of a tearful Mavis Dockree, who was emptying the personal effects from her desk under the supervision of Sergeant Cecily White (of the Women and Children Team). Mavis, the woman who had so often told herself that she held a position of power, had finally been put in her place. She had been suspended from her post and she made for a pathetic sight as she got her things together. Mavis was about to be unceremoniously escorted from the building.

Before Pratt could knock on the door of Stockwell's office, he was intercepted by Cooper, who led him down to the town hall canteen. He explained that, in about an hour, and once Mavis had left, they would have a meeting with the superintendent to discuss a strategy for managing the press.

Around midday, they found themselves sitting across the table from Tom Stockwell. There were teas and coffee on the table in front of them. Cooper wondered where these had come from now that Mavis had "had her arse kicked". Stockwell was clearly pleased about the outcome, but he wore a look of resignation on his face and was obviously conflicted.

'Very well done, Albert,' said Stockwell, congratulating Cooper on a successful operation. 'Thank you, sir.'

'It is a sad situation, though, all the same. She's been with me for a few years now, and she was good at her job. But we can't have that kind of thing. A complete breach of confidentiality. It is corrupt practice, plain and simple.'

'Absolutely, sir.'

'Albert, you explained the *prima facie* case to me, which was enough for us to take the correct action in relation to Mrs Dockree. There are just a few things that I wanted to satisfy myself on,' declared Stockwell. 'So, let's go through it again, shall we?'

Cooper gave a full summary of the evidence against Mavis.

'The meeting between DI Brown and myself was taped to record the content so if there is any argument it could be checked and compared against the detail in the *Recorder*.'

'That's good practice. Well done,' said Stockwell.

'During her lunch hour on Friday, Mavis was followed to the Home and Colonial shop in Head Street, where she was seen to meet another woman to whom she handed an envelope. The other woman was then followed to the office of the *East Anglian Recorder*, where she was seen to enter the building. She remained there until about 6.15pm, after which she walked to a house on the outskirts of the town. We later ascertained that this is the home of Gladys Munson, who is the crime reporter on the *Recorder*. That, taken together with the dissemination of the facts of our "sensitive meeting", leaves little room for doubt that Mavis was the source of our leaks.'

'Of course, Albert, it will be a matter for the Headquarters Complaints and Discipline Department to make a case for the dismissal of Mavis. It's bound to be endorsed by the chief constable. But, in my view, there's no benefit in taking her before a court of law. I have already spoken to the chief and he agrees with me. He also takes the view that it would be counterproductive to try to make a case against Munson. The papers would just construe it as the police interfering with the workings of a free press, and would, very likely, create a political maelstrom. No, it's better to face down the press in a conference, deny knowledge of any suspect called Bernard Connelly, and let Munson suffer the embarrassment and judgement of her peers.'

'Part of the story we used was that Connelly was a gravedigger at St Saviour's. Do you have any concerns about the press bothering Father O'Leary at all, sir?'

'No. No concerns at all. I don't think they'll bother him, Albert. And even if they do, worse things have happened in Christendom. It might just make the Church cooperate and recognise the victim, as one of their own. Our aim was to plug the leak of confidential information and you have been successful in achieving that objective. I am pleased that you have got to the bottom of the problem and so is the chief constable. I shall be speaking to Superintendent Egerton at Braintree, to pass on my thanks to DI Brown.'

'Thank you, sir,' said Cooper.

'Albert, there was something else that I have been meaning to speak to you about. If you would leave us for a few minutes, Sergeant.'

'I'll go back to the office, sir, and meet you there.' Pratt withdrew.

'Oh, and Brian,' said Cooper, calling after him, 'please don't say anything about this to the team, for now.'

'Right you are, governor.'

Pratt closed the door behind him.

'Albert, I wanted to speak to you about Linda Collins. I should have done so earlier. The fact is, she's my niece.'

'I know she is, sir.'

'Really? But how?'

'My aunt Sadie is a friend of your sister. Apparently, they went to school together. She's been on at me about Linda for a few weeks now, only she got her name wrong and was calling her Brenda. She does like to matchmake on my behalf, and it was only when I pushed her on the detail that she came up with the surname Collins, that her mother's maiden name was Stockwell, and she had a brother called Tom. I finally made the connection and it has left me with something of a dilemma, so I had to speak to Linda about it. She was a bit embarrassed.'

'I'm sure she was,' said Stockwell.

He stood, gazing out of the window, and was silent for a few seconds pondering over his words. He turned and looked Cooper in the eye. 'Albert, I really must apologise for putting you in that position. Her mother made mention of Linda's aspirations and I must admit that I rather took it upon myself to give her this opportunity. On reflection, it was rather unprofessional of me.'

'To be fair though, sir, Linda has made a very good start.'

'That's nice to hear. And your aunt Sadie was matchmaking, was she?'

'Yes, sir. She was, I'm afraid.'

'Don't be afraid, Albert. You're a single man, aren't you?'

'Yes, sir.'

'Well, what do you make of Miss Collins? Professionally, I mean.'

'She's very capable, conscientious and bright, sir. I'm pleased to have her on the enquiry. I was a bit worried about the possibility of the others finding out and maybe thinking that she had been underhand in not telling them that she's your niece. Particularly with the problem of the leaks. Personally, I now think it would be an excellent idea to call a meeting and tell the others, just to deal with the elephant in the room, so to speak.'

'I agree. At least, that way she's being open. After that she will just have to survive on the power of her own personality.'

'Would be best, sir. She's well liked and I'm sure that the others would appreciate her candour.'

'Then that's what you should do, Albert. As for matchmaking, I know that you are a man of discretion. I'll leave it to the pair of you to decide whether you are compatible. Just don't let it have a negative effect on your day-to-day work or I'll have to think about moving one of you.'

'Yes, sir. Understood.'

As Cooper made his way back down the High Street, he had an extra spring in his step, but he also felt that it would be wise to tread carefully with Linda Collins and take a slow approach to any personal relationship. Though, he wasn't at all sure that he could manage it.

'Somethings going on,' said Rogers, 'I can feel it in me water.'

'What are you going on about now, Tom?' said Jane Stewart.

'Well for a start, I saw Brian Pratt and Linda Collins go into the boss's office about half an hour ago, and they shut the door behind them. They're still in there. I put me ear to the door, but I couldn't hear anything.'

'I wouldn't do that if I were you Rogers, you'll end up getting the sack,' said Ian Mills, who had just joined them at the CID table in the canteen.

'If it helps to satisfy your curiosity, the office meeting's going to be attended by Mr Stockwell and before that the governor wants us to have a short meeting to discuss something else,' said Mills.

'What's that going to be about, Sarge?' said Stewart.

'There's been a breakthrough of some kind, I think.'

After tea, the team filed down to the training room where they found that Cooper, Pratt and Linda Collins were already present and awaiting their arrival. Linda looked tense. Jane walked up to her and placed a friendly arm around her shoulder.

'You all right, my lovely?'

'Yes. Fine thanks, Jane.'

'Come in folks, take a seat,' said Cooper, anxious to get started. 'We've something to discuss before Mr Stockwell arrives.'

After they had got themselves seated at the conference table Cooper opened the meeting. 'Right, as you know, Linda here has been with us for a couple of weeks having been posted from the Women's Police Department, and that was on the insistence of Mr Stockwell. When I first saw him about staffing the enquiry, I asked for six detective constables. As we are short on the division he wouldn't let me have that number, but he offered up Linda and Jane to help us with the investigation. Linda has since been to see me as she has been worried about something that has been troubling her. She has found herself in a difficult position and she wants to tell you about it herself. Over to you, Linda.'

'Thank you, governor.'

There was a brief pause as Linda gathered herself. The others were on the edge of their seats brimming with curiosity. She spoke slowly, deliberately and almost teasingly.

'Before I tell you, I want you all to know that I really enjoy working with you and I hope that you'll forgive me for not telling you this earlier. But it's difficult and I hope that it won't change things between us.'

'What is it then?' said Rogers.

'It's the fact that… Superintendent Tom Stockwell is my uncle.'

'Thank God for that Linda!' said Jane, 'I thought you were going to tell us that you're pregnant!'

'Oh. Thanks very much, Jane!' Fortunately, Linda saw the funny side of the remark and in a mixture of humour and relief, she burst out laughing.

The comment punctured the tension in the room and they all laughed.

'Is that all? Bloody hell! You had me going for a minute,' said Rogers.

'You can choose your friends, but you can't choose your family, Linda,' said Mills.

'Just thought that I ought to let you know, that's all. Just in case you found out some other way and thought that I was a spy in the camp,' said Linda.

'Don't be daft,' said Jane.

'The teas are definitely on you later, then,' said Rogers.

'Tom, if I must do your typing for you, we'll call it evens.'

'Fair dos,' said Rogers.

'Good. So, that's that out of the way then. We carry on as before,' said Cooper.

'Absolutely,' said Jane.

'Is that the breakthrough we've been hearing about?' said Rogers.

'No, Tom. There's more to tell. Wait until Mr Stockwell arrives. While we have a couple of minutes, if anyone needs the lavatory, now is the time to go.'

The girls left the room.

After another five minutes, Superintendent Stockwell arrived in the training room and they all stood as a sign of respect. As they did so the members of the team all looked at Linda Collins and gave a mischievous smile.

'Good morning, ladies and gentlemen, thank you, please be seated. Over to you Inspector.'

'Thank you, sir,' said Cooper, 'Ladies and gentlemen, we will have a longer and fuller meeting this morning. I want to take stock of where we are with the investigation and the outstanding enquiries that have yet to be completed. Also, there have been two things that have happened in the last couple of days that we need to make you aware of, not least of which are the so-called "press leaks". Mr Stockwell has something to say to you on that subject. So, I will hand you over to him.'

'Thank you, Inspector. By the way, smoke if you want to, ladies and gentlemen.'

Mills, Pratt and Stewart all lit up.

'As you know, there has been an unfortunate series of leaks to the press, which have culminated in the name of a suspect being published in the *East Anglian Recorder* this morning. I know that you are all aware of that development and that, this morning, you were told to ignore the name "Bernard Connelly" for the purposes of this investigation. The suggestion that anyone with this name is responsible for the murder is totally erroneous. I can now tell you that my secretary, Mavis Dockree, has been suspended from duty regarding the leaks, and the matter is under investigation by Headquarters. I am telling you this now to clarify the situation for you. There is compelling evidence against Mrs Dockree, but I am not at liberty to say any more to you than that.'

Stockwell then appealed to his audience.

'But, I want you to think on this. Unfortunately, this series of leaks undermined not only what you were doing but you as individuals. It's a sad fact, but you were all under suspicion. This kind of thing creates bad feeling and a toxic atmosphere in the workplace, and in extremis it can put officer's lives at risk. Anyway, it has now been dealt with, and I want you to know that I am proud of the team and have faith in you all. Now let's put this unfortunate situation behind us and see if we can get our murderer. Thank you, ladies and gentlemen. It's back to you now I think, Albert.'

'Thank you, sir.'

The team broke into a spontaneous round of applause and Cooper thought that he could see a moistening around the eyes of Mr Stockwell as he left the room.

'OK, I will just reiterate what the boss said then. The press do not have a right to know how we managed to solve this problem. Mr Stockwell and I will deal with it if any potential conflict arises from the situation. In fact, we're due to have a press conference at 4.00pm. I anticipate that, as far as the press are concerned, we'll have to manage a certain amount of disappointment.'

'Finally, and before we move on to general matters, and I make no apologies for repeating myself here, nobody is to speak to the press on any issue, and if you are approached, I expect you to come to me or one of the sergeants in my absence.'

'Right. You've had the gypsies warning.'

The press conference would be the final stage of the operation to plug the leak. It was decided that advanced details were to be disseminated to the various press organisations by Ian Mills working from the sheaf of telephone logs that had been completed by the front-office staff when fielding the many telephone enquiries that morning. He had to remain steadfast and stick rigidly to the script over the telephone, as, in some cases, the recipient of the advanced details, tried to pump him for more information. The conference was to be held in magistrates' court number three, which would be vacant as the court would have no normal business scheduled for the day. Stockwell prepared a form of words as a statement to be made at the press conference:

"Essex Constabulary are currently engaged in a murder enquiry to identify and bring to justice the killer(s) of Sister Margaret, a Carmelite nun. The murder was committed on Tuesday 12th July 1949, in the grounds of Beaumont Hall, a stately home in the village of Beaumont-cum-Moze. The name of a man called Bernard Connelly has been brought to our attention as a possible suspect for the murder in this morning's edition of the *East Anglian Recorder* Newspaper."

Cooper considered that the choice of Colchester Magistrates' Court, as the venue for holding the press conference, was something of a masterstroke. Apart from the fact that it was available space, the very purpose of the building would hopefully instil some discipline into what was likely to be a volatile event. However, to be sure, a section of uniformed officers would be on hand to deal with anyone who became inordinately exercised.

Brian Pratt was acting as the usher, as the doors were opened by him at 3.45pm. The fact that he was nearly injured in the stampede led him to shout out, 'Please take it easy, ladies and gentlemen. There's plenty of room for all. Let's have fact on the right, fiction on the left!' One or two groaned at this merry quip. Gladys Munson had turned up with a colleague. She was looking rather smug and had ensured they could grab a couple of seats in pole position on the front row.

At 4.00pm precisely, Superintendent Stockwell, somewhat magisterially, entered the court with Cooper, and he took the chair usually occupied by the chairman of the bench. Cooper sat alongside him. Stockwell had also taken the prudent decision to have a court stenographer present in the room to record the proceedings.

'Thank you, ladies and gentlemen. May I have your attention, please?' said Stockwell. He introduced himself and Cooper, and then went on to explain their reason for being there. 'Ladies and gentlemen, we have called a press conference today to deal with the matter of a person, one Bernard Connelly, who has been named as a suspect in our investigation into the murder of Sister Margaret. This revelation was led by the *East Anglian Recorder*, in their morning edition, with some fanfare.'

'Mr Stockwell, my name is Richard Timmins of the *Argus*. Can you give us some more specific detail on this development?'

'No, Mr Timmins. We can't give you anything. We simply have nothing to give you.' said Stockwell.

There was an audible gasp from the assembled members of the press and the room erupted.

'But the public have a right to know!' shouted a voice from the back of the room, with outrage and indignation.

'I couldn't agree more, sir,' said Stockwell, who was warming to his task. The tactic was working. They were starting to bite.

Gladys Munson, who having penned the article for that morning, felt it incumbent on her to challenge Stockwell and force "the truth" out into the open. This was her moment, so she got to her feet.

'Superintendent, I am Gladys Munson of the *East Anglian Recorder* and I am the author of the piece to which you are referring. Are you denying that you have arrested a man called Bernard Connelly for the murder of Sister Margaret?'

'Yes, I am. Perhaps you can tell us more Mrs Munson? For instance, how you managed to come by this information?'

'Well, as I'm sure you know, Superintendent,' said Munson, who was playing to the gallery, 'I am under no obligation to divulge the details of journalistic sources.'

'Quite right, too. But if your source has any other information that might help our investigation, I am sure that we would be most grateful to them for their assistance. After all it is a citizen's duty to help the police,' said Stockwell with heavy sarcasm.

'We understand that Bernard Connelly works as a gravedigger at St Saviour's Catholic Church in Beaumont. Are you saying that you have never heard of this man?' said Munson, who was not prepared to give up easily.

'That's exactly what I am saying. This is a name that we do not recognise. We have no Bernard Connelly in custody, nor does any such person have a bearing on the investigation of this murder,' said Stockwell, vehemently.

'Anyway, that's all for now. Thank you, ladies and gentlemen, when we have some information to give you, we will let you know.'

Stockwell and Cooper both rose from the bench to walk out of the court.

The anger in the room was palpable. Much of it was directed at Gladys Munson and her "silly provincial rag".

The press had been well and truly stuffed. But, would it end there? Was this fiasco a story, in itself?

Cooper followed Superintendent Stockwell from the court and out through the connecting door, into the magistrates' retiring room. As they reached the sanctuary of the back room he saw Stockwell punch the air.

'God! I enjoyed that, Albert!'

This man, who had once seemed so dour and defeatist, was going up in Cooper's estimations.

15

DAY FIFTEEN

Tuesday 26th July 1949

The national newspapers had a field day at the expense of the *East Anglian Recorder*. The criticism of their provincial cousins was largely over the fact that they didn't appear to have carried out any due diligence to verify what their source had told them and had simply taken it as being totally reliable. In fact, Munson had spoken so highly of her informant, emphasising their level of placement and access, that her editor had allowed himself to be bullied into immediate publication. Furthermore, he was so intent on stealing a march on his competitors that he had taken a reckless punt on the veracity of the information. He and Munson were about to pay the price.

So, it was the turn of the national newspapers, led by the *Daily Sketch*, to make their own enquiries to try to get to the bottom of the suspect named as Bernard Connelly. They were certainly not going to take the word of mere country coppers. They were convinced that there was a story to be distilled from the mess presented by the *Recorder*.

There was only one place to go to pursue their interest, St Saviour's Church, where Gladys Munson had stated that the suspect Bernard Connelly was employed as a gravedigger.

It was midday and several members of the press were camped outside St Saviour's. Some had taken it upon themselves to ring the doorbell of the parochial house, and on each occasion the door had been opened by the housekeeper, Mrs. Maloney. She had flatly denied that there was anyone employed at St Saviour's called Bernard Connelly and denied that there were any priests in the house, before she slammed the door. Disgusted, she crossed herself on both occasions for her sin and walked to the foot of the stairs where she shouted up to Father O'Leary. 'You can't hide in your bedroom forever, Father!'

'Yes, I can,' whispered O'Leary, 'and keep your voice down, they'll hear you.'

After working in the vestry due to having been tipped off about the arrival of the press by the housekeeper, Father O'Leary, had left the church through the crypt and had sneaked into the house via the back garden. He had since been hiding in his room. Various reporters and camera men had been camped on his doorstep since early morning and the front doorbell had been ringing off the wall. Father Thomas O'Leary was deeply disturbed by all the attention. What on earth would his parishioners think? He only had himself to blame. He had been flattered when first contacted by Cardinal O'Mara and had readily obeyed when he had sworn him to secrecy. Father O'Leary knew that his old friend held a position of influence in the Vatican, as it was said that he carried out the projects that Pope Pius XII would entrust to no other. O'Leary now regretted the fact that hubris had stopped him from telling his bishop about the presence of Sister Margaret in the village. Although he could have done nothing to have prevented her murder, Irma Caro, a young Swiss woman who was in a strange land, had been entrusted to his care. Despite her being an adult, she was an innocent, so he was firmly of the view that he was expected to act *in loco parentis*. He had failed her and consequently he felt very guilty about the situation.

O'Leary decided that he would send a telegram to the Vatican requesting that the Cardinal contact him urgently. As for the bishop, he could wait.

Lord Jeremy Roding was sitting alone with a rug over his knees and a jug of Pimm's on the table at his side, the content of which was down to its last couple of inches. It was a fine, still, sunny afternoon and Jeremy was seated in the shadow cast by the summerhouse. Although it was the middle of the day, it was almost as if his lordship was keeping vigil in memory of his recently departed house guest.

Cooper and Pratt were once again at Beaumont Hall and were being led through the garden by the butler, Jenkins. His lordship looked up from his book as he saw the group approach him and then with laughter said, 'Ah! The intrepid detectives. I need to speak to you.' He pointed an accusatory finger. 'What is this I have been reading in the paper about an arrest?' Lord Jeremy sounded as if the Pimm's had started to get the better of him.

'I take it, my lord, that you are referring to the suspect named in the *Recorder* as Bernard Connelly?'

'Yes, Inspector, that's the chap. I've never heard of him. Has he been charged?'

'No, my lord. The whole business is a complete nonsense. Newspaper speculation, I'm afraid. On the back of a so-called journalistic source. We are totally sure that the person named could not have been responsible for the good sister's murder.'

'Oh. How disappointing. Well, I should like to have been kept informed all the same,' said Lord Jeremy, almost sulkily.

'Well, that is one of the reasons for my visit today, my lord. A bit late in the day, I will admit, but we had to get to the bottom of it first,' said Cooper somewhat disingenuously. He continued, 'But putting that aside, my lord, we wanted to ask you some more questions about Sister Margaret. Did she ever speak to you about her family or any of her friends at all?'

'No, no,' he said ponderously. 'She always insisted that the church and the Carmelite Order were her family.' He went silent for a few seconds and he appeared to be concentrating his thoughts. 'Now! How silly of me! Something has just occurred to me. I do know that she visited Father O'Leary at St Saviour's in the village on a couple of occasions and it was he who brought her to Beaumont Hall in the first place. Oh, please forgive me, I've only just realised. My memory seems to be getting worse. Don't get old, Inspector; your brain starts to freeze over.' He shook his head in despair.

Cooper did not share the fact that enquiries with Father O'Leary had already been carried out, although he imagined that, Beaumont being a small and close community, it would probably have already reached his lordship's ears.

'What about her painting? Did she ever sell or exhibit any of her work in this area?' asked Pratt.

'No, not to my knowledge. Though she was quite prolific, and I know she took a lot of pleasure from her painting. In fact, she was something of a perfectionist and I'm sure she would not have dreamed of selling a piece of her work unless it was absolutely to her liking. She seemed to destroy as much as she created, you know. Typical woman. Never satisfied, you see. The only example of her work that remains, apart from the landscape she was working on, is the painting still hanging in her room. She framed and hung it herself. Seems she was quite satisfied with that one,' explained Jeremy.

'Do you think that we could see it, my lord?'

'Yes, of course. I will have Jenkins get the key to her room and escort you. I'm not too good on the old pins these days I'm afraid, so I will leave it to him if you don't mind.' Jeremy poured himself another glass of Pimm's.

They followed Jenkins to the kitchen, where he took a key from the desk drawer in the office. He then led them up two flights of stairs, and, as they reached Sister Margaret's room, he produced the key from his pocket and unlocked the door. The room looked much as they had left it with the additional signs of fingerprint powder that had been tactically smeared on various surfaces.

The painting was hanging above the bed, which had, by then, been stripped of linen and consisted of just the frame and mattress. Cooper pulled the bedstead away from wall and stepped around it. He stood and admired the painting for a few seconds then removed it from the wall and placed it on the dressing table.

The painting depicted an image of Jesus Christ rising from the midst of a dense pine forest. To Cooper's untrained eye it appeared to be a very skilful piece of work. Even for one as thick skinned as himself, he realised that there was some spiritual meaning to it and he wondered about the inspiration behind it. Had she really painted it herself or had she just acquired it from somewhere?

He turned to Jenkins and said, 'Do you know anything about the provenance of this painting, Mr Jenkins?'

'Yes, Inspector. It's all her own work. She painted it during her time here at the Hall. I actually remember complimenting her when I saw her working on it in the summerhouse.'

'Did she make any comment to you or say anything about the meaning behind it at all?'

'Nothing that I recall, beyond her just saying a polite thank you.'

To his knowledge, there were no pine forests in the area and so Cooper came to the obvious conclusion that the picture had been painted from her memory or her imagination. He turned the picture over to examine the reverse side of the frame. On running his fingers over the rear of the canvas he detected a raised area in both bottom corners.

'Have you got a pen knife on you, Brian?'

'You are not going to damage the painting, are you, Inspector?' said Jenkins plaintively.

'No, Mr Jenkins. I assure you I won't cause any damage unless it's absolutely necessary.'

Cooper took the knife offered to him and he unfolded one of the blades. He then used it to make an incision around the inside of the relevant corner of the frame and removed the backing sheet, which released a wallet-sized bundle of papers.

'Hello. What have we got here, Brian?'

Cooper, with Pratt at his shoulder, examined the articles, which consisted of a passport and a ticket. He examined the front of the passport, which was light blue in colour and bore the words "Vatican State" in gold leaf. On opening it, he saw the face of Sister Margaret staring back at him. It occurred to him that she had been a very attractive young woman and that she could probably have got a lot more out of life. *He chided himself for being so shallow minded.*

The name and the other details were very interesting. She had held the name of Sr Margaret of the Sacred Heart of Jesus. It showed that she had been born in Graz, Austria, on 23rd March 1919. Furthermore, that the passport was issued as a diplomatic passport (under the Vatican Citizenship Code of 1929) on the 8th May 1949. There were only three immigration stamps on the inside pages. The first evidenced the holder's entry to the Netherlands on 16th May 1949 and her departure from Hook van Holland on 17th May 1949. The final stamp evidenced her entry to the UK at the port of Harwich on 18th May 1949.

On examining the ticket, Cooper found that it related to a one-way sailing from Hook van Holland for the night of 17th May 1949 aboard the *MV Koeningin Wilhelmina* for arrival at the port of Harwich the next morning. There were no payment details shown on the ticket.

Cooper returned to the rear of the canvas and ran his fingers carefully within the backing sheet. He produced a small bundle of bank notes. On examining them, he saw that they were denominated in Austrian schillings, deutschmarks and Dutch guilders. 'We shall have to take the painting as well as the passport, cash and ticket, Mr Jenkins,' stated

Cooper, 'Clearly, they are likely to be of evidential value. But, of course, we'll give you a receipt for all of the items.'

In company with Jenkins, the two detectives returned to the garden to share their revelation with his lordship. Since they had only seen the victim following her demise, they showed him the passport photograph for his identification. He had seen her in life and had spent a lot of time with the woman.

'Yes, that is our dear Sister Margaret,' He said sadly, almost breaking down in tears.

'Did she ever show this passport to you, my lord?' asked Pratt who held it open to prevent his lordship from touching it.

'No. I haven't seen it at all, before now.'

Jenkins agreed that he had never laid eyes on the documents either.

'My lord, we just need to take a few lines from Mr Jenkins and yourself in relation to this discovery, and then we will leave you in peace.'

They each set to work taking a witness statement from his lordship and Jenkins to prove the provenance of the painting, and, in Jenkins' case, to also confirm the discovery of the documents. Pratt issued a receipt.

In the presence of Jenkins and Lord Jeremy the officers were at pains to maintain an air of quiet dignity and professionalism. However, after taking their leave and on their way back to the police station, they could not wipe the grin from their faces. They were elated.

'This takes us a lot further forward, Brian. Now we can wave this under the noses of the Catholic Church; that should get a response!'

At last they had some positive news for the troops and it would raise morale no end.

16

DAY SIXTEEN

Wednesday 27th July 1949

'Stockwell speaking.'

'Good morning, sir. DI Cooper here. I thought I would call you and just bring you up to date on some good news to do with our murder enquiry.'

'Sounds encouraging, Albert. Go ahead.'

Cooper related the details of the visit to Beaumont Hall and described the items found in the picture frame.

'What kind of passport was it?'

'It was a diplomatic passport issued by officials at the Vatican. I must confess, I didn't even know that the Vatican State issued diplomatic passports.'

'What name was on the passport?'

'It gives her name as Sister Margaret of the Sacred Heart of Jesus. It shows that she was born in Graz, Austria, on the 23rd March 1919. The passport itself was issued on 8th May 1949.'

'It sounds like it was issued specially for this particular journey,' observed Stockwell.

'Yes, it does, sir. I think this represents our first bit of luck.'

'Indeed, Albert, but I wonder why Scenes of Crime didn't find it when they searched her room the first time.'

Oh, for Christ's sake, Thought Cooper, *why don't you just try to be positive for once?*

'To be fair, sir. It was well hidden, and these things do sometimes get missed.

'Well, I suppose so. But one wonders why, if everything was above board, she would need to hide her passport?'

'Yes. A good point. Why indeed, sir.'

'We need to get to the bottom of this woman.'

Yes, of course we do. That's bloody obvious.

'I'm going to get Miss Collins to make some enquiries with Immigration at Harwich. That might reveal something more about her status.'

'Good. I would imagine that it's not every day that a Vatican State passport is produced at Harwich Passport Control let alone a diplomatic one, so they should remember her. If Immigration get a bit precious, let me know and I'll get Special Branch on to it.'

'How much does the foreign currency come to?'

'Well, sir, there were one hundred and fifty deutschmarks, sixty schillings and twenty-five guilders. All in notes.'

'Probably comes to about 150 to 200 pounds. A not insignificant sum. Please make sure it goes into the admin safe, will you?'

Cooper shook his head in despair.

'Will do, sir.'

'Oh, and Albert...'

'Sir?'

'Well done.'

In the absence of Cooper, Brian Pratt briefed the team about the finding of the passport and ferry ticket, and he highlighted the relevant dates of travel through the Netherlands to Harwich.

'Job for you Linda, I think,' said Ian Mills. 'We need you to go Parkeston Quay to see what Immigration have on her arrival in this country.'

'See me afterwards, Linda, and I'll give you the details,' said Pratt.

'Is it right that you recovered some foreign currency at the same time, Sarge?' asked Jane.

'Yes, one hundred and fifty deutschmarks, sixty Austrian schillings and twenty-five Dutch guilders. All in notes. They were also in the back frame of the painting.'

'Seems to indicate that she spent some time in Austria and Germany. Otherwise why have marks and schillings at all?' said Linda.

'Unless she was going on to those countries after she finished her work at Beaumont Hall,' suggested Mills.

'Possible, I suppose,' said Pratt.

'Who had the job to speak to the taxi firms?' asked Mills.

'I've got it now, Sarge,' said Rogers.

'Any joy there?'

'Not yet. I'm about half way through them. Do you want me to visit the Harwich taxi companies as well now?' said Rogers displaying uncharacteristic initiative.

'Please do,' said Mills. 'Right, what else was there? Enquiries to be made in respect of the two anonymous calls and the information regarding James Davidson. Who had those jobs?'

Linda Collins put her hand in the air. 'I had both the James Davidson job and the one for Raymond Jenkins, Sergeant.'

'Let's take Davidson first.'

'Yes. Well, I went to see Master Davidson at the Hall and I asked him about the allegation that he was caught out of bounds in private quarters by Sister Margaret. He was quite straightforward and said that it did happen, but that it was not long after she had arrived at the Hall herself. He did genuinely think that there was an intruder and he is adamant about it.'

'Fine. So, you are happy with him, then?'

'If you're asking whether I think that he could have committed the murder, I would say not.'

'Even if he was creeping around, out of bounds, it doesn't make him a murderer,' added Jane Stewart.

'Also, a major point is that, although he was the one who found her, he had no blood on him. Whoever killed her would have been heavily blood stained. He would have had no chance of changing his shirt; also, he was under the watchful eyes of Mrs Aldis and Jenkins during the relevant time.'

'That's a fair point, Linda. I think that we can rule him out,' said Pratt.

'And what about Raymond Jenkins?'

'That was pretty straightforward. Yes, he does sometimes stay over at Bedford Square when her ladyship needs him for an engagement the day after he has delivered her there. His lordship doesn't need the Rolls much himself these days. As for the nun, he said that she was pleasant enough as far as he was concerned, but she was rude to the junior members of staff. As for being besotted with her, he said that that was complete nonsense.'

'Thank you, Linda. Do we have anything on the missing crucifix?' asked Pratt.

'Nothing on that, Brian,' said Ian Mills, 'Bob Scott and his team did a thorough search over a quarter mile radius of the scene. Nothing was found at all. But you'll remember that Scenes of Crime did find a couple of loose links under the body that seem to indicate that the crucifix was wrenched from her neck.'

'OK. Unless there is anything else folks, we'll leave it there for now. Thank you.'

The officers filed out of the room to get on with the day's business.

'What the bloody hell am I going to do now, Glad?' said Mavis, tears streaming down her face. She was nursing a glass of ginger wine, which her sister had provided for her, and they were both on their third cigarette. They were sitting in the front room of Gladys Munson's terraced house, in Chapel Street, which was located only a stone's throw from the town centre.

'I've only a few pounds in the bank and I've got to pay the rent somehow.'

'Well, if you find that you can't pay the rent, you can always move in with us for a while. I'm sure Colin wouldn't mind too much,' said Gladys, tongue in cheek, knowing that her husband Colin couldn't stand Mavis at any price.

She felt, privately, that this was the least she could do for her sister having coaxed her continually to provide titbits of information from her job at the police station. By any objective assessment, Gladys had used her sister for her own ends. Now, having pushed her too far, it had come back to haunt them, and Gladys felt terrible about it.

It was now obvious to her that the police, having had their suspicions, had set Mavis up by feeding false information in her direction and that Mavis had taken the bait. Consequently, Mavis was now suspended from her job, and would be lucky not to face prosecution on charges of corruption. Apart from Gladys though, Mavis only had herself to blame.

Compounding her own humiliation was the fact that Gladys had been embarrassed in front of her peers during the so-called "police press conference", when her "exclusive" report for the *East Anglian Recorder* had been torn to shreds. Following this excoriating experience, her editor, Tony Swayze, who had held her in such high regard, had given her a very serious dressing down on her return to the office. Only two things had saved her from the sack. Firstly, Tony Swayze and Gladys Munson were lovers, and they had been so for a couple of years. As Swayze did not relish the possibility of his wife finding out about their relationship, he didn't dare dismiss Gladys and he needed to contain the threat. Secondly, Swayze, had been aware of the information from the outset and he should have ensured that some enquiries were undertaken to verify it before publication. To that extent, he would also be culpable in the eyes of his directors should they learn of his lack of due diligence.

Swayze knew the identity of the source, and had, on several occasions, been on the end of Gladys's entreaties about Mavis and her unrivalled access to command decisions. He had to accept the fact that familiarity and his own poor judgement had allowed this situation to develop. He was going to have to, somehow, find redemption or draw a veil over the matter.

So how would they redeem the situation? After Swayze's attack on Gladys's professionalism and the resultant tears, they kissed and made up. He was on a very sticky wicket indeed and felt that the only course open to them was to make a concerted effort to get to the bottom of the nun's murder by sound investigative journalism based on verifiable information.

He resolved that the next time they went to print on this subject, the product would be explosive and beyond scrutiny.

17

DAY SEVENTEEN
Thursday 28th July 1949

'But why don't you just get a taxi, my love? It would be far easier than having Jenkins go all the way to London just to drive you to a social function, wouldn't it?'

'Yes, darling, but the function is in Richmond. It's too far out for a taxi. It would cost a bloody fortune,' said Fanny.

'Well, if it's so far out, why agree to attend the blessed thing simply because someone invited you? You don't have to go to every function that you are invited to, surely?'

'But, Jeremy, darling, I did promise Felicity that I would attend, and I really don't want to let her down. Not only that, I shall be coming home tomorrow, and you know what the trains are like these days: they are a bloody disaster. This way Jenkins can drive me to the function and then home tomorrow. It does make sense, darling.'

'Well, let me ask Jenkins if he is able to fit this all in. He does have a life of his own, you know, and he has plenty to do here.'

His lordship put his hand over the mouthpiece of the telephone.

'Jenkins, her ladyship wonders whether it would be possible for you to go to London today to drive her to a function in Richmond this evening. It would entail you staying overnight in Bedford Square and bringing her back to Beaumont tomorrow. Would this cause you a problem?'

'No problem at all, my lord. I am sure that Adina would be able to make herself available to assist you while I'm away.'

'Thank you, Jenkins.' His lordship returned to the telephone. 'OK, so be it then, darling. What time will you need Jenkins to be there?'

'About 5.00pm.'

'Fine, 5.00pm. That's settled then. Have an enjoyable time this evening. I will look forward to seeing you tomorrow when you come home. Perhaps, if you'd like, we can have dinner together. I will speak to the cook and get her to prepare something nice. Bye then, darling.' Lord Jeremy replaced the receiver.

'Now, Jenkins, it's a lovely day. While I still have you here, you may take me for a spin around the garden.' He released the brake on his wheelchair.

'My lord, if I may crave your indulgence. Before we go into the garden, may I first just go and tell my wife the arrangements for later?'

'Yes. How thoughtless of me, of course you must.'

Jenkins left the room to go back to his quarters. He knew that Adina was not going to be happy and by now she surely must be starting to suspect that his regular jaunts with Lady Fanny were indicative of a closer relationship. He had always managed to compartmentalise his life and keep his affairs discreetly separate; however, he was enjoying the thrill of it all and he no longer saw much of a future for himself with Adina. This was making him reckless.

Executive Officer Justin Wood of HM Immigration Service was sitting in his office at Parkeston Quay, Harwich. He had just put the telephone down after being informed that he had a lady visitor at the front desk. Wood examined himself carefully in the mirror and he made a few minor adjustments before leaving the room to walk the short distance to the front of the building.

There were a few people in the foyer, and, on seeing him come through the office door, the receptionist pointed out his young lady visitor, who was sitting on one of the benches. Wood strode across to her, and, by holding his head high and straightening his back, he tried to maximise his height of five feet five inches. He was a good-looking man, by conventional standards, but, unfortunately, he was vertically challenged. He made up for his lack of height in other ways. At least, that was what his mum had always told him.

On seeing Justin Wood approaching, Linda Collins got to her feet and immediately exceeded his stature by a good four inches. She extended a hand, 'Mr Wood?'

'Yes, PC Collins, I believe.'

The introductions having been made, Wood showed her through the connecting door and after arriving at his corner of the office, he offered her a seat. 'Can I get you some tea or perhaps a coffee, PC Collins?' asked Wood, anxious to make a good impression.

'Yes, tea please, two sugars. And, please, call me Linda.'

Wood was happy to do so. She was rather lovely.

'I'm Justin.'

Yes, I imagine you probably are, thought Collins.

Wood made a quick visit to the next room to order the drinks, and then he returned and sat behind his desk.

'Tell me, how may I help you, Linda?'

'We're investigating the murder of a nun that was committed a couple of weeks ago in Beaumont. That's just this side of Colchester. I don't know if you know the place?'

'Yes, I do. I live in Thorpe, actually, which is quite close by.'

Collins continued, 'Yes, right, well, you'll know where we are then. Essential to the success of the investigation is our knowledge of the nun's background and how she came to be in this country. We have reason to believe that she was sent here from Rome and we're seeking any information that might give us confirmation of the purpose of her visit. We know that she entered this country through Harwich Port.

'I see, Linda. I'll be happy to help if I can. Can you just let me have her name and some details?'

'Yes. We believe that her given name was Irma Caro, but in the Catholic Church she was known as Sister Margaret of the Sacred Heart of Jesus. She was born in Graz, Austria, on 23rd March 1919.'

'Have you got her passport?'

'Yes, we have, but it's locked away for forensic examination. I can tell you the details though.' Linda consulted her notebook.

'She had a Vatican State diplomatic passport.'

'Did she really?' said Wood, expelling a whistle of surprise, 'We don't see those every day.'

'It was stamped on entry to Harwich on the 18th May this year.'

'Which vessel did she come in on? Do you know?'

'The *MV Koeningin Wilhelmina* from the Hook of Holland.'

'That should give me enough, thank you, Linda. If you sit tight for a short while, I'll see if I can find her landing card in the archive.'

Wood was inspired. He was always nervous around beautiful women and he was anxious to do his best to impress this one. He left the room with such élan that he almost collided with the admin assistant who was on her way in with the teas.

He re-emerged after about ten minutes and declared triumphantly, 'I'm pleased to say that the system works. I found her card. It looks like the control officer was my old colleague, Bill Latham. The details are as you said. She was given three months limited leave to remain in the UK.'

'When does Mr Latham come back on duty?' asked Collins. 'Only I need to ask him what he remembers of the woman.'

'He won't be. Well, at least not here anyway. He works at our Tilbury office now, so you would have to speak to him there. However, there's one additional piece of information that I can give you.'

'Really?' said Collins, intrigued.

'She wasn't alone.'

'Who was she with?'

'One Monsignor Tarquin Crecy. I have his landing card here. It says that he's based at an address in Westminster, London.'

'Can I see the cards please?'

Wood passed the cards to Collins. On examining them she saw that they were indeed both dealt with by the same officer, and although Sister Margaret was travelling on a Vatican State diplomatic passport, Monsignor Crecy was on a more modest Irish passport. The dichotomy of their ranks and passports was a fact picked up by Linda straight away.

'How do we actually know that they were together?'

'Luckily, the cards for each movement are stored together in the archive. They were certainly both on the *Wilhelmina* and both cards were signed by Bill Latham, so we can assume that they were also in the same channel of passport control as they entered the country.'

'Justin, I know that I'm splitting hairs here, but we can't really be one hundred percent sure that they were together, without speaking to your colleague Mr Latham.'

'No, I suppose that must be right,' agreed Wood, feeling chastened and reduced in her estimations.

'Justin, do you think you could let me have the telephone number for your Tilbury office so that I can contact him?'

Wood reached into his bottom drawer and withdrew the internal directory. After thumbing through it for a few seconds he wrote down the main telephone number for the Immigration Service in Tilbury on a scrap of paper. He handed this to Collins.

'He'll probably remember them. You don't get many clergy and certainly not many nuns coming through the port.'

'I don't suppose you do.'

'One other thing that I could do for you, if it helps, is to speak to the shipping line, and find out where the passage was booked and how it was paid for.'

'That would be good. Thank you.'

'It may take a day or so, but if you give me your number, I could phone you with the result,' said Wood enthusiastically and with a sweet smile. *Good. I'm on the front foot again,* he thought to himself. Esteem restored.

'That would be very helpful. Thank you,' said Collins. Her complexion turning red. *Is this man flirting?* she asked herself. *I'm never very sure about these things.*

She then quickly channelled her thoughts and made a start on taking a witness statement from Wood. It would explain the system for the control of arrivals and formally producing the landing cards as exhibits. She was thankful for the fact that Wood could lay his hands on the cards. It did seem that they employed an old-fashioned system to store passenger records, but it was certainly effective, all the same.

After finishing with Justin Wood, Linda took the train from Parkeston Quay for the half-hour journey back to Colchester North. As the locomotive made its progress, she looked out of the window of the carriage, and, through the steam billowing out from the engine, she could see the beautiful sight of the Stour Estuary with its sailing boats and wildlife. She was saddened by the thought of Irma Caro making the same journey and seeing the English countryside for the first time. It occurred to her that, although in the company of Monsignor Crecy, she would probably have felt quite isolated and alone. Now the Catholic Church were denying her very existence. The idea of it made Linda angry.

❖

On arriving back at the police station, she could not wait to seek out Cooper to pass on the information she had managed to glean. She went straight to his office. As usual, Cooper's door was open. She knocked, and he looked up from his paperwork with a smile.

'Have you got a minute, sir?' she said shyly.

'Yes. Come in, Linda. Close the door and take a seat. How are you getting on?'

She was bursting at the seams, 'Fine thanks. I've just been making enquiries with the Immigration Service at Harwich and they have Sister Margaret's landing card covering her arrival on 18 May. It basically confirms what we already know.'

'Good, good.'

'But they also have a landing card for Monsignor Crecy, who got off the same boat at the same time. I just need to confirm with the officer who checked their passports to see whether he can recall them, and whether they arrived separately or whether they were together.'

'Brilliant! That's good, Linda, well done.' Cooper was so chuffed, he wanted to hug her, but he stopped just short. He was having trouble maintaining his dignity before his young colleague, but he was delighted for her and he knew that it would help raise her self-esteem as an investigator. 'Do the landing cards say what types of passport were produced by them on entry?'

'Yes. She had a Vatican State diplomatic passport, as we know, but his was a standard Irish Republic passport. A bit strange that. If anything, I would have thought it would be the other way around.'

'Yes, I agree, Linda. I think it's beginning to look like Monsignor Tarquin Crecy was more than just a consultant and that he was acting on behalf of Cardinal O'Mara to ensure that Sister Margaret was able to get into the UK. Hence, her being supplied with a diplomatic passport, which virtually guarantees entry.'

'Sorry, sir, but who is Cardinal O'Mara?' asked Linda, not quite up to speed.

'He was the man who was named in Father O'Leary's statement as the person who sent Sister Margaret to England to convert Lord Roding,' explained Cooper, patiently.

Straight away she remembered the significance of O'Mara, felt silly and the florid complexion returned to her cheeks. Cooper didn't mind. He had a lot of time for this girl.

'Yes, of course, governor. Sorry, I remember now. And, of course, Monsignor Crecy died recently, didn't he?'

'Yes, Linda, he did. You know, it could all be quite innocent, of course, but, given the fact that we are investigating her murder, we need to know more about why she was here and not only that…' Cooper hesitated, 'It would do us no harm at all to find out more about Crecy's death.'

'Do you think that it was suspicious, then?'

'Not necessarily, but we simply don't know the circumstances surrounding his death, and, given that he was the catalyst for our victim's arrival at Beaumont Hall, it would be logical to consider the possibility of the two deaths being connected in some way.'

'Do you suspect that the same person or persons killed them both?' asked Linda.

'No, it's just that I'd like to know what Monsignor Crecy did for the Church by way of a job. Was he just a senior priest or something more than that? The difference in passports looks very suspicious. Very suspicious, indeed. The problem is, and this might sound strange, who do we contact in the Catholic Church that we know we can trust?'

'Stockwell speaking.'

'Superintendent Stockwell?'

'Yes, speaking.'

'Good morning, sir, my name is Trevor Lloyd-Davis, I am a Detective Chief Inspector working in Special Branch at Scotland Yard. It has been brought to our attention that you are investigating a murder involving a Catholic nun. Is that correct?'

'Yes. That is the case, Chief Inspector, and it's no secret. It's been covered by the national press consistently enough over the last couple of weeks.'

'Quite so, sir. Our department has been monitoring it in the papers. The thing is, we have an interest in your case, but I can't speak to you about it over the telephone, so I'd like to come and see you when it's convenient, sir.'

'Yes, of course. The officer in charge of the case is Detective Inspector Albert Cooper. A good man. When would you like to come?'

'How about this afternoon sir, say, 2.00pm?'

'Yes. Fine, as far as I'm concerned. I suppose I'd better check with DI Cooper to make sure that he's available. I'll have him call you later, Mr Lloyd-Davis,' said Stockwell.

They exchanged details and then ended the call. Stockwell immediately telephoned Lloyd-Davis's commander at Scotland Yard to confirm his bona fides.

That afternoon saw DCI Lloyd-Davis and his sergeant, Frank Nattress, sitting in the reception area of Colchester Town Hall. They were eventually shown into Superintendent Stockwell's office by his temporary secretary, Lucy Bonney, an attractive redhead who had been moved across from the staff office at Headquarters. Cooper was already in attendance.

The introductions were made, and tea was served.

Stockwell began, 'Well, gentlemen. Sorry to have kept you waiting, I was rather tied up on another matter. How may we help you?'

'Well, sir, as you know, the *raison d'être* of Special Branch remains the protection of the realm and particularly our ongoing problem with the so-called Irish Republican Army [IRA],' said Lloyd-Davis.

'Yes, I appreciate that,' said Stockwell impatiently. He was apparently having one of his "off days".

'We have, over a period of some years, been conducting an intelligence operation against certain individuals who, as we understand it, have been involved in the movement of people wanted by the authorities in Ireland. Central to the operation are certain members of the Catholic Church. One of our suspects was the late Monsignor Crecy, who I believe features in your case.'

'So, you know that he died recently then, sir?' said Cooper.

'Yes. We were made aware of that.'

'Forgive me for asking such a direct question, but how did you find that out?'

'We have our confidential sources of course,' replied Lloyd-Davis somewhat patronisingly.

'Is your source anything to do with our investigation?'

'No. They are quite separate, I can assure you of that.'

'So, what precisely does your operation have to do with us?' asked Stockwell, wishing that Lloyd-Davis would cut to the chase.

'We have reason to believe that Monsignor Tarquin Crecy was doing the bidding of others more senior within the Catholic Church.'

'In what way was he involved?' asked Cooper.

'Let's just say that he was facilitating the movement of people from jeopardy to positions of safety.'

'When you put it like that, it sounds quite the Christian thing to do,' said Stockwell.

'Well, if that is what he was doing, he is out of the game now,' said Cooper.

'Yes, that's true,' said Lloyd-Davis with a wry smile.

'So how and where did Monsignor Crecy die exactly?'

'Apparently, he died of a heart attack, although I am told that his death was initially treated as suspicious and it attracted the attention of the local CID. He was staying at the Royal Horseguards Hotel in Westminster,' said Lloyd-Davis.

'I see. Very nice too. Returning to my original question, though, Mr Lloyd-Davis, how may we help you?' said Stockwell.

'Sir, I think that the death of Monsignor Crecy and him featuring in your investigation are factors that present us with an opportunity. It gives us a chance to broaden our knowledge by using your case as a cover to make direct enquiries with those who worked with him. Not ourselves you understand, but, sir, with your permission, hopefully your officers acting on our behalf. If the name Special Branch were mentioned, I am sure that the Church authorities would withdraw any cooperation.'

'What sort of information would you need my officers to collect for you?' said Stockwell.

'We could learn a lot from general information. For instance, we need to know where he laid his head and where he kept his belongings. It might seem naïve, but did he keep a diary? And, maybe as pertinent to your investigation as it is to ours, what stamps has he got in his passport? Who was he visiting and associating with at home and abroad? We know that he travelled extensively.'

'Well, for a start,' said Cooper, 'We know that he came into Harwich from Holland on 18th May and we believe that he was travelling with our victim, Sister Margaret. That bit of information came from our enquiries with HM Immigration in recent days.'

'That is exactly the sort of information I am talking about, Mr Cooper.'

'Clearly your idea has some merit,' said Stockwell, pompously, 'It is good, sound thinking, and I am sure that we could be of considerable assistance. But, who would we approach within the Church to get access to the Monsignor's worldly goods?'

'I would suggest that you make your approach to somebody at a junior level. An approach to the office of the archbishop at this stage would most likely create a political situation that could get out of hand. That's why we can't make the approach ourselves,' said Lloyd-Davis.

'I thought that Special Branch would have a contact in most institutions,' said Stockwell.

'Yes, sir. We probably do in most institutions. But I must say that the Catholic Church is something else entirely.'

'That's true enough,' said Cooper. 'They're not good at returning phone calls, for a start. We've been trying to get in contact with them for a couple of weeks now.'

'We'll just have to persevere,' said Stockwell, who continued, 'Being a murder enquiry, where a nun is the victim, there is no doubt that our investigation could be used as a cover to gather the information that you require, particularly as Monsignor Crecy was responsible for her coming to the UK in the first place.'

'So, what would be your way in?' asked Lloyd-Davis.

'I'd suggest that the coroner's officer dealing with Monsignor Crecy's death should have a named point of contact with both the Church and the police. That would be our way in,' said Cooper. 'Best speak to the local CID who dealt with the case first.'

'Yes, that does sound logical and we could have done that ourselves, but we need to stay one step removed.' said Lloyd-Davis.

'So, would you have any idea which mortuary covers the area where Crecy died, sir?'

'Probably St Pancras,' he replied and turned to his sergeant, 'Frank, any idea?'

'Yes, St Pancras, it is, sir.'

'Sergeant Nattress was on CID at Cannon Row before he came to us, sir.'

'Does the name Cardinal Pat O'Mara mean anything to you?' asked Cooper.

'No, that doesn't ring any bells.'

Cooper explained the role that Cardinal O'Mara and the Vatican Special Assignments Unit had in relation to Sister Margaret's passage to the UK. Also, the fact that she was there to assist Lord Roding in his conversion to Catholicism.

'Vatican Special Assignments Unit – it sounds rather like the Spanish Inquisition,' commented Lloyd-Davis.

Cooper reminded himself that that was exactly what he had made of it, in an earlier conversation.

The two sides agreed to liaise closely during the conduct of the investigation. Lloyd-Davis and his colleague then left to return to London.

18

DAY EIGHTEEN

Friday 29th July 1949

Cooper was sitting alone in his office and, unusually, he had his door closed. He was looking out of the window marvelling at the picturesque view across the rear yard to the bus station. Doris had been and gone, and he was carefully sipping from a hot mug of tea.

It had been a busy week, and he was allowing himself time to sit and get his thoughts and priorities into some sort of order for that day's team briefing, which was due to commence shortly. Cooper was looking forward to the weekend, particularly Sunday. He was thinking of suggesting to Linda that they might go sailing together. *But would she be interested?* he wondered, *Sod it! What's the worst that can happen? She could say no, I suppose.*

Cooper was starting to feel that they might be getting somewhere with the murder.

Special Branch having a wider interest might just provide the key to understanding the reasons behind the death of the victim. But their involvement created something of a dilemma. It was not that Cooper didn't trust his team, of course he did, but they simply did not need to know of the Special Branch connection and heaven forbid that it should ever reach the ears of the press.

Cooper decided that he would carry out this aspect of the enquiry with Brian Pratt, so he called him into the office and gave him a brief outline of what Lloyd-Davis had said during his visit. 'Thing is, Brian, we need to keep the involvement of Special Branch between ourselves and Mr Stockwell. Any actions that flow from what they tell us must be written up carefully and kept separately in my safe. As you know, information coming into an investigation needs to have an audit trail. So, we'll have to convince the team that any enquiries they are instructed to make into Monsignor Crecy are a logical progression of some other action, otherwise they'll question their validity and they'll sense that there's some other agenda.'

'Understood, governor. Now, how would you like some more good news?'

'Go on then, Brian. Spoil me.'

'I spoke to the people at St Pancras mortuary, who put me on to the officer dealing with Crecy's case. I've just been on the blower to Detective Superintendent Wiseman in Westminster and I took the liberty of making an appointment for us to see him at Cannon Row nick at 2.00pm.'

'OK, and what's the good news?'

'Crecy's belongings are still under lock and key in the property store at the police station. They haven't yet got around to handing them over to the Church authorities. Not only that but they have his passport.'

At this, Cooper almost leapt out of his chair.

'Brilliant, Brian!'

'Thought you'd be pleased governor.'

'Pleased! I'm fucking delirious!'

Just before 11.15am, Cooper gathered up his papers and made his way into the main CID office, where the team were all seated at their desks. They all appeared very alert and they had expectant looks on their faces.

'Good morning, boys and girls. Smoke if you want to,' said Cooper. Ian Mills and Tom Rogers lit up.

'Day eighteen of our enquiry and our victim is getting more enigmatic, the more we dig into her, no joke intended.'

Everyone laughed regardless.

'We now know that on 18th May of this year she entered the UK at Harwich, having got off the night boat from the Hook of Holland. But something even more interesting is that we now know that on the same boat was Monsignor Tarquin Crecy, the man, who you will recall, was the person with whom Lord Roding arranged the victim's attachment to Beaumont Hall. I don't think it unreasonable for us to assume that they travelled together.'

'Do you think they shared a cabin governor?' said Rogers.

'Dirty little sod,' said Janet. The team laughed.

'No, Janet. For once, and probably quite by accident, Young Tom here may have stumbled on something relevant,' said Cooper. 'We do need to know whether they took a cabin, either separately or together. Will you arrange for an enquiry to be made with the shipping company, please, Ian?'

'Yes, governor.'

Linda Collins put her hand up.

'Yes, Linda. Your man at Harwich Immigration. I believe he was going to speak to the shipping company for you, wasn't he?'

'Yes. He was, governor.'

'Fine,' said Cooper, 'Tom, you and Linda need to get your heads together after the meeting. Our friend ought to be able to find out about their cabin arrangements for you.'

'Yes, governor.'

'Anyway, to continue, we've still had no direct contact with the Church authorities, but, according to Lord Roding, they denied all knowledge of Sister Margaret when he called them to speak to Monsignor Crecy. We'll have to pay them a visit. We need to go above Father O'Leary. I take it that Father Thomas has still not been in contact, Brian?'

'No, he hasn't, governor.'

'Do we know how Monsignor Crecy died, governor?' asked Collins.

'Well, I'll be going up to London with Sergeant Pratt to speak to the Metropolitan Police about Monsignor Crecy later today. I expect we'll find out more specific detail then. What we do know, though, is that he was found dead in a hotel with a head injury. It was later put down to "death by natural causes".'

'Presumably they would have had dealings with somebody from the Church, wouldn't they, governor?' asked Mills.

'Yes, I'm sure they would have. We'll let you know how we get on.'

'Have we got a date for the inquest yet, governor?'

'No, Ian, but I'm sure it'll be coming up soon. In the meantime, we must establish a point of contact with the Church authorities. The buggers still haven't answered Mr Stockwell's letter, and the coroner will certainly expect us to have made contact, since, to all intents and purposes, they were her family.'

'Linda, have you managed to speak to Mr Latham at Tilbury Immigration yet?'

'Not yet, governor. Apparently, he's back on duty this afternoon.'

'Good. Tom, what about the taxi firms?'

'I've been in touch with all of them, governor, and they're going to speak to their drivers. I'll give them a few days and contact them again, if that's all right?'

'That makes sense. I'm sure it'll take a few days. Keep up the pressure though, Tom. If you make a bit of a nuisance of yourself, word will get around that much quicker, and we all know how good you are at that.'

'Thanks, governor. I'll take that as a compliment.' Tom laughed, and the others joined him.

Cooper then addressed his remarks to Brendan Withers of Scenes of Crime who had managed to get away from his desk at Headquarters. 'Brendan, have you been able to identify any of the fingerprints lifted from the victim's room?'

'We're gradually working our way through them, governor. We fingerprinted the body after the post mortem, and, as one might expect, there were plenty of the victim's marks present in the room. We also found one left by Raymond Jenkins. That was on a corner of the mirror on the dressing table. You'll want to ask him about it, I'm sure. But, as you know, he's the key holder for all of the rooms and has legitimate access anyway.'

'Is that a full mark or a partial?' asked Cooper.

'A full mark.'

'Thanks, Brendan.'

'Right, folks, any other business?'

The replies being in the negative, the meeting was closed. As the officers filed out of the room Cooper called back Linda Collins. After satisfying himself they were alone he asked her a question, 'Linda, did you do any sailing when you were in the Wrens?'

'As a matter of fact, I did, governor. Especially when I was in Malta.'

'Well, my parents live on Mersea Island and they're away this weekend. I shall be looking after the place and they have a dinghy. I wondered whether you'd like to come sailing with me on Sunday?'

'I'd love to, but won't we be working?'

'I'm hoping that, unless something momentous happens, the team will have the day off.'

She shifted her poise from one stockinged leg to the other and, drawing loose strands of hair behind one ear, she replied, 'Yes. That would be lovely. Thank you, governor.'

'I'll let you know the details later.'

'I'll look forward to it.'

As she glided out of room, she was fighting to contain her excitement and expectation. *God. I want this man. What took him so long?*

'Immigration. Mr Latham speaking.'

'Good afternoon, Mr Latham. My name is Linda Collins, I'm a constable with the Essex Constabulary at Colchester. I was given your name and number by Justin Wood at Parkeston Quay Immigration.'

'Yes, Miss Collins. Justin rang me earlier and explained to me what you were enquiring about. How may I be of assistance?'

'Did Justin tell you that we are investigating a murder at a stately home in our area, then?'

'He did. Murder of a nun, wasn't it?'

'Yes. The victim was called Sister Margaret. She came into the country from the Hook of Holland during May. According to the landing card, you spoke to her at passport control.'

'Yes, indeed. I've been racking my brains, such as they are. I remember Monsignor Crecy. In fact, he's a regular traveller. I do recall him coming in at Parkeston with a nun a couple of months ago.'

'Do you remember what kind of passport she produced?'

'I do indeed. A Vatican State diplomatic passport. They are as rare as hen's teeth.'

'Can you describe her?'

'Yes. She was wearing a habit, obviously. She was very pretty, for a nun. Something you don't expect. About twenty-eight to thirty years of age. Five feet six or so. Quite slim, although you can't really tell a woman's shape properly under a garment like that.'

'I know that I told you the name of our victim, but, allowing for the possibility that she was a different person from the one you spoke to on passport control, would you have remembered her name?'

'No. It was the type of passport that really stuck in my mind.'

'Did she speak at all?'

'Not much. I don't think she spoke English. As I recall Monsignor Crecy mostly spoke for her. I can't remember exactly what he said, but it was enough to satisfy me to allow her entry.'

'And Monsignor Crecy, what do you remember about him?'

'Well, he was in his cassock. He's a frequent traveller. He always says hello. A nice man. In fact, last Christmas he very kindly presented us with a bottle of Irish whiskey. That's all I can say about him really, other than I know that he has something to do with Westminster Cathedral.'

Unfortunately, he's now dead, thought Linda. *But I think I'd best keep that myself.* She thanked Latham and rang off.

After a torturous journey to London by British Railways that had involved two cancellations, Cooper and Pratt were sitting in the foyer of Cannon Row Police Station, waiting to see Superintendent Wiseman. If the scramble to get to Westminster on time was not enough to wind Cooper up, the ensuing twenty-minute wait made him decidedly pissed off. He had to have a serious word with himself to prevent him from airing his discontent. Finally, a side door was opened, and a young detective stood in the entrance, who asked 'Mr Cooper?'

Cooper responded 'Yes, and this is my sergeant, Brian Pratt.' They showed the officer their credentials.

'I'm DC Eric Cattermole, sir. Sorry to keep you waiting, but Mr Wiseman was unexpectedly called in to see the commander.'

Cooper nodded and said nothing in response.

'If you'll just follow me, please, I'll take you upstairs to Mr Wiseman's office.'

They were taken up two flights of stairs and along a corridor, which had windows facing out onto Whitehall.

Eventually, they found the door of the superintendent's office. Cattermole knocked.

'Come in,' said a disembodied voice.

They were shown into the room where they saw a giant of a man loom up from the other side of a desk, which was located almost immediately behind the door.

'DI Cooper and Sergeant Pratt from Essex, sir,' said the young constable.

'Good afternoon, Mr Cooper, Sergeant Pratt; Nigel Wiseman, I am, for my sins, head of CID for Westminster. We spoke on the phone earlier, I believe, Sergeant.'

'Yes, we did, sir.'

'Thank you, Eric. Please take a seat, gents.'

The three of them were left alone in what was a particularly pokey little office, in dire need of a lick of fresh paint. Wiseman noticed that Cooper was examining his surroundings. 'Please forgive the accommodation, gentlemen, but, at present, we're being reorganised. Or so I'm told. I'll probably end up with an even smaller office.' He laughed somewhat philosophically. 'Still. It'll have to do for now. Anyway, how may I help you?'

'Sir, you'll recall we were speaking on the telephone about Monsignor Tarquin Crecy who was found dead in the Royal Horseguards Hotel.'

'Yes, Sergeant. As I said on the phone, we thought that we had a murder to begin with. Bit disappointing, really. Murders are quite rare in the Westminster Division nowadays. I always find that it's good for morale if we can get most of the team working on one case. Focussing on one job seems to do away with their moaning about trivial issues. Anyway, I digress. Monsignor Crecy was found lying on the floor with a head wound, by a cleaner. Not much blood, which surprised us at the time. But it was explained when the post mortem revealed that he had suffered a massive heart attack. He then collapsed, hitting his head on the wash basin as he fell to the floor. We treated it with a full Scenes of Crime examination, fingerprints, photographs and the like.'

'How long was he at this hotel for?' asked Cooper.

'Well, it was a bit of a home from home for him, really. Apparently, he travelled quite a lot on behalf of the Church. Locally, they have a bit of a problem because their accommodation was bombed out a few years ago, and they haven't replaced the building yet. So, their headquarters staff, if I may call them that, are all dispersed around the area. Some are in digs, some in other parishes and, of course, the very top people have their own houses. To answer your question, I think on this visit, he'd only been there for a few days.'

'Was anyone else staying in the room with him?'

Wiseman laughed, 'No. He was a good priest. He was quite alone.'

'As I told you yesterday, we're dealing with the murder of a nun who was known to Monsignor Crecy, and we'd be very interested to know who you liaised with from the Church on your job?'

'Well, ironically, as Crecy was the assistant to the nuncio, it would ordinarily have been he, himself, in cases such as this. Or at least that's what we've been given to understand.'

Wiseman opened the box file sitting on the desk in front of him and he rifled through various documents. 'Ah, yes. I remember now. It was Father Michael Thomas. He's based at Westminster Cathedral and worked closely with Monsignor

Crecy. I believe he was nominated to deal with us by the archbishop of Westminster.'

'What was he like to deal with? Helpful, was he?'

'I only met him the once. Nice chap, though. He seemed to take it all in his stride. He came to the police station on the one occasion I met him. I gave him the findings of the post mortem. We've been meaning to give him back Monsignor Crecy's effects and I believe we did make one appointment to do so, but, for some unknown reason, it was cancelled by one of their staff. We haven't heard anything from him or the Church since. DC Cattermole has Crecy's belongings in the office. I'll take you down there, when we finish here.'

'Do you know what kind of role Monsignor Crecy performed for the Catholic Church sir, as the assistant to the nuncio?'

'Well, he certainly moved around quite a bit. I know that. Apparently, he'd just come back from Ireland. I suppose you might call him a liaison officer, or even some kind of public-relations man.'

'Did he have an office at the cathedral?'

'Yes, he did. I believe he shared it with Father Thomas.'

'Did you visit them at the cathedral at all, sir?'

'No, we dealt with Father Thomas here on just that one occasion and he identified the body at the mortuary. Given the choice, I wouldn't go there myself, anyway.'

'Why is that then, sir?' asked Cooper, intrigued.

'Well, our family name is Weismann changed to Wiseman. And as a good *Yiddisher mensch* I wouldn't want to, if I didn't need to. Know what I mean? And, to be perfectly frank, I can't stand churches and places of worship of any kind. I don't even attend my own synagogue these days. Not since the war, anyway. Like a lot of people, I've rather lost faith in the whole shebang.'

'I see. Obviously, we must go there ourselves, sir, and I'd be obliged if you would give me the telephone number you have for Father Thomas, please? We've been trying to get in contact with him for a few days now, but we've had no success at all.'

'Certainly, Albert. We had the same difficulty with them ourselves. They appear to operate on an extended timeframe, to put it kindly.'

Wiseman opened the file, found the number, wrote it down on a piece of paper and handed it across the table to Cooper.

'Do you think we could see Monsignor Crecy's personal effects now, sir?'

'Yes, of course. I'll take you down to see young Cattermole. He's got the boxes ready in his office.'

Wiseman led them along the corridor to another room, which was not much larger than his own. It contained enough desks for six occupants. As they entered the room Wiseman was, once again, apologising for the state of the place.

'As you can see, gentlemen. The lads are even worse off than me. There are six desks in here for ten detectives. They have to indulge in what they like to call "hot desking"!'

Cooper looked around the room and compared it to their own accommodation, he realised that he and the Colchester team had been truly blessed.

'Yes. Welcome to our humble abode, gentlemen,' said Cattermole.

There were two cardboard boxes on the table in front of him. Both of which lay open. There was a large box that contained items of civilian clothing and vestments. A smaller box contained personal items such as a pipe and tobacco pouch, papers, and sundry books, including a 1949 diary and an Irish passport.

'Would you be happy for us to take some time to go through these, sir? Only, it would save us from having to take away items that have no real relevance to our case.'

'Yes, feel free. Shortly I must go to a meeting at Scotland Yard, so you're more than welcome to use my office in my absence. If you feel that there's anything of value for your investigation and you need to take anything away with you, please speak to DC Cattermole here and he'll let you have the items against signature.'

'Very much obliged to you, sir,' said Cooper. They all shook hands and Wiseman left the room. Ten minutes later, Cooper and Pratt were examining the contents of the boxes in Wiseman's office.

They started on the clothing and made a list of the garments. Each was searched thoroughly in case something had been missed or left. There was nothing found in the pockets, and the garments were of no interest.

'Now for the documents,' said Pratt.

They examined the passport, which was stamped as having been issued in Dublin. The face of a handsome man in his early fifties stared back at them from the page. The details were listed as "Tarquin DeVere Crecy, Born: 5th January 1895 in Co. Wicklow, Occupation: Clergyman".

Cooper thumbed through the pages of the passport. It contained date stamps galore, each providing evidence of visits to various countries in Europe, including the Vatican State. He examined the stamps on the last page and, although there was some smudging, he could make out entry and exit stamps for the Netherlands. They were identical to those they had seen in the passport that had belonged to the victim. Same dates and the same border points. This provided them with conclusive evidence that they had travelled together.

The next stamp, going back in time, was an entry stamp to Wien Flughafen (Vienna Airport) dated 14th May 1949. An adjacent stamp showed that the passport holder had left Rome on the same day.

'Bloody hell, governor. He certainly got around, didn't he? I wonder what he was in Vienna for. He seemed to have an exciting life.'

'I would hope that, in due course, the Church might be able to tell us, if it becomes relevant. It wouldn't be a bad idea for us to get someone to draw up a schedule of his travel movements using the diary and the passports as the source documents. Certainly, Special Branch would find it useful,' said Cooper.

'I'll get onto it when we get back, governor,' volunteered Pratt.

'Brian, as we need to take them with us we ought to prepare a receipt for DC Cattermole. Will you go and see him, explain what we intend to take and borrow a typewriter?' said Cooper.

'Yes, governor, will do.'

'And while you're doing that I'm going to phone DCI Lloyd-Davis at Special Branch. I think we should go and see him, and tell him what we have found, before we get the train back to Colchester. I think he's going to be chuffed.'

Pratt opened his briefcase. He pulled out a folder containing stationery and, ever efficient, he produced a blank receipt bearing the Essex Constabulary heading. He then went along the corridor to see Cattermole.

Within half an hour, they were sitting in the Special Branch office at Scotland Yard sharing the product of that day's enquiries.

'Blimey. You have done well, Albert,' said Lloyd-Davis in a slightly patronising tone.

'I'd prefer it if you didn't call me Albert, please, Trevor. Only my mum calls me that, and normally only when I've been a naughty boy.'

'And, so does Mr Stockwell, it seems,'

'Yes. That's right. I'll have to have a word with him about that,' said Cooper laughing.

As they spoke, the diary of Crecy, and the passports of both Crecy and Sister Margaret were being examined by Special Branch officers, and all details were recorded. Copies were also taken of both passports, using some modern technology that had recently been made available to their department.

'Good result though, Alby?' said Lloyd-Davis, drawing on his pipe.

Cooper nodded his consent for use of the soubriquet.

'From our point of view, there are some very interesting stamps in his passport and they go back quite a while. It must have been almost ready for renewal.'

'Yes. Your man certainly seemed to have got around "representing the Church", didn't he? It was more of a Hollywood lifestyle. But, from our point of view, we're wondering what Crecy was up to in Vienna on the 14th May? And taking it a stage further on, both Crecy and the sister have date stamps showing entry to the Netherlands on the 16th May. That was at a place called Venlo, which is, in fact, on the border with Germany.'

'If Crecy landed in Vienna two days before that, where did they meet? Vienna? Maybe they met somewhere else in Austria or even in Germany? But why were there no stamps for her before Venlo?' said Lloyd-Davis.

'After what you told us about the activities of Monsignor Crecy, Trevor, I'm beginning to suspect that our Sister Margaret may have been smuggled across at least one border. But why on earth should that be?'

'Why, indeed. It's certainly consistent with our intelligence about him. I'm hoping our intelligence people will learn something from their contacts in Vienna to help put the whole thing into perspective.'

'Trevor, have you done a Special Branch check on the name Irma Caro, at all?'

'Yes, we have, but she's not on our records. However, we're sending a message to the security department at the British Embassy in Vienna requesting they make enquiries into Crecy and Irma Caro. They have contacts locally, and we've had some excellent results from them in the past. We'll mark the message as urgent, so I expect we'll get an answer back soon. We'll let you know as soon as we've had a reply from them.'

After recovering the documents from the Special Branch officers, Cooper and Pratt made their way along the Thames embankment, stopping at a café next to Embankment tube station. They treated themselves to tea and a sandwich, and sat in the window, people watching. Pratt lit up a cigarette, he gasped with pleasure and inadvertently blew smoke all over his boss.

'Bloody hell, Brian, I do wish you would give up that filthy habit,' spluttered Cooper.

'Sorry, governor, but it's one of my few pleasures in life. It helps me concentrate.'

'Well, what are you concentrating on now, exactly?'

'That's not the point. It provides me with an all-embracing sense of calm and wellbeing, so that, when I do have something to concentrate on, I'm on the ball.'

'Bollocks,' said Cooper.

'Well, I don't drink like you do, governor.'

'Cheeky bugger. You drink plenty when you're in the mood. Anyway, at least beer has some food value, whereas, with fags, you're just burning money. Might as well just set light to a ten-bob note.'

Cooper continued studying the passers-by. There were office workers hurrying back and forth. Most of the men were "suited and booted", and many of the younger women were looking very alluring, some of whom wearing what was apparently now in vogue. He suddenly thought of young Linda Collins and how she might fare working in this type of environment. She had a fine figure and would certainly be able to carry off the styles.

Cooper flirted with the idea that working in the City of London might be quite a pleasant existence compared to chasing villains around the provinces, but he quickly dismissed the notion. He knew that boredom would soon get the better of him. He enjoyed the day-to-day uncertainty of being an operational detective, and seriously doubted whether, even if he were to reach a higher rank, he would find it at all fulfilling. He would be like most office workers in London: desk bound.

After a short break, they walked down to the Underground and caught a Circle-line train to Liverpool Street. They were both feeling pleased with themselves after a very fruitful day, and, given the fact they had a half hour to wait for the next train, Cooper decided to treat his colleague to a pint in Dirty Dicks. Strangely, Pratt didn't argue.

19

DAY NINETEEN
Saturday 30th July 1949

'Telephone call for you, governor,' shouted Brian Pratt.

'Who is it?'

'Lucy, Mr Stockwell's secretary.'

Cooper walked back to his office and took the receiver from Pratt. 'Cooper speaking.'

'Hello Mr Cooper, I have Mr Stockwell for you.'

'Hello Albert. I tried to get hold of you yesterday afternoon, but you were out of the office. I just wanted to let you know that I received word from the chief's office authorising an article in collaboration with the *Tatler*. So, I've dictated a letter to inform them of the fact.'

'Thank you, sir. That was quick.'

'I want you to deliver it in person, Albert.' said Stockwell, 'In that way, we can ensure that it hits the intended target.'

'Will do, sir. I'll send one of the lads up to collect it.'

'We don't want any unnecessary delay with *Tatler*, but I expect that, unlike the Church, it's in their own interests to cooperate with us.'

'Yes, of course, sir. I know they're very keen.'

'I'm mindful of the fact that the coroner will want to interview a representative of the Church or at least know that the Church have sent one to the inquest. Time is rather running out for them in terms of getting back to us. When is the inquest exactly?'

'Next Monday, sir. The 1st August.'

'Well then, there's no time to lose.'

'No, on the contrary, sir, if I might say so. There's no urgency really, as far as the inquest is concerned. All that will happen on the first date is that the case will be opened and then it'll be adjourned automatically until much later. Hopefully, before the next hearing, we'll have caught our murderer. But we do need a reply from the Church to give us her background.'

'OK, keep me posted.'

'Thank you, sir,' said Cooper.

Linda Collins was sent to the town hall to collect the letter. On her return, she took it to Cooper, who read it for himself:

'Addressed to "The Editor, Tatler, 35-37 Winton Street, London W1.

"Dear Sir or Madam, I write further to our recent conversation with your Mr Quentin Smallpiece regarding the murder of the late Sister Margaret of the Sacred Heart of Jesus. I have sought and obtained permission from the chief constable to liaise with *Tatler* regarding an exclusive article (or series of articles) on the investigation of said murder.

"Subject to a contract being prepared by the Essex County Council Legal Department, the force is prepared to release information to *Tatler* concerning said murder investigation. The editing and timing of publication will be solely at the discretion of the chief constable of the Essex Constabulary. Our legal department will be in contact with you in the coming weeks.

"Yours faithfully,

"Thomas Stockwell, Superintendent.'"

Cooper left Linda in his office to read the letter for herself and walked through to the sergeants' office, where he found Brian Pratt.

'Brian, I've just received the letter from Mr Stockwell about our collaboration with *Tatler*. I would like it to be delivered to them by hand.'

'Not by me, governor, I'm afraid.'

'Why not?'

'I arranged to have this afternoon off to take the wife to her see her sister in the maternity hospital, if you remember?'

'Yes, of course. OK, I'll do it and take young Miss Collins with me then.'

Within the hour, Cooper was, once again, on his way to London by train.

The day held the potential to be a very interesting one indeed, covering the higher echelons of the social scale, with, on the one hand, a sobering visit to Westminster Cathedral and, on the other, a visit to the bastion of gossip and frivolity; that was, the high society magazine, *Tatler*. Linda Collins had taken the prudent step of telephoning to ensure that Quentin Smallpiece and his colleague would be in the office on a Saturday. Furthermore, Cooper had miraculously reached Father Michael Thomas by telephone. They were due to see him at Westminster Cathedral at 2.00pm.

Cooper told himself that, by taking Linda Collins with him, it would give her useful experience. It also had the added benefit of his being able to observe her in a more testing environment. There was something about this young woman that attracted him, not only on a personal basis but as an investigator. Female detectives, even in 1949, were somewhat rare, and, from what he had seen so far of the confident way that she conducted herself, he could see potential for her making a valuable contribution. He was eager to indulge her and to help her develop her talent. Besides, the very thought of her brightened his day.

They caught the London train early and it was only midday when they arrived at Liverpool Street Station. As time was on their side, Cooper elected to visit the canteen at Bishopsgate Police Station, which was just across the road from the railway station.

Throughout the inward journey and during the meal, their conversation was chiefly about the case and the job in general, but, these topics having run their course, the conversation turned to matters more personal.

'Have you told your aunt that we have met each other yet?' asked Linda.

'Yes, Brenda.'

'I'm not going to hear the last of this "Brenda", am I?' she declared.

'Well, actually, it's a name that quite suits you,' he teased, 'I'll have to have a word with Sadie about getting her details right though.'

'What? You mean, for the next girl she chooses for you?' she said.

'No, Linda. I don't want her interfering in that way anymore.'

Linda was horrified, 'Please don't do that, governor. I don't want to embarrass her and I'm sure she meant well.'

Cooper decided to change the subject. 'So, are you a Colchester girl as well, then?'

'Yes. Dad was in the military and the family originally came from Aldershot. He was posted to Colchester quite a few years ago, and it's where I was born.'

'How long ago was that?'

'Probably not as long ago as when you were born,' said Linda, giggling.

'Of course, forgive me. You shouldn't ask a lady how old she is.'

'No. That's quite right.'

'So how much do you weigh, then?'

Linda collapsed in fits of laughter. 'Cheeky.'

'So, what do you want out of this job?'

'I want to get on the CID permanently.'

'Really? Well, you won't get very far taking the piss out of the DI like that, will you, young lady?'

'Sorry, governor. I stand rebuked,' said Linda Collins laughing.

'So why not get married and have children? Does that not appeal to you?'

'Blimey, governor. That was a bit sudden. I hardly know you. I'll have to think about it.' She laughed so heartily that Cooper could see her breasts struggling against her blouse. Embarrassed? He certainly was.

'Sorry, I didn't mean it to come out like that.'

'That's OK, governor. Don't mind me. It's just my wicked sense of humour. To answer your question, I might eventually, I suppose, if I meet the right man. I just want an interesting life, really. I know that it was forced by circumstances but being in the Wrens really wet my appetite for adventure.'

'So, you enjoyed it in the navy, then?'

'I loved it. It was work hard, play hard. That sort of thing.'

'Do you still work hard and play hard?'

'With respect, governor. You should know the answer to the first part of that question, shouldn't you?'

'Yes, I do. You do.' He stumbled over his words. *Cooper, get a grip*, he thought. *You are starting to sound like a right soppy date.* He had never been confident with attractive women. He had been badly hurt in the past and, although he was attracted to this woman, he was wary. Where could it all end?

'So, what do you do to unwind when you're not at work?' asked Linda.

'Go to the pub. Read a bit. I used to play football regularly, but I'm getting a wee bit old for that now.'

'Oh dear, governor, that sounds a bit tragic.'

'Yes, I suppose it does, when you say it like that, doesn't it?' he laughed, nervously.

'No other ladies in your life, then?' she said, teasing him.

'Only my mum, Sadie and my landlady, Pearl.'

'Oh dear, that's a shame. You have a relationship with this Pearl, do you?'

'No, nothing like that,' said Cooper with a grimace. 'I just threw her name in for good measure.'

'Do you think there could be enough room for one more then?'

'You know you don't have to ask that.' He smiled, shook his head and looked away.

'Sorry, governor. I know I'm a bit forward. I don't believe in wasting time. The war and the navy made me like that, I'm afraid.'

'Listen. You can drop the "governor" bit, when we're out on our own, so long as you don't keep teasing and tormenting me all the time. I'm very sensitive,' he said, feigning shyness.

After lunch, they made their way by tube to Westminster and, as they emerged from the steps of the Underground, they found themselves facing the "Mother of all Parliaments". It was a sunny day outside and they felt the warmth hit them as they reached ground level. They turned right and crossed Whitehall. Time was still on their side, so they strolled across Parliament Square and on up Victoria Street.

Cooper felt like holding hands with the young beauty who was walking beside him. It almost seemed like they were together, on a holiday. He had to slap himself down and make a conscious effort to remain professional and concentrate on the job.

As he walked in silent contentment, Cooper reflected on the fact that, like most people, a holiday was something he hadn't had for many a long year. The war had seen to that. Although he'd been abroad at the time, the years of captivity didn't really count as leisure. It got very boring, being in the same place, with the same "happy campers" and the same food, day in, day out.

After ten minutes or so, they arrived at the front steps of Westminster Cathedral and as they were unable to locate an obvious "business entrance", they ascended the few steps at the front of the building. They entered the main doors, walked through the vestibule and were met with a vision of pure majesty.

As they stood looking up at the ceiling they were casually approached by a young priest who nodded to them and said, 'Beautiful isn't it?'

'Magnificent,' said Linda.

'Can I be of any assistance, sir, madam?' There was a trace of an accent Cooper was unable to place.

Cooper made the introductions, 'Yes. Thank you, Father. We're police officers from Essex. We have an appointment with Father Michael Thomas.'

'I see. If you would care to take a seat for a moment, I will go and see if I can find him for you.'

The priest walked away along the nave, to the rear of the building, and turned left disappearing behind the choir screen. After about five minutes, a tall, slim priest in his early thirties, taking the same path as his colleague, walked back towards them.

'Inspector Cooper?'

'Yes, Father,' replied Cooper. He gesticulated towards Collins and continued, 'And this is my colleague Detective Constable Linda Collins.'

She subconsciously grew in stature as the sudden promotion registered with her.

Cooper reached into the inside pocket of his jacket and retrieved his wallet, which contained his warrant card. He offered it for the priest's inspection.

'Father, we are from the Essex Constabulary. I spoke to you earlier on the telephone. We're investigating the brutal murder of a nun in our area. We believe she had something to do with your late colleague Monsignor Crecy.'

'Yes. Was this on the estate of Lord Roding?'

'Yes, it was, Father.'

'Only I spoke to him on the telephone a couple of weeks ago, when he contacted our office. Was this Sister Margaret?'

'Yes, it was.'

'And she was said to be from the Carmelite Order. Yes, it's a great shame Monsignor Crecy is no longer with us. He passed away recently. But I'm sure he would have been able to tell us all about her. Unfortunately, even though I made extensive enquiries at the time of Lord Roding's contact, we simply know nothing of her. I had to leave it like that, I'm afraid.'

'Did your secretary pass you the letter that one of my sergeants delivered here a couple of weeks ago, which was intended for Archbishop Mahoney?'

'Yes, Inspector. I delivered it to his office myself and gave it to his secretary. He was abroad at the time and has only recently returned. I dare say he'll reply shortly.'

'I understand you shared an office with Monsignor Crecy. What was his job, exactly?'

'He was a type of liaison man, I suppose you could say. Before he was sadly taken from us, Monsignor Crecy's role was to maintain contact on behalf of the archbishop of Westminster, that is, Archbishop Mahoney, with the Church in other countries and the Holy See.'

'The Vatican?'

'In essence. Yes, the Vatican.'

'Do you know of a Cardinal Patrick O'Mara?'

'I've heard of him. He's in the Vatican, I believe. Tarquin Crecy has spoken of him in the past. I understand he carries out papal projects.'

'What sort of projects are they, then?' asked Collins.

'I am really not privy to that kind of information, I'm afraid, miss,' said Father Thomas.

'We were informed by HM Immigration at Harwich that Sister Margaret entered this country in May, from Holland, in company with Monsignor Crecy. Do you know anything about that?'

'No, I don't. He was often gallivanting around Europe, but he didn't confide in me at all, I'm afraid.'

'We have been given to understand that the purpose of her visit was to assist Lord Roding with his conversion to Catholicism. Is that something that happens a lot?' asked Cooper.

'You mean to say that she came from abroad just to do that?' asked Father Thomas, with a tone of incredulity.

'Yes, Father, and that is according to Lord Roding himself, apparently; it was the sole reason she was here. She even had a Vatican State diplomatic passport.'

'Something is definitely wrong there, I must say. You might think the Catholic Church has money to burn, but, believe you me, Inspector, we're always being told to tighten our belts and try to curb our costs. They wouldn't send somebody all the way from Rome for a task like that, I can assure you.'

'What is the normal procedure for this sort of thing then?' asked Collins.

'The normal procedure is that the local parish priest would take that kind of pastoral role and not a nun brought all the way from Rome. The very idea is ridiculous.'

'Well, Father Thomas, the formal letter from our chief officer that I referred to is addressed to the archbishop. It sets out our position and that of the coroner. We'll need the Church to take on responsibility and act for Sister Margaret. Do you think you would be able to speak to the archbishop and try to speed up his response?'

'Yes, I can certainly try. I can assure you of that, Inspector.'

'As you have said yourself, the whole idea of her being seconded in this way is somewhat irregular. Would you be able to assist us by making the necessary enquiries with the Vatican to ascertain whether they know anything about her?'

'I could certainly take care of that for you. It may take a little time though.'

Cooper showed Father Thomas the victim's passport, so he could take down the details.

'Do you think you could find out whether this passport is genuine?'

'Yes, I can, of course. I assure you these enquiries will be carried out as quickly as possible, Inspector, and I will speak to the archbishop. We can't have our people murdered like this and be seen to be sitting on our hands. True, the Church is a vast organisation, which is spread out over many countries, and the lines of communication are long, but we can move swiftly when we want to. I'll be in touch.'

Cooper and Collins were both comforted by Father Thomas's attitude and response. They bid the priest farewell, took their leave and walked out onto Victoria Street, where they tried to hail a cab.

'What do you think of all that then, Linda?'

'He certainly means business. By the way, thank you for the promotion. It was very sudden and unexpected,' she said, with a beaming smile.

'My pleasure DC Collins. I was only expressing a personal wish, and, of course, I'll have to speak to the head of CID to get his sanction on it. So, don't tell anybody else about it, as it's nowhere near official yet,' he said with a grin.

Linda Collins felt encouraged. In more ways than one.

After standing at the side of the street for a full five minutes or so, Cooper finally managed to flag down an empty cab and they sped off to their next appointment.

On arrival at the offices of *Tatler*, they were provided with a welcome cup of tea in the reception area, where, after a short wait, they were joined by Quentin Smallpiece.

'Hello Inspector. Nice to see you again. I see your new assistant is far more attractive than the last one,' observed Smallpiece, who nodded towards Collins.

'Thank you, Quentin. Meet my colleague DC Linda Collins who is on the murder team with me at Colchester.'

'Yes. Miss Collins, we spoke on the phone, didn't we?'

'We did indeed.'

Smallpiece shook hands with them both.

'I have a letter here from Mr Stockwell, in which he sets out the terms regarding our cooperation on an "article".'

'Splendid,' said Smallpiece. He took the letter from Cooper and briefly gave it the once over before putting it back in the envelope and sliding it into his pocket.

'Thanks for that. I'll read it in more detail later and pass it on to our legal department for their attention. Is there anything we may help you with in the meantime?'

'Yes, we have an interest in a Monsignor Tarquin Crecy who was connected to our victim, Sister Margaret. We wondered whether you might have anything in the archive on him, at all.'

'How are you spelling that?'

Cooper provided him with the details.

'I can certainly have a look for you. It'll take a day or two, as the archive is located out in Pinner. I would want to go out there myself rather than entrust this type of task to somebody else. So, if you'll leave it with me, I'll let you know as soon as I can.'

'We are much obliged, Quentin.'

There was nothing else to discuss at this juncture, so Cooper and Collins, having declined the offer of more tea, left *Tatler* for the tube station, citing their wish to beat the rush hour.

They made their way back to Liverpool Street Station and found that they were in luck. There was only a wait of ten minutes for the Colchester train, and an hour later they were walking out of the front door of Colchester North Station. It was now 6.00pm, and Cooper felt they had done enough for one day.

Cooper found a telephone box nearby and he put a duty call into the CID office to ascertain whether anything was happening. Jane Stewart answered the telephone. Apparently, all was quiet and there were no messages for either of them. Cooper had Jane mark both him and Collins off in the duty book. Now their time was their own.

'Right, we're off duty,' said Cooper as he exited the telephone kiosk, 'You can go home now, if you want to, Linda.'

'I will. But what about I buy you a drink first?'

'Fine, DC Collins. Good idea,' said Cooper. A little taken aback.

'You can call me by my Christian name now, then. Can't you, Albert?'

'Yes. I think that I could manage that, Brenda.'

Linda feigned a punch to Cooper's arm.

'Do I really look like a Brenda?'

Cooper just nodded, smiled and didn't answer.

They walked across the road to the Norfolk Arms where they entered the snug and spent a couple of hours in fun and self-indulgence over a few drinks. They found they were happy and relaxed in each other's company, and they confided details of family, their wartime experiences and hopes for the future. On leaving the pub, Cooper escorted Linda to her home, which was only a fifteen-minute walk away. As they strolled arm in arm through the quiet streets, Cooper came to a decision. He knew he was besotted with Linda, but, for now, their relationship would have to be hidden from their colleagues, and be one of slow and careful progression. Both their careers would be blighted if, God forbid, their personal relationship was ever allowed to interfere with their work.

It was late afternoon and Lord Jeremy was lying in his bed reading. Also in the room was his nurse, the ever-devoted and flexible Adina Jenkins. She was sitting by the window, looking out across the gardens. It had been a mild day with a few clouds breaking up the sunshine. They had the window open and all that could be heard was the rustle of the leaves as the air moved through the trees. All was calm and peaceful.

They were quite alone as Raymond Jenkins had once again been called up to London to convey her ladyship to yet another society function. Jeremy was always grateful to Jenkins for his willingness to adapt his schedule at short notice. He reflected that Jenkins really was a very patient and obliging man, and that he was fortunate to have secured his services.

Jeremy put his book down and laid it on the eiderdown. He watched Adina for a while as she moved around the room. She was a very attractive woman, with classic Mediterranean looks. She had a nice figure, a particularly alluring bottom and shoulder-length, black hair that was flecked with grey. Jeremy hoped, that in the years to come, she would not run to fat, like many mature women from that part of the world. But for now, she was perfect.

One thing that had struck him about her was that she had very deep brown eyes, which were very expressive. She was the type of woman who found it almost impossible to hide her thoughts and feelings. It was all in her face. There was no doubt in his mind that she had a kind heart. The way that she cared for him was testament to that. But, now, he could see that she was deep in thought, troubled even.

'Is everything all right, Adina?'

'I'm OK, my lord. I'm just thinking about my family in Romania. I miss them a bit, you know, especially my mother.

'Who do you have there?'

'We had a big family at one time, but not many now. The Germans, they kill some of them. The Russians kill others. I still have my mother. She is Hungarian. Also, I have a younger sister, Natalia, and two cousins.'

'Where do they live exactly?'

'In a little village near Bucharest.'

'Why don't you go and visit them?'

'I have spoken to Raymond about going to see them, but he says we have to save money.'

'I could pay for you to have a visit, you know.'

'That is nice of you, my lord. But when do we have time? Raymond is in London a lot these days and I have my work here.'

'I'll speak to him,' said Jeremy.

'Anyway, it is time for your medicine.'

Adina walked into the bathroom, opened the cabinet and took a large brown bottle from inside. She rinsed a teaspoon in the basin and proceeded to load it from the bottle. She then re-entered the bedroom slowly, with an open palm beneath the spoon, taking care not to spill the contents on the carpet.

'Open wide your mouth, my lord.'

Jeremy swallowed the contents of the spoon, after which she again rinsed it in the basin. She re-emerged from the bathroom drying her hands on a towel.

'I am just going to the kitchen to see Mrs Aldis about your dinner. What would you like to have, my lord?'

'She served up a nice steak and kidney pudding last night. I really fancy some more of that, if there's any left, with gravy, roast potatoes and peas,' said Jeremy, almost salivating.

'Good. You're hungry. That is a good thing.'

Adina left the room and walked off along the landing.

Jeremy felt among the covers for his Bible, and in doing so, he heard a thud as it fell off the bed and hit the floor.

'Damn and blast!' said Jeremy to himself.

He didn't want to wait for Adina's return and he couldn't be bothered to get out of bed to retrieve it. Thinking that, with a minimum of effort, he could lean out of the bed and reach his book, he slumped heavily down the side between the bed and the dressing table but found he couldn't quite get there. Then suddenly, it happened. He became dizzy and couldn't focus his eyes. There was a ringing in his ears and, down one side of his body, he felt quite numb. Jeremy became distressed and began to panic. He tried to call out for help, but he just could not articulate his words. He could only groan and make the noise of alarm.

My God, he thought to himself. *Is this how it's going to end?*

It was.

Jeremy, 7th Lord of Roding, lost consciousness. And it was never to be regained.

When Adina walked back into the room she immediately saw that Jeremy had his head and shoulders awkwardly bent out of the bed. She rushed around to the far side and managed to pull his upper body back to an upright position. She tried hard to revive his lordship, but he did not respond to her efforts. Adina rushed downstairs to the kitchen to tell Mrs Aldis, who ran immediately to the study to telephone for an ambulance and then the doctor. Both arrived in quick time, but there was nothing that they could do to help the situation. The master had gone.

✦

At 9.50pm, later that evening, PC Richard Bentlow of the Metropolitan Police was waiting at the front door of Roding House in Bedford Square. He had been sent to deliver what, in police parlance, was often referred to as, an "agony message".

The door was opened by Maisie, the house maid.

'Can I speak to Lady Roding, please?'

'No, I'm sorry constable. I'm afraid she's gone out for the evening.'

'Is there anybody else at home from the family?'

'No. There's only me and a couple of other members of staff.'

'Can you tell me where she is?'

'She's at the Windmill Theatre, where they're holding a reunion do.'

'Is that the one in the West End?'

'Yes, it is.'

'Is she alone?'

'No, not as such. Mr Jenkins, her chauffeur, has taken her. He'll be close by, I expect.'

'Well, miss, we need to speak to her quite urgently. We'll try to find her at the Windmill Theatre. If she should come back in the next couple of hours and she hasn't spoken to the police, will you please get her to telephone Whitehall 1212 and ask for Inspector McCoist, who, after 10.00pm, will be the night-duty officer in charge at Tottenham Court Road.'

The constable wrote down the details on a piece of paper and he handed it to her.

'Can't you let me know what this is all about?'

'I'm not at liberty to do that, miss; we'll have to wait for her ladyship to come home, I'm afraid. If we don't hear from her, we'll send someone back to try again in the morning.'

Maisie was somewhat bemused. She made her way to the kitchen to inform Mrs Barber, the housekeeper.

20

DAY TWENTY
Sunday 31st July 1949

At 2.20am, in the early hours of Sunday morning, a very tipsy Lady Fanny Roding arrived back at the house in Bedford Square. She was assisted through the front door by Raymond Jenkins, who had effectively been shepherding her all evening. He was exhausted. They were met in the hallway by Maisie.

'My lady, we had the police here last evening. They told me they have an urgent message for you. Did they find you at the Windmill Theatre?'

'No, they didn't, Maisie. Do you know what it's all about?'

'They wouldn't tell me, my lady. But they left me this note for you.'

She handed the note to Lady Fanny who immediately thrust it into the hands of Jenkins.

'Oh Raymond. I really can't be doing with this tonight. Call them for me, will you? It's probably just the burglar alarm gone off at the gallery again.'

Lady Fanny went upstairs to her bedroom.

Jenkins took the note into the study so that he could use the telephone. He first rang the number for Scotland Yard and the operator put him through. After waiting for a few minutes, he finally managed to get through to the duty inspector at Tottenham Court Road Police Station. He introduced himself as the butler to Lord and Lady Roding. 'I understand that you have an urgent message for her ladyship,'

'Yes, Mr Jenkins. We did send an officer to the Windmill Theatre last evening, to try to find her but she wasn't there.'

'No,' said Jenkins. 'She went there for a couple of hours, then on to somewhere else. So, what is the message please, Inspector?'

'I really ought to give it to her personally, Mr Jenkins,' said the officer.

'She is indisposed at present. I am Lord Roding's butler after all. Perhaps you can tell me, and I can assure you that I will deal with it expeditiously.'

'Fair enough. Well, I must tell you, sadly, that your master, Lord Roding, passed away yesterday afternoon. The Essex Constabulary sent a message to us to have her ladyship informed.'

'I understand, Inspector. That is sad, but not unexpected. His lordship wasn't a well man. Can you tell me where he was when he died?'

'He was in his bed, I believe.'

'Let's hope he didn't suffer any pain. Do you know where his lordship's body has been taken to?'

'I believe that he's been taken to the mortuary at the Essex County Hospital in Colchester. The Colchester Police attended the house. A Sergeant Myall dealt with the matter.'

'Thank you, Inspector. I will inform her ladyship.'

Jenkins put the telephone down. He considered the situation for a few minutes. Life would certainly change for himself and Adina. They would most likely be out of a job. He was sad for his master, of course he was, but he also wondered what kind of fist Fanny would make of the future. He shook himself from his reverie and he dialled the number for Beaumont Hall. It was answered by Adina.

'At last. Raymond, where the hell have you been?' Adina sounded very unhappy.

'I've only just heard the news. Her ladyship wanted to go all over the bloody place. We didn't get back until gone midnight. I still haven't told her about his lordship's death yet. What is happening at the Hall now?'

'Nothing, it is all quiet here now,' said Adina, 'and they have taken his body in the ambulance to the hospital. I was with him just before he died. I think he had a heart attack or something. I was only out of the room for a few minutes. I went down to see Beryl in the kitchen about his dinner and when I got back he was dead.'

'I'll have to break it to Lady Fanny now, but she's a bit drunk.'

'Good luck. I'm going to bed. Will you be back here in the morning, Raymond?'

'Yes. I will see you then my love.' Jenkins put the phone down.

He went to the kitchen and made himself a cup of tea. After fifteen minutes or so, he went up to Fanny's bedroom and knocked on the door. There was no response. After several further attempts to rouse her, he tried the handle. Luckily, the door was unlocked, so he crept in. The bedside lights were still on and Jenkins saw that Fanny was still in her evening dress, curled up on the bed. She was sound asleep and snoring loudly.

He now had something of a dilemma: to wake her or not to wake her. She was inebriated, and she was in no fit state to receive the news he was duty bound to deliver. Truth be told, he wasn't at all sure how she was going to react to the news. However, he was not going to leave Fanny on her own, so he turned her on her side, which appeared to alleviate the snoring. He covered her with the eiderdown, undid his tie, took off his shoes and laid down next to her. He would break the news to her in the morning.

It had been a busy week and the investigation had reached a stage where the urgent enquiries had been exhausted, so Cooper judged it prudent to give the team another rest day. Cooper arranged with the duty officer that, should anything arise to do with the murder requiring immediate attention, he would contact Brian Pratt at home.

Cooper had experienced an interesting week as far as his private life was concerned. He was now about to take Linda out for a day's sailing around Mersea Island in his father's dinghy. He couldn't have been happier. His parents were away for a few days and it had been agreed he would stay at their house on the island to look after their border collie, Buster. His mum and dad, having gone off in their Austin Seven, had left Cooper their motorbike and sidecar. Cooper senior had owned the combination since the young Albert was in his teens, so he and the bike were well acquainted.

He was a bit embarrassed about using the bike as it wasn't the most glamorous of vehicles, but, as he had no car of his own, he reassured himself that it was at least preferable to the bus.

At 10.00am he found himself knocking on the front door of Linda's parent's house in town, as had been arranged. He was bursting with anticipation, as was apparently the object of his desires. She was at the door in an instant.

It was a warm, but breezy morning with some light rain, and Linda was dressed for the weather. She looked beautiful in a pair of light-blue slacks with a matching dark-blue blouson top bearing the WRNS insignia, with a scarf around her neck. On her feet were a pair of pumps and she carried a bag, over one shoulder, which appeared to have been packed to the gunwales. Cooper noticed the telltale neck of a bottle protruding tantalisingly from one corner of the bag.

'Good morning, sailor.'

'Good morning, miss. Care for a pleasure cruise around the island?'

'That would be lovely. I have packed the necessary provisions.'

Cooper, somewhat sheepishly, indicated the motorbike and sidecar, which stood at the kerb behind him. 'Your carriage awaits. Three wheels rather than four, I'm afraid.'

'Don't be silly, governor darling,' said Linda. 'It looks like great fun.'

'Not what one might expect on a first date, though, is it?'

'That's what this is then, is it?'

Cooper's face reddened.

'Just teasing, governor darling.' She gave him a hug and a peck on the cheek.

After she had declined the use of a helmet, Linda slid into the sidecar and they were off. They were soon out of town and into the country lanes. Although there was very little traffic, Cooper kept his speed to a reasonable level. Not only did he not want to frighten the girl to death, he was not at all confident that the aged motorcycle combination should be tested to its limits.

After nine miles, they were crossing the Strood, the causeway connecting the island to the mainland, which, at high tide, is completely covered by water. Cooper, was a local lad who had been caught out by the tides too often, so he had timed their arrival carefully. They were soon at the boatyard standing alongside the *Essex Skipper*, the family sailing dinghy, and, after preparing the vessel and floating it off its trailer, they were into the water and away.

Cooper, after a minimum of consultation with Linda, decided they would sail across to the small town of Brightlingsea and along the River Colne. It soon became clear that she was no stranger to sailing and her time in the WRNS had not just been spent in the radio room. They were on the water for three hours or so, and she appeared to be loving every minute of the experience.

During the day, they stopped for a lunchtime drink at the Rose and Crown, a riverside pub in the old fishing village of Wivenhoe. As Linda walked along the quay to fetch some chips, Cooper went inside the pub for two pints of beer. They were intending to sit on the side of the river and dine *al fresco*.

He had only just entered the saloon bar and arrived at the counter when he caught sight of Gladys Munson, who was at the other end of the bar, sitting in the snug. She was deep in conversation with a man: a dark, handsome individual. He recognised the man as being the colleague who had accompanied her to the press conference a few days earlier. Cooper could tell from their body language that there was a mutual attraction. A horrifying thought then struck Cooper, *if Munson spots me with Linda she will want to know who she is and why we are together. This could make life very uncomfortable indeed.*

However, any thoughts of a discreet withdrawal were wasted as Munson's companion looked up from the table and caught his gaze. An exchange of words passed between them that Cooper was unable to hear. She looked up, followed her friend's eyeline and, seeing Cooper standing at the bar, she gave an acknowledging wave of the hand. Cooper nodded and smiled in response. *Bollocks. That's just what I don't need.* He quietly ordered the drinks and left the bar quickly to thwart any notion that Munson might have of coming across to speak to him.

As he got back outside the pub, with the beers, he saw Linda had returned from the fish shop. There were a couple of upturned vessels on the quayside that would provide perfect cover, so he walked behind them and placed the pints on the ground. He then beckoned Linda to join him.

'Oh, governor darling! What are you up to?' she said flirtatiously.

At this he walked back to her, grabbed her free hand, compelling her to follow him behind the boats. He put his finger up to his lips, urging her to remain quiet.

Linda was bursting with curiosity, she just had to ask. 'Alby, what are you doing? You naughty man!'

'There was someone in the pub who I didn't want to see us.'

'Who was it then?' asked Linda, thinking in terms of an ex-girlfriend.

'Gladys Munson of the *Recorder*. She's with a bloke.'

'Why would that be a problem?'

'She might start asking questions about why we are in each other's company, clearly off duty. Not only that, she might make the connection between you and your uncle Tom.'

'Why worry about it? Has our relationship really anything to do with her?' said Linda. She wondered why he was being so cautious.

Cooper treated it as a rhetorical question, but stored the image of Munson's friend away in his mind. Just in case, at some time in the future, he needed to "return fire".

'Right, let's have these and get back to the boat.'

'Aye aye, Captain.'

They made it back to Mersea Island with the wind in their favour and in what seemed like half the time of the outward voyage. Then it was back to the bike. Linda had always been a good sailor, but although the motorcycle combination was a novel mode of transport, she had suffered some motion sickness on the earlier ride from Colchester and was not looking forward to the journey home. The distance from the boatyard to the house turned out to be mercifully short and this time she rode pillion.

Linda wasn't sure what she had been expecting, but she soon learned that Cooper's parent's house was very impressive.

It stood on an acre of land, with a five-bar gate across a gravel drive, and beautifully maintained gardens. They abandoned the bike outside the gate and Cooper led her towards the house, which was a large construction with white stucco walls topped with a thatched roof. To one side of the house was a pond with ducks, and there was a well-stocked chicken coop. Linda's impression was such that she imagined it to have once been the centrepiece of a thriving farm.

Cooper unlocked the front door of the house and he entered the porch.

'Linda, I have to warn you now. Buster doesn't bite, but you need to stay back and wait until I call you forward.'

He opened the inner door and, as he did so, he was hit by a large, black, beast. He only just managed to stay on his feet.

'Good boy, Buster! Good boy!'

Cooper grabbed Buster by the collar and then turned to pull a lead from the coat rack that was hanging from the wall, just inside the front door. He quickly attached it to the collar and this made the dog easier to control. He tried to push the dog's hind quarters into a sitting position that he was very reluctant to adopt.

'Now you sit! Be a good boy! Aunty Linda is here to see you.'

After a few seconds or so, Buster, a border collie, appeared finally to get the message.

'I think he'll be all right now, Linda. If you come forward and stroke him, he'll calm down and realise that you are a trusted friend.'

Cooper steered the dog into the house and Linda followed on behind them into the kitchen.

Linda stroked Buster for a while, during which time Cooper had prepared the dog's food and had laid his bowl on the kitchen floor. On seeing this, Buster instantly lost interest in his new friend and made straight for the food.

'Can I get you a drink of some kind Linda? A beer, Scotch or anything?'

'A drink would be nice. I've brought some of mum's parsnip wine with me. Shall we try some of that?'

'Yes, sounds good. Let's try that.'

'I warn you, Alby. It's a bit strong.'

'Even better.'

Linda reached for her bag, pulled out the bottle and passed it to Cooper, who searched the kitchen for glasses and a corkscrew. He took her by the hand and led her into the sitting room, where he set the glasses on a table, opened the bottle and poured the drinks. Linda made herself comfortable on the settee. She was soon joined by the dog, who settled down at her feet.

'Relax now, Linda. I'm going into the kitchen to prepare some dinner. Can I take it you like fish?'

'Lovely, darling. I'll eat anything.'

She took another sip of her parsnip wine, took off her pumps and rested her feet on Buster, who was laying on his back. She was soon asleep.

An hour later, dinner was served. Cooper had acquired some cod fillets from a local fisherman and these were served with boiled potatoes, peas and parsley sauce. He later realised that Linda had come armed with two bottles of the parsnip wine and not just the one. After dinner, they both lay in each other's arms talking until the early hours. Eventually, Linda fell asleep again. He was too intoxicated to drive her home and he didn't want to wake her. They would just have to leave earlier for work the next day.

The Rolls Royce arrived at the front door of Beaumont Hall, having been driven, in stately fashion, along the drive. All the members of staff were standing in two ranks, formed up either side of the front door. Dressed in their best uniforms and wearing black armbands, they had assembled to show their support for Lady Fanny and pay their respects to the master, who had already joined Sister Margaret at rest in the mortuary. They sensed that this represented the end of an era and, quite apart from the sadness of losing his lordship, they all feared for their future.

Quite unexpectedly, after exiting the vehicle, and on the arm of her butler Jenkins, Lady Fanny addressed the staff. 'Thank you, ladies and gentlemen. His lordship would have been extremely proud to see you all looking so smart today. We have all lost a fine man and it was an honour to have known him, but we have to carry on.'

Jenkins took her inside. She spent the rest of the day in her bedroom, and, as it was Sunday, she got Jenkins to take her to the evening service at St Saviour's. He had made a point of telephoning Father O'Leary to inform him of his lordship's passing.

The next few days would involve Fanny dealing with the family solicitor and making the arrangements for Lord Jeremy's funeral. Jenkins was full of admiration for her as she appeared to be holding up remarkably well.

Just look at her. Bitch! Who does she think she is? Putting on her airs and graces. I don't know who's worse, that common tart or the so-called nun. I have half a mind to deal with her as well. Still, we will see. It won't be long now.

21

DAY TWENTY-ONE

Monday 1st August 1949

'Governor, guess what,' said Pratt.

Cooper had that Monday morning feeling and was in no mood to play games.

'Go on then, what?'

'Lord Roding died on Saturday afternoon.'

Cooper was suddenly alarmed and, for a second, he believed they might have another murder on their hands.

'Really? Who told you that?'

'Alf Lewis, the local beat PC.'

'Why weren't CID informed about it?'

'Apparently, PC Lewis called out Inspector King, who attended Beaumont Hall, but as there were no suspicious circumstances it was just treated as a normal sudden death.'

'How did that happen, then?'

'He died in his bed during the afternoon and was found by his nurse, Adina Jenkins.'

'Is that right? said Cooper, relieved. 'Poor old devil. Sad. But it was no secret that he wasn't a well man. He spent half his time in a wheelchair. Probably a welcome release for him. Not to be unkind though, it doesn't help our investigation one little bit, does it?'

'Blimey, governor. You had a bad weekend?'

'No, not really. I'll snap out of it as the day goes on. Go and get me a cup of tea, will you? That'll cheer me up.'

'Walked into that one, didn't I?'

Not only had Cooper been losing sleep over the case, he had Linda Collins on his mind. He was worried that she might have received some stick from her parents over the fact that she had stayed out overnight. He had only just dropped her off at home with the bike, so she could get changed for work.

While Pratt went for the tea, Cooper thought about Jeremy Roding. Death certainly seemed to follow him around. His first wife, his son, Sister Margaret and now himself. He had not been a lucky man. It then dawned on him that, to add insult to injury, Lady Fanny, his wife of only a few years, was likely to inherit the entire estate. He imagined the lengthy queue of suitors and chancers who would soon be beating a path to her door.

Pratt, who had just come across Doris further along the corridor, reappeared with the two teas. He placed them on Cooper's desk and sat down.

'I've just been thinking about Lord Roding,' said Cooper. 'He didn't have any blood relatives left, after the death of his son, did he?'

'No, he didn't. The Honourable Teddy was the last of the line.'

'Now his widow is going to inherit the whole estate and she's only been with him five minutes.'

'Yes. Doesn't seem right, does it? I'm thinking of pimping myself out around the House of Lords to see if I get lucky.'

'You always have been a tart, Brian. Right, down to business. We're in the coroner's court at 11.00am for the preliminary hearing.'

'Never been to one of those. I'm quite looking forward to it, just to see what happens.'

'It's a short hearing, really. The coroner opens the case, there's a bit of spiel, then it's adjourned until a later date.'

'Do you think the Church will send anyone?'

'No. Not at this short notice. We only went to see them a couple of days ago, and they haven't even claimed ownership of her yet. I think I'll just call Father O'Leary anyway and see if he wants to come.'

Cooper dug out the telephone number from the file and picked up the phone.

Mrs Maloney answered the phone and went off to find the priest.

'Father O'Leary speaking.'

'Good morning, Father, this is Inspector Albert Cooper of Colchester CID. How are you today?'

'Busy. I had Mr Jenkins from Beaumont Hall on the telephone to inform me of the passing of Lord Roding over the weekend and now Lady Fanny is pressing me because she wants to know if we can do the funeral. He's only been dead a couple of days. Anyway, how may I help you?'

'Yes. Obviously, we were made aware of that ourselves, but in this instance, I'm calling about Sister Margaret. I wanted to inform you that the coroner will be holding a preliminary hearing at the town hall at 11.00am today. It's not essential, but we wondered whether you would want to be present?'

'Thank you for the kind thought, Inspector. I could come in a private capacity, but I really can't come as a representative of the Church as I haven't been authorised to do so. I did send a telegram to the Vatican for the attention of Cardinal O'Mara to inform him about the situation and to seek his guidance. That was ten days ago, and they still haven't done me the courtesy of an acknowledgement. I sometimes think the Catholic Church is run by bloody heathens!'

'As a matter of interest. Will you be holding his lordship's funeral at St Saviour's?'

'I don't think we can, Inspector. He didn't complete his conversion, you see. That is something else I need to take advice on. I must leave it there, I'm afraid. I'm halfway through a meeting with one of my parishioners. I will try to be with you at 11.00am.'

The inquest went exactly the way that Cooper had predicted, although he hadn't expected there to be any representatives from the press. In the event, sitting in the well of the court, were Gladys Munson and her editor, the dark and swarthy Tony Swayze.

At 11.00am sharp, the coroner opened the hearing by giving the basic facts of the death of Sister Margaret. There were no witnesses called by the court, other than Cooper, who was asked by the coroner to provide an outline of the enquiry.

He did so, adding that there were doubts about Sister Margaret's status. The plain truth being that they had not conclusively identified the deceased as the Catholic Church did not appear to recognise her. As for the murderer, nobody had been identified. The Catholic Church was not represented at court.

For the benefit of the few people present, the coroner read the pathologist's report aloud, citing the cause of death. He then gave a summary of the case as it stood and adjourned it for three months.

On their return to the police station, Cooper phoned Stockwell to bring him up to speed on the inquest, after which he went over Saturday's business with Brian Pratt and Ian Mills.

'Well, chaps, the people at Westminster Cathedral certainly didn't know her,' said Cooper, 'and Father Thomas, the priest we spoke to, put no store by the notion that she'd come all the way from Rome merely to help Lord Roding with his conversion.'

'So, what Lord Roding told us about them not knowing her was right after all then,' observed Pratt.

'Yes, it was, but Father Thomas is going to follow it up with the Vatican, to see if they know anything.'

'One other piece of news,' said Mills. 'The shipping company have come back to us. It turns out that Monsignor Crecy did have a cabin on the boat, but she didn't have one herself.'

'You don't suppose they shared it, do you?' said Cooper with a mischievous smile.

'Blimey! I wouldn't have thought so, governor. But nothing would surprise me with this case. It would be a bit weird though, wouldn't it? A nun and a priest sleeping in the same cabin.'

'Perhaps they got to know each other in the biblical sense.'

'I don't think you're going to go to heaven now, governor,' laughed Pratt. 'Oh, and the other thing was that he booked both their fares in his name and paid for them by cash at the terminal at the Hook of Holland.'

'Good. So, that clinches it, as far as the question of their travelling together is concerned.' Cooper was pleased with the revelation.

'Anyway, whatever our dirty minds might suggest, governor, we can only speculate about who used the cabin. Perhaps he was just being a gentleman.'

'Maybe so. But, again, it begs the question, where did they meet?'

'What do you mean, governor?'

'Let's just think about the passport stamps. They both have one entering the Netherlands on the 16th May. If you examine the stamp it tells us this was at a road crossing. A place called Venlo. I looked it up in the atlas and I discovered that Venlo is on the border with Germany. He landed at Vienna Airport two days before that on the 14th May and the passport shows nothing in between. So where did they meet? Did they both travel from Vienna, or did he meet her somewhere else in Austria or Germany?'

'And, governor, if they met somewhere between Austria and the Netherlands. What form of transport did they use?'

'A car would be obvious, I suppose, Brian, but I wonder how readily available the fuel is over there these days. The railway is another option or perhaps they used a combination of the two. And then, of course, there is the possibility that somebody else drove them.'

'But why were there no date stamps in the passport covering that stage of the journey?'

'Given what we have been told about Crecy, I'm starting to think she was actually smuggled across borders.'

'Why on earth would she have to do that?'

'Use your loaf, Brian! Isn't it obvious?' said Cooper, *a large penny starting to drop.*

'Not really governor, no.'

'Well, given what Special Branch have been telling us about Crecy and what the Church have said about her, I think we can safely assume that she wasn't a nun at all and she never was a fucking nun!'

They were both sat in silence trying to come to terms with the reality that was now facing them. Cooper started the self-flagellation.

'I should have worked it out long ago, with her attitude to those around her. The fact that nobody in the Catholic Church in London has heard of her at all. The association with Monsignor Crecy, who was of interest to Special Branch for moving wanted people. And, according to her ladyship, she hardly ever went to church for Christ's sake! Am I getting thicker as I get older or what?'

'So, if she wasn't a nun, what was she?'

'What indeed. We know she wasn't Irish; she was from Switzerland. So, I doubt that it has anything to do with Irish Republicanism. But somebody was after her.'

'Her passport shows she was born in Austria, though. So where are her family? Where is the child she gave birth to?' said Pratt.

'Of course, we only have Father O'Leary's statement saying she was born in Switzerland. That either could have been a lie on her part or down to poor memory on his.'

'I'm inclined to go by what it says in the passport, Brian.'

'What about Father O' Leary? Do you think that he knows about her real status, governor?'

'No, I don't think he really knew what was going on.'

'Surely he must have suspected something was amiss?'

'Cardinal O'Mara of the Special Assignments Unit of the Vatican contacted him, and he told him to expect the arrival of Sister Margaret, who was on an assignment. O'Mara is apparently a man he holds in high regard and he was proud to serve. He simply did as he was told and didn't question it.'

'I mean, it wasn't much of an assignment, was it, just preparing Lord Jeremy Roding for conversion to Catholicism? What is so special about that?'

'Well you have to realise that he was a peer of the realm. It still carries a lot of influence, even today. There aren't that many Roman Catholic peers in the House of Lords. The more the better as far as the Catholic Church is concerned.'

'Yes, I suppose so.'

'So, Lord Roding consulted Monsignor Crecy on the fact that he wished to convert to Catholicism. Crecy obviously saw it as an opportunity to move Sister Margaret and he discussed it with Cardinal O'Mara. It seems they exploited the situation to get her over here for a few months, so that she could hide in plain sight.'

'But why?'

'That's what we need to find out, Brian. Do you remember the other day when I said to you her death looked like a punishment?'

'Yes, I do. You could be right.'

'One thing that does occur to me is that I think we would be far better off just concentrating on the name Irma Caro. This bloody "Sister Margaret" lark is wearing a bit thin, don't you think?'

'What about the enquiries with the Vatican?'

'I think Father Thomas is genuine enough. He'll do his best, I'm sure. But I don't think the "powers that be" at the Vatican will have heard of her, and the only issue they are likely to be interested in is the misappropriation of one of their diplomatic passports.'

'Yes. How did that come about, I wonder?'

'My money is on the probability that Cardinal O'Mara arranged to get someone in the Vatican to steal the passport and have it forged in her name. As for him, naturally, he'll deny all knowledge of the passport and the sister.'

'Anyway, Brian, I've got to go to see Mr Stockwell and bring him up to date with how we're getting on.'

Fifteen minutes later, Cooper and Stockwell were sitting in the comfy chairs in the superintendent's office. Coffees were on the table in front of them.

'A few things to tell you, sir. I went with Miss Collins up to Westminster Cathedral on Saturday where I saw Father Michael Thomas. I spoke to him about the letter you sent to the archbishop and explained the situation. He told me he would chase it up. But, on the face of it, they have no knowledge of our nun.'

'And what do they say about this man Crecy?'

'Apparently, Monsignor Crecy was something of a liaison man between London and the Vatican. Father Thomas is going to discuss the matter with the archbishop and make enquiries with someone senior at the Vatican.'

'What about Cardinal O'Mara? I hope they'll make their enquiries with somebody senior to him and more trustworthy.'

'One would hope so.'

'I made some enquiries of my own with the Foreign and Commonwealth Office. They told me about a man they hold in high regard, a Cardinal Maglione, who is the Vatican secretary of state.'

'I'm told they'll also speak separately to Cardinal O'Mara.'

'Good, Albert. I'll be interested to see what comes back from that.'

'Perhaps the Foreign Office might speak to their contact for us?'

'I hope that it won't come to that, but it's something we might have to fall back on. I don't know about the Catholic Church, it seems that it's more like we're dealing with the Mafia.'

Cooper then went on to explain the basis for the suspicion that Sister Margaret was not in fact a real nun. Stockwell was aghast.

'I think that, in light of what you have managed to learn in recent days, you need to contact DCI Lloyd-Davis at Special Branch and bring him up to date. I agree this situation doesn't sound like it's connected to the IRA, but he may have a view on the circumstances and how you might take your enquiries forward. They have contacts on the continent who could prove useful.'

'Thank you, sir. I will do so.' *As if I haven't already thought of doing just that,* thought Cooper.

He then went on to explain that he had also delivered the *Tatler* letter, and that he had asked them to search the archive for Monsignor Crecy and was awaiting a result of their search.

The superintendent expressed his satisfaction at the apparent progress of the investigation and thanked Cooper for his efforts.

'So, Irma Caro it is then.'

'Yes, sir.'

'One other thing before you go, Albert. How is Miss Collins getting on?'

'She's doing very well, sir. I've found her to be keen, bright and hard working. I know she's not been with us for long, but, on what I've seen of her work so far, I would be happy to have her remain with us with a view to her being a permanent member of the department.'

'I am pleased to hear that, Albert. I trust your judgement. Thank you.'

A lump formed in Cooper's throat. He liked the girl a lot. Apart from fraternising with a junior female officer off duty, he hadn't done anything wrong, but he wasn't going to tell "Uncle Tom" that he and Linda were getting on well or that he had taken her sailing at the weekend. As he walked back to the police station, Cooper considered the possibility that, if things were to really take off, one day he might even marry the girl. He chided himself for being silly. All the same, if it were to happen, would he have to call Stockwell "Uncle Tom?" Cooper laughed out loud, and a lady passer-by crossed the road to avoid him.

22

DAY TWENTY-TWO

Tuesday 2ⁿᵈ August 1949

It was 9.30am and Linda Collins found herself alone in the CID office, as everyone else had disappeared out to pursue their individual tasks and enquiries. She had grabbed a mug of tea from Doris, and, as there was nobody else in the main office, she had taken one into Cooper.

Linda was back at her desk and was just settling into some paperwork. Although it was early days, Linda felt that she was becoming accustomed to life in the CID, and the support of Alby Cooper had given her comfort and confidence. The department had a complement of two detective sergeants and ten detective constables, although the office was now rather depleted due to sickness, annual leave and the ongoing murder enquiry. That being the case, she allowed herself to believe that she had half a chance of remaining where she was and to become established as a detective.

There was certainly some jealousy over her attachment to CID, and some unfortunate remarks by her erstwhile colleagues on the Women and Children's Team were starting to reach her ears. The women's unit consisted of a bitch of a sergeant called Cecily White and five woman constables. Their room was on the ground floor of the police station, adjacent to the front office and one would have to pass it when en route to the back door. Consequently, she had been in receipt of some "stage whispers", but had chosen to ignore them.

She got on with most of the girls, but a couple of them were sour and two faced, and she had been given the silent treatment on a few of occasions when she had gone back to the office to check her pigeon hole. *Still, I can deal with that kind of nonsense,* she thought to herself. *They want to try being in the WRNS. Some of those women were evil. This lot wouldn't have survived a week with them.* She laughed at the memory.

Linda had lived with her parents for a while and they were beginning to get on her nerves. She had started to think about finding herself digs in town. Her father had given her a dirty look when she had popped home to change her clothes following her night at Alby's. He hadn't said anything, but he knew full well that she had not been working late. She anticipated that she would get the third degree later when she arrived home from work. *I'm a grown woman,* she told herself, *Not only that but a police officer and ex-Wren. If he starts, I'll tell him where to get off!*

Linda reflected on the lovely time she had spent with Alby. She liked him a lot. The fact that he was now her boss was a bit tricky, and, taken together with the Stockwell factor, life had the potential to be difficult indeed. But she was going to do her damnedest to make their relationship work.

Linda was an intelligent and confident young officer, but if there was one thing that made her nervous about her present position it was being caught in the CID office alone when the telephone rang. Would she react in the right way if something serious came down the line or would she be found wanting? Linda's nerves were tested when the phone burst into life on the desk in front of her.

'CID. WPC Collins. How may I help you?'

'Ah, DC Collins. It's Quentin Smallpiece here at *Tatler*. How are you?'

'Ah, good morning, sir.'

'Oh, do call me Quentin, please.'

'Yes, Quentin. What can I do for you?'

'You wanted us to delve into the archive for anything to do with Monsignor Tarquin Crecy. Well, I went over to Pinner yesterday and I think I've found some items you might be very interested in. I've brought them back to the office, so you're welcome to come and have a look at them at your convenience.'

'That sounds exciting, Quentin. Can I have your phone number, please? I will find Mr Cooper and I'm sure we'll come back to you quickly to arrange something.'

Smallpiece gave Linda the telephone number for *Tatler* and then rang off.

Linda walked along the corridor to find Cooper, who was sitting in his office reading a report.

'Sorry to interrupt you, governor, but I've just had Quentin Smallpiece of *Tatler* on the phone. He sounded quite excited. He told me he has something from the archive to show us that we'll find very interesting. I said I would speak to you and come back to him ASAP.'

'That sounds good, Linda. I'm getting swamped with bloody paperwork here and I could do with a bit of fresh air. Will you call him back, please, and ask him if he has time to see us this afternoon?'

'Will do.' She rushed back to the main office, made the call and returned after a few minutes.

'He says it would be convenient up to about 4.30pm.'

'OK, Linda. Give me twenty minutes to sort myself out and then we'll go.'

At 2.45pm Cooper and Collins were sitting in the waiting room at *Tatler*.

On the train journey up to town, their conversation was a mix of business and pleasure. They were both conscious that they were on duty and they had to work hard to maintain a professional approach. But Alby was nervous. He liked Linda a lot. She was just the kind of woman he needed. He was all too aware that he would soon be in his forties and therefore inclined to view any girlfriend as a long-term proposition. He had absolutely no intention of playing games or wasting his time by engaging in casual affairs, but their relationship would have to be a slow burner. As for Linda, she was fearful that her relationship to Stockwell would ultimately put the mockers on things and that Alby's interest in her would wane.

One thing that did sustain them during the journey was the sense of anticipation as to what lay in store for them at *Tatler*. Smallpiece had teased Collins with the comment that they might find his discovery "very interesting". She hoped that his description wasn't an exercise in overstatement. So, as they both sat in the waiting room, having arrived at *Tatler*, time passed slowly until, finally, Smallpiece put his head around the door.

'Good afternoon, folks. Hope you are well? If you would like to come with me, we'll go and find young Mr Grimes.'

Smallpiece moved swiftly and he virtually danced along the corridors. He clearly couldn't wait to disclose the fruits of his research.

On entering the studio, they were greeted with a wave by a smiling Grimes, who was using the telephone. When he had finished his call, he ushered them across the room to a long table. Stretched out before them were photographs and news cuttings. Smallpiece provided a commentary.

'Luckily, our people at the Pinner archive building have designed a very comprehensive indexing system, so I was able to go back over the last ten years or so quite quickly. What I found was very interesting.'

He showed a group shot of two men who were standing either side of one central figure, who was wearing a smart business suit. Smallpiece pointed to the man, standing on the right, who was also wearing a black suit but with a clerical collar.

'That is your Monsignor Tarquin Crecy enjoying himself at a party in London at the end of 1937. He is identified in the article.'

'Quite a handsome man, wasn't he?' said Collins. Cooper looked sideways at her, more out of curiosity than jealousy.

'Who is the man in the middle? He's obviously acting as the host.'

'That, folks, is Joachim von Ribbentrop, German ambassador to the Court of St James. He was hanged at Nuremburg a couple of years ago, after having been convicted in the war trials.'

'Bloody hell. Crecy certainly did get around, didn't he?'

'Who is the other man in the photo?' asked Collins.

'The other one is Fritz Luther the renowned Berlin interior designer. The occasion is to celebrate the opening of the new German Embassy in London. He was responsible for the design and layout.'

'Do you think that we could have a copy of these?'

'Certainly, Linda. In fact, we have prepared a copy of everything for you to take away with you. But we haven't quite finished yet. We have a little bonus,' said Smallpiece.

'What, Quentin? You've got Crecy with even more Germans?'

'No, Inspector. Something else entirely,' said Smallpiece, jovially.

He indicated another table on the other side of the studio.

'Young Grimes and I were out on our perambulations on Saturday, and we covered the Windmill Theatre reunion. We anticipated that our friend Lady Fanny might be there. And she was. Not only that, she had another man in tow. They appeared to be very intimate. We're hoping that you might recognise him.'

They were treated to another series of photographs. Fanny was surrounded in most of the shots by a group of tarty-looking women who were obviously contemporaries from her theatrical days. In addition, there were other shots of Raymond Jenkins having a high old time with Lady Fanny, arm in arm, cuddling, dancing and apparently sharing passionate kisses. He was obviously performing well beyond the call of duty.

'Oh, Raymond Jenkins! What the butler saw!' said Cooper.

'What the butler did!' said Collins laughing.

'Well, I can certainly identify the man to you, gents. That is Raymond Jenkins, his lordship's butler and chauffeur.'

'Thanks for that, Albert. I think we may have the makings of a story there, Harry, don't you?' said Smallpiece.

'Yes, Skipper.'

Then a worrying thought came to Cooper's mind.

'When were you thinking of using these photographs, Quentin?'

'Probably in the next edition. Why?'

'Were you aware that, unfortunately, on the afternoon that these were taken Lord Roding died at home in his bed?'

'Blimey! No, we weren't aware of that,' said Grimes.

Smallpiece said nothing and the self-satisfied grin left his face.

'Yes, he did. Although it's not yet confirmed, he very probably died of natural causes. Of course, these are very interesting photographs from our point of view and they might have implications as far as our murder investigation is concerned, but to publish them in *Tatler* at this time would be very cruel, don't you think?'

'Yes, of course. Well, we won't do that. Not for a week or so anyway,' said Grimes.

'*What?*

'Sorry, just a joke.'

'Bad taste, dear boy,' said Smallpiece.

'Yes. Indeed, it is.'

'Just a thought though, Inspector. If it turns out that it would prove useful to your investigation to put the photographs into the public domain, we could slip them into a future edition for you.'

'That might be something to think about. Thank you, Quentin.'

'Is there anything else that we may help you with, Albert?'

Given the existing legal agreement, Cooper thought he would take a risk, and tell Harry and Quentin something about the victim. The fact that she had been in the UK for about two months, and the fact that she had travelled and entered the country with Monsignor Crecy. The two journalists were agog.

'You were very successful in finding valuable information on Monsignor Crecy in the archive. Would you look to see whether she is in there as well?'

'Yes, indeed,' said Smallpiece. 'What details do you have for her?'

'She was known as Sister Margaret of the Sacred Heart of Jesus. Her earthly name was Irma Caro. She had at least one child, whom we have not yet traced, but Caro might be a maiden name. She was born in Austria in 1919.'

'Leave it with us,' said Smallpiece, eager to please.

'Forgive me for stressing this, Quentin, but her real name is not in the public domain and we want it to stay that way,' said Cooper.

'We shall be very discreet. You have our assurance on that.'

Grimes handed Collins a pre-prepared bundle containing copies of the material they'd been shown.

'Gentlemen, we are very grateful to you for your help. It's a bit early in the day now, but perhaps next time we come to see you we can time it so that I can buy you both a pint.'

They shook hands on the idea, and then left for the return journey.

Cooper was intent on going straight back to the office to place the bundle safely under lock and key. It certainly wouldn't do for such explosive material to be left unattended or mislaid.

Back at the police station, Alby and Linda signed off duty, but, before they were able to go their separate ways, Linda entered his office and closed the door behind her.

'Governor, darling. I want to speak to you. Could we go somewhere quiet for a drink?'

Cooper agreed, and so they made their way to the Abbey Arms, which was just a few streets away. As they entered the snug, Cooper was pleased to see that, as it was a Monday evening, the place was as empty as he had hoped it would be. He went to the bar and bought a pint for himself and a half of stout for his companion.

As he returned to the table he saw that Linda was sitting on a high-backed pew with her back to the wall. It had plenty of room for two occupants, but for appearances sake, lest they be seen by a colleague, Cooper elected to sit, across the table, facing her.

'So, having tricked your way into me buying you a drink, Linda, what is it you wanted to speak to me about?' said Cooper, light heartedly.

'I just wondered whether there had been any feedback after my announcement at the meeting.'

'Only from your uncle Tom.'

'*What?*'

'Yes. He spoke to me the other day and he said, "Listen, Cooper, I know you're seeing my niece and you'd better look after her or else!"' he said teasingly.

'He didn't! Did he?'

'Of course, he didn't, you, daft ha'p'orth.'

'Well what did he say, then?'

'I was just giving him an update in his office after we had got back from our trip to the cathedral. I happened to mention that you'd been with me. He asked how you were getting on with being attached to the CID. I told him you were doing very well and that you're an asset to the department. I even went so far as to say that I would be happy for you to be a permanent member of the team…'

'You said that?'

'Yes,' said Cooper.

'Oh, Alby. That's lovely.'

'Thing is, it's early days. We've only been out a couple of times socially. So, it wouldn't do to get ahead of ourselves and worry about it, would it? I know that you want to be on the CID, and I certainly wouldn't want to expose you to the possibility of being accused of benefitting from favouritism or nepotism. So, we must just take things slowly and carefully. But, to put it simply, I don't want to lose you, either way.'

Linda got up from her pew and walked around the table. She placed a hand each side of Cooper's face and kissed him passionately on the lips.

'I'm going to powder my nose, you gorgeous man. She left Cooper to his pint. When Linda returned to the table she had a few questions to put to him.

'Is it still totally taboo for a senior officer to have a relationship with someone more junior in rank?'

'Yes, I suppose it is, if the senior officer is a part of the same team. What the job would normally do would be to split them up. They've even been known to split up married couples if they happen to have been on the same team before they got married. If it causes a disciplinary problem, it'd be regarded as a display of poor judgement.'

'I see. And that wouldn't be good for your prospects, would it?'

'I suppose not, such as they are. But, of course, it would only be a problem if we make it a problem.'

'Do you want to keep me a secret, then?'

'Well, we don't have to tell all and sundry about our relationship. It's our business. We can always go over the border into Suffolk if we want to have a day out somewhere. If we carry on like that for now, at least until we finish the murder enquiry, and then I might have to put in to transfer to another division.'

'You would do that for me?' said Linda.

'Let's just see how we get on, shall we.'

They remained in the pub until closing time. Cooper told Linda about his family and how they had come to find their dream house on the island. He was completely beguiled by this young woman and he even suggested that, now they'd returned from holiday, they might pay his parents a visit, so that he could introduce her to them. But, for this evening, it was enough just to be able to walk her home.

'Beaumont Hall, Mr Jenkins speaking, may I help you?'

'Yes, Mr Jenkins. It's Geoffrey Green, Lord Roding's solicitor. May I speak to her ladyship, please?'

'Just one moment, sir. I will try to locate her.'

Green heard Jenkins' footsteps on the wooden floor as he walked away from the telephone. After a few seconds, he returned.

'Hello. Mr Green. Her ladyship will be with you shortly.'

Fanny entered the room in her dressing gown and slippers. She'd had a busy night. She took the receiver from Jenkins.

'Hello, Fanny Roding speaking.'

'Good morning, your ladyship. This is Geoffrey Green, Lord Jeremy's solicitor. I understand that you called the office late yesterday afternoon. I am sorry for not coming back to you sooner, but I have been at the high court in London on another matter.'

'Yes, Mr Green. I did wonder. I was telephoning to speak to you about the reading of the will. To be honest, Mr Green, I would like to get it over and done with as soon as you can possibly manage it.'

'Well, as you know, Doctor Stevenson had been attending his lordship on a regular basis and his medical condition was well established. Lord Roding's death was certainly consistent with that diagnosis and the treatment he was receiving; however, given the fact that the police are still investigating a murder at Beaumont Hall, the coroner has taken the precautionary measure of ordering a post mortem.'

'I see.'

'So, I am sorry to say that the reading of the will might be delayed for a few more days.'

'That's bloody inconvenient, I must say.'

'Furthermore, my lady, I must just mention that his lordship spoke to me about some alterations to his will during the final days of his life and the will has been changed.

'What kind of alterations are these?' asked Fanny.

'Nothing to alarm you, my lady. They just relate to bequests to a member of the domestic staff, and they are in accordance with his wishes, I can assure you.'

'Well, please hurry it up, will you? I need some money to pay bills, suppliers and such. They are pressing us for payment.'

'I will do my best, my lady. I can clear up the bequests to the staff quite quickly. Those are quite straightforward. It would just entail me coming to the Hall and speaking to each of them individually and handing them a letter with a cheque.'

'OK, so when would you like to come?'

'May I, perhaps, come and see you this afternoon. Would that be agreeable?'

'Yes, how about 1.00pm?'

'Yes, that would be fine.'

'Who do you need to see then?'

'Mr Raymond Jenkins and Mrs Adina Jenkins, Mrs Beryl Aldis, and Mr Stephen Savage.'

'I'm not sure if they're all available, but I'll make sure that they are informed, Mr Green.'

'Thank you, my lady. I will see you at 1.00pm.'

Jenkins was lurking by the study door.

'Did you hear that, Raymond? The reading of the will has been delayed. Bloody nuisance. We need the money to pay bills, don't we?'

'Yes, and some people are becoming rather impatient.'

'Apparently, his lordship made some changes to the will. It seems that he left you something, also Adina, Mrs Aldis and Savage.'

'Did I hear you say that he is coming here at 1.00pm?' said Jenkins, stifling his glee.

'Yes, Raymond, will you make sure the others are available for when Mr Green comes? He needs to give you all a letter and a cheque.'

'Yes, my lady. Thank you.'

'Oh, and when he does get around to reading my part of the will, I think it would be best to have a witness. Would you help me with that and sit in?'

'I'd be glad to be of service, my lady.'

'Oh, and by the way…'

'Yes, my lady?'

'I do need you, you know, and not just as an employee.'

Jenkins shut the study door, so they could speak in private. Now that they were alone, he could revert to calling her Fanny. He didn't always know where he stood with her, as when the mood took her, she could be very cold and ruthless. At other times, she could be amorous. Alcohol was usually the factor that made the difference. They'd been intimate, but she professed guilt that they had gone behind Adina's back. Fanny had, on at least two occasions, in her passion, declared that she and Raymond might be together, were it not for his marriage. He held high hopes for their relationship. Raymond felt he could say almost anything to her. So, he took his opportunity.

'Fanny, I haven't had much chance to speak to you alone since the death of his lordship. How are you holding up?'

'I'm getting used to the situation, Raymond. Let's just say that I'm taking it one day at a time.'

'Have you had any thoughts about the future?'

'In what way do you mean? You and me?' asked Fanny.

'You know how I feel about you. But, I mean, things in general: the estate, the staff. They're all worried, you know.'

'I'm sure they are, but I really don't know what I want to do yet. As purely an exercise in taking stock I'll have the estate, the Hall and the land valued. I think there are eighteen acres, in all. There's also the house in Bedford Square. I just want to know how much I'm worth.'

'Do you think you might sell up, then?'

'We'll have to wait and see. I've got no plans to go anywhere, Raymond. I just need to get a grip on what Jeremy has left me. I'll find out more later when the solicitor finally gets around to reading the will.'

'The staff need to be reassured, Fanny. As you know, there are seven staff here and three at Bedford Square whose lives are on hold. They deserve some indication about the future, don't you think?'

'Let's just get the will over with and I'll have a better idea, OK?'

Fanny got up and left the study to go to her room to bathe and get dressed.

Raymond was sick to his stomach. He'd never felt so uncertain about the future. And what form would that future take? Would he be central to Fanny's life? She'd told him that she was not interested in the usual fops she came into regular contact with and that he was her man. He felt very insecure. What of Adina? He wasn't at all sure he wanted to be with her any more. Raymond knew that soon he was going to have to take a difficult and probably painful decision, and, for that, he would need to know where he stood.

Raymond got on with his day, which consisted of washing and polishing the Rolls. Since the passing of his lordship, he was at something of a loss. There was no longer a gentleman for him to look after and Fanny tended to look after herself. As for Beryl, she was now only cooking for one.

At 12.55pm precisely, Geoffrey Green arrived at the Hall. He was shown into the dining room by Jenkins, and soon after they were joined by Fanny.

'Good afternoon your ladyship.'

'Good afternoon, Mr Green. I hope you've some good news for me. God knows, I could do with some.'

'There is no change to the situation as I explained it this morning, I'm afraid, my lady. Although I must confess that it is a slight change to the usual format, my dealing with the bequests separately; however, I thought that the members of staff might need the money to tide them over.'

'My husband made no mention of any changes to the will.'

'He gave me to understand that, due to his illness, he did not expect to live many more years and he was anxious to get his affairs in order. The staff bequests were a very recent addition to the will. It was all signed off by his lordship; I can assure you of that, my lady.'

'But why the delay?'

'Unfortunately, these things take time.'

Fanny did not begrudge the staff their individual bequests, but she knew when she was being patronised. She realised she had no other option but to go along with the solicitor and his approach to administering the family estate.

The solicitor placed his briefcase on the table and he undid the buckles. He withdrew a folder from the inside of the case. The will, written on parchment, was placed in front of him and he smoothed the pages down.

Green asked to speak to Raymond Jenkins and the others. Fanny summoned Jenkins, who escorted the solicitor to the kitchen, where they were met by Adina, Mrs Aldis and Savage. Green used the office to speak to the individual staff members in private. He handed each an envelope containing a letter and cheque made out in their favour in the sum of their individual bequest. Lord Roding had been very even handed in his largesse, with each of his four senior members of staff receiving a cheque for three hundred pounds.

They all reacted with surprise, gratitude and respect. Beryl Aldis, when told of the sum that had been left to her, was very emotional.

At the conclusion of this supplementary piece of business, Jenkins escorted Geoffrey Green to the front door. Jenkins was again left with a feeling of nausea. He was pleased to receive the money, of course he was. But the *ex gratia* payments seemed to have an air of finality about them. He was sure that they were kindly meant, but, in his eyes, they represented a pay-off. Life was about to change for them all, one way or another.

23

DAY TWENTY-THREE

Wednesday 3rd August 1949

'Raymond, will you fetch my suitcase? It's in the bedroom.'

'Yes, my lady. Then I'd better go to the garage to collect the Rolls.'

'No, Raymond. I shan't be needing the Rolls today.'

Fanny had appeared in the hallway, dressed in her finery. Although she was totally dressed in black, she looked stylish and elegant.

'Don't you want me to drive you, my lady?'

'No. I'll get the train.'

'But, isn't it my job to drive you wherever you want to go?'

'Not for much longer.'

'I'm sorry. What does that mean?'

'Look, Raymond, I'm thinking of making a few changes anyway. I know his lordship loved it, but I won't be needing such an expensive motor in future.'

'Does that mean I shall be out of job?'

'I've not made up my mind yet. We'll have to see how we get on. Anyway, you can run me to the station if you want to.'

Raymond felt as though he'd been punched in the stomach. He didn't dare question her further or show his lack of confidence. He simply didn't know whether she was speaking as his employer or hinting at some enhancement of his future position as her lover. He drove her ladyship to the railway station in silence. It was clear that she had her mind elsewhere and didn't want to talk. Her ladyship was about to take herself off to London to "sort a few things out".

The train was already at the platform, so he dutifully followed her, carried her bag and placed it inside the first-class carriage. Fanny stood at the open door and having first checked that there were no witnesses, she thanked him by kissing him on the cheek. *That was a positive sign,* he reassured himself.

He had walked on to the platform believing that now he was no more than her ladyship's butler, but as he walked away he allowed himself to dream that he was still her ladyship's lover. He realised, though, that he was subject to her whim and fancy, and this diminished him as a man. Whichever way it went, unless he took charge of his life, he would remain at her mercy. He had never felt such turmoil.

Raymond and Fanny had engaged in intercourse on two memorable occasions after he'd driven her to society functions. She had always found them intimidating, and could never throw off the feeling that she wasn't worthy and didn't belong. She was of the hoi polloi, and she was constantly reminded of the fact. On those occasions when she had been drinking heavily, she would seek the company of Jenkins, who would be only too happy to provide comfort and satisfy her needs. Unfortunately, he'd made the fatal mistake of reading too much into their stolen sexual encounters. He cursed himself for ever having dared think he might be a part of her future. He felt anxious, excluded and surplus to requirements.

He reflected on the fact that he was over twenty years older than her, yet here he was, totally dependent on her every mood. He hated being in this position. He vowed that he was going to begin a new life in which he would exercise more control. A better life. A life alone.

'Well, that's her ladyship on her way,' said Jenkins as he entered the kitchen. He hung up his coat and joined Beryl Aldis and Stephen Savage at the table. As Beryl poured him a cup of tea, Jenkins reached across to the sideboard and switched on the wireless. 'Don't mind, do you, Beryl? The news will be on in a minute.'

'No. Carry on.'

'Anyway, that's one fewer mouth to feed,' said Jenkins.

'I feel a bit redundant to be honest, Ray. There's only us servants left. And, as for young James, I'm having to find jobs to keep him busy and I'm running out ideas. He's starting to become a bloody nuisance.'

'In what way?'

'He won't leave the twins alone. They think it's hilarious, and they keep flirting with him and leading him on. He keeps trying to get one or other of them on their own. I don't think he knows which one he's talking to at any one time. It's like a game to them.'

The twins were happy enough in their own way and quite oblivious to what was happening around them. There was still a house to clean and they would just carry on as if nothing had really changed.

'If he's at a loose end, send him out to me I'll give him something to keep him out of mischief,' said Savage, 'Anyway, have we got a date for the funeral yet, Mrs A?'

'Not yet,' interrupted Jenkins, 'the funeral is still to be arranged. And, as tradition has it, it will be followed by a wake, so we'll have that to sort out. I must say I'm not looking forward to it and I'm at a loss as to who we should invite.'

'I must say I'm dreading it, as well' said Beryl.

'Well I've yet to receive any instructions from her ladyship regarding the form or scale of the funeral. The master and Lady Fanny had few mutual friends, and there are no family members to invite, so it's likely to be quite a modest affair. Sad really, he deserves better than that.' said Jenkins.

'Yes, we're at the end of an era, all right. Things are going to be a bit different around here. It's the youngsters I feel sorry for. Do you think that her ladyship will sell up the Hall and the estate, Raymond?' asked Beryl.

'I took the liberty of asking her what her plans are, only this morning. I don't think she even knows what she wants to do herself.'

'If the worst does come to the worst, Sidney and I could start a new life with our money. We'll probably open a tea shop,' said Beryl.

'Very nice too,' said Jenkins.

'When my cheque clears, there'll be three hundred pounds winging its way towards me. I could do quite a lot with that, I reckon. That's, of course, provided the police don't charge me with something,' said Savage.

'That won't happen, Steve. You should have never been arrested for the sister's murder in the first place. I told the police and anyone else who would listen that you wouldn't do such a thing,' said Beryl.

'Thank you, Beryl. Much obliged.'

Beryl couldn't quite work out whether Savage was being sarcastic.

'I really would like to find a woman and get married,' said Savage, 'Get our own cottage and a small holding. Maybe I could even still have one or two children. I'm pretty sure there's life in the old pecker yet.'

'Sounds lovely, Steve. Do you know any women?'

'I've got a couple of irons in the fire, Beryl,' said Savage, tapping his nose.

'Best of luck with that,' said Jenkins. 'Anyway, what have you been doing with yourself the last few days?'

'Just keeping myself busy walking the dogs and looking after the game birds. Trying to keep the poachers at bay. I don't think Lady Fanny cares much about the garden, so I'm just doing the lawns and leaving the flowerbeds to look after themselves, for now. As for the summer house, I still can't bear to go near the bloody place.'

'Anyway, Raymond, I've got an idea,' said Beryl. 'Whatever her ladyship's intentions are, why don't we hold our own wake in memory of Lord Jeremy?'

'Why are you asking me, Beryl? It sounds as though you've already got something planned, as usual?'

'You're right, I've been thinking. As you know, I'm always careful where food is concerned. I hate waste. Well, the larder is full to the brim with meats and things, and if we don't use them up in the next couple of days, they'll go off and will have to be thrown away. His lordship wouldn't have liked that at all. So, why not have a banquet of our own to pay our respects to his lordship's memory?'

Savage smiled broadly. 'That's a smashing idea, Beryl, but won't we have to ask her ladyship's permission first?'

'No, she wouldn't mind, but she needn't know about it, anyway. Kitchen management is my job. We're only using up our surplus stock, after all. So, how do you fancy a meal just for the staff? I'm sure they'd enjoy it and it'd cheer us up no end.'

'Well, I think it's a marvellous idea,' said Jenkins. 'There might also be a few bottles of beer in the cellar that are on the turn as well. We could use those up at the same time.'

After the news had been and gone, Jenkins walked through to his office intending to examine the accounts. Beryl followed on behind.

'How are things with the household expenses, Ray?'

'Not too bad. I'll need to speak to her ladyship again and ask her for an injection of cash into the household account. It's getting a bit low now. She's having to wait for the reading of the will before she has the money released and we can pay the bills. If we do hold this wake, will we have enough food for the week?'

'Yes, I think so. There's plenty of tinned stuff, fresh fruit and veg. That'll see us through to the end of the week, Ray.'

'I'll give her a call later and ask her to transfer some

money, even if it's only a small amount to cover the staff wages. They must be paid first. Of course, we need to pay our suppliers, but if it comes to it, they'll just have to wait a bit longer. The sooner we find out what she's going to do, the better. I hate this not knowing.'

'Tell me about it. Have you paid your cheque in yet, Ray?'

'No, not yet.'

'I was just thinking that we ought to keep the fact that his lordship has left us some money to ourselves. The youngsters won't have received anything in his lordship's will. It's a shame, but it's all about time served.'

'I'm sure we'd have heard about it by now, if they had. Lord knows what young James would do if he were to be left three hundred quid,' laughed Jenkins.

'No, but, anyway, we don't want to rub their noses in it, do we?' said Beryl.

'I agree. The reality is, though, that they could be out of a job.'

'So, what do you think? Shall we do lunch or dinner?'

'Lunch on Saturday I think. We don't want things getting out of hand, and I'll expect to see everything cleared away by 5.00pm.'

'Right you are. I'll aim for a 2.00pm sit down. Will you tell Adina?'

'Yes, Beryl, if you'll tell the others, and I'll deal with any callers during the afternoon, should there be any.'

24

DAY TWENTY-FOUR
Thursday 4th August 1949

'He sounded like a lovely young man, Father. I must be getting old. But they do say, don't they, that when policemen look young, that's a sure sign you're getting old. Now you can add young priests to the list. Although I only heard him speak, but you can tell what people look like from their voices, I always think. He sounded a charming person and he had a lovely way about him.'

'Woah, woah, please, Mrs Maloney. Hold your horses. What did he actually say?'

He had been out cycling around the parish and, on his return, he'd just put his head around the door of the kitchen to ask if there had been any callers. As it was a Thursday, Father O'Leary had made his regular visit to the old people's home in the village. He liked to join in their activities and he'd nearly become inveigled into a game of "strip dominos" until common sense told him he was having his leg pulled. He'd come away, tutting to himself. *Old people of today!*

Here he was, back at the parochial house, trying to debrief

Mrs Maloney on a simple message. The process was becoming torturous and frustrating.

'He will call back in an hour and speak to you then.'

'How long ago did he call?'

'Oh, I don't know. Half an hour ago, maybe more. Would you like something to eat while you're waiting, Father?'

'Yes, please. That would be nice. I have to be getting on with my sermon, so if you don't mind, I'll have it while I'm working.'

He ran into his office, sat at his desk and removed his cycle clips. He got on with some work, and every now and then caught himself staring at the telephone. *This is silly,* he told himself. So, he chose to ignore it. Within a couple of minutes, the phone rang.

'Beaumont Parochial House. Father Thomas O'Leary speaking.'

'Good afternoon, Father. This is Father Michael Thomas calling from the staff office at Westminster Cathedral. I am looking, on behalf of the archbishop, into the death of a nun called Sister Margaret, who I believe was with you recently. Are you aware of the matter?'

'Yes, Father. A sad situation indeed. I introduced her to the late Lord Jeremy Roding, who was the local lord of the manor. She was recently found murdered on his estate. Apparently, she was beaten to death with a garden spade.'

'Yes. Well, I wasn't told exactly how it happened, but I learned of this when the police came to see me a couple of days ago. They wanted to know more about this Sister Margaret and how she came to be in Beaumont. I have made enquiries and we simply know nothing of her.'

'Well, Father, the first I heard of Sister Margaret was when I was contacted by Cardinal Pat O'Mara of the Special Assignments Unit of the Vatican. Pat O'Mara and I go way back to when we both entered the priesthood.'

'I see. And how did Cardinal O'Mara know how to reach you, exactly?'

'Pure coincidence. Of course, it was all about Sister Margaret and Lord Roding. Not me. Anyway, I had heard on the old "bush telegraph" that he carries out projects for His Holiness the Pope. He told me what he needed, and he swore me to secrecy. I was quite happy to do my duty.'

'And this Special Assignment was about the conversion of Lord Roding. Is that correct?'

'Yes, it was. I feel so guilty about it all now. She was effectively in my care. I was tasked to keep an eye on her.'

'Did you ever speak to my late colleague Monsignor Tarquin Crecy about her?'

'No. I've heard the name, but I've never spoken to him.'

'Well, he passed away recently. I've been tasked by the archbishop to make enquiries into this case. In the first instance, we received a call from Lord Roding himself telling us about Sister Margaret following her death. I asked around at the time, but nobody here knew anything of her. He cited Monsignor Crecy, but, unfortunately, this was at a time just after the Monsignor's death, so we couldn't ask him about her either. Lord Roding maintained that the attachment was organised by Monsignor Crecy. Since the police contacted us I've made more enquiries, and, I must say, I am still no further forward. The woman is a complete and utter mystery.'

'Did you speak to Pat O'Mara?'

'Yes, and he said that he knows nothing about her.'

'Well, I can't understand that at all. I'm sure it was Pat O'Mara I spoke to. I recognised his voice.'

'Well, he is adamant. So, you see…'

O'Leary became agitated and jumped in. 'So, are you telling me that, in the eyes of the Church, Sister Margaret was not a nun and therefore she is not our responsibility?'

'Precisely.'

'Well, I met her, and she convinced me. We even prayed together, and I can tell you this, Father: she knew the scriptures and the passport that she used to come to this country was a Vatican State diplomatic passport.'

'And?'

'And, it is in the hands of the police now, but, as I understand it, it was genuine in as much as it was authentic. But, apparently, it has never been officially issued by the Vatican. So, we just wash our hands of her, do we?'

'That's about the size of it, Father, yes.'

'But look at the evidence, Father. Lord Roding said that it was organised by Monsignor Crecy.'

'Yes, but they couldn't testify to anything. They're both dead.'

'She was real. I met her and introduced her to his lordship.'

'She's dead.'

'It was initiated by Cardinal O'Mara.'

'He denies it. I'm sorry, Father, but that is the position the Church has to take.'

'Will you tell this to the police?'

'In fact, that is my next unpleasant duty. I am instructed by Archbishop Mahoney to telephone them tomorrow morning, so if you see them in the interim I would be grateful if you don't tell them we have spoken.'

Father Thomas brought the call to an end. Tom O'Leary sat back in his chair. He was shocked. All his faith in the Catholic Church had drained away in the course of one telephone call.

'Blimey, anybody would think you'd won the football pools, Mrs A!' shouted James Davidson. Mrs Aldis was rooting around in the pantry, checking on various foodstuffs in preparation for Saturday's celebration. As she went about her business she was singing "Wish me luck as you wave me goodbye" in a passable imitation of Gracie Fields. Mrs Aldis' mood had certainly changed in recent days. Not only that, but without anybody to cook for but themselves, things in the kitchen were a lot more relaxed. James was certainly happier, since, at the behest of Mr Jenkins, he was not required to be at work until 8.00am rather than his usual time. Yet, and this he could not fathom, he would be paid the same wage as usual.

It was now midday, and, for some reason best known to herself, Beryl Aldis was in high spirits. Although alone, she danced a conga back into the kitchen.

James watched her in amazement, as she danced off into the scullery and returned carrying a bottle of sherry. Then, having selected two beakers from the cupboard, she poured drinks: one for herself and one for James.

'Get that down you, boy. It'll put hairs on your chest.'

James obeyed her to the letter. He downed it in one gulp and then coughed as though his rib cage was about to explode.

'That's bloody horrible!'

'I didn't mean down it in one, silly bugger! It should be sipped slowly and savoured.'

Beryl demonstrated the correct method of imbibing. 'Ooh, lovely!'

She put her arm around James's shoulder and hugged him.

'Ooh! My little James! We're going to have such fun! For once we're going to do as we like. I'm going to make us a lovely meal. Her ladyship's not coming home until next week, so, apart from keeping the house clean and tidy, the time is our own.'

Beryl took the bottle, topped up her glass and grinned broadly. Suddenly, to young James, the reason for Beryl's dancing became clear.

'It's only me!' called Jenkins as he closed the front door behind him. 'Are you up yet?' He walked through to the bedroom where he saw Adina, who was sitting up in bed, in her dressing gown. She was examining some documents that were lying on the bedspread in front of her. At a glance, he recognised the Green and Green Solicitors letterhead and the two cheques she was holding in her hand.

'I was just looking at the cheques the solicitor gave to us, Raymond,' she said excitedly.

Raymond Jenkins suddenly became enraged. 'I see. You've opened my envelope as well, have you?'

'Yes, I didn't think you would mind, darling.'

'Well, I do. It's my business, not yours. You had no right to do that.'

'It's all our money. It belongs to both of us, I'm your wife, remember? His lordship wanted us to be happy together. You trust me, don't you?'

'That's not the point. One cheque is for you and one is made out to me, and it was done like that for legal reasons.'

'OK, if you feel like that, Raymond. You keep yours and I'll keep mine. I'll put it in my own bank account. I know where I stand. I suppose you will want to spend it on your lady friend, won't you?'

'Don't be silly, Adina. You don't know what you're talking about. I have no lady friend.'

Jenkins snatched his cheque from her hand, folded and tucked it in his waistcoat pocket. The red mist had come down heavily, she had unwittingly cited a home truth, and he felt like strangling her, but he retaliated with words.

'Anyway, it wouldn't surprise me one little bit if you caused his lordship's death. You and your special treatment. You probably gave him too much excitement, I expect. You dirty cow!'

Adina poured forth a stream of Romanian invective and burst into tears.

'Don't say that, Raymond,' she sobbed. 'I did not touch him. I went downstairs to see Beryl and when I came back to the room he was lying over the side of the bed.

'Really?' said Jenkins, cynically.

'Yes, I was out of the room when he died.'

'Well, we only have your word for that, my sweet!'

'He was such a nice man. He did not deserve to die.'

'Just remember, Adina, one word from me and I could get you into serious trouble.'

'But you still love me, don't you Raymond?'

Good, thought Jenkins, *I've got her on the back foot. All I have to do to keep her where I want her is keep turning the screw.*

'Of course, I still love you, silly girl.'

She grabbed his arm and pulled him down onto the bed. He laid alongside his wife and wrapped his arms around her. He knew that he still cared for her, but he was damned if he was going to trust her. It took him some time to calm down and relax. His mind was racing, and the fact was that, whether it was Adina or Fanny, he was tending to love the one that he was with. Emotionally, he was a mess, but he was prepared to ride his luck and see where fate would take him.

Raymond knew Adina had a ruthless streak that, he had always imagined, must have entered her psyche as a result of her wartime experiences. He reflected on the fact that they probably deserved each other and should never have children. God only knew what kind of monsters they might create. They cuddled for a while, and then Jenkins remembered the meal that he and Beryl were planning for the staff.

'By the way, Adina, Beryl and I are holding a dinner for the staff at 2.00pm on Saturday to celebrate Lord Roding's life. I think you should be there.'

'I don't feel so well at the moment, but I will come to the dinner party, if it makes you happy, Raymond.'

'It would. I know his lordship would want you to be there. Who knows? You might even enjoy it.'

Adina had her doubts on both counts, but she would show her face.

Before that, though, Adina had her own plans. There was a cheque for three hundred pounds that was burning a hole in her handbag. She was due to meet her "Romanian friend" in Colchester for coffee that very morning. The poor fool was deeply in love with her and she knew he would do anything she asked. She would ensure that he would pay the cheque into her bank account as soon as possible. She would soon need the money. Her future depended on it.

25

DAY TWENTY-FIVE

Friday 5th August 1949

Raymond thought it advisable to telephone her ladyship straight away about the household account, rather than take a chance on her calling him during the luncheon the following day. Besides, he wanted to be able to relax and enjoy the occasion himself. He knew that she would be quite reasonable about the fact that the staff were having their own wake, should she hear of it, but, depending on her mood or mindset, she could turn nasty. He would require a clear head for this conversation.

Cooper dialled the number for the Bedford Square residence. As luck, would have it, Fanny was at home.

'Good morning. Raymond here.'

'Good morning, Raymond. How are you, my darling?'

'Fine, thank you. And how are you today, my lady?'

'Don't start that "lady" lark again, Raymond. You know how it embarrasses me. Plain Fanny will do.'

'There's nothing plain about you, Fanny.'

'Thanks, Raymond. You always say such lovely things. I must say, you're lucky to catch me. I was just on my way out to South Kensington to the gallery, but my taxi hasn't arrived yet.'

'Another exhibition?'

'No, a meeting. Marcus wants more money.'

'Funny you should say that,' said Jenkins. 'Only I rang to ask you to transfer some money into the household account to cover bills and staff wages.'

'OK, but I'll just have to speak to the solicitor about that. I need to get him to free up some funds, but the will is taking some time to go through and they might have to wait for another week or so. If you give me the household bank account details, I'll arrange to have a money transfer made from my private account. How much do you want?'

'Thirty quid should cover it. Only, we haven't paid our suppliers for a few weeks now and they're starting to get a bit chirpy.'

'Can't have that, can we? Bloody vultures. They wouldn't have dared to complain when his lordship was alive. I'll go to the bank this morning.'

'If you would, please, Fanny.'

'Anyway, when are you going to come up to see me, Raymond, darling? I'm missing your hugs.'

'Well, perhaps we can arrange for you to attend another social function.'

'I'll look at the calendar and see if there's anything due to come up.'

'When are you coming back to Beaumont?'

'I have to be back for Tuesday. I got a call from Geoffrey Green, the solicitor, this morning. He wants to read the will and it's not before bloody time, I must say.'

'So, the post mortem has been held, has it?'

'Yes. His lordship died of natural causes. It was a pulmonary embolism. A type of stroke involving his lungs.'

'So very much in keeping with his respiratory illness, then.'

'Yes, it was.'

'Do you want me to be a witness at the reading of the will, again?'

'Yes, Raymond. I'd be grateful if you would. Only, this time, he wants me to go to his office in Colchester. Why the lazy sod can't come to the Hall, I don't know.'

'Perhaps your money is too heavy for him to carry.'

'Yes, if it's in threepenny bits,' Fanny laughed aloud. 'Anyway, I'll speak to you soon, darling. Young Maisie is waving to tell me that the taxi's outside. I must dash now. Bye.'

The telephone went dead.

Jenkins sat and thought for a few minutes. It was obvious to him that their relationship was not doomed after all. He smiled, got to his feet and walked down to the cellar to select some bottles for the luncheon. He believed that his life was back on track.

'Have you got anything I can be getting on with, Sarge?' said Linda Collins, 'I'm up to date with all of my enquiries and I haven't had any new jobs for a few days now.'

'It's always like this towards the end of an enquiry,' said Ian Mills. 'If there hasn't been an arrest and the enquiry runs out of steam, we start to reduce the size of the team. Other jobs come in and they start to take priority.'

'Yes, life goes on,' said Rogers attempting to act the sage in front of Linda, who was one of the few officers who was junior to him.

'We're not quite at that point yet though,' continued Mills, 'The boss has called a meeting for 11.00am and I'm hoping we might pick up some new work from that.'

At the appointed hour, the whole team were assembled, and, for once, nobody was missing.

They stood up as Cooper came into the main CID office. Hot on his heels came Brian Pratt, who had just put the phone down from speaking with Father Michael Thomas. He didn't look happy. Cooper, who had obviously picked up on his agitation, gave him a quizzical look.

'I think we'd better let you go first, Brian, before you bust a gut.'

'Thanks, governor. I've just put the phone down from speaking to Father Thomas at Westminster Cathedral. He was delegated the task of making enquiries to pin down and identify Sister Margaret. It seems that nobody there has heard of her and she is not on any record.'

'So, Monsignor Crecy takes his knowledge of her to the grave,' said Cooper.

'Has Father Thomas been in touch with the Vatican?'

'Yes, governor, and they say the same. Never heard of her.'

'What about Cardinal O'Mara who allegedly contacted Father O'Leary in the first place?'

'Apparently, he denies all knowledge of her.'

'So, Father O'Leary is being made out to be a liar, then,' said Rogers.

'Yes, I suppose he is. In a way,' said Cooper.

'What about the Vatican State diplomatic passport?'

'Apparently, Father Thomas managed to check on that and it's the genuine article, governor,' said Pratt, 'but it's never been officially issued by the Vatican State authority.'

'So, it seems that it was stolen, and the details added later?'

'Yes, governor.'

'What is the position of the Church regarding Sister Margaret's burial?' asked Cooper.

'They no longer wish to get involved with that. They're washing their hands of her.'

Callous bastards, thought Cooper.

'So, that means that she's a non-nun then,' said Rogers. For once, most of the team laughed at one of his jokes.

'Thanks for that, Tom,' said Mills, dismissively.

'I think the Church need to reconsider. In the eyes of the public, Father O'Leary and Lord Roding, Sister Margaret was a nun attached to Beaumont Hall. It won't do the image of the Catholic Church any good at all to take such a position,' said Pratt.

'Nor would it hurt them to cover the cost and send someone along to the funeral. The coroner will want them at the inquest, as well. Brian. Did Father Thomas say they'll confirm their position in writing?'

'Yes, governor. He did.'

'We'll monitor that. If they fail to do so, we'll speak to the coroner. I'm bloody sure that he could bring pressure to bear. If our friends in the press learn about it, they'll have a field day. Any other business?'

Brendan Withers of Scenes of Crime put his hand up.

'Fire away, Brendan.'

'Thanks, governor. We've been working through the fingerprints that were lifted from inside the victim's bedroom. You'll recall that last time I said there were several marks that were identified as hers. Also, there was one on the corner of the dressing table mirror that was identified as Raymond Jenkins.'

'Yes, and you raised the point that he holds spare keys to all the rooms in his capacity as butler,' said Cooper.

'Yes, but we've now checked four more marks, all of which have been identified as belonging to Adina Jenkins.'

'Really?' said Cooper. 'Interesting. Where were they?'

'On the windowsill. They consist of four fingers of one hand and they were found in a position indicating that the hand was pointing in the direction of the window frame.'

'Ian, will you get Adina Jenkin's witness statement out for us, please?'

Mills went to the cabinet and retrieved a file. He selected the document and passed it to Cooper who gave it a quick read.

'Linda, you took this one. She's says she hardly ever spoke to the victim and she has said nothing about going into her room.'

'That's right, governor. She was very firm on the fact. Mrs Jenkins said she hardly ever spoke to her. I don't think that they really got on that well.'

'Given the fact that both must have spent some considerable time with his lordship, you'd have thought, even if they didn't get on with each other, they would have had to have liaised in some way,' said Cooper.

'What did you make of her, Linda? Do you think she would have it in her to have committed the murder?'

'I think, like a lot of people, she had a tough time during the war. Struck me as being quite a strong woman who knows her own mind. If she did do it, it would give her a reason to try to push it on to Savage.'

'On its own, it's not enough to bring her in, but it gives us a start. What would have been her motive for killing Sister Margaret though?' said Cooper thinking aloud, 'She did have the means available and, being in the general vicinity, she might have had the opportunity to do so, but what could have been her motive?'

'Brendan, were there any other outstanding marks?'

'No. As per usual there are plenty of smudges, but the ones that have enough detail have all been checked now,' said Withers.

'Were there any partial identifications?'

'No, sir. Everything has been checked and done.'

'Governor, don't you think it might be an idea to interview her again? After all, she did falsely accuse Savage, in her statement, of being with the victim at 4.30pm on the day of the murder,' said Pratt.

'Not yet. Let's hold off for now. I'd like to have a word with her husband first. We don't know much about her history. I'm sure he'll be able to fill us in on a few details.'

'She came originally from Romania,' said Linda. 'They met when her husband was stationed abroad at the end of the war.'

'The Romanians were on the side of the Nazis, weren't they?' said Rogers.

'They were for a while, Tom,' said Cooper, 'but I want to hear about her past from her husband. He could be holding some significant information about her. Not only that, I want to push his buttons by showing him the *Tatler* photographs. See how he reacts. It might just loosen his tongue'.

'Going back to the subject of fingerprints,' said Pratt, 'I'd like to hear what he says about his fingerprint being found on the victim's dressing table mirror. Just because he holds all the keys doesn't make it necessary for him to go into all of the rooms.'

'Fair comment, Brian. Another thing, did we get the statements from the Winthrop sisters?'

'No, governor,' said Ian Mills.

'Right, let's get on with it. I want to know if the victim's room was cleaned before she occupied it in February, and how thoroughly. Linda, will you see the twins for me and let me know when their statements have been taken?'

Collins nodded and smiled, 'Yes, governor.'

Linda Collins didn't waste much time and she didn't have to be asked twice.

A few minutes after the meeting had ended she was straight on the telephone to Beaumont Hall and spoke to Raymond Jenkins. He arranged for Linda to see the twins at midday. She had intended to interview the girls by herself, but she was unable to arrange transport to get her to the Hall. That being the case she thought she'd exert her influence on Tom Rogers and she called to him across the office.

'Tom.'

'Yes, darling,'

'You know the governor wants me to get statements from the Winthrop sisters?'

'Yes,' said Rogers warily.

'Well, the thing is, I'm not yet qualified to drive police vehicles and I can't get any transport. Would you be a poppet and run me to Beaumont Hall in the Wolseley?'

'Only if you buy me a tea.'

'Of course, I will, Tom. Goes without saying.'

After a roller coaster of a ride to Beaumont Hall, Rogers dramatically skidded to a halt outside the staff entrance. Linda regretted asking Rogers to drive her. He had spent most of the journey trying to impress her with his "response driving", and all the while she had been forced to grip the sides of the seat tightly with both hands. She was now suffering from motion sickness. Not an ideal condition to be in when about to conduct an interview. Linda could have throttled him.

James Davidson answered the door and he showed the officers through to the dining room. They did not have long to wait before there was a knock on the door, and in walked Amy and Cecily. They both wore the regulation maid's uniform, complete with bonnet, and, as identical twins, they were both red heads, each with a pale complexion and freckles. They were quite pretty. But they were so alike, it was almost sinister. After making their introductions, Linda explained to the girls the purpose of their visit and what they intended to do.

Linda decided to interview Amy, and Tom took the other twin, Cecily, to an ante room where he interviewed her by himself. On seeing that Amy was rather nervous, Linda tried to put her at her ease before putting questions to her.

'How long have you worked here, Amy?'

'Two years now. Cecily and I started on the same day. It was Mrs Aldis who got us the job. We'd been cleaning the village hall for a few weeks as a favour. We weren't getting paid, but did it to help Mum and Mrs Aldis, who are both on the committee. When the jobs came up here, Mrs Aldis suggested to Mum that they'd be ideal for Cecily and me.'

'And how old are you?'

'Nineteen.'

'Do you like working here?'

'It's a job and the people are friendly enough. Although it doesn't matter too much as Cecily and I tend to go our own way. We keep ourselves to ourselves.'

'Who is the eldest out of the two of you?'

'I am, according to Mum. Only by ten minutes. I try to boss Cecily around and pull rank. It doesn't work though. She just either ignores me or tries to give me a Chinese burn.' She laughed aloud.

'Who is your boss?'

'We come under Mr Jenkins and Mrs Aldis. She's nice. He's quite strict. He checks our work to make sure that things have been done properly. Cecily calls him Hitler, but not to his face, of course.'

'Did you know Sister Margaret? Or ever speak to her?'

'No, not really. Sometimes if she was coming along the hall to go to her room and we were cleaning, she'd say hello or good morning. But she didn't speak to us apart from that.'

'Did Sister Margaret get on very well with the other members of staff at the Hall?'

'We didn't see much of her really. We're normally gone by 2.00pm. She used to spend most of her time with Lord Jeremy.'

'Did you clean her room for her?'

'No, she cleaned that herself. We cleaned it just before she arrived in May, but we didn't go in there after that.'

'Was that on the instructions of Mr Jenkins?'

'Yes. He made a right old fuss about the fact that there was going to be a nun living here, and everything had to be clean, and spick and span for her arrival. The room hadn't been used for a few years, and it looked like it when we first went in there as well. It was in an awful state with thick dust everywhere and ragged curtains; they even had to get a glazier in to replace a couple of the window panes.'

'Did Mr Jenkins inspect your work after you'd cleaned her room?'

'Yes. He came just when we were finishing putting the new curtains up. He gave the room the once over and locked the door behind us as we left.'

'Have you seen him or anyone other than Sister Margaret go to the room after that?'

'No, nobody.'

'Are there any other rooms occupied on that landing?'

'No. One or two are used for storing things, that's all.'

'So how often were you up on that floor?'

'When she was there, it would be every day. We would just check that everything was all right and clean a couple of times a week when we found something that needed doing.'

'Do you have much to do with the other staff?'

'We know Mrs Aldis, obviously. James Davidson, we were at school with. There's Mr Savage the gardener; he's all right. He lets us make a fuss of the dogs when we see them.'

'Have you ever seen Mr Savage sitting or talking with Sister Margaret?

'No, not that I can remember.'

'What about Mr Jenkins? Did he have much to do with her?'

'I don't really know, but I suppose he must have done.'

'Do you have anything to do with his lordship's nurse, Adina?'

'Is that Mrs Jenkins?' asked Amy.

'Yes, it is.'

'We would see her moving about the place with his lordship. She always seems a bit sad, really.'

'Losing Lord Roding might have something to do with that, don't you think?' said Linda.

'No. She was always like that. But she used to say hello and wave. She wasn't stuck up or anything. We often used to see her sitting on the side of the well.'

'Sitting on the where?'

'On the side of the well,' said Amy.

'Which well would that be?'

'The one in the back garden. It's not far from the kitchen.'

'She would often sit there, thinking and staring into it. Cecily used to say it was almost like she wanted to make a wish, but couldn't make her mind up what to wish for.'

'Does she still do that?' asked Linda.

'Haven't seen her there for a couple of weeks, come to think of it, but there's been a lot going on hasn't there?'

Linda then put pen to paper to take down Amy's witness statement. After completing the statement, she had finished with Amy and, having sent her on her way, she walked next door to check on progress with Tom Rogers and Cecily. She found Rogers sitting alone as Cecily had already departed.

They made their way out of the house via the kitchen, where Linda spoke to James Davidson. 'James, I understand that there is a well near the kitchen. Will you show us where it is, please?'

James guided them to an area some thirty yards from the kitchen door behind an outbuilding. The well was part of a rockery, which was surrounded on three sides by a hedge. A small path led to the one exposed side, but, for persons unaware of its existence, it would have been easy to carry on along the main path and miss it altogether. Linda gazed into the mouth of the well, but she couldn't see the bottom. She picked up a small pebble and tossed it into the darkness. There was a splash after a second or two, and she estimated that it would be a drop of around twenty feet to the surface of the water.

'Tell me, do you use the well to draw water for the kitchen?'

'Not now, miss. They used to in the olden days, but now the Hall is connected to the water mains. I think Mr Savage still uses it sometimes to collect water for the garden.'

Linda thanked the young man and they made their way to the car.

Some poor devil is going to have to go down and search it, she thought to herself.

Trevor Lloyd-Davis sat in his office at Scotland Yard, studying a document with a self-satisfied grin. He had just been given lunch in the House of Commons dining room by a couple of MPs who were opposing a security bill soon to be tabled in Parliament. They had wanted to pick his brains and never one to waste an opportunity, he had been pleased to oblige them.

Now, just when he thought the day could not get any better, he had been given some good news in the form of a secure telegram, handed to him by one of his sergeants, who was now standing at the side of his desk, waiting for instructions.

'Shut the door, Archie, and have a cigarette.'

The sergeant walked to the door and back across to the boss's desk and accepted a cigarette from the silver box Lloyd-Davis was offering up.

'Thank you, sir. The people at SIS have done bloody well for us this time. Who would have thought it?'

'Yes. The CID at Colchester will be pleased. Now they'll know who they are dealing with. Doesn't reflect particularly well on the Catholic Church though, does it?'

'Do you want me to call Colchester and tell them the good news, sir?'

'No, I'll call their DI, Albert Cooper, and tell him, in general terms, that we have an interesting result for him. Then I want you to take the telegram to Colchester and give it to him by hand.'

The security officers (MI6) working at the embassy in Vienna had indeed made themselves busy. Following the referral from Special Branch, in relation to Monsignor Tarquin Crecy and Irma Caro, they had fully utilised their local contacts. The scenario, as described to them was a familiar one. There was one common driver for people wishing to flee Austria by unconventional means, even in 1949, and that was to avoid being held to account for their actions during the war.

It was, therefore, a logical step to have made enquiries with the Jewish Historical Document Centre in Linz. They had come back quickly with a positive result having identified their subject from the details given:

"Irma Regina Caro, née Kurz.

"Born in Graz, Austria, on 23rd March 1919. *Stabsunteroffizierin* in the TK Waffen SS Support Service.

"Wanted for war crimes of murder in Mauthausen Concentration Camp, Linz."

Brian Pratt had just returned to the office having shown DS Archie Ferguson to the front door. It was now 6.30pm. Ferguson had declined Cooper's offer of hospitality, preferring to pursue some personal agenda of his own.

'I can't believe it, Brian,' said Cooper, 'A Nazi war criminal disguised as a nun on our patch.'

'Yes, and it looks like she finally got what she deserved, governor,' said Pratt.

Alby Cooper suddenly became very earnest, 'Brian, I think it best we keep this between ourselves for now, mate. We need the team to remain objective. We can't have them switching off at this stage just because they think she had it coming to her.'

'No, sorry, boss. I agree, of course. Just my automatic reaction.'

'I think that now would be an appropriate time for us to speak to Mr Raymond Jenkins. Don't you? We'll pay him a visit first thing tomorrow morning.'

'What about Mr Stockwell, governor?'

'As luck, would have it, he is on leave until Monday.'

26

DAY TWENTY-SIX

Saturday 6th August 1949

Adina slipped into the study and silently closed the door behind her. The room was dark, save for the moonlight shining through the french windows. She stood for a few seconds to adjust her eyes to the darkness, listening to the sounds of revelry coming along the corridor from the kitchen. The 5.00pm deadline, as set by Raymond for the end of the planned festivities, had been abandoned under pleading from Beryl Aldis and the event had gathered momentum.

Adina's heart was pounding. She was acting on impulse and had not had time to think up a cover story for her reason for being in the room, should she be discovered. Satisfied that the noise was consistent and contained within the bounds of the kitchen, she moved slowly across to the desk, sat in the chair and lifted the telephone. There was just enough light for her to make out the numbers on the dial. She picked up the receiver and rang the operator.

'Operator. May I help you?'

'Yes, I would like Highgate 1354, please.'

'One moment please, madam.'

There was a pause of a few seconds, which was enough to make Adina feel anxious. She realised that her hands were shaking.

'Highgate 1354,' announced a female voice.

'Hello. May I speak to Mr Chaim Herzl, please?'

'Hold on, caller, I will try to put you through.'

Another excruciating pause.

'Herzl,' said a male voice.

'Chaim, it's Adina.'

'Adina, how are you, darling?'

'Not good. I need to come in as soon as possible.'

'I understand. Where can we collect you from?'

'Come to the Hall and wait at the front. If you come in the morning at 6.00am, Raymond will still be asleep. I will be ready for you.'

'We will see you then. Sweet dreams.'

Adina replaced the receiver, slipped out of the room and went up to the apartment.

27

DAY TWENTY-SEVEN

Sunday 7th August 1949

Beryl sat in front of the open hearth in the kitchen enjoying tea and toast, and the equilibrium that it was bringing to her digestive system. She was suffering from the mother of all hangovers.

Although she had washed her face and hands in the sink, Beryl felt grubby and uncomfortable as she was wearing the same clothes that she'd had on the previous evening. Still, she consoled herself with the thought that she wasn't going to see anyone important and she was due to finish work around midday. Her thoughts turned to the staff lunch of the previous day, which, by her own estimation, had been a roaring success. It had gone on well into the evening and had ended around midnight when Raymond, Savage and herself had finally polished off the bottle of whisky. She reminded herself that the lunch had been held in memory of their late lord and master, and smiled at the thought that, apart from a toast proposed by Raymond Jenkins, Lord Roding's name was barely mentioned. It had become more of a wake to mourn the probable passing of their jobs.

Beryl was woken from her thoughts by the arrival of James Davidson.

'Morning Mrs Aldis.' He appeared to shout the words and he was annoyingly chipper. Beryl's thumping head seemed to maximise the sound.

'Blimey, James. Do keep your voice down.' She instinctively looked at the clock and realised that James was early. 'Couldn't you sleep?'

'I slept well, actually, Mrs A.'

'I thought you weren't due in until 8.00am. Given the amount you were drinking last night, I'd have thought you'd make the most of the lie in.'

'No. I woke up at my usual time and I'm feeling good. So, I thought I'd get up and get on with things. A good do, though, wasn't it?'

'Yes. Shame we can't do it more often.' Beryl gave a rueful grin.

'How are you today?'

'I must say, I've felt better, boy.'

'Bit too much cooking sherry, eh?'

'Something like that.'

'You cooked a lovely dinner, though.'

'Yes. I think we used up most of the food, so that was good. Did you manage to see the girls home all right?'

'Yes, their mum wanted them home by 10.00pm and we managed that OK. I think I'm in love, Mrs Aldis.'

'Really? Which one, Amy or Cecily?'

'Do you know? I can't remember. We had a good night, though.'

Beryl sensed a possible upset on the horizon, as she suspected that the twins had been playing games with the young man.

'Just you be careful with those two little minxes.'

'It's OK, Mrs A. I'm a big boy. I can look after myself.'

I doubt that very much, thought Beryl.

'What time did you finish up?'

'Well, Adina had too much vodka and she went up just after you left, about 9.30am. Then me, Mr Jenkins and Savage finished off the Scotch. So, it would have been around, oh, midnight, I think it was.'

'It wasn't really worth going home at all then, was it?'

'No, so I didn't. I slept here, in the chair.'

James thought better of making any comment and just nodded.

Beryl got to her feet and stretched her shoulders. They were clearly giving her some gip.

'Fancy a cup of tea?'

'Yes, please. And some toast if there's any going.'

'Don't push your luck, young man. You know where the bread is. You can make it yourself.'

'Mrs Aldis, there is something I wanted to ask you.'

'Go ahead, then. No time like the present.'

'Do you think that I can have Tuesday morning off?'

'I don't know. What do you want the morning off for?'

'I got a letter yesterday morning from his lordship's solicitors. They want me to go to their office about a quest or something. I have to be there at 11.00am.'

'I think that would be a "bequest", not a "quest".'

'They want me to take my birth certificate with me. So, I've got Aunt Ruby trying to dig it out. She keeps all my important stuff, medical card, school reports and that kind of thing.'

'Anyway, what's a bequest when it's at home?'

'It's a pleasant surprise. I'll write it down for you and then you can go into the study and look it up in the dictionary.'

'So, is that a yes then?'

'Yes, but make sure you're back to clean up after lunch. Her ladyship will be back from London on Tuesday.'

Beryl was pleased for the lad, but she wasn't about to tell him about her own good fortune. These things led to jealousy.

She shuffled across to the sink to fill the kettle. 'Hello. Who's this coming up the drive?'

James joined Beryl at the sink. They both looked through the window and saw a black Buick limousine coming slowly up the driveway towards the Hall. Unable to make out who was inside the vehicle, they watched it until it moved, out of sight, around to the front of the building.

'Oh, my word,' said Beryl, 'I hope it's not her ladyship come home unexpectedly. We're in one hell of a state. Mr Jenkins can't answer the door; he'll be snoring his head off. Smarten yourself up, James. You'll have to go and see who it is.'

Panic had set in; James and Beryl ran around the room gathering up bottles and glasses, and other evidence of the previous evening's celebration, and they unceremoniously dumped them in the pantry. He quickly checked himself in the mirror and spat on his hands to smooth down his hair. He then walked through to the vestibule, and opened the front door expecting to welcome her ladyship or receive some other visitor. He was surprised when after a few minutes nobody had made any approach. He altered his position to investigate further and moved out onto the front steps just in time to see Adina Jenkins embrace a smartly dressed man, who kissed her on both cheeks. She handed him her suitcase and climbed into the back of the vehicle. The man placed the suitcase into the trunk at the rear before climbing into the back of the car himself. The Buick then moved off down the drive at a modest speed. James walked back to the kitchen to tell Mrs Aldis about what he had seen.

'Panic over,' said James.

'Well, don't keep me in suspenders. Who was it?'

'Mrs Jenkins. She's just gone off with some strange men. She had a suitcase with her.'

'Did she look as if she knew them?'

'Yes, she was quite happy to go with them. In fact, one of them kissed her on both cheeks.'

'Well that's foreigners for you,' said Beryl. 'They do that kind of thing all the time.'

'Shall we tell Mr Jenkins?'

'No,' said Beryl. 'None of our business.'

It was early morning when Adina Giurgiu silently closed the door of the south wing of Beaumont Hall. She had one suitcase and she carried it purposefully across the gravel forecourt to the limousine. The driver had brought the Buick to a halt as close to the south wing as he was able, and he kept the engine running while his boss got out of the car to deal with the business at hand.

As she got to the vehicle, Adina was met by her "friend" Chaim Herzl, who placed his hands on her shoulders, they embraced each other, and he kissed her on both cheeks. She got into the back of the vehicle and Chaim placed the suitcase in the boot. Raymond would have been oblivious to her departure. She had left him lying prostrate on the settee in the living room, where he was sleeping off the effects of the alcohol from the previous evening. Adina had anticipated that this would be the likely outcome, as he was already inebriated when she had made her excuses to leave the party the night before. After telephoning her "friends", she had returned to the apartment, packed and hidden her suitcase. She had spent a restless night in anticipation of her departure and her impending flight to freedom.

In the front of the limousine were two Israeli soldiers, both smartly dressed in suits and wearing fedora hats. One of them was the driver and the other a bodyguard. Although Adina was unaware of the fact, both were armed with handguns. She had first met her "friend" Chaim Herzl several months before at the Bevis Marks synagogue in London. He had been responsible for facilitating the regular payments from Adina to her mother, which had been channelled through her local synagogue. The money had provided something of a lifeline for the family.

Adina was now on her way to London and then, she hoped, on to a new life. Chaim had already agreed that he and his organisation would provide the means of transport, and he had arranged for her to be issued with an Israeli passport. As a heroine of the State of Israel, nothing was too good for her.

Meanwhile, Stephen Savage was in heaven. In fact, he was in clover. Lying alongside him was the fair Sister Margaret, who, for once, was topless, her blonde hair was flowing free and she was without her wimple. She thrust her ample breasts into his chest and laid across him. She gently kissed his forehead, sniffed his hair and licked his face. He was the happiest he'd been for a long time. Oh, how he loved this nun. He then became aware of the disgusting smell of her breath.

In startled disappointment, he opened his eyes, focussed and found himself considering the face of Colin, one of his black Labradors. 'Shit! My head is killing me! What was I drinking last night?' he said aloud.

The Labrador was joined by his brother Nigel, and they both stood staring at Savage expectantly. He struggled to his feet, looked at his surroundings and realised that he had been sleeping on the lawn in his front garden.

On seeing that the front door to his cottage was wide open, he remembered that when he had returned home from the party, he was intent on feeding the dogs and had let them out for a run in the garden. He could remember nothing after that point. Just as he was getting his thoughts together, his attention was drawn to the sound of a motor engine, which was coming from the road beyond his garden gate.

He just caught sight of a black car that had entered the drive and had passed his cottage on its way up towards the Hall. Savage, for reasons not even known to himself, did not like the look of the vehicle. Knowing that her ladyship was in London, he wondered what business its occupants could possibly have at Beaumont Hall. He had been taken by surprise when the car had driven onto the estate and did not have a chance to make a note of the registration number. He resolved to do so when it made its return journey back down the drive. In fact, he would do better than that. He would speak to the driver. Savage rushed inside the cottage to collect his shotgun. He eventually found a pen and paper and took up a position sitting on the garden wall. He did not have long to wait. After barely a few minutes had elapsed, the Buick made its way back down the drive towards him. It was moving at no great speed and this give him the chance to surreptitiously jot down the registration number of the vehicle. As the car got to a point some twenty yards away, Savage stepped into the road and held up his right hand bidding the driver to stop. The shotgun remained broken open and slung over his left forearm. Savage saw that there were two men in the front of the vehicle and he could see the look of apprehension in the driver's eyes. The passenger appeared to give the driver an instruction, and the car swerved onto the grass verge to avoid Savage and it moved off down to the main gate, gathering speed. Savage was a lucky man. He had no notion of the fact that the Israelis were armed. It was likely that, had he pointed the shotgun at them, he would have been killed on the spot. Totally oblivious to his brush with death, Savage walked up to the big house to see Beryl and report what he had seen.

At 10.15am, having been woken from a deep drunken slumber, Raymond Jenkins opened the front door of the apartment to Cooper and Pratt. They were the very last people that he wanted to see. He was not feeling at all in tiptop condition. Before going to the door, he had quickly washed his face and hands in the kitchen, and he feared that he probably reeked of

whisky. He felt fragile and vulnerable, but he tried to put on a businesslike front and feigned bonhomie. He was still wearing the previous day's clothes and had not had a chance to change out of them. He looked awful.

'Good morning Inspector, Sergeant. This is an unexpected pleasure.'

'Good morning Mr Jenkins. I trust that you are well?'

'I've felt better. We had a bit of do last night in memory of his lordship. If you wanted to see her ladyship, she is away up in town, I'm afraid, and not expected back until tomorrow.'

'It's actually you we've come to see, Mr Jenkins. We need to have a bit of a chat about the murder. It might take some time.'

'I see. Does that mean you are arresting me?'

'No, that really won't be necessary. Do you want to speak to us here or do you want to come down to the police station?'

'I think I'd better come down to the police station. My wife is still asleep in the bedroom. I don't want to disturb her, if I can help it.'

Jenkins shut the door to the apartment, left with the officers and asked them to wait at their car while he quickly walked to the kitchen to speak to Beryl Aldis. He found her lying on the floor, scrubbing out the stove. She looked, for all the world, like a garage mechanic carrying out an oil change. Beryl was completely unaware of the presence of the police officers and Jenkins very much wanted it to stay that way.

'I'm just popping out to town for a couple of hours, Beryl. I'll see you later.'

Beryl acknowledged him. A few minutes later she went out to the bins and caught sight of Jenkins talking to Cooper. She watched as they both climbed into the rear of the unmarked police vehicle, which then disappeared off down the drive.

On arrival at the police station Jenkins was taken before the station sergeant and then to an interview room on the ground floor. He was supplied with tea and a cigarette by Pratt, who was intent on cultivating a basis of trust and confidence.

Cooper began, 'Mr Jenkins or may we call you Ray?'

'Ray is fine.'

'Before we start the interview, thank you for agreeing to come down to the police station, Ray. This shouldn't take too long.'

'That's OK, Inspector. I'm happy to help.'

'You may call me Albert if you like. Tell us about your job at Beaumont Hall. It is that of butler, isn't it?'

'Yes.'

'Would you say that you occupy a key position at the Hall?'

'Yes, I think so, or at least I thought I did. That's changed somewhat since the death of his lordship. I'm no longer a "gentleman's gentleman" as such.'

'I'm sure that things have changed quite considerably since his lordship's passing. So, does that mean you act as butler to her ladyship now? Is that your role?' asked Cooper.

'No, it isn't. I am looking after the household for her because she spends most of her time in London. So, I suppose I'm going to be more of a manager now, really.'

'Is she going to sell Beaumont Hall, do you think?'

'I don't know. I would say that she's presently taking stock of her life. She's just about to inherit a large estate and I think that she's still coming to terms with the responsibility of it all.'

'Quite an undertaking for her, I should think.'

'It's going to affect her enormously. The thing is, until the solicitors get their finger out and read the will, we won't know the full extent of any changes that may come about. It's causing a lot of concern, particularly among the younger members of staff.'

'Why should it be different for the younger members?'

'Well, my wife Adina and I were lucky in that Lord Roding left us six hundred pounds between us. That should give us a good start elsewhere, if necessary. Beryl and Savage were also left money. The youngsters weren't so fortunate.'

'Do you think you'll lose your job, then?'

'None of the servants really know what the future holds. But, if she sells up, I suppose, yes, I'll be out of a job, and, of course, with his lordship's passing, Adina has automatically lost her job.'

'Do you have a date for the reading of the will?'

'I understand that her ladyship is coming back to Beaumont for the reading of the will next Tuesday.'

'Ray, you'll recall that we spoke to you when somebody made an anonymous phone call about your relationship with Sister Margaret and your frequent visits to the Roding House in Bedford Square. The caller also implied that you have a close relationship with Lady Fanny. Is that correct?'

'We get on well. She's from the East End, like me, and she has a lively sense of humour. She's nice to work for.'

'We believe that you have a closer relationship with Lady Fanny than just that of employee. Why don't you tell us about it?'

'Well, I suppose we have quite a close relationship. I give her support and act as a confidante, if she needs help.'

'Come on, Raymond. It's a bit more than that, isn't it?' said Cooper.

'No, it isn't. What are you suggesting?'

Cooper opened an envelope, took out the contents and laid the *Tatler* photographs on the table in front of Jenkins.

'Raymond, I would like you to look at these photographs. They are of you and Lady Fanny on a night out together.'

Jenkins examined them. Cooper could almost see the blood drain from his face.

'These show you in a number of intimate embraces with Lady Fanny. They were taken at a reunion function at the Windmill Theatre on the day that Lord Roding died.'

Jenkin's jaw dropped. He instantly realised that, in the wrong hands, the photographs would be compromising. Furthermore, given the significance of the day that they were taken, they could be extremely damaging for both he and her ladyship.

'These photos were taken by a society magazine. The irony is that, were it not for Lord Roding's death, they would have been published and your relationship would have been aired in public. It's all about timing and luck, really. We saw them just before they went to press, and we were able to prevent that from happening. We've saved your bacon, Raymond, so I think that a bit of honesty is required. Don't you?'

Jenkins said nothing. He was shaken to the core.

'Now, let's just try again, shall we? What is the nature of your relationship with Lady Fanny?'

Jenkins realised that anything less than total frankness would not do. He sat in silence for a few seconds before giving his response.

'I am her employee; yes, we do have a close sexual relationship; and, with all due respect to my late lord and master, I am hoping that now he has gone we can have a future together.'

'And your wife?'

'What about her?'

'It goes without saying, doesn't it? She's not going to be happy with you going off with Lady Fanny.'

'Of course not, but, now everything on the estate is going to change, that may not even happen. I'm not sure what the future holds.'

'What does Lady Fanny say about the possibility of you being together?'

'She blows hot and cold, to be honest.'

'So, the situation is very uncertain, then?'

'I suppose it is. Tell me, what will happen to these photographs?'

'We'll keep them locked away. For now.'

'What about the magazine who took them? Are they going to publish them?'

'We have asked them not to, for the present. But we might have to get a court order further down the line.'

'And the negatives?'

'We are not in possession of the negatives, but I think we could get them, if necessary. What is your relationship with your wife, Adina, like?'

'Not very good. I think our marriage is coming to an end. I don't really want to be with her anymore, and I suspect that she feels the same way about me.'

'Why? What's wrong with her?'

'She can be very moody and even violent, at times.'

'Violent? Towards whom?'

'Me. I think she has suspected for some time that I'm seeing someone else. She keeps probing and when she gets frustrated she goes into a rage.'

'What was her relationship with Sister Margaret like?'

'Adina wouldn't speak to her.'

'Why not?'

'I can't tell you.'

'You can't tell us, or you won't tell us?'

'I won't. She's my wife. You'll have to ask her.'

'OK, Raymond. I am arresting you for the murder of Sister Margaret.'

Cooper cautioned him.

Jenkins slumped in the chair with his head bowed. He looked utterly defeated. They sat in silence for a few seconds.

'Do you need time to think?'

'Yes.'

Jenkins was taken before the station sergeant and Cooper related the facts of the arrest. The sergeant noted his details on the detention sheet. Jenkins' property was taken from him along with his belt and shoe laces, after which he was placed in a cell.

A couple of hours had elapsed when Cooper was passed a message that Jenkins wanted to speak to him. He was collected by the gaoler from the cell and taken back to the interview room, where he was seen by the detectives, who were brimming with anticipation.

'I understand you want to speak to me, Ray,' said Cooper.

'Yes. I've thought long and hard about this, and now I realise that I've got to tell you what happened. Whatever the state of our relationship, Adina only has herself to blame. She's brought it all on herself.'

'OK then. Fire away.'

'Sister Margaret.'

'Yes. What about her?'

'Adina was convinced that she knew her from the time she spent in the concentration camp. In fact, it became an obsession with her.'

'Did Adina name her?' asked Pratt.

'She called her Irma Kurz. She said that she was a corporal in the SS and that she was a guard at the camp.'

'Which camp was Adina in?'

'I can remember the exact name of it, as, coincidentally, I had the unfortunate pleasure of visiting it at the end of the war. It was Mauthausen, near Linz in Austria.'

'Why did you have to visit the camp?'

'I was posted to the British Mission, which was operating from Vienna. We were sent there as part of the humanitarian effort to try to save and rehabilitate the inmates. We were also tasked to check whether there were any British or Americans in the camp.'

'Did you meet Adina there?'

'No, that came later in Vienna.'

'Tell us about Adina. What nationality is she?'

'Adina is of Romanian extraction, although her mother is Hungarian. She is Jewish, but she doesn't go to the synagogue much these days; what with all the things she witnessed during the war, she's lost her faith.'

'Where did you first meet her?'

'She is a qualified nurse and I first met her when she was working as a nurse in Vienna at the end of the war. She was working for the International Red Cross caring for survivors of the Holocaust.'

'So how did she come to be in a concentration camp?' asked Cooper.

'It was towards the end of the war when she was arrested by the Germans in Linz. She was caught with others forging and handing out ration cards, and then somebody denounced her for being Jewish.'

'And how did she manage to get out?'

'She was lucky because within a month the camp was liberated by the American army and she was moved to a hospital in Vienna. She has told me that, over time, many of her family were killed in the camps. She's got a lot of pent-up hatred and she has terrible nightmares; she has arguments in her sleep, and kicks and thrashes about.'

'What did she tell you about Sister Margaret?'

'She said that she would beat people with a club, including children. Sometimes beat them to death. She hated her, but, at the same time, she was scared to death. She felt that, somehow, she still had power over her.'

'A bit of a coincidence, wasn't it?'

'Yes, it was. I refused to believe it at first. I thought she must have it wrong; for a concentration-camp guard to turn up in the same village as one of her victims in Essex was, for me, just too much of a coincidence to accept. But Adina insisted that she knew who she was, and she made a very compelling argument.'

'Did Adina ever go to her room?'

'I don't think she would have dared. I did. I had to make sure it was cleaned for her before she moved in. Then, when she realised she was here, Adina wanted me to use the key to have a look around to see if there was anything with her name on it, a passport or some clue as to who she really was. She was obsessed and very afraid. She kept on about it. In the end, to try to set her mind at rest, I went in and had a quick look around, when she was out in the garden with Lord Roding. I didn't find anything, though.'

'Do you think your wife killed Sister Margaret?'

'I have fought against it in my mind. I didn't want to believe it, but now I know that she must have done.'

'What makes you so sure?' asked Cooper.

'On the afternoon that she was murdered, when I returned to the Hall, I entered through the main door. This was about 5.20pm. I went up to the apartment and I saw Adina. She was just coming out of the bathroom. She was wearing a blouse, and I noticed that she had specks of blood on her chest and down the front of her uniform. I asked her about it and she told me she'd had one of her nose bleeds.'

'Nose bleeds?'

'She does tend to suffer from those due to high blood pressure. Anyway, I left her to tidy herself up, and I went to make a cup of tea and a sandwich in the kitchen. After that, I went back downstairs to the dining room to carry on working. Then all hell broke loose.'

'You saw the body and all of the blood. Didn't it occur to you the death had been caused by your wife?'

'Not immediately. There was too much going on. When it had quietened down and I'd had time to think about it, I sort of knew. But I was in shock and I didn't want to believe it.'

'Did you ask her about it?'

'Yes. When I finally went back to the apartment, I saw she had cleaned the place from top to bottom, then she had taken to her bed. She pretended that she was asleep, but I shook her awake and told her about Sister Margaret.'

'What did she say to that?'

'She told me she had confronted Kurz and told her that she knew who she was. Kurz had just laughed in her face and said that nobody would believe her.'

'And how did she react to that?'

'She said what came next seemed to be like it was a dream and was happening in slow motion. She lost control. She said she found the spade outside, and then went back and hit her around the head with it. Several times.'

'Did Adina say anything else?'

'She said there was nobody else about. She didn't think anybody had seen her and the sister arguing, so she ran back to the apartment.'

'Did she say anything about taking something from her?'

'Yes. She said that during the struggle between them, she grabbed her crucifix and pulled it off. Then, on the way back indoors, she was in a bit of a daze. She realised she still had it in her hand, so she threw it away.'

'Did she say where she threw it?'

'She threw it down the well.'

'Is that in the garden?'

'Yes. You have to walk past it, along the path, to get back to the house and the apartment.'

'So, what happened to Adina's uniform and the rest of her clothing?'

'I don't know. I didn't see it when I went back into the apartment. I suppose she must have washed it.'

'To be fair, I think that I should caution you at this point, Raymond. You are not obliged to say anything unless you wish to do so, but whatever you say will be taken down in writing and may be given in evidence.'

'You could have told us all about this at the time that you made your witness statement. Why didn't you?'

'Well, I didn't lie. I just didn't say anything. What could I do? She's my wife and she went through hell during her time in the concentration camp. I felt so sorry for her. I mean, it was so sudden. It's not every day that you get faced with a situation like this, is it? I needed time to think. How can you inform on your own wife?'

'You still need to think about your position, Ray. So, in fairness to you, we're going to arrange for you to have a solicitor. My colleague, Brian, will stay with you for now. If there is anything else that you remember, tell Brian or your solicitor.'

Cooper left the room. He needed to get some officers together and go to the Hall to find Adina.

Beryl Aldis answered the door to find Cooper on the doorstep with Linda Collins and Jane Stewart. Apart from the plain

CID Wolseley, which was parked on the gravel drive, there were two marked police vehicles containing uniformed officers and a van from the Scenes of Crime Department. She viewed the whole spectacle with some amusement.

'Good morning Inspector. Mr Jenkins is not here at present, but, since I saw you take him away this morning, I assume that you already know that.'

'Yes, Mrs Aldis. Mr Jenkins is helping us with our enquiries at the police station.'

'Oh dear. So, you have him in custody, then?'

'Yes, but we're here to see Mrs Jenkins and he has given us the key to their apartment. Have you seen her today, at all?'

'The last I saw of her was when she left our party about 9.00pm last night. She had a few too many vodkas and wasn't feeling well. Although she can't have been that bad because young James told me that he saw her leave the house this morning with some men in a black car.'

'Is that right? What time was that?'

'Not long after 6.00am. We both saw the car come up the drive. I thought it was her ladyship at first, come home early.'

'I need to speak to James. Is he here?'

'Yes. He's working in the kitchen. If you'd like to come with me, I'll take you through.'

Cooper and his two colleagues followed Beryl into the house. She led them through the hallway to the kitchen at the rear of the building, where they came across James who was busy banking up the fire. He straightened up as they came into the room.

Beryl opened the conversation, 'James, tell the inspector what you saw when that car came up the drive this morning.'

'Yes. It was just after six o'clock. There was a black Buick. Mrs Aldis and I saw it through the kitchen window coming up the drive. It parked on the forecourt. We thought it might be her ladyship home early, so I went through to the front hall to open the main door. Mr Jenkins would normally do it, but he wasn't about at the time. I opened the door, but nobody came, so I went out onto the steps to see what was happening. I saw Mrs Jenkins get into the car with a couple of men.'

'Did you recognise them?' asked Cooper.

'No, sir. I've never seen them before.'

'What did they look like?'

'A bit foreign looking. They were dressed smartly in suits and they had on trilby hats. They were a bit like the American gangsters out of the films you see at the pictures.'

'Did you hear them say anything?'

'They did speak, but I couldn't really hear what they were saying. But before she got in the back of the car one of the men kissed her on the cheek, and then he took her suitcase and put it in the boot.'

'A suitcase, you say?'

'Yes, sir.'

'So, did she get into the car willingly?'

'Yes, sir. She seemed quite happy to go along with them and she was all dressed up as if she was going somewhere important.'

'Did you get the number of the car?'

'No, sir. I'm sorry, I didn't. But Mr Savage did, and he held on to it for safe keeping. He gave me the number as well. They nearly ran him over, you know.'

James put his hand in a trouser pocket, produced a scrap of paper and handed it to Cooper.

'Thank you, James. Was Mr Savage injured?'

'No, sir. He wasn't hurt.'

'And they drove straight off along the drive, did they?'

'Yes, sir. Mr Savage came up to the house after the car went off and he told us that he'd tried to stop it on the drive. But the driver wouldn't stop for him, and just drove around him, up on the grass verge and away. He was quite shaken up about it.'

'Thank you, James,' said Cooper, who turned his attention back to Beryl. 'Mrs Aldis, may I take it that there are only yourself and James here in the house at present?'

'Yes, Inspector. The twins aren't at work today, and Mr Savage is probably back at the cottage or out in the grounds somewhere.'

'What about her ladyship? Is she not back from London yet?'

'No. She's up there till tomorrow.'

'Linda, will you get one of the constables from outside to come and speak to me? I want him to go and find Mr Savage, and ask him to come up to the house. I want to ask him if he saw anything of the people in the car, and we need that original piece of paper with the car number on it.'

'Yes, sir.'

'We're also going to have to search the well. So, Linda, while you're out there, will you get another one of the lads and show him where the well is.'

Linda Collins went to the uniformed officers who were waiting outside and gave them the necessary instructions. One officer went away with Linda towards the well, the other marched off to speak to Cooper, who pointed him in the direction of Savage's house.

After they had finished with James and Mrs Aldis, Cooper made his way to the south wing with Linda and Jane. On their arrival at the Jenkins' apartment, Cooper knocked on the front door several times with ever-increasing vigour, just in case Adina Jenkins had made it back home, unseen. There was no reply. Finally, Linda took the bunch of keys from her handbag and she opened the front door.

'Hello! Mrs Jenkins! It's the police!' No answer came back to them.

They strode through the apartment, which consisted of a hall, living room, kitchenette, two bedrooms and a bathroom. They found there was nobody present in any of the rooms. The double bed had not been made, but things, generally, appeared to be clean and tidy. Linda and Jane had a browse around, casting a female perspective on the condition of the place.

'Well, I think she's definitely gone for good,' announced Linda.

'How can you tell?' said Cooper.

'Linda's right, governor,' said Jane. 'There are no lady's clothes in the wardrobe or any of the drawers, only men's things, and there's nothing in the bathroom except the usual soap and shaving stuff. No make-up.'

'Jane, before we go any further, we need to get Brendan Withers and his team up here to do a careful forensic examination of the apartment. Will you go outside and ask them to come up, please?'

'Will do, governor.'

'We need to take care because this flat is technically an extension of the murder scene. So, let's not touch anything else, Linda. They'll need to carry out a search to see if they can find any traces of the victim's blood.'

A few minutes later, Brendan Withers appeared at the door to the apartment with two of his colleagues. They were fully briefed by Cooper on the parameters that he had determined for the search, and Withers was already conscious that Cooper and the other members of his team intended to carry out a physical search of their own. But that would have to happen later. For now, Cooper and the ladies withdrew and went back to the kitchen, leaving Scenes of Crime to their task.

'Have you any idea where she might have gone to, Beryl?' asked Cooper.

'Not really. She does go up to London quite regularly. I know that. She's got a Romanian friend up there.'

'A friend! What kind of friend?'

'I really don't know whether they're male or female, if that's what you're thinking about,' said Beryl, 'but she goes up there about once a month and she sends money back to her mum in Romania. Whether that's got something to do with her absence, I don't know.'

'How do you know about that, then?'

'Raymond told me about it.'

'With the greatest of respect, Mrs Aldis, why would he want to tell you about something as personal as that?' asked Collins.

'I suppose you could say we've built up a level of trust between us over the years, and, after all, we're of a similar age. Raymond told me, on more than one occasion, that he was worried that Adina might be having an affair with someone from her own country and that she might leave him.'

'The so-called "friend", you mean?'

'Yes.'

'Does she have anyone who visits her here at the Hall?'

'I haven't seen anybody.' There was a pregnant pause while Beryl, who was standing at the sink, stared into the middle distance and thought about the question.

'I appreciate that you haven't seen anybody yourself, Beryl, but were you aware of anybody coming to visit her? Has anybody made mention of it at all?'

'No, not at all. Well, not until this morning, anyway. Fancy a cup of tea?'

'Thank you, Beryl. If you think of anything else, please let us know. I need to use your phone while you put the kettle on.'

Beryl directed Cooper to the study. The others remained in the kitchen awaiting tea and further instructions.

The call was urgent. Cooper finally got through to Brian Pratt, who'd been in the cell area and had to be fetched by the station sergeant.

'Brian, Mrs Jenkins is not in the flat or anywhere to be found on the estate. Apparently, she went off, quite freely, with some men in a black limousine around 6.15am. We think she's probably scarpered.'

'Blimey! That's not very good, governor,' said Pratt, stating the obvious, 'Do you want me to speak to Raymond about it?'

'Yes. He may be able to shed some light on where she might have gone. If he doesn't know anything, then we'll need to get her details circulated to all ports. Get one of the lads to liaise with Linda.'

'Might sound a bit obvious, governor, but as you haven't been able to search the flat yet, is there any possibility she might have left a note anywhere?'

'We didn't notice one, but I'll let Scenes of Crime know to keep an eye out. I'll also get Linda to search the flat for a decent photo to circulate. Will you ask Raymond where she might be able to lay her hands on one?'

Cooper put the phone down and he redialled the operator.

'Operator. May I help you?'

'Yes, madam. I am calling on behalf of the Essex Constabulary. My name is Detective Inspector Cooper. Will you please tell me where your exchange is located?'

'Yes, sir. We are based at the post office in Thorpe-le-Soken.'

'We are conducting a murder enquiry. Tell me, do you keep records of calls made through the exchange?'

'Yes, we do, sir.'

'Good. I'm going to arrange for one of my officers to come and see you shortly. Her name is WPC Jane Stewart. If you would be good enough to inform your supervisor, please. She will be with you within the hour.'

'Certainly, sir.'

Cooper replaced the receiver and went to rejoin Jane and Linda.

'Linda, I've just spoken to Brian at the police station and he's going to talk to Raymond Jenkins to try to ascertain where Adina might have gone. Not only that, but he's also going to ask him where there might be a decent photograph for us to use to circulate. I want you to take the lead on that and ensure that it gets done, please.'

'Certainly, governor,' said Linda. She very nearly said "Certainly, darling", but just managed to stop short. She fancied him like mad, but she was also in awe of his decisiveness and air of command.

'And, Jane, I want you to go across to the telephone exchange at Thorpe Post Office and see the supervisor. I want to know if there have been any calls put through by them from Beaumont Hall in the last couple of days. You can take the Wolseley.' Cooper handed her the car keys.

Cooper became aware of DC Peter Smith, a Scenes of Crime officer, who appeared in the entrance to the kitchen. He knocked on the door jamb, 'Sorry to interrupt you, but have you got a minute, governor?'

'Yes, Peter.'

'It's just to give you an update on our search of the apartment. We have found some traces of blood in the bathroom, around the base of the taps of the wash basin and on the floor.'

'Good. Was it visible with the naked eye?'

'No, governor. We used luminescent spray on various surfaces.'

'What's that when it's at home?'

'We spray a substance called luminol as a presumptive test for blood. If any is detected, it glows.'

'Thanks for that, Peter. That's something else I've learned today. How long before we're able to establish the blood group?'

'We should be able to give you that before the day is out, governor.'

'Obviously, we have the blood group of the victim. We also need that of Raymond and Adina,' observed Cooper, 'Hopefully, Raymond will provide us with a sample while we have him at the station.'

'Anyway, governor, we just thought that you'd like to know. We're working on the kitchen next and then we'll move to the other rooms,' said Smith. 'So, you can come in behind us and carry out your own search of the apartment, whenever you want.'

'Just one thing, Peter. Have you come across a note from Adina Jenkins during the search so far?'

'No, we haven't yet, governor, but I'll speak to the others and we'll keep a good look out for one.'

'Thank you, Peter,' said Cooper, 'we'll speak to you later.'

Smith moved off along the corridor to return to the apartment and Jane Stewart left to make her enquiry at the exchange.

'Linda, while we are waiting for Brian to come back to us, let's just finish our tea, and then go outside and find out how they're getting on with the search of the well.'

The two of them left the kitchen and walked into the yard to be treated to the sight of a uniformed sergeant leaning over the edge of the well. He had both feet off the ground and his position looked precarious indeed. He was shouting into the darkness. It was a comical scene, and as Cooper and his young lady colleague stood observing the spectacle, they had to work hard not to descend into fits of laughter.

There were three other uniformed officers who had adopted a kind of tug-of-war stance, holding a rope that was leading into the mouth of the well. It was under severe stress, and they appeared to be struggling. At one point, they nearly lost their grip completely and the rope shot forward a few feet before they regained control of it.

An urgent voice of alarm came from down below.

'Oi! Don't let go for Christ's sake. It's full of water down here!'

'How deep do you reckon it is then, boy?' shouted the sergeant, who was apparently unconcerned about the man at the end of the rope.

'I reckon I'm about three feet above the surface of the water, Sarge. If you just keep me in this position, I'll drop the plumb line in and try to gauge how deep it is.'

There was a pause of a few seconds.

'If I stand in it, it'll be up to my waist!'

'Well, what are you waiting for then?' shouted the sergeant, 'You can swim can't you?'

'Bloody hell, Sarge. I'm going to get soaked!'

'We've still got you on the rope, so stop bloody moaning and just get on with it, will you?'

There was nothing else for it but for the constable to get under the water and perform a gradual fingertip search along the bottom of the well. This went on with him shouting, 'Going in!' every time he submerged himself. After he had dipped himself for a fifth and final time, he returned to the surface and shouted triumphantly, 'Got it!'

'Got what?' shouted the sergeant.

'The cross!'

The tug-of-war team slowly and carefully pulled him back to the top. PC Wally Blackmore, whose vest and uniform trousers were completely saturated and covered in mud, emerged from the mouth of the well, triumphantly carrying his prize.

Cooper strode across to him, saying 'Well done, boy!' He patted the constable on the back.

'Is this what you wanted, sir?' said Wally holding up the crucifix for Cooper's inspection.

'That's it precisely. You've just found a crucial piece of evidence in the solving of a murder. Well done, boy,' said

Cooper, who was grinning broadly. He took the crucifix from the young officer, placed it into an evidence bag and got him to sign the exhibit label. 'I shall be recommending you to Mr Stockwell for a commendation, young Wally.' Cooper reached into his trouser pocket and took out a half-crown piece. He handed it to the officer. 'Here, get yourself cleaned up back at the nick, and buy yourself a cup of tea and a sandwich.'

The young officer accepted the money gratefully. 'Thanks very much, governor.'

'Well, Jenkins was right about that, wasn't he?'

'Yes, Linda. He knew where it was all right, but I think we do need to be careful. He's not totally alibied himself, and, perhaps I'm being over cautious, but his wife has suddenly gone missing,' said Cooper.

'Yes, but the kitchen porter James was convinced that she went off willingly with the men in the car.'

'I agree, Linda. But why wouldn't they stop for Savage?'

'I know. Strange behaviour. If the situation were innocent.'

'Not only that, we've found blood in his apartment. We need to establish the blood group and ascertain whether it might have come from the victim. This case is not cut and dried by any means.'

Cooper became aware of Savage, who was lurking with a young constable by the kitchen door. He sent Linda across to speak to them and she returned a few minutes later.

'I'm going to take a witness statement from Mr Savage, governor. As you know, he took down the registration number.'

'Brilliant. Now we've confirmed it, we need to get it circulated and checked for the details of the owner. I'd like to know who we're dealing with.'

It was a clear, sunny morning and the Buick, having made its way through the Essex countryside, was now passing through North London. As it was a Sunday, there had been very little traffic on the roads; nonetheless, the driver had driven sensibly within speed limits so as not to draw the attention of any passing police patrol. The driver and bodyguard were separated from the rear compartment by a glass partition, so Adina felt that she could speak freely.

'I really want to thank you, Chaim. You are my saviour. It has been a very stressful time for me. I don't know what I would have done without you.'

'You don't have to keep thanking me, Adina. You have done a great service. If only the people knew, they would always be very grateful to you.'

'I would be happier if, for the moment, you said nothing to anybody else about it until I am completely safe.'

'Yes, of course, Adina.'

'What will happen now?'

'Arrangements will be made for your mother and sister to be taken to Vienna, where they will meet us in a few days when we fly out. Then we will all travel on to Israel together.'

'We?'

'I will travel with you. We will travel as husband and wife, and you will have an Israeli passport.'

'You mean I have to marry you?'

'No, that won't be necessary,' he said laughingly. 'It's just a cover to help you get safely through passport control. It should make our passage much easier. That's all.'

'Where will I be until we make our journey?'

'You will stay within the Diplomatic Mission complex. It is safe there and the British authorities cannot touch you. It is like a little piece of Israel.'

'And when we get to Israel?'

'We will find you and your family a house and a job within the Government Service.'

'And you?'

'I expect that I will be reassigned somewhere. I might even go to America, I don't really know. I go where they send me.'

Adina was content and not a little relieved. She sat back in the luxurious leather seating of the Buick and looked across at Chaim. He was dark and very handsome. She wondered what the future held for them both and whether they might even be together.

As they passed through the streets of Islington and on up the Holloway Road, Adina noticed a signpost indicating the way to HM Prison Holloway. Her stomach became knotted with fear and she was suddenly gripped by nausea. She imagined the noose. It reminded her that her fate was not yet assured.

'We can only have missed her by a couple of hours, Raymond,' said Cooper.

'If only I'd made the effort to check on her before I left with you this morning. We might have stood a better chance of finding her.'

Cooper was in no mood to be charitable.

'Yes, Raymond, but if we had, you probably wouldn't have told us the truth about her committing the murder. Would you?'

'Probably not.'

Jenkins was sitting at one end of the wooden bed in his cell, with his shoulders hunched over. He looked grief stricken, and, due to him suffering from claustrophobia, he'd had a dreadful time in the cells.

'She didn't say anything about going anywhere yesterday. But we had a row a couple of days ago and she wasn't happy. She's been talking recently about going back to Romania to visit her mother.'

'What was the row about?'

'I was annoyed because she was going through my writing bureau and interfering with my papers. The other day we were each given a letter by Mr Green, his lordship's solicitor, which contained a cheque for three hundred pounds. She opened it. When I argued with her about going through my private papers, she told me to keep my cheque and she'd pay hers into her own account.'

'And, did she pay it into her account?'

'I don't know, but I don't think she'd have had much chance. It was only given to her in the last few days.'

'Where does she have her bank account?'

'Well, she doesn't know that I know this, but I once saw a letter in her handbag. Its Martin's Bank in Shoreditch.'

So, you are quite content to go through her handbag, thought Cooper, *but you don't like her going through your papers.* Cooper wasn't going to press the point with him. He had to try to keep him on side.

'Which is where you drop her in London to see her friend?'

'Yes, that's right.'

'Do you think that she might have gone to see this "friend" of hers?'

'Maybe. I can't imagine that she's gone anywhere else. She doesn't really know anybody else outside of Beaumont and she hasn't got much money. Well not until her cheque clears at the bank anyway.'

'What do you know about this friend?'

'I think he's Romanian, and Jewish, because he was always arranging to get money sent across to her mother through the synagogue.'

'This is a man that she meets in Shoreditch, is it?'

'Yes.'

'Didn't you mind her meeting a bloke?'

'I wasn't too happy about it, to be honest, but I had to trust her. I couldn't lock the girl up twenty-four hours a day, could I?'

'No, I suppose not. Do you know where they used to meet?'

'No, not really. It was normally just in a café somewhere, but I don't know which one. After they'd had their meeting, she would go along to Liverpool Street, get the train back to Colchester and then get the bus to Beaumont.'

'What sort of passport has she got?'

'Romanian.'

'Is it still in date?'

'Yes, I think it's probably still got a couple of years to run.'

'Raymond, I know you've now had access to a solicitor and he's advised you to cooperate with us, which you're doing, but we need you to stay here for a little longer. We also need you to give a blood sample. Are you happy to do that?'

'What for?'

'To check against the blood found in your apartment.'

'You found blood in our apartment? Where did you find it?'

'In the bathroom. It could be Adina's blood, for all we know.'

'Why should it be Adina's blood? I haven't done anything to her.'

'I'm not saying that you have, but you told us earlier about her nosebleeds.'

'Yes, OK. Well, I suppose on that basis it could be hers. Whatever you want.'

'Do you happen to know her blood group?'

'No, but she was under Doctor Graham Bull, at the Beaumont practice. He might be able to tell you. She saw him a few times about women's problems.'

Cooper exited the cell and locked the door behind him. Mindful that Jenkins had expressed that he was prone to claustrophobia, he left the small window flap open. He went upstairs to the main CID office where the team were assembled.

'Right, folks, as you all now know, it appears that Adina Jenkins is the person responsible for the murder of Sister Margaret. But, unfortunately, she left home before we got to Beaumont to arrest her. However, just because we missed our murderer, it doesn't mean that we can't find her again. Let's look at what we've got to go on. First, anything on the blood found at the apartment?'

'No, governor, not yet,' said Mills.

'OK, perhaps it's a bit early. Just bear in mind that we haven't yet been able to make comparisons with the blood of Adina or Raymond Jenkins anyway. It could just as easily belong to them.'

'How are we going to get her blood type, boss?'

'Good point, Ian. Although she is at large, we might be able to get her blood type from medical records. She is under the Beaumont surgery. What have we got on the Buick?'

'We got the registration number of the Buick from Mr Savage, as you know, and we found that it's registered with Middlesex County Council. I had to make a series of phone calls to identify the keyholder and get him out of his home on a Sunday to check their files. He wasn't a happy man. But it seems the car is registered to the Israeli Diplomatic Mission at their Embassy in Kensington.'

'Christ!' said Cooper, 'That's all we need.'

'Doesn't stop us from arresting her if we find her though does it, governor?'

'No, Ian, it doesn't. What about your enquiries with the telephone exchange, Jane?'

'Very interesting, governor. It seems that only one call was made from the Hall on Saturday. That was to the number Highgate 1354. This apparently relates to the Israeli Diplomatic Mission at an address in Highgate, North London.'

'Right. We do know that she's of Jewish extraction and it rather looks like the Israelis have got her. Ian, have Brian and Tom Rogers left to go to Croydon Airport yet?'

'Left about an hour ago, governor. They've got a good recent photograph of her and we've already spoken to the Metropolitan Police and Immigration.'

'Right. When they phone in, we need them to go on and have a look at the Highgate address and sort out an OP [Observation Post].'

'Leave it with me, governor.'

'Good. That's that covered then. I managed to speak to the Special Branch duty officer at Scotland Yard earlier. Apparently, they don't have a good relationship with the Israelis, and because the embassy and the Highgate address are diplomatic premises, we can't just walk in without an appointment.'

'Can't we just make a direct approach with a phone call, governor? She is wanted for murder after all,' said Mills.

'No, Ian. As it stands, the Israelis think that we have no knowledge of their involvement. I want to keep it like that. Once we get the OP sorted out, we'll keep the Highgate address under twenty-four-hour observation for a few days to see if we can get sight of her. The moment she steps out on the street, she's in play. I need you to organise a rota.'

'Yes, governor.'

'We do know that she was given a cheque for three hundred pounds, left to her by Lord Roding. She banks at Martin's in Shoreditch. The cheque will take a few days to clear and she is going to need the money. That probably represents our best chance of getting her. So, tomorrow morning, I'm going up to London to see the people at the bank. Linda, I want you to come with me.'

'You were going to say something about the victim, governor,' said Ian Mills.

'Yes, thanks, Ian. I must confess that I was in two minds as to when to disclose this information to you. Now, I'm going to tell you something that I've been aware of for a few days. It is imperative that you tell nobody outside of this room. Throughout the investigation we have been liaising with Special Branch at Scotland Yard. They have been running an intelligence operation for some time into certain members of the Roman Catholic Church who have made it their business to hide and move members of the IRA and Nazi war criminals. We have it on the highest authority that Sister Margaret's real name was Irma Caro née Kurz. During the war, she was an SS concentration-camp guard at Mauthausen Camp near Linz in Austria.'

The team were stunned at this revelation. Jane Stewart was the first to ask the obvious question.

'What the hell was she doing here, governor?'

'She was hiding, Jane. She is wanted for war crimes, including murder.'

'But she was Swiss.'

'No, she was Austrian,' said Mills.

'Now we know who and what she was, it does explain something else.'

'What was that, governor?'

'During the post mortem, the pathologist drew our attention to some scar tissue which was under her left arm, between her elbow and armpit. He put it down to an injury sustained during the war. Can't blame him for that; after all, we believed that we had a dead nun on our hands.'

Linda was agog and just wished Alby would spit it out, 'What was it?'

'I have since learned that, during the war, members of the *Schutzstaffel*, the SS, all had their blood group tattooed on their left arm in the exact same place. Many also had SS insignia accompanying the blood group. At the war's end, those who could had the details eradicated medically. Some cut them out themselves.'

'With respect, governor, why didn't you tell us this information earlier?' asked Jane.

'Apart from the fact that we don't want it to be put into the public domain, it's fair to say that some of us, myself included, suffered at the hands of the Nazis during the war. So, we know what it means to people.'

'We wouldn't have said anything, governor,' said Jane, registering her disappointment.

'I don't suppose you would, Jane, but it's not just that. We don't want anybody to soft pedal on this case just because she was an Austrian Nazi. I recognised that it would be quite natural for people to think that "she had it coming to her", but we must be professional. The case is almost solved, and that's due to your dedication and painstaking work. I want us to see it through to the end.'

'So, why was she murdered then, governor?' asked Jane.

'Well, it was a clever move on the part of Cardinal O'Mara to have Crecy bring her over so that she could hide in plain sight. But you would certainly have bet against the fact that one of her concentration-camp victims, namely Adina Jenkins, was already living at the Hall.'

'Bit of a coincidence, wasn't it? said Jane.

'According to Raymond Jenkins, he thought the same. But, Adina, who is Jewish, told him that she recognised her from her days in Mauthausen. In the end, she confronted Kurz, who didn't deny who she was and just laughed in her face. Adina lost control and beat her to death in a fit of rage.'

'He said all that during interview, did he, governor?' asked Ian.

'Yes, he did, and quite without prompting he came up with the name Irma Kurz and Mauthausen Concentration Camp, which corroborated what Special Branch managed to find out from their enquiries.'

'Sounds pretty conclusive then, boss,' said Jane.

'It does, but we need to just bear in mind that there are bloods still to be compared and that Raymond Jenkins would have had a half-hour opportunity to have killed her himself. After all, he did tell us where to find the crucifix. Only the killer or someone they had informed would know about its location.'

'But he had no obvious motive,' said Mills, 'and Adina would have had a strong reason to have killed her.'

'Quite right, Ian. Anyway, before we do anything else, I'm going to call Mr Stockwell at home to apprise him of the situation and try to get some more troops.'

The team filed away from the meeting, still amazed at what they had heard and saddened by the fact that Cooper hadn't felt able to trust them until then, but totally understanding his reason for playing his cards close to his chest.

28

DAY TWENTY-EIGHT

Monday 8th August 1949

'If you and your colleague would like to go through, Inspector. Mr Blenkinsop will see you now.' The secretary ushered Cooper and Collins into the secure area of the bank and directed them towards an open door that stood at the end of a corridor. Framed within it was Alan Blenkinsop, the branch manager of Martin's Bank, Shoreditch. As the officers reached the door, they introduced themselves. They shook hands and, after again producing their credentials, Blenkinsop offered them a seat.

'How may I help you?'

'We are investigating the murder of a nun in Essex. The suspect we are trying to trace, and arrest is, we believe, one of your customers.'

'Good Lord. Really? Which one would that be?'

'A lady by the name of Adina Jenkins.'

'I can't say that I can bring her to mind, Inspector. The name doesn't ring any bells with me.'

'She is married to a Mr Raymond Jenkins, although we have reason to believe that she holds the account alone. Mrs

Jenkins, herself was originally from Romania. She has the maiden name of Giurgiu.' Cooper spelled the name out for him and he wrote it on his notepad.

'No, I still can't place her. Do you have an address for the lady?'

'Yes, Beaumont Hall, which is a stately home belonging to the late Lord Jeremy Roding in a village called Beaumont-cum-Moze, near Colchester. Her husband Raymond was his lordship's butler.'

Blenkinsop jotted down the address. He then rose from his seat, opened the office door and shouted along the corridor, 'Lawson, would you come into my office, please?'

Shortly thereafter, 'You wanted to see me, sir?' said a rather timid young man who, after knocking, had put his head around the door.

'Yes, Lawson. I want you to look up a personal account for me. Will you check to see if the ledger shows any recent activity as well? These are the details.' Blenkinsop handed his scribbled note to the young man who promptly disappeared along the corridor.

'We believe that Mrs Jenkins is somewhere in the London area having left her home over the weekend. We also understand that she received a solicitor's cheque last week for three hundred pounds and that she is likely to try to draw against it over the next few days. Would she have to come to your branch to do that?'

'Yes, she would, of course, unless she has an arrangement with the bank to draw money elsewhere. Not only that, if it were for a significant sum, she would have to gain special clearance, even if it was at her own branch.'

'Would you be made aware of any such arrangement, Mr Blenkinsop?'

'Most certainly. It must be compliant, and I or my deputy would have to authorise it. Also, we would probably have to order the money in.'

'You see, we think that Mrs Jenkins is likely to try to flee the country. Would you be able to inform us if she were to arrange to draw funds from the bank?'

'There is, of course, such a thing as customer confidentiality, but I am permitted to use my discretion, and, in view of the serious nature of the investigation, I'm sure we could keep you informed. As I said, any significant sum would require special clearance.'

'What would you call a significant sum?'

'Anything above one hundred pounds.'

A knock came on the door and the young clerk re-entered the room. 'I found the account, sir.'

'Well done, Lawson. Which name is it in?'

Lawson made an abortive attempt to pronounce the name Giurgiu. Collins wanted to laugh and purposely avoided Coopers gaze to prevent herself from doing so. She was embarrassed for the lad, but he appeared to remain unabashed.

He continued, 'It's listed at the address given, sir. The ledger shows that a cheque for three hundred pounds was paid in last Friday. It has been sent for clearance.'

'Did you find the deposit voucher?'

'Yes, sir. It was paid in by another individual with a surname beginning with H. I couldn't read the signature, but I have compared it with the customer's signature and it's definitely not hers.'

'What other activity is there on the account?'

'The customer doesn't have a cheque book. It's a savings account, sir. Apart from the uncleared cheque, she has a balance of fourteen pounds, three and sixpence.'

'Thank you, Lawson. You may leave us now.'

The young assistant left the room. 'So, that confirms what you told me earlier, Inspector. I will expect the cheque to have cleared on Wednesday, at the earliest.'

'Is my understanding, correct? If Mrs Jenkins wants to draw against the cheque a sum of more than a hundred pounds, she must do so by arrangement?'

'Yes, and in that event, I would be able to inform you so that you can meet the lady.'

'Excellent. Obviously, if you could buy as much time as you can for us, we'd really appreciate it. That way we can get our people in place.'

'I'll do what I can without arousing suspicion, Inspector.'

Linda supplied Blenkinsop with the relevant contact telephone numbers and after thanking him, she and Cooper left the bank.

'Looks promising,' said Linda as they got back to the car.

'Yes,' said Cooper, 'I only hope that they give us enough notice. I should hate for us to miss her again. If that happens, I'll be writing reports about it from now until Christmas.'

'Couldn't we get whoever's in the OP to cover it, if we get short notice?'

'Yes, that's a possibility. Right, young miss, let's go and see what the Highgate address looks like. You've got the A to Z. Show me if you can navigate on land as well as at sea.'

'I'll do my best, governor darling. Cheek.'

The Wolseley was moving slowly along Hampstead Lane with Linda in the front passenger seat peering through the window at the various large properties on her nearside.

'I think this is it here. Yes, Roman Hill House.'

The house was contained within a compound surrounded by high walls of at least ten feet in height, which were topped with razor wire and fronted by large double gates. To the right of the gates was what appeared to be a porter's lodge.

'Good. We'll find the nearest telephone box and call Brian in the OP. Then we'll have a walk around and get the lay of the land.'

Cooper drove on to the next telephone kiosk, leaving Linda in the car while he made a call to the number that had been provided by Brian Pratt.

'Hello.'

'Brian. It's Alby Cooper.'

'Hello, governor. Where are you?'

'In a phone box, up the road from the Highgate address. Where's the OP?'

'We managed to get into the offices above the undertakers.'

'Is that covert enough, do you think?'

'Quiet as the grave, governor.'

'What have you told the undertaker about your reason for being here?'

'There's only the undertaker and his daughter here. I told them that we're trying to arrest somebody who's been doing a series of burglaries in the area. He's quite happy to have us on the premises. Makes him feel secure, I think.'

'What sort of view have you got?'

'We're on the second floor. We can see right over the wall into the compound and the front steps to the house.'

'Any security around?'

'Yes. There's the guardhouse by the front gates, which is always occupied, and we've seen a picket patrol moving around inside the grounds. All in all, it's on about two acres of land.'

'Have you seen the Buick?'

'Yes. We've seen it a couple of times, but only with the driver in it.'

'And any sign of Adina Jenkins?'

'No sign of her, governor.'

'It's a bit short notice, I know, Brian, but are you OK to stay put there until we can get you relieved at 7.00am tomorrow?'

'One moment, governor.'

Cooper could hear Brian checking with his colleague in the background; he then came back on the phone.

'Yes, we're both fine with that. We are warm enough, with plenty of food and drink. I anticipated that we might have to stay longer, so I've already primed the owner, Mr Payton, and he's agreed to it. They're keeping us well supplied with cups of tea.'

'OK. Linda and I are just going to walk around the area for a while to get our bearings and see if there are any other entrances. Then we'll go to the local nick to make some phone calls. I'll call you later.'

'Righto, governor.'

Cooper left the kiosk and walked back to the car. He chuckled to himself. '"Quiet as the grave", indeed.'

❖

Adina was standing by the window of the apartment, peering through the net curtains. She had been in the, so-called "safe house", for barely a day and had kept an almost constant look out for any signs of police activity. Although Adina felt safe within the confines of the Diplomatic Mission, she was suffering from anxiety and felt very restless.

'Do come away from the window, Adina,' said Chaim Herzl.

'I can't help thinking that they'll find me. I just want to go now, get to the airport and get on the plane.'

'You are perfectly safe, Adina. Nobody will find you here, and, even if they did, they're not allowed to enter the Mission.'

Herzl walked across to her, wrapped his arms around her from behind and kissed her on the cheek. He then took her by the hand and led her back to the sofa.

'I can't stop thinking about Raymond. He must be very worried about me. He'll be wondering where I am.'

'You can't afford to worry about him, Adina.'

'I know.'

'And you can't afford to telephone him either. It would only complicate things for you. He must not know where you are. Promise me you won't try to call him,' pleaded Herzl, with slight impatience in his tone.

'I wasn't going to call him. I just want the bank to clear the cheque, and then I can have my money and I can leave the country.'

'It's not just the money that is causing the delay, Adina. We need to coordinate the movement of your mother and sister for them to arrive in Vienna on the same day as you. We must get them out of Romania first, then we can all go on to Israel together.'

'Still, I need to go to telephone the bank to find out when the cheque will clear and what they will need from me.'

'I will take you to a telephone box at the back of the complex and I will be with you when you make the call. We can't have the police tracing the call back to here. The less they know about our involvement the better.'

Herzl escorted Adina to the rear of the Mission and they left the compound through a small service gate for which he held the keys. This led to a quiet, tree-lined avenue bordering Hampstead Heath. They walked to a telephone kiosk that was barely thirty yards from the gate, and, armed with the necessary change, Adina dialled the number for Martin's Bank in Shoreditch. She was finally put through to the branch manager.

'Blenkinsop. May I help you?'

'Yes, Mr Blenkinsop. My name is Miss Adina Giurgiu. I have a savings account at your branch. A colleague of mine paid a solicitor's cheque into your branch last Friday and I am waiting for it to clear. Can you tell me how long it will take?'

'That would take about five days, madam. Today is Monday, so it should be cleared by Thursday, all being well.'

'I see.'

'How much is the cheque for, madam?'

'Three hundred pounds. It was money left to me by my employer, Lord Roding, who has died. The original cheque is on the account of Green and Green Solicitors. I would like to draw the money out in cash. Can you do that for me?'

'Yes, we can certainly do that, madam.'

'What do you need from me?'

'A letter requesting the payment in cash. If you would prefer, you may deliver that to us on the day you draw the cash. We will need you to have your savings passbook and your passport. Would you like us to telephone you when the cheque has cleared?'

'No, thank you. That won't be necessary. I will call you again on Thursday morning.'

Adina ended the call and Herzl shepherded her back into the compound, returning her to her accommodation. Adina was starting to worry, and, on reflection, she was concerned that her wish not to receive notification by telephone might have aroused suspicion. However, she reassured herself with the knowledge that the cheque was valid; and the account was her own. The bank couldn't possibly know of her situation. Within ten minutes of her replacing the receiver, Blenkinsop had related the details of the call to Linda Collins.

29

DAY TWENTY-NINE

Tuesday 9ᵗʰ August 1949

It was to be a red-letter day for the company of Green and Green Solicitors. Geoffrey Green, the senior partner, had arrived early, and he had twice mulled over the final will and testament of Lord Jeremy Roding. At 11.00am today he was due to read the will to interested parties and he was not looking forward to it. He anticipated that Lady Francine Roding was going to be unhappy with what he had to tell her. Green was going to need support, and as soon as his junior colleague, Reginald Cohen, arrived for work he called him into his office.

'I'm going to require your help this morning, Reginald.'

'What for, sir?'

'The reading of Lord Roding's will.'

'What time is the appointment?'

'It's at 11.00am.'

'I think I've got an appointment at 11.00am, sir.'

'No, you haven't, young man. I've checked.'

'Do I really have to deal with that bloody awful woman, sir?'

'Yes, Reginald. She is our client, after all, or at least her late husband was. A good man was Jeremy Roding, and a great bon viveur in his day. I dined with him on several occasions. He kept a good table.'

'Pity he didn't have good taste in women,' said Cohen.

'Now do keep a respectful tongue in your head. We made you a partner at a relatively early stage in your career. You can't just pick and choose to deal exclusively with the more pleasant clients. This is going to be difficult and I am going to need your support.'

'Sorry, sir.'

'Anyway, here is the will. You had better read it and then you'll realise where the conflict is likely to arise later.'

'Very good, sir.'

Geoffrey Green left the room to visit the lavatory. On his return, Cohen was just finishing reading the document.

'I see what you mean, sir,' said Cohen, taking a long draw on his cigarette. 'Wouldn't it be better to just have a constable on standby in reception?'

'Where on earth is everybody this morning, Mrs Aldis?' said her ladyship as Beryl placed the plate of bacon and eggs in front of her.

'Raymond has gone into Colchester, Adina has gone away for a couple of days to stay with one of her Romanian friends and young James has the morning off to accompany his aunt to an appointment.'

Beryl was feeling in a particularly mischievous mood this morning. She knew about James' impending visit to the solicitor's office and that Raymond was helping the police with their enquiries. But she was going to disclose the minimum of information and she would let her ladyship find out the full details for herself. As far as Beryl was concerned, her future did not lie at Beaumont Hall and she was past caring. Now that she had her nest egg of three hundred pounds, life was about to change for the better and she would soon be setting up her own tea shop. Lady Fanny Roding could go to hell.

'I see, and did Raymond take the Rolls?'

'No, my lady. It's still sitting in the stables.'

'So how did he get into town?

'He got a lift. Raymond has been working hard on the Rolls, preparing it for sale, so he probably didn't want to take it out.'

'He was supposed to be coming with me to the solicitor's this morning, I hope he's back in the next hour, otherwise I'll have to go on my own by taxi.'

Fanny had arrived back at Colchester on the last train the previous evening and had not thought to inform Raymond. She now regretted digging her heels in about the use of the Rolls and wished that she had let Raymond drive her to London. *Still, never mind,* thought Fanny, *things are about to change and they're all going to have to get used to it.*

As the time approached 10.15am, there was still no sign of Raymond, so Fanny ordered a taxi, which arrived at the solicitor's just before the meeting was due to begin. As she entered the reception area, Fanny immediately caught sight of James Davidson, who was seated with his aunt Ruby.

'Aren't you supposed to be at work, young man?' said Fanny, with a tone of disapproval.

Both James and his aunt got to their feet, and Ruby spoke in his defence. 'He got permission to take the morning off, my lady. He has to see the solicitor.'

'I see,' said Fanny, 'I suppose his lordship has left you some money as well. There'll be none left at this rate. Well, you can earn it, since you are here, by acting as my witness in the absence of Mr Jenkins, when the time comes.'

At this point, Reginald Cohen stepped into the room, introduced himself and, having checked the identity of Ruby Gedge and the fact that it was she who had been James's legal guardian, he ushered them all into the office, where they were greeted by Geoffrey Green. They were seated, and Green spread the pages of the will out across the table in front of him.

'Thank you for coming, my lady, Mr Davidson, Miss Gedge. I shall get straight down to the business of reading the last will and testament of his lordship, the late Jeremy John Beaumont, 7th Lord of Roding, which was sworn under oath by his lordship on the 18th July 1949. Right, if you are ready my lady,' said Green.

'Let's just get on with it shall we,' said Fanny in exasperation.

Geoffrey Green read the document aloud. He went through the usual terms of Lord Jeremy Roding being of sound mind, etc. Fanny wanted him to cut through the niceties and get down to the detail. *What has my husband left me with, you boring little man?*

Green summarised the total estate, of which Fanny anticipated that she would be the sole beneficiary:

'"The estate known as Beaumont Hall, with the main house, its contents and outbuildings, four tied cottages, eighteen acres of parkland and the sum of one hundred thousand pounds, which is held on account by Coutts & Co Bank, 440 Strand, London WC2, I bequeath to my son and heir James Davidson."'

There was silence in the room. James and Ruby turned to each other, but they were stunned and just couldn't find the words to express themselves.

Not so, in the case of Fanny, who erupted, 'Have you gone bloody mad? There must be some mistake surely?'

'No mistake, my lady. Please stay calm, I haven't finished reading yet.'

'"To my dear wife, Lady Francine Roding, I bequeath Roding House in Bedford Square, London WC1, with all contents and the sum of ten thousand pounds, which is held on account by Coutts & Co Bank, 440 Strand, London WC2."'

'We are duty bound to inform all principal beneficiaries of the terms of the will in writing, in due course. The terms being in force from this moment.'

'It's not right. It's not right. I'm not having this!' Fanny leapt to her feet.

'I have here letters written by his lordship that are addressed to you both individually.' Green handed the letters across. 'My lady, should you wish to challenge the terms of the will you would be able to do so through the high court. However, we would not be able to act for you. That is all I am at liberty to say. Mr Davidson, if you would stay behind, there are some matters that we need to discuss.'

'You won't hear the last of this!' Fanny stormed out of the building onto the High Street. She found a quiet spot in Castle Park where she could sit, read and digest her letter.

"Dear Fanny, if you are reading this, you will know that I have finally passed on to a better place. My dear friend and solicitor, Geoffrey Green, will by now have read my last will and testament. I expect that you will be unhappy that the London house and the sum of money are all that I bequeath to you, but this should help you to pursue life in London. Something that I know you have always cherished. However, the family name must go on, and I have been aware that James Davidson is my natural son since the day of his birth. My name is not shown on his birth certificate as his biological father, since I needed to hide the fact from Bettina. I did, however, sign an affidavit and place it with my solicitor at the time of his birth. James' mother, Evelyn, was the sister of Ruby Gedge. We had an affair and James was the result. Bettina was unaware of our relationship. When Evelyn was killed during the war, young James came to live with his aunt Ruby in the village. Although I have been unable to declare the nature of our relationship, I have provided modest financial support throughout his life. It is a fact, therefore, that his aunt Ruby has always known that I was his natural father. As for the relationship between you and I, my dear, I have known, for some time of your closeness to Raymond Jenkins.

"Sister Margaret made me aware of the fact and counselled me about the state of our marriage. It does not matter now. You are free to follow your own path. I wish you well for the future and hope that you find happiness. Yours sincerely, Jeremy."

Fanny sat on the park bench in silence, trying to assimilate the implications of the letter. The reading of the will had presented her with an unwelcome surprise, but the more she thought about it, the more she realised that she would only have had the bother of managing the estate. A costly and time-consuming responsibility, requiring her to spend much of her life at Beaumont Hall. Fanny reminded herself that she had come from humble stock and had started life with nothing. This way, at least, she would still be able to live her life in London and have the man of her choosing. The house was a very valuable piece of real estate in a prime part of Central London and ten thousand pounds was not an inconsiderable sum. Life was indeed about to change, and she was beginning to look forward to it.

DAY THIRTY-ONE

Thursday 11ᵗʰ August 1949

Over a period of three days, the OP was manned constantly with staff on twelve-hour shifts, and, while they had seen the comings and goings of the Buick, there had been no sightings of Adina Jenkins in or around the Highgate complex. This fact did not trouble Cooper too much, as Adina had clearly stated that she would contact the bank on Thursday and he believed that, true to her word, she was likely to visit the bank and claim her bequest. However, Alby Cooper was leaving nothing to chance. He and his team would have the area in and around Martin's Bank well covered.

The bank was due to open for business at 9.30am sharp. Earlier, Cooper, Linda Collins and Tom Rogers had arrived, and had taken up position. They were given a room at the rear of the bank and a telephone with its own outside line, putting them in direct contact with the OP team, consisting of Ian Mills and Jane Stewart at Highgate. Brian Pratt was ensconced in an office above the shop immediately opposite the front door of the bank, from where he could give an early warning of Adina's arrival.

Adina had endured a troubled night. Due to a combination of anxiety and eager anticipation, she had managed very little sleep. She was up at the crack of dawn, laying her things out on the bed and checking the necessary documentation. She just wanted to get on with the day's business. Chaim joined her for breakfast, and, even though they had discussed their plans late into the previous evening, they went over the details yet again.

At 10.00am, Adina put her call into the bank from the telephone kiosk at the rear of the Mission complex.

'Hello. May I speak to Mr Blenkinsop, please?'

'Blenkinsop.'

'Hello Mr Blenkinsop. Adina Giurgiu speaking. I am telephoning to find out if my cheque has been cleared yet.'

'Ah yes, Miss Giurgiu. If you would wait just one moment, please, I will find out what the position is for you.'

Blenkinsop quickly walked along the corridor to fetch Cooper. On their return to his office he snatched up the receiver. 'Miss Giurgiu, your cheque has cleared, and you may draw against it today, if you wish. If I may just remind you that you need the letter that we spoke about the other day, and your passbook and passport for identification purposes. When would you like to come in to draw down the money?'

'I should be able to come to the bank just before midday. Thank you very much for your help, Mr Blenkinsop.'

'It is my pleasure, madam. We will see you later.' The call was ended.

'Thank you for that, sir. Did I hear correctly that she's coming in to the bank today?' asked Cooper.

'Yes, that's right. Just before midday.'

'How did she sound?'

'She did sound rather nervous. She sounded foreign, although I'm not too good on accents, and wouldn't have been able to place her as coming from Romania, or anywhere else, for that matter.'

'Did she give you any indication as to where she was phoning from?'

'According to the girl on the switchboard, she was calling from a telephone box, but beyond that I couldn't say.'

Cooper was animated. As he walked back to the room to inform the other members of the team, he had to stop and take several deep breaths to calm himself. If the operation was to be a success, he needed to maintain control. One thing was certain, they could not afford to miss her this time.

The telephone rang in the bank office at 11.20am and Linda Collins picked up the receiver. 'It's the OP, governor,' she said, handing it to Cooper.

'Hello, Ian?'

'The Buick is at the gates of the complex now, governor. Usual driver with a woman in the back. Turning onto Hampstead Lane and away south towards Holloway. Out of sight now.'

'Thanks Ian. Stay in position and keep us informed of any other developments.' Cooper put down the phone.

'Right, it looks like she's on the move in the Buick with only the driver. She's sitting in the back. She knows you, Linda, so you'd better stay out of sight with me for now. It'll probably take them about twenty minutes to get down from Highgate. Will you let Brian over the road know, please?'

'Yes, governor.' She picked up the receiver and dialled.

'Tom, I want you behind the counter with the two tellers. As soon as they get sight of her paperwork, they'll give you the nod. I'll be able to see you at the counter from my position, but we'll have to move quickly. We don't want her to be spooked and get back to the Buick, and us having a car chase.'

At 11.47pm, the telephone rang in the office.

'The Buick is pulling up outside, governor,' said Brian. 'Engine still running. The driver is opening the back door and our lady is getting out. She's now on the pavement. She's wearing a light-blue, two-piece suit with a matching hat. Looks very elegant. She's going in now. The driver is standing just outside the doorway to the bank.'

Cooper moved along the corridor to take up a covert position that afforded a view of the counter. He could see the outline of Adina Jenkins, who was standing second in the queue. When the first customer departed, she approached the counter and produced some documents for the teller. Although Cooper was unable to hear what was being said, he saw the teller make the agreed hand signal to Tom Rogers, who then slowly moved towards the door leading to the banking hall. He passed through the doorway and walked to a position immediately behind Adina. He was then joined by Cooper, who touched her on the arm. She spun around in surprise and a look of fear came across her face.

'Adina Jenkins, I am Detective Inspector Cooper of the Essex Constabulary. I am arresting you for the murder of Irma Kurz, otherwise known as Sister Margaret, in

Beaumont on the 12th July 1949.' He then began to caution her, but before he could finish, she had collapsed at his feet.

They were joined by Linda who knelt on the floor next to Adina and tried to revive her. She was carefully helped up from the floor and taken to an interview room at the side of the banking hall. A few minutes later they were joined by Brian Pratt.

'Well, the driver didn't hang around. One minute he was standing in the doorway, then he saw what was going on inside the bank and he was off like a long dog.'

'What documents did she produce at the counter, Tom?' asked Cooper.

'A letter addressed to the bank requesting a bank draft for three hundred and fourteen pounds, and a savings passbook and Romanian passport both in the name of Adina Giurgiu. The letter authorises the bank to hand the draft to the bearer.' said Rogers.

'Sorry to say, governor, but having now seen her close up, it's no surprise to me,' said Linda. 'I know she looks very much like her, but this isn't Adina Jenkins.'

'What!' said Cooper. 'Who the hell is it then?'

The suspect lapsed back into unconsciousness. They couldn't tell whether it was feigned or otherwise. As a precaution, she was taken to St Bartholomew's hospital by ambulance where she was kept under police guard.

It was 12.30pm. "Mrs Adina Herzl" and her "husband" were being delivered by one of the embassy drivers to the front entrance of Croydon Airport. As they entered the terminal building, they made their way immediately to the British European Airways check in desk, where they deposited their luggage and collected their boarding cards. Although their flight to Vienna was not due for take-off until 2.00pm, a combination of superstition and hyper-vigilance compelled them to walk immediately through to the departure lounge.

Although outwardly calm, Adina felt that all eyes were upon her as they walked through the building. She chided herself for the fact that, in her excitement at making such a momentous journey, she had dressed as elegantly as her wardrobe would allow. Adina now wished she had adopted a frumpier look. Before reaching the departure lounge, they stopped off at a newsagent's stand to buy a paper and cigarettes. However, on leaving the stand they had got no further than a few yards when a male voice shouted from behind them.

'Just a moment, miss!'

They stopped in their tracks and turned around. The voice belonged to a uniformed constable. Adina's immediate impulse was to run, but she stayed rooted to the spot.

'You've dropped your glove.' The officer held out the offending article at arm's length.

Chaim stepped forward, and he accepted the glove and thanked him with all the charm that he could muster. Adina nodded and was just able to force a smile. They carried on walking. Not a word passed between them until they had reached the departure lounge and were well out of earshot of any third party.

As they sat together, attempting to regain their composure, Chaim realised that Adina was in shock. But, after some soothing words, he managed to restore her to a state of calm. Luckily, their decision to make an early transit to the departure lounge had proved beneficial, as, at this stage, they were quite alone.

'My God. We don't want too many encounters like that. I almost had a heart attack,' said Adina softly. 'Give me one of your cigarettes please, Chaim.'

'But you don't smoke, Adina.'

'Now would be a very good time to start, don't you think?'

Chaim lit her a cigarette and passed it across to her. She sat and puffed at it, displaying all the smoking experience of a ten-year-old girl.

After another fifteen minutes, they were joined by other passengers and members of the ground crew, but time appeared to be passing very slowly.

Finally, at 1.30pm, they were approaching Gate 2, which was open for the boarding of Flight BE345 to Vienna. Adina Herzl produced her new Israeli passport and boarding card for the benefit of the official who was checking passengers' papers at the gate. He gave the documents a cursory inspection and then did the same with those of Chaim Herzl.

The body language of the man on the gate showed a distinctly *laissez-faire* attitude. Since Mr and Mrs Herzl were leaving the UK, and not entering the country, the official did not seem particularly interested in them. The demeanour of the immigration officer had been much the same when, a few minutes earlier, they had passed through immigration control.

The happy couple were escorted to the aircraft which was parked on the apron of the airfield with its engine already running. This was as much a precautionary measure, to minimise the possibility of passenger decapitation, as it was a matter of courtesy. The aircraft was a British European Airways De Havilland Dragon Rapid, a bi-plane capable of carrying only eight passengers.

A stewardess was welcoming the passengers on board and she showed the Herzls to their seats. Adina caught herself studying the others and willing them to deal with their hand luggage and take their seats as quickly and efficiently as possible. As far as Adina was concerned, the aircraft could not take off quickly enough and she had to work hard to supress her anxiety. 'Are you all right, miss? Have you not flown before?' asked the stewardess.

Chaim answered for her, 'My wife doesn't speak much English. She hasn't been on an aircraft before, so she is a little nervous.'

'Perhaps it will help if, when we are airborne, she sucks on some of these.' The stewardess offered a bag of boiled sweets.

Adina took a few and mouthed the words, 'Thank you.'

Adina knew that once they had taken off they would soon be out of the UK jurisdiction and free from any intervention by the British authorities. She relaxed back in her seat.

Adina spared a brief thought for Raymond. She had finally reconciled the fact that he had had designs on the so-called "Lady Fanny Roding", all along, and, now his lordship had departed, they would be able to get on with their romance unencumbered.

She had loved Raymond once. But, increasingly, she had felt herself to be in the way as he seemed to spend more and more time at her ladyship's beck and call. At first, she had told herself that Raymond was merely doing his job and that he was having to cater for Lady Fanny's needs purely because of his lordship's incapacity. It was Lord Jeremy himself who had, quite innocently, alerted her to the possibility that there was something going on between them. He had marvelled at Raymond's devotion to duty and his willingness to make himself available, saying, 'It's almost as if they are a courting couple and he is devoted to her; he's a good man.' Adina finally saw the situation for what it was. It seemed that the old booby did not.

She wondered what would become of their relationship now that Fanny was free to play the field, and there was no longer a need for deceit and discretion. After all, Fanny was now a very wealthy woman in her own right. Raymond, on the other hand, had no more than three hundred pounds to his name. By any objective assessment, he had little to offer her ladyship, and Adina imagined that his days as her paramour were surely numbered.

As for Irma Kurz and the fact that she had savagely beaten her to death, Adina felt only pride. She had, albeit in an uncontrolled and sudden fit of rage, gone some way to avenging the women and children who had suffered and died at the hands of Kurz in Mauthausen Concentration Camp.

Although she, herself, was of the Jewish faith, Adina had become enraged by the fact that Kurz was masquerading in the guise of a Catholic nun and woman of God. As if her evil deeds could be forgotten and forgiven by a contrived change of life and false repentance. It was the hypocrisy, and the callous sense of entitlement, displayed by Kurz that had tipped Adina over the edge.

But, Adina had no regrets. She knew she had carried out

a noble, even heroic, deed on behalf of the Jewish people.

At the end of the flight she would be met at Vienna Airport by her mother and her sister Iribka, and if they did not know about the death of Kurz already, she would tell them about it in due course. Adina had been assured by Chaim Herzl that they would already have been aided in their passage through Hungary and on to Vienna. They would all later be assisted on the final leg of their journey to Israel, a new country, where a fresh and happier life awaited them.

EPILOGUE

DI Albert Cooper found himself with something of a dilemma. The young woman arrested at the bank was identified as Claudia Ben-Bassett, a middle ranking official of the Israeli Government Service. She didn't reach the police station, but later that day, when she'd recovered, she told Linda Collins, at her bedside, that she'd merely been acting as a courier, to collect the bank draft, and hadn't attempted to pass herself off as Adina Giurgiu. Meanwhile, strong representations were being made to the Metropolitan Police commissioner by the Israeli ambassador, who, when pressed, refused to acknowledge the name Adina Giurgiu or Jenkins. However, he claimed that Miss Ben-Bassett was subject to diplomatic immunity and should be released from custody. She was freed within the hour.

At that time, Raymond Jenkins was still sitting at the police station. He'd told them, during his interview, that Adina had admitted to him that she'd beaten Irma Kurz to death, outside the summer house. If this was to be believed, it also had to be considered that he'd said nothing about her being the murderer when he'd made his initial witness statement to the police. However, this didn't make him an accessory to murder, and there was no evidence to suggest that Jenkins had done anything to assist his wife, other than maintain his silence. Certain additional pieces of information had been related to the police by Jenkins, not least of which was the fact that Adina had told him that she'd snatched the crucifix from the victim's neck and had thrown it into the well. She wasn't, however, available to be questioned on this revelation. What if Raymond Jenkins had committed the murder himself? He would also have known of the location of the crucifix, wouldn't he? Cooper wondered whether the timeline of Jenkins' alibi had provided him with enough of an opportunity to have killed Irma Kurz and to have cleaned himself up before returning to the study. He had serious doubts about that hypothesis, and, anyway, what would have been Jenkins' motive for doing so? After consulting the county prosecuting solicitor, it was decided that Raymond Jenkins should be released without charge.

There were several pieces of evidence fundamental to his decision: the fact that Sister Margaret was Irma Caro née Kurz, a Nazi war criminal and fugitive from justice; Adina Jenkins having been a prisoner at the same concentration camp where Kurz had served as a guard, and this providing a clear motive for the murder; the presence of Adina's fingerprints in the victim's bedroom; and traces of blood, of the same type as that of the victim, being found in the bathroom.

Albert Cooper, Stockwell and the solicitor all agreed that, to their satisfaction, the murder of "Sister Margaret" had been solved. As for the prospect of ever prosecuting

Adina Jenkins, were she ever to be traced and arrested, the solicitor took a pragmatic view. Given the victim's history, he doubted that it would be considered in the public interest to do so. Furthermore, "Sister Margaret" was not recognised by the Catholic Church. Monsignor Crecy and Lord Roding, both of whom were key witnesses, were deceased, and, as the law stood, Raymond could not be compelled to give evidence against his spouse. The chances of a conviction would be slim indeed. So, Albert Cooper and his team had to accept the wisdom of this decision and move on to their next challenge.

When Raymond Jenkins was released from the police station, he was driven back to Beaumont Hall, where he immediately went up to his apartment in the vain hope that Adina might have returned. There was still no trace of her. It was almost as though she had never existed.

Lady Fanny returned to the Hall later that day and she stayed in her rooms for a week, ostensibly as a guest of James Davidson. After much consideration, she decided against appealing the terms of the will, since she was likely to amass heavy legal costs in the process of doing so. Fanny, resolved to be satisfied with her lot, and she returned to the Bedford Square house, never visiting Beaumont Hall again.

James Davidson and Ruby Gedge moved into the Hall, and occupied the apartment vacated by Adina and Raymond Jenkins. It took them some time to settle down to the new status quo, and, although the fact that he was the illegitimate fruit of Lord Jeremy Roding's loins went unchallenged, James, at no time, assumed the role of lord of the manor. He would rather be known as the owner, and, with the help and guidance of Beryl and Raymond, James developed the Hall into a country house hotel, complete with twenty-five guest rooms, bar, restaurant and tea rooms. It was, after all, what they had been doing for Lord Jeremy, but on a far grander scale.

Whether James would become the 8th Lord of Roding was yet to be seen, but there was a feeling of optimism at Beaumont Hall, and a common determination to forgive, forget and look to the future.